T0157973

TAKING THE DARE

Gabe saw the same vulnerability that had been there the night of the potluck streak across her face. And damn it, it brought the protector out in him. No matter how much he tried to look at Raylene as an assignment, she got to him. And despite his better judgment, he pulled her over the seat into his lap.

"You'll be fine, Ray."

She straightened her spine. "Damned right I'll be fine."

He smiled because the woman was as stubborn as he was—and as proud. So damn proud he couldn't help but admire her. "That's the old spirit."

They sat there for a few seconds, her legs awkwardly splayed across the console, and it seemed like the best thing to do in that moment was kiss her. He cupped the back of her head, pulled her in, and claimed her mouth. That was the thing about Ray, she couldn't resist a dare. And the kiss was definitely a dare.

I dare you to kiss me back.

And she did, long and slow...

Books by Stacy Finz

The Nugget Series
GOING HOME
FINDING HOPE
SECOND CHANCES
STARTING OVER
GETTING LUCKY
BORROWING TROUBLE
HEATING UP
RIDING HIGH
FALLING HARD
HOPE FOR CHRISTMAS
TEMPTING FATE

The Garner Brothers
NEED YOU
WANT YOU
LOVE YOU

Published by Kensington Publishing Corporation

Tempting Fate

Stacy Finz

LYRICAL SHINE
Kensington Publishing Corp.
www.kensingtonbooks.com

LYRICAL SHINE BOOKS are published by

Kensington Publishing Corp.
119 West 40th Street
New York, NY 10018

All Kensington titles, imprints, and distributed lines are available at special quantity discounts for bulk purchases for sales promotion, premiums, fund-raising, educational, or institutional use.

Special book excerpts or customized printings can also be created to fit specific needs. For details, write or phone the office of the Kensington Sales Manager: Kensington Publishing Corp., 119 West 40th Street, New York, NY 10018. Attn. Sales Department. Phone: 1-800-221-2647.

Lyrical Shine and Lyrical Shine logo Reg. U.S. Pat. & TM Off.

First Electronic Edition: December 2018
ISBN-13: 978-1-5161-0394-2 (ebook)
ISBN-10: 1-5161-0394-7 (ebook)

First Print Edition: December 2018
ISBN-13: 978-1-5161-0395-9
ISBN-10: 1-5161-0395-5

Printed in the United States of America

Chapter 1

"That girl has some nerve showing up in this town after all the trouble she's caused."

"I was surprised Logan and Annie even invited her to the wedding."

Raylene Rosser huddled behind a display of canned goods, trying to make herself as small as possible while eavesdropping. She recognized Donna Thurston's voice. The Bun Boy owner always was a sanctimonious bitch. But Raylene expected better from Ethel. She'd known her since before she could walk. Donna, too.

Then again, it would've been foolish to think she'd be welcomed back to Nugget with open arms. She hadn't exactly left on the best of terms. Nope, instead of burning bridges, she'd blown them up with a hand grenade.

That's okay. As soon as Logan and Annie tied the knot, and Raylene found what she was looking for and sold the last of her inheritance, a prime piece of Nugget real estate, she'd get in her truck and leave this dusty, godforsaken town. Forever. Let Logan carry on the Rosser legacy—such as it was. She had places to go and people to meet. Without Butch, the worst husband in the annals of bad husbands, she was free to roam. Free to do whatever the hell she wanted. And if it all worked out, she could dig herself out of the mess she'd buried herself in. But for right now, she wanted to be with Logan on the most important day of his life.

Funny, that. Last summer, she'd hated him on sight. Her daddy's secret love child. But then Logan Jenkins swooped in and helped her clean up her train wreck of an existence and they connected like only blood can. And Annie...the woman was a saint. Earth mother rolled in sugar and spice and everything nice. And the best part: she accepted Raylene, warts and all. No judgment.

So no way was Raylene missing their wedding, even if the town busybodies wanted to burn her at the stake. She strained to hear if Donna and Ethel were still talking about her. Apparently neither of them knew she was in the store. Or perhaps they didn't care.

"Who are you hiding from?"

Raylene jumped at the voice, a deep baritone with more than a hint of New Jersey. A voice that irritated the hell out of her. She whipped her head around and put her finger over her lips. "Shush."

Gabe Moretti leaned against the spaghetti sauce shelf, a six-pack in one hand and a bag of Ruffles in the other, a smile playing on his lips. "You can run, Ray, but you can't hide."

"Don't call me that." It was her father's name, and Ray Rosser had been a mean son of a bitch. Probably still was, even six feet under. "Now go away."

He didn't budge, just continued to stand there, all two hundred and twenty pounds of him. The man was a brick house who moved like a freaking ghost. The way he'd snuck up on her…well, she was lucky he hadn't given her a heart attack.

"Don't pay attention to them," Gabe said. "Small town, small minds."

The truth was she deserved every ounce of their venom, and more. That was what was so hard about being here. Every day was like looking in a mirror and seeing something you didn't like staring back. At least in LA, no one knew her and she could be anyone she wanted, even if it meant living on ramen and letting out rooms in her beach rental.

"I thought you liked it here," she said.

"Love it." He jabbed the bag of potato chips at the front of the store. "Love those two old biddies, but they don't know you like I do, Ray."

"You've met me exactly twice." Three times, if she counted now. "Neither time did we say more than three words to each other." The first time, he and Logan had come to Denver to help her get away from Butch. The second time was yesterday, at a small, pre-wedding gathering at Logan and Annie's place.

"Yep." He winked. "But both times I made a lasting impression on you." His lips ticked up in an arrogant grin. If he weren't her brother's best friend and business partner, she'd wipe that smirk off his face. "Are you planning to stay in canned goods your whole life?"

She pretended to study the various brands of tomato paste. "Annie asked me to pick up a few things for the party tonight. I'm trying to decide which one is best."

"Annie cans her own tomatoes." He lifted his brows in challenge, then slid a glance at her empty basket. "Coward."

"I am not." She stuck her chin out with false bravado, because she *was* a coward. The worst kind of coward. "They can all go to hell."

"Isn't that the kind of attitude that got you labeled the wicked witch of the west in the first place? Why don't you just go out there, smile, and say, 'Fine afternoon'? It's called diplomacy."

"They teach you that in SEAL school?"

"It's BUD/S, not SEAL school." He pushed himself away from the shelf. She noted that he had on a stupid straw cowboy hat and a pair of pointy boots. Gabe Moretti was as much a cowboy as she was Snooki from *Jersey Shore*. "It's after Labor Day, by the way." She nudged her head at his hat.

"Yeah, so?"

"Felt in the winter; straw comes out Memorial Day. You want people around here to laugh at you?"

"People around here love me, sweetheart. You, not so much."

He had a point, at least about her. She had no clue how the people of Nugget responded to Gabe. According to Annie, they loved Logan. He'd gotten the good Rosser genes—if there were any. Or maybe he just took after his mom, a woman Raylene had never met. Soon she would, when Maisy got here for the wedding. The whole thing would be very strange. Meeting the other woman, the one who'd been her father's mistress right under Raylene's mother's nose.

"Just trying to help you pull off the look," she said. "No self-respecting rancher wears a straw cowboy hat in December, just saying."

"Good thing I'm not a rancher."

"Good thing."

His eyes took a long, leisurely stroll down her Wranglers. You could take the girl out of Nugget, but you couldn't take Nugget out of the girl. She had a closet full of designer jeans in every color. In LA you could easily pay three hundred dollars for denim. But nothing got between her and her Wranglers. From the gleam in Gabe's eye, he wished he could. But she was done trying to impress men. Her father, Butch…she was done.

He lifted his gaze to her face. "You better hurry if you're planning to make dinner."

She glanced at her watch. There was still plenty of time to pick up the items Annie needed. The whole point of this expedition was to get out of the house and avoid the neighbors, who were over at the farmhouse to help Annie set up for the dinner. She and Logan had been in remodel hell since they bought the place last summer and had only recently moved in. Annie had wanted an August wedding but they'd had to speed things up a bit, otherwise the bride would've had to walk down the aisle in a maternity dress. Raylene shuddered. A baby Rosser. Crazy.

"Are you bringing that?" She pointed at the beer and Ruffles.

"Yeah, why? You think I should get barbecue, instead?"

She rolled her eyes and grabbed the bag. Sour cream and onion. "Hey, you're the best man. If you think bringing potato chips to pre-wedding festivities is appropriate, there's no hope for you."

"Give me a break, Ray. I'm bringing a case of Veuve Clicquot." He held up the Ruffles and the six-pack of Bud. "These are for me."

She gave Gabe a quick scan. The man could eat chips and drink beer until the cows came home. Washboard abs under his thermal shirt, lean hips encased in denim, and not an ounce of fat on him. Butch had had to switch to light beer because he was getting a gut. He used to stare at himself in the mirror until it made Raylene nuts. Poor Butch, no longer able to reel in the young rodeo queens as easily as he once had.

"Well, nice chatting with you." She waited for him to leave, hoping he'd take a hint so she could figure out a way to sneak out of the market sight unseen. Graeagle was just a few minutes up the road; she'd buy her groceries there. They were probably cheaper there anyway, and she had to make her money last.

But Gabe stayed put. Either he was dense as Denver or he wanted to witness her humiliation.

"If you want, I'll help you finish your shopping and walk you to Ethel's cash register." He winked. "Safety in numbers."

"No thanks, I'm good." She dropped the basket on the floor and told herself screw it. There was a time in this town when the residents bowed down to a Rosser. She'd walk out of the market with her head held high.

She marched past Gabe, through the center of the store, and watched as Ethel and Donna did double takes. They immediately exchanged glances, probably wondering if she'd heard every cruel word they'd said.

Raylene pasted on one of her old barrel-racing smiles and flipped her hair from her collar. "Spill on aisle five."

Outside, in the parking lot, she let the cold air wash over her, relieved to leave the stuffy market behind. She'd nearly forgotten how frigid Nugget was in the winter. Southern California rarely dipped below fifty degrees. She headed to her truck, noting that Gabe's big-ass SUV was parked next to her Ford F-150. Knowing her brother, he'd probably bribed Moretti to babysit her and keep her out of trouble. Old reputations were hard to shed.

Yes, there'd been a time when she liked to stir things up. She and her father had left a lot of carnage in their wake. That's why she knew there'd be daggers out for her the minute she crossed the Plumas County line. Raylene couldn't fix what she'd broken. As soon as the wedding was over, as soon as she got what she came for, she could leave. Go back to Los Angeles and start searching for a ranchette in the San Gabriel Valley to raise her cutting horses.

In the meantime, she could handle the dirty looks and the nasty comments spoken behind her back. With practically the whole town coming to the wedding, there would be plenty of whispering. But Rossers were made of stern stuff, she told herself, pressing her clicker to unlock her truck.

Except for a charging station for an electric car and a few new shopping cart storage docks, the parking lot was the same as she always remembered. Like her, it was a little frayed around the edges. The letters on the market sign could use a new coat of paint and the building a power washing.

From the corner of her eye she saw a dark-haired woman leaning against her Outback, giving Raylene a steely stare. Cecilia Rodriguez—now Stryker, according to Logan—hadn't aged a bit. Those high cheek bones still slashed across olive skin on a wrinkleless face. A face Raylene knew as well as her own mother's.

Raylene stood there awkwardly, letting the seconds stretch to minutes. Finally, Cecilia flipped down her sunglasses from the top of her head and walked away. Raylene watched until she disappeared inside the automatic sliding doors of the Nugget Market, then she let out a breath and climbed into the cab of her Ford. She didn't realize she was crying until Gabe tapped on her window.

Shit.

She rubbed her eyes, smearing black mascara down her face. Great. When she didn't immediately respond, he tapped again. Persistent cuss.

She started the ignition and cracked the window just enough to say, "What?"

"You okay?"

"Why wouldn't I be?" She swiped her cheeks with the back of her hands, hoping to conceal evidence to the contrary.

"Dunno, you tell me."

"I have something in my eye." She tilted the rearview and held her eyelid up, pretending to look for a lash. It was easier than telling the truth. Gabe was the only person in this town who didn't know the full story of her past, and she wanted to keep it that way. It was bad enough that he knew the shoddy way she'd treated Logan when she first found out about him.

All those years, Ray had abandoned his only son and kept any knowledge of him a well-guarded secret.

"Let me see." He tried to squeeze his big hand through the opening, but it wouldn't fit.

"There," she said. "It's gone. All good."

"I called Annie and got the things on her list." He held up a grocery bag. "You don't have to worry about it."

She should've been thankful that he'd saved her a trip to Graeagle. Instead, she felt a sting of humiliation for not being able to stand up to Donna and Ethel. For letting Gabe see her run out of the Nugget Market with her tail tucked between her legs.

"You want to get a cup of coffee?"

"Cawfee?"

"You making fun of my Jersey?"

She took another pass at her face with the back of her hand. It was hard to be a smart ass with raccoon eyes. "You do know the nearest Starbucks is in Glory Junction? That's thirty minutes up the road."

"Forty-eight minutes to Dunkin'." He grinned, and the dimple in his chin became more prominent. It looked like someone had shot him with a BB gun.

She motioned her head at his bag. "The groceries will spoil."

"There's nothing perishable."

"You have an answer for everything, don't you?" The truth was she wanted a stiff drink. Badly. Caffeine was a tolerable substitute, she'd learned during the last few months. "We're not going to the Bun Boy." Donna Thurston might order one of her employees to pee in Raylene's cup.

"That only leaves one place."

"Meet you there." Raylene didn't wait for a response, just backed out of her parking space and headed to the square to the only sit-down restaurant in town, which also happened to be a bar and a bowling alley.

At least the owners of the Ponderosa hardly knew her. They'd moved up to Nugget from San Francisco, bought the place and rehabbed it while Raylene was still living in Denver with TAB—That Asshole Butch—though her reputation likely preceded her.

She found a spot in front of the Lumber Baron Inn, a Victorian B&B that took up a quarter of Nugget's business district, such as it was. The hotel was decked out in holiday decorations, as was the entire square. Lights, boughs of holly, and big red bows flocked with a smattering of leftover snow. She suspected the garland and ribbons would be coming down soon, since it was mid-January, and she would've stopped to take it all in but it was too cold to loiter. There were a lot of memories in this square. Farmers' markets, festivals, and concerts. In high school, after a game, they'd all pile into someone's truck and meet at the Bun Boy, where they'd blare music and eat burgers at the outdoor picnic tables.

Back then, she and her family had been the closest thing to royalty this town ever had. And she'd been the reigning princess, the girl most likely to have everything. Beauty, wealth, and the Rosser's Rock and River Ranch. A rusty laugh bubbled up in her throat, because all of it was gone. *Look at me now. Dull, poor, and alone.*

A blast of welcome heat and a Dixie Chicks song hit her as she entered the restaurant. Gabe had already claimed a table—she didn't know how he'd beat her here—and waved her over.

"Did you fly?"

Again with the obnoxious grin. "Nope, I'm just faster than you."

She took off her scarf and jacket, draped it over a chair, and took a quick look around.

"Doing a little recon?"

The man didn't miss a trick, and it was kind of spooky. Retired from the Navy, he and Logan owned a private security firm and still did a lot of top-secret missions for the government.

"Just reliving my misspent youth."

She watched Gabe scan the long, intricately carved bar. According to rumor, it had been salvaged from a Gold Rush bordello. But people around here liked to make up colorful stories, so the bar could've come from Ethan Allen for all Raylene knew.

"So this was your stomping ground, huh?"

She shrugged. "It sure didn't look like this." Back when she was a kid, the place smelled of cigarettes and cheap beer and looked like an old-man bar. Now it resembled one of those gourmet tap rooms on Nob Hill. Lots of dark wood paneling, period wall sconces, red velvet curtains, and pleather banquettes. Yet they'd still managed to retain the saloon's cowboy vibe. A vibe that reminded her too much of her father.

"Sophie and Mariah take pride in the place, that's for sure." Gabe perused the menu. "You hungry?"

"We're gonna eat in less than three hours." It was potluck, which, knowing the good folks of Nugget, meant enough casseroles to fill the grange hall. The evening would likely prove to be the most trying dinner of Raylene's life, depending on who attended.

"Yeah, so what's your point?"

A server came to the table. No one Raylene knew, thank God.

"You want coffee, a cocktail, or a glass of wine?" Gabe asked her.

A vodka tonic. She sat on her hands so they wouldn't shake. "Coffee's good."

Gabe got coffee as well, and a plate of sourdough bread and butter for the table. The waitress quickly returned with their order and left a carafe of piping hot caffeine in the middle of the table.

"How much did Logan pay you to be my minder?"

He tossed his head back and laughed. "Ah, Ray, you really have to work on your self-esteem."

She couldn't help herself and flipped him the bird. "Seriously, I don't need a keeper."

"What, you don't like my company?"

She was probably the only woman on God's green earth who didn't. Though to be truthful, he was funny. And good-looking, if you liked muscular men hopped up on cockiness and attitude. She'd had enough of those to last her a lifetime.

"I don't mind the accent," she said. "The rest of you, I could take or leave."

"A: I don't have an accent, you do. B: Logan didn't pay me." His lips curved up. "He threatened to break my legs if I didn't keep an eye on you."

She shook her head and emptied a couple of packets of sugar into her coffee.

"According to Logan, and town gossip, you've got quite a history here. You mind filling me in? I'd like to hear your side of it."

"Uh, no." She sipped her coffee while he stared at her with those chocolate brown eyes of his, waiting for an answer. It wasn't any of his business. "People here are batshit."

He leaned closer to the table. "People around here?" He lifted his brows in a not-so-subtle jab at her own sanity. "I know you tried to screw Logan out of his inheritance, and there's something about you having a drunken meltdown at the Gas and Go the last time you visited town. 'Do you know who I am?'" Gabe laughed. "Please tell me you didn't really say that to a cop, Ray."

"Did you suggest coffee to torture me?" Raylene didn't want to talk about it. She'd spent the last couple of years trying to forget the things she'd said and done.

"Just trying to figure out what went down."

"Well, don't." She reached for a piece of the sourdough and shoved it in her mouth. If he was buying, she was eating.

Someone got up and put a few quarters in the jukebox and an old George Jones song came on. George had always been one of her dad's favorites.

He'd played "Tennessee Whiskey" and "Why Baby Why" so many times Raylene knew them by heart. He might've been a son of a bitch, but he'd always had good taste in music.

The door swung open and the only person who could make this day any worse strode in. He took off his hat and searched the dining room, skimming over her. For a second, she thought she was safe. Then, just as quickly, they locked eyes and she felt a trickle of sweat roll down her back.

She calculated how fast she could get to the door without causing a scene and took a deep breath.

"Stay cool." Gabe put his hand on her shoulder. "I've got you covered."

Chapter 2

Gabe had heard twenty different versions of the story, each one more elaborate than the next. Despite its many configurations, he'd basically discerned the general gist. And it wasn't good. By all accounts, Raylene Rosser was a wackjob. But she was also his best friend's half sister. Gabe and Logan had been through thick and thin together. BUD/S training, two wars, and too many tight situations to count.

So when Logan asked him to look after Raylene during the wedding festivities, he reported for duty. No questions asked. That didn't mean he was siding with her against his new neighbors. All it meant was that he'd give her a broad back to hide behind when things got socially dicey.

And things had just moved to DEFCON 1.

"Kiss me," he whispered.

"Are you out of your mind?"

He'd only said it as a joke to defuse the situation before she made it any worse. Already people were starting to murmur among themselves, obviously anticipating a showdown. Lucky Rodriguez stood there, still as a statue. Gabe couldn't tell if Lucky was planning to kill Raylene or was simply stunned to see her, though it was no secret she was in town.

Raylene grabbed Gabe and covered his mouth with hers, fisting his shirt in her hands. Her lips were full and soft and giving. And without thinking, he kissed her back. When she twined her hands around his neck, he felt his body leap to attention and tried to shut it down.

They were in a public place, and Raylene was Logan's sister—not to mention nuts—but she tasted good and felt even better. Small, compared to him, but the woman had some curves. Her long blond hair tickled his neck, and her firm breasts, breasts he distinctly remembered being much larger the first time he'd met her, smashed against his chest.

"Is he gone yet?" she asked.

Gabe snapped to attention and slowly turned his head to look. "Yep." And just like that, she pushed him away. "Thank God."

He glanced around the room to find that most of the diners had gone back to their meals and private conversations. Nothing to see here. But by tomorrow it would be all over town that he and Logan's crazy sister had been sucking face in the middle of the Ponderosa. He'd come to learn that that's how it worked here in Nugget. Everything was up for public scrutiny. They were probably over at Owen's barbershop talking about it now. He didn't care what the townsfolk thought, but Logan was protective where Raylene was concerned. To say he'd be pissed was an understatement.

"A little extreme, don't you think?"

"It was your idea, not mine," she protested.

"It was a joke, Raylene. Something to lighten the tension."

"Well, it worked." She shrugged.

"What happens the next time you run into Lucky?" With a population of less than six thousand, it was bound to happen. Besides, Lucky and his wife, Tawny, were invited to the wedding.

She huffed out a sigh. "You know about it then?"

"Ray, this is Nugget." He pinned her with a stare and she turned away, unable to hold eye contact with him.

"I'm only here for a few days, a week at most." Long enough to find Levi's Gold.

"Okay." He pushed his empty cup away and reached for his wallet. "Just don't turn Logan and Annie's wedding into your personal drama."

"I wouldn't do that."

Right. The first time he'd met her, she and her husband stood in their driveway, embroiled in an epic screaming match in front of the entire neighborhood. He and Logan had had to pull her out of there before one of them went to jail. Granted, the ex was a real jerkoff. But Raylene was no angel. "Good, because it would really suck if you did. Let's go." He handed her her scarf and jacket.

She followed him out to the square. His SUV was parked in front of the police station, and he took the long way around so he could walk Raylene to her truck. "I'll meet you at the farm."

She nodded and unlocked her door.

He trailed her to the main road out of town, but she hung a right instead of a left, heading in the opposite direction of Logan and Annie's house.

"Goddammit! Where the hell is she going?" Hey, it was her business, he told himself. The woman could drive wherever she wanted.

Back at the farm, Gabe found Annie at the kitchen table studying a seating chart. "Do you think it's a bad idea to put Owen next to Donna?"

What did Gabe know about seating arrangements? "Maybe. Where's Logan?"

Distracted with her chart, Annie motioned toward the living room, where Logan was messing with a set of speakers.

"What you got there?"

"They're supposed to work with voice control. But they're pieces of shit." Logan lifted his head. "Where's Raylene?"

Gabe hitched his shoulders. "We were both headed here from town, but she must've forgotten something, because she went the other way."

"Back to Nugget?" The farm where Logan and Annie lived, which was also the home of L&G Security, was fifteen minutes away from town.

"It looked like she was headed to Reno, but who knows with her."

Logan pierced Gabe with a look. "Why Reno?"

"Beats the hell out of me. She probably needed something she could only get in a big town, like a lobotomy."

Logan checked his watch. "She's cutting it close for the party. It's a forty-five-minute drive each way."

"She's a grown woman, Jenk."

"I know, but being back here…it's hard for her."

Gabe sprawled out on the couch and rubbed a spot out of his new boots. "She had a couple of run-ins in town. First, she overheard Donna and Ethel talking about her at the Nugget Market, and while we were getting coffee at the Ponderosa, Lucky came in."

Logan put down the speaker and gave Gabe his full attention. "What happened?"

"Nothing, really." No way was he telling Logan about the kiss or whatever the hell that was. "It got a little tense, then Lucky left."

Logan let out a breath. "Lucky and Tawny decided it was better if they didn't come tonight, but they'll be at the wedding."

"There'll be enough people that Raylene can avoid him and vice versa. When's your mom and Nick getting in?"

"Not until tomorrow. That might be weird, too."

Ya think? "Jenk, why'd you have to invite her?"

"She's my sister. Her mother's a damned space cadet, and I'm all she has. I couldn't leave her out even if I'd wanted to, which I didn't. She's come to rely on me."

The truth was Logan was the softest badass Gabe had ever known. The man was one of the best spec op warriors in the business, but he cried watching a Hallmark movie. Last summer, Logan assigned himself the job of being Raylene's guardian, which in Gabe's opinion was a full-time gig. "All right, I'll try to run interference as much as possible." He got to his feet. "I'm grabbing a shower over at headquarters. Anything you want me to do before I leave?"

"Nope, Annie and I have everything under control." Logan began fiddling with the speaker again.

On Gabe's way out, he stopped in the kitchen to check in with Annie. "You have that seating situation handled?"

"I think so. Gia will help me as soon as she gets here." She gazed out the window. "I hope the weather cooperates."

To Gabe it felt too cold for snow. "I guess you couldn't wait until summer." He patted her stomach and grinned.

"Nope." She hugged him and her whole damn face glowed.

"I think you and I should run away together."

From the other room came a crashing sound. "Fuck you, Alexa."

Annie rolled her eyes. "He's been at it all day. Whatever happened to turning the music on by hand?"

"I'm out of here, before he starts shooting the thing. See you in an hour."

Gabe let the screen door slam behind him, got in his truck, and took the driveway to the end of the property where he and Logan had built L&G from the ground up. It was a small compound compared to many security firms, but it was efficient as hell, with an indoor shooting range, a gym, a wing of small offices, and a big-ass conference room. They used a landing strip outside of town when they needed to get to assignments fast, which was pretty much always.

The rest of the sixty acres Annie farmed, and she sold much of what she grew at a farm stand on the main road. The setup was unusual, to be sure, but it worked for them, and Gabe had come to love rural life. He could fish, hunt, and hike whenever he wanted, and the nights in his small apartment felt like camping with the convenience of electricity and indoor plumbing.

And the Sierra Nevada was the most beautiful place on earth. Mountains and valleys, lakes and rivers, and trees as far as the eye could see. In four hours he could be in San Francisco, and it was less than three to Sacramento. And there was gambling and women just across the Nevada state line, an easy drive from Nugget.

The whole arrangement had turned out perfectly. Best of all, it had made it possible for Logan to have both of his dreams: Annie and L&G.

They'd remodeled the old dilapidated farmhouse on the property and had transformed it into a real home. And soon they'd be bringing their first child into the world.

Gabe had been elected godfather.

He spent the next twenty minutes in the locker room shower, practicing his Marlon Brando impression. Then his thoughts drifted to Raylene and the kiss. It hadn't lasted long, but the woman packed a punch. She was also *pazzo*, as his Italian grandmother liked to say. Crazy as a fucking loon. Hot, though. Big blue eyes, full red lips, and an ass that wouldn't quit. Under normal circumstances, she'd be his type. For a night.

Any more thoughts of Raylene got cut short by the ringing of Gabe's phone. He hopped out of the shower, reached for a towel, and managed to grab his cell in time to take the call.

"Moretti."

"You mind bringing an extension cord when you come back?" It was Logan.

"Roger that. I'll be over in a few minutes. Anything else?"

"Nope. Just get your ass over here."

Gabe quickly dressed. He'd brought over everything from his small apartment in town, that way he'd be close and on hand to help with any party preparations. Most of the time—when he wasn't on a mission—he lived out of the office anyway. But with the holidays and Logan's wedding, they hadn't taken on any new projects. It would be nice to have a few months off to catch up on paperwork. And to sleep, something he didn't get much of with the frenetic pace of the job. But he wouldn't trade it for anything.

He searched the equipment room for an extension cord and drove back to the house, noting Raylene's truck was still MIA. Where she'd disappeared to was beyond him. Frankly, he didn't want to know. Hopefully he wouldn't have to bail her out of the can. According to the big mouths in town, she'd nearly gotten arrested for the crap she'd pulled a couple of years ago. Her old man had gotten a life sentence for his overarching role, which included killing a cattle rustler and trying to pin the murder on Lucky Rodriguez. Ray Rosser had died in prison. That's how Logan had learned the whole sordid story about his paternity and had come into his inheritance, which included a nutso half sister.

The kitchen was filled with people and about a hundred casserole dishes when he got inside. Donna, Brady Benson, and Emily McCreedy were rotating pans in the oven as Samantha Breyer was checking off a list. All this for a freaking potluck. If Gabe ever got married, he was eloping. Between his Irish mother and his Italian stepfather, he had a bazillion siblings, half siblings, stepsiblings, and relatives. Weddings in the Moretti family were like the Macy's Thanksgiving Day Parade. This nearly rivaled it.

"Hand me that extension cord," Logan called to Gabe across the room. "Annie wants to project a slide show of all the work we did on the farm."

Nice idea, Gabe thought. For months they'd all been working to rehabilitate the place, which had previously been owned by a hoarder who'd let the house go to pot. Annie, who had a fancy degree in agriculture and worked as farming consultant, had whipped the land into shape. Now, she grew all kinds of shit, half of which they'd be eating for dinner.

"Raylene's still not here, huh?" Gabe didn't want her screwing up Logan and Annie's pre-wedding festivities, and from everything he'd heard—and seen—she was like a battering ram, causing mayhem wherever she went.

"She called and is on her way."

"Where'd she go?"

Logan shrugged. "Annie talked to her. I suspect she needed space. This town holds a lot of bad memories for her."

Gabe spent the next thirty minutes helping Annie's brother, Chad, with the bar. Her parents had made the two-hour trek from Yuba City, where they grew rice, and were spending the night. It would be a full house at Chez Jenkins tonight. Gia and Flynn, who now owned Raylene's dad's old ranch, had offered to lend their guest cottage. Until recently, Logan and Annie had lived there while their farmhouse was being redone.

"Hey, were you two part of that UFO study group?" Owen pointed to Gabe and Logan.

As usual, Gabe didn't know what the old man was talking about. The local barber lived in an alternative universe, as far as Gabe could tell. Plus, he was early. Guests weren't scheduled to arrive for another ten minutes.

"You smoking weed again, Owen?"

"It's all over the news…the Pentagon's Advanced Aviation Threat Identification Program. So don't try to deny it."

"I'm not denying it, I just don't know anything about it."

"Of course you do. You"—he nudged his head at Logan—"and him know more than you let on."

Yeah, and the Starship *Enterprise* was in the backyard. Gabe put his finger to his lips. "Don't blow our cover, or it could mean death to the whole town."

"You're a real wiseacre, aren't you?"

Gabe laughed. "Where's Darla and Wyatt?"

"Wyatt's finishing up his police shift, and Darla had to close the barbershop. They'll probably be late. Those two couldn't be on time to save their lives."

Like you, who came early, Gabe wanted to say, but he liked the guy too much to keep razzing him. "I've got to bring in some extra folding chairs. I'll catch you later."

Gabe headed to the garage to give Logan a hand. "Chad seems good."

"Yeah, he's done a lot of growing up." Annie's kid brother hadn't been much better than Raylene. Both disasters. But he owned a thriving restaurant now and appeared to have gotten his shit together. "Knockers is making a killing. Chad's talking about franchising."

"Good for him." Gabe put Logan in a headlock. "You okay?"

"Never happier."

"Good. It's a lot, though. Marriage, a baby, a mortgage."

"You ought to try it." Logan punched Gabe in the chest. "A little responsibility would do you good."

"Someday, but not anytime soon." Gabe liked his life just the way it was. When he wasn't working, he could take off to places unknown. Do a little sightseeing, a little clubbing, a little partying. After twelve years in the Navy, he liked his freedom just fine. "Who knows? Annie and I may decide to leave your ass."

"Annie's got good taste, Moretti. You're the last dude she'd pick."

He'd only known Annie since last summer and already loved her like a sister. The woman was salt of the earth.

They both lifted their heads when they heard a vehicle pull up, and Gabe peeked outside to see who it was. Raylene. She let the engine idle in the carport longer than necessary, and he got the sense she was psyching herself up to go in.

"I'll go talk to her," Logan said.

"Nah, it's your party. I'll take care of it." Gabe handed the extra chairs to Logan and ambled over to Raylene's truck.

"Where'd you go?" he asked as she stepped out of the cab.

"I had an errand." She turned her back on him and started for the house. "I've got to get ready."

"Okay. Just making sure everything's okay."

"Everything's fine," she said, but her hands were shaking.

Chapter 3

Raylene made a beeline for the bedroom she was using. She desperately wanted to wash off the day's grime and suit up in her best armor—a little black dress—for judgment day. No matter what she wore, she'd get talked about. Might as well do it in style. She'd bought the dress in a small, exclusive shop on Montana Avenue in Santa Monica when her bank account was still full, and it had been languishing in her closet ever since. It was high time she took the dress out for a stroll.

She locked the door and took a few seconds to breathe and stop her hands from trembling. The meeting had been good. Just what she needed, yet the desire for a drink still nagged at her. A little voice kept telling her that one vodka tonic was all she needed to get through this thing and she could go cold turkey tomorrow.

Nope. She wasn't going to ruin this for Logan and Annie, and alcohol made her do bad things. Or maybe she was just bad and the combination was noxious.

She sat on the edge of the bed and recited, "God, grant me the serenity to accept the things I cannot change, courage to change the things I can, and wisdom to know the difference," hoping the words would give her strength.

All she had to do was make it through dinner. If she designated herself dishwasher or oven monitor, she could hole up in the kitchen and pass much of the evening without having to talk to anyone. That was her plan, anyway.

She took a quick shower, shimmied into her dress, and did her makeup, steering away from her usual dark, smoky-eyed look. Butch had told her that it made her look like a whore. Instead, she went with a neutral palette. It was big in LA. Kind of a natural, dewy face thing. Since she didn't have a job, she'd spent a lot of time shopping, emulating the styles of the chic women in Los Angeles. It was amazing how fast someone could piss through a fortune. Between Butch—who'd robbed her blind—her divorce attorney's fees, the lease on her beach house, breast implant removal surgery, and her patronage of Lucy's House, a women's shelter, she was down to nearly nothing.

In the new year, though, she planned to start her own company with the money she got from her land—and hopefully the gold. She wanted to raise and train cutting horses for competition and working cattle ranches. It was a lifelong dream. All she needed was the money, property, a barn, an equestrian center, and some good stock. The last part was easy. The Rossers had owned one of the largest cattle operations in California. She knew her horse flesh and every breeder west of the Mississippi. It was the right property that would be hard to come by, not just because real estate in California cost a fortune, but the land had to be zoned to allow a commercial horse farm, be accessible to buyers, and close enough to a town to buy supplies. Sort of a tall order in Southern California.

But she liked it there. The ocean, the beaches, the weather, and the fact that it was hundreds of miles away from Butch, Nugget, and her past.

On her way out, she took one last look in the mirror and saw a presentable woman staring back. It wasn't as if it mattered. Her reputation was already so scarlet, nothing would change it.

At the bottom of the stairs, Gabe waited for her as if he'd been standing sentry there for the last forty minutes. Either that, or he'd put a tracker on her to know her comings and goings. She wouldn't doubt it.

"What took you so long?" he asked, acting put out. But his eyes told a different story. Male appreciation gleamed there. Though Raylene had been appreciated more times than she wanted to admit, something about having Gabe look at her that way gave her courage.

"I told you, I had to change."

"Well, the party has already started. You're late."

"Big deal. It's not like I'm the main attraction," she said, though she wasn't so sure about that. People were probably tripping over themselves to watch her humiliation. "Is he here?"

"No, he's not coming."

She jerked in surprise. Annie was friends with Lucky's wife, Tawny. And by Nugget standards the Rodriguezes were neighbors, even if they lived a few miles away. In the country, it was a cardinal sin not to invite your neighbor to an event like this. "It's because of me."

Gabe gazed down at his boots but didn't deny it. She'd give him points for honesty.

"He'll be at the wedding," he said. "Now let's go in. Annie has you seated next to her."

Annie Sparks, soon to be Jenkins, was Mother Teresa. If Raylene's brother ever hurt his wife, she would personally kill him. The thing was, he wouldn't. Ever. Logan was as good as Annie, and why these two kind souls had taken her in, Raylene would never know.

"You go first." She nudged him.

"Nope, age before beauty." But he took her hand and they walked into the dining room together.

Maybe it was Raylene's imagination, but she could've sworn there was a gasp from someone sitting at one of the banquet tables that had been lined up from one end of the room to the other and draped in mismatched linens. Annie waved to Raylene from across the room, pointing to an empty chair.

To get there, though, Raylene would have to run the gauntlet. Gabe squeezed her hand and led her through the dining room.

"Thank you," she whispered and sank into her seat between Annie and her brother.

Gabe took the chair across from her. It was as if they'd formed a protective wall around her.

"The tables look great," Raylene told Annie for the sake of something to say. But the truth was she liked Annie's quirky style, a combination of thrift store, farmhouse, and shabby chic. She'd grown up in a house where even the candles had to match the china.

"They do, don't they? Everyone brought stuff, including Emily, who has a treasure trove of tablecloths and dishes."

"Hello," Emily said from across the table. Her voice was far from friendly and her smile didn't quite reach her eyes. "I don't think we've officially met."

Emily wasn't originally from Nugget. She was a cookbook author and was now married to Clay McCreedy. Raylene knew that because the McCreedys had been the Rossers' closest neighbors before her father had been forced to sell the ranch to pay his defense lawyers. Like Ray, Clay was a cattle rancher.

Raylene cleared her throat. "I was happy to hear the news about your daughter."

"It was our Christmas miracle," Emily said, and turned to look at the end of the table where a group of children sat.

Raylene didn't know the whole story, only that Emily's little girl was abducted years ago and had recently been found living with a dying woman in Idaho. Unsure what was appropriate to discuss at the dinner table, she left the topic alone.

Out of the side of her eye, she saw Gabe watching her. "What?" she whispered.

"Nothing." He filled her glass with pinot noir. "Pass the potatoes, would you?"

She handed him the huge crockery bowl and tried to ignore the red wine that seemed to be pleading with her to drink it.

"I hear you live in Santa Monica," Annie's brother, Chad, said. "I'm thinking of opening a restaurant there."

The area had more restaurants than one person could eat at in a year. Even more than her old trendy neighborhood in Denver. "Really?"

"Good demographics." He grabbed a roll and seemed to remember his manners. "You want one?"

"No, thank you."

The guests who sat directly near her proceeded to make small talk. Raylene noted that most of them were either newcomers or from out of town, while the old timers sat at the other end of the table. Raylene was sure Annie had planned it that way. Another reason to love her soon-to-be sister-in-law.

She got into a lengthy discussion with Annie's father about rice farming. Although her family's specialty was livestock, she knew enough to keep up. A few times, she caught Harlee Roberts, owner of the *Nugget Tribune*, staring daggers at her. Harlee was besties with Tawny, so it stood to reason that she hated Raylene's guts.

She checked the clock on the fireplace mantel. It was only five minutes past the last time she'd looked.

"Relax." Gabe had switched to her side of the table, grabbing Logan's chair while her brother and Annie made the rounds, talking with their guests.

"I am."

"Could've fooled me." He stabbed a piece of steak on her plate with his fork and put it in his mouth. "That was nice, what you said to Emily."

"I'm not a complete ogre." When the story hit the news, Raylene had cried. She noted that Emily had gotten up to talk to Donna and asked, "Is the little girl okay?"

"Yeah. I mean it's been a hard transition, but physically…she's fine."

"How did they find her?"

Gabe nudged his head at Clay, who'd wandered to their end of the table. "Let's talk about it later."

"Hi, Clay." He was standing right next to her, so it wasn't as if she could ignore him, even though he was ignoring her.

"Raylene," he said tightly.

"How are you?"

"Best Christmas ever." For a second, he dropped his reserve and smiled. But just like that, the grin was gone. He didn't like her, and on several occasions in the past he'd made it known that he thought she was a spoiled brat. She supposed it was better than what he thought of her now. But for the sake of Logan and Annie, he was being cordial. It didn't take a particularly astute observer to know that.

Raylene was relieved when he moved on to talk to Rhys Shepard, the police chief. That glass of wine still sat at her elbow, teasing and tempting. *Just one sip.*

"You want dessert?" Gabe asked her. Members of the Baker's Dozen, a cooking club, had baked enough cakes and pies to feed the entire state of California. Someone had even brought homemade ice cream.

"I'll get it." She needed to stretch her legs and wished she'd taken up smoking. Then she'd have an excuse to go outside for a cigarette break.

The sweets were laid out on the counter, and several people stood huddled around the assortment, trying to make their selections, Raylene noted as she entered the kitchen. She'd just started to exercise an about-face when she heard the whispers.

"I still can't believe her audacity."

"This has to put a pall over the whole wedding. But Logan and Annie are too sweet to turn her away, even though I can't imagine them wanting her here. For goodness' sake, she and Butch tried to sue Logan and steal his inheritance."

"The scheming bitch should've gone to prison like her daddy."

From their backs, Raylene couldn't tell who they were. Not Donna or Ethel—too young. Quietly, she slipped out of the room, wended her way back to the table, and grabbed her wineglass. The powder room in the hallway was empty. She ducked in and quickly locked the door, leaning her back against the pedestal sink.

She pushed the bowl of the glass underneath her nose and inhaled. After all this time, she'd forgotten how good wine smelled. Like fruit and earth and freedom. Her father used to sneak her sips of the Russian River pinots he liked so much behind her mama's back when she was just a little girl. She'd giggle and he'd laugh. Their own private joke. Later, he'd slip her shots of whiskey. If you were a Rosser, you held your liquor. Inebriation was for the weak, he'd say. But she'd always been a lightweight. A sloppy drunk who danced on tables, took off her clothes, and wept until she passed out.

"To you, Ray." She held up the glass in a salute, letting the rivulets catch the light. "May you rot in hell."

* * * *

"You okay in there?" Gabe knocked. He'd seen her go in at least ten minutes ago.

The toilet flushed and Raylene emerged, holding an empty wineglass.

"You drinking alone, Ray?"

"I'm not feeling well."

"What's wrong?"

"Stomachache. I think I'll go up to my room."

He gave her a long, hard look. "I thought you were tougher than that."

"You want me to throw up on you?"

He rolled his eyes. "There's that flair for dramatics you're so famous for. You can't tough it out another hour? By then, I'm gauging everyone will go home."

"No, I need to lie down."

She looked fine to him, but he couldn't force her to stay. She'd surprised him by holding her own over dinner. She'd been subdued, gracious, even friendly, despite the death glares that had been thrown her way. For a minute there, he thought Clay McCreedy was going to bite her head off. And Harlee's resting bitch face would've scared an entire SEAL team.

"All right," he told her. "Take care of yourself. We've got a long three days ahead of us."

"Night." She handed him the wineglass.

Okay, apparently he was a waiter now. He watched her climb the stairs in her little black dress, a few inappropriate thoughts flitting through his head. She was Logan's sister—and *Nightmare on Elm Street*.

Try to remember that, idiot.

He turned to go to the kitchen and bumped into Rhys. "Hey, Chief. What's shaking?"

"All's quiet on the Western front." He motioned at the stairs. "Stay away from her. She's bad news." And with that, he moved on to join a group of old dudes who everyone called the Nugget Mafia.

Gabe had always gotten a kick out of that. To him, Owen, the mayor, and the rest of their cadre were more like a barbershop quartet. Then again, he was from Jersey, home to real wise guys.

"Where's Raylene?" Logan took the glass from Gabe and stuck it on the counter.

"Uh, she wasn't feeling well and went upstairs."

"I'll go up, see how she's doing." He started to walk away, but Gabe grabbed him by the shoulder.

"Let her be, man. This is...a lot, Jenk. People here have long memories."

"Yeah, well, she left a lasting impression. But she's changed. She's really trying."

Gabe wondered. Helping her late father set up an innocent man on a murder rap was pretty unforgivable in his book. But she was Logan's blood, and Logan was Gabe's brother from another mother.

"She'll be fine," he told Logan. "I'll handle Raylene. You focus on the wedding and Annie."

Logan's face lit up. It usually did at the mere mention of his fiancée. The man was smitten.

The party wound down and, as Gabe had predicted, people started heading out not long after Raylene went to bed. Most of the folks in Nugget were either ranchers, farmers, railroad workers, or business owners. It was that whole early to bed, early to rise thing, which took some getting used to. Then again, Reno was only forty-five minutes away.

He helped clean up and took off to his duplex apartment in town. He rented the place, a no-frills cabin that had been divided into two separate one-bedroom apartments, from the police chief and his wife, Maddy. The other apartment was vacant for the time being, so it was nice and quiet. Sometimes too quiet.

He pulled down the driveway and did a three-point turn so his SUV faced the road. That way, if he had to go in a hurry, he could rocket out of there. A habit he'd picked up in the military. The minute he walked in, he jacked up the heat. It had to be twenty degrees, meaning there was a good chance of snow. Luckily, the wedding would be indoors.

It was too early to sleep and too late to do anything else, at least in this town. Gabe plopped down on the couch, propped his feet up on the coffee table, and channel surfed. There was nothing good on. He wound up watching a program about a couple who'd won the lottery. They were shopping for homes in Tuscaloosa.

Around two in the morning, he fell asleep in front of the TV and was up by nine to take his run. Afterwards, he headed to the Ponderosa for breakfast.

"No snow yet." Sophie, one of the owners, led him to a table near the fireplace.

"Nope, but it's coming. I can feel it."

"Great party last night."

"Sure was." Only a rehearsal dinner and a wedding left to go, then Gabe could hang up his party hat.

A few tables down, Gabe spotted Clay, Emily, their baby and two boys, and the girl, Hope—now Harper—having breakfast. He nudged his head their way. "How's that going?"

"Baby steps, but I think there's progress. She's finding her way, not easy for a thirteen-year-old whose whole life has been turned upside down."

All Gabe knew was that she'd been abducted when she was six. Over Christmas, the FBI found her, safe and sound, living with a woman who'd died shortly after the discovery. He and Logan had just come back from an overseas assignment and had missed much of the news reports about it, but he'd gotten some of the story from Annie.

"I can't imagine," he said. "I hear the ex-husband bought a place here."

"Over at Sierra Heights. He and his wife are planning to live here part-time so Harper doesn't have to travel back and forth to the Bay Area. Emily is over the moon about it."

Gabe wondered if the same went for Clay. Being part of a blended family, he knew firsthand the travails of divorce. The good news was that he, his steps, and half brothers and sisters all loved each other like crazy.

"That's good," he said. "I'm guessing the kid could use some stability."

Sophie nodded in agreement. "You want coffee?"

"Yes, please. And eggs over easy, bacon, and those biscuits Tater makes."

"Coming right up."

He checked his phone while he waited for his food and returned a quick email to a tactical equipment manufacturer that he and Logan were doing business with. Things were slowly getting back to normal after the holidays. Before he knew it, it would be February. Tonight, he was joining Logan and his parents for dinner. It had been a year since he'd last seen Nick, Logan's stepdad. The guy, a kickass former frogman, had good stories about the teams back in the day. Gabe never tired of hearing that shit.

Friday was the rehearsal dinner, and Saturday the wedding. After that, Raylene would go back to LA and his chaperone duties would be officially over. So far, it hadn't been too terrible. For all her faults, she made him laugh with that attitude of hers, especially the way she poked fun at his accent.

Logan said she was talking about starting some kind of horse ranch in SoCal, which would suit her. Supposedly, she was quite an equestrian and a former rodeo queen. Gabe didn't know how someone went about getting the title, but he figured it had something to do with her riding skills. Or maybe it was based on beauty. She had that, too.

His breakfast and coffee came and he devoured the entire meal. He was just about to pay his bill when Rhys came in and grabbed the seat next to him.

He waved to the McCreedys, then said, "You have time to take a ride with me?"

"Sure. What's going on?"

"Not sure yet but I'm a little short staffed. The flu...vacations."

"Dude, you've got to hire more cops."

"Working on it, but it's not easy getting good people up here."

No question the town was isolated, but it was a fine place to raise a family. That had to be a good selling point, Gabe thought. "Let's go."

He slapped a twenty down on the table, shrugged into his coat, and followed Rhys outside. The temperature had dipped ten degrees since yesterday, too cold to snow.

Rhys led Gabe to his SUV. All the officers in the Nugget PD drove one. They were all-wheel drive, with plenty of bells and whistles. For a tiny force, the equipment was top of the line.

"Where we going?"

"You'll see," Rhys said. "You carrying?"

"Nope. Should I be?"

"Maybe," was all he said, then he started his engine.

Chapter 4

Raylene walked into Nugget Realty and Associates. The office had been there since before she was born, but she'd never been inside. It had a professional appearance—new carpeting, taupe walls, a few plants, and a television screen that played a loop of house listings. She stood in front of it for a few minutes, watching. There were a couple she recognized, homes of kids she'd grown up with who had since moved away. Their parents probably wanted to be closer to them and the grandkids.

After Ray was busted, her own mother had relocated to Denver, just a few minutes from Raylene. Why, she never knew. It wasn't as if they were close. When Raylene left Butch, it was Logan and Gabe who came to help her put all her things in storage. Her mother had been too busy pretending that everything was fine. Raylene supposed that's what weak women did when they were married to cheating, abusive husbands. She ought to know, having been married to one and the daughter of another.

"Raylene?"

Raylene recognized the woman from the dinner party the previous night, though they hadn't been introduced. She wasn't much older than Raylene. Maybe in her mid-thirties. Very polished in a black pantsuit and a red silk scarf.

"Yes. Are you Dana?" Raylene had hired Dana over the phone to sell her property.

"That would be me," Dana said, then stood up to shake her hand. "I meant to introduce myself last night but the time got away from me. I'm glad to finally meet you in the flesh."

Dana was a newcomer, otherwise she wouldn't have been so friendly. Then again, she stood to make a great deal of money from Raylene.

"Come sit down. Can I get you a cup of coffee…a soda?"

"I'm fine, thank you. I figured your message to meet you here was because you want to lower the price." They'd listed the land last summer and hadn't gotten so much as a bite.

"No." Dana grinned. "We actually have an offer. Apparently, the interested party talked to your dad about buying the parcel before he…"

"Went to prison," Raylene finished. There was no need to protect her delicate sensibilities, because she had none. The ranch, the Rosser legacy, had to be sold to pay Ray's legal bills. And, to be fair, the leftover money had made them all wealthy. Raylene hadn't been too smart with her share, though, and now it was gone.

"Right," Dana said. "But he wouldn't sell."

No, because he'd promised the two hundred-acre parcel to her and Butch along, with Levi's Gold—if they could find it. "How much are they offering?" she asked and took a deep breath.

"Full price, as long as the environmental impact report is approved and the well is still good."

"How long will those tests take?" She desperately needed the money, but she also needed time to search the place, something she should've done when Ray died. But she'd been too busy fighting Butch for full ownership of the land in the divorce.

Now he wasn't entitled to one red cent of it, though she'd paid dearly to win that battle.

"They want to do this quickly. And I suspect you do, too," Dana said, but she didn't seem particularly enthusiastic about the deal. Or maybe, like everyone else, the real estate agent was unenthusiastic about Raylene. She'd like the big fat commission she got, though.

"They'd like a thirty-day escrow," Dana continued in the same dour tone that was starting to annoy Raylene. "They're willing to lift their inspection contingency in ten working days. It's an all-cash deal so nothing's hinging on the financing."

An all-cash full offer sounded a little too good to be true. But the price of the land was nothing compared to Levi's Gold. If the legend was true, she'd never have to worry about money again.

"Ten days. Does that mean they'd start with their inspections right away?" She didn't want anyone mucking around on the land until she'd examined every acre with a magnifying glass.

"As soon as you accept their offer."

Raylene didn't want to lose the deal, but she needed a few days. "Can I sleep on it?"

Dana seemed surprised. "Of course."

"It's the only thing I have left of my daddy," Raylene said by way of an excuse, deciding that she'd start digging first thing in the morning. Ray had sworn by the legend and had considered the gold his secret reserve, telling her and Butch that when the crash came and the banks failed, like they had during the Great Depression, he'd have Levi's buried treasure to save him.

It's safer in the ground than it is in a savings account.

Her father had always harbored a distrust of financial institutions. Still, Raylene suspected he simply hadn't wanted to turn over a big chunk of the gold to the IRS. And it wasn't as if Ray had needed the money. Growing up, Raylene had never wanted for anything other than her parents' hard-won affection. Her mother was too caught up in her own misery to give Raylene a second thought, and her father was difficult to please, always pushing her to meet his ever-increasing expectations. She'd convinced herself that making him proud was synonymous with love. Only now did she realize that a parent's love should be unconditional.

"Are you interested in who the buyers are?" Dana asked, and Raylene got the sense she was being tested.

Her mind had been spinning so fast she hadn't thought to ask. She assumed it was a cattle rancher. It was just bare land, after all. Albeit prime usable land with Feather River frontage, but little else to recommend it other than an excellent well that would support an agricultural venture and a good road close to the highway. There was already one of those golf course communities in town. From what she'd heard, the owner was having trouble unloading the homes. She doubted a developer wanted her land for the same purpose. Or any purpose, for that matter.

"Who are they?" she asked.

"Moto Entertainment. They develop motocross parks." Dana let that sink in for a second.

"They want to turn the land into a racetrack?" What the hell did she care? As soon as Raylene got her gold, she was leaving. The land was far enough away from Logan and Annie's place that it wouldn't impact them. As far as the others...not her problem. "Isn't it zoned for agricultural use only?"

"Nope. Your father got a variance after he annexed the parcel from the rest of Rosser Ranch." Dana rolled a pen back and forth on her desk. "It's my job to represent you and get you the best price possible but...I'm glad you're sleeping on it."

Several seconds of silence stretched between them. Raylene needed this deal—she'd promised a sizeable chunk of the sale to Lucy's House—and told herself that a motocross park would be good for Nugget. It would bring people and money. Progress. And who was she to stand in the way of progress?

Raylene put the sale out of her mind and took her time driving back to the farm, wanting to give Logan and Annie some private time before the hordes descended. Today, Logan's mom and stepdad were due in. They were driving their Winnebago from Las Vegas. Raylene was nervous about the meeting. Even though she hadn't been born when Maisy and Ray had had their affair, coming face-to-face with the "other woman" would be weird and awkward.

She thought about Gabe a few times and wondered what he was doing today. He seemed to keep his own hours and didn't talk much about work. Most of what he and her brother did wasn't for public consumption. And because she didn't pay much attention to the news, she probably wouldn't have understood it anyway.

As much as she gave him a hard time about being her constant shadow, a secret part of her was thankful. He'd become her security blanket through this whole ordeal. Unlike most men she knew, he didn't demand anything from her. And even when he was trying to keep her in line for Logan's sake, she felt in control. Which was a first.

And for a guy who could have any woman he wanted, he was pretty self-deprecating. More importantly, that New Jersey accent kept her entertained for hours.

She got off the highway and made her way to Rosser Ranch like a homing pigeon. *It's someone else's now*, she thought as she passed the large iron gates and felt a wave of melancholy settle over her. The ranch had been her hell and her haven and her family's pride and joy since the Gold Rush. Her great-great-grandfather had built the house with his own two hands after making his fortune, selling beef to the miners. Her grandfather had brought the house into the twentieth century, and her father had turned it into a showstopper. Ray Rosser had always lived large, and the ranch exemplified his excesses. The Olympic-size swimming pool, the two-story stable fit for the best horseflesh money could buy, the wraparound porch with its sixteen ceiling fans. Ray never did care much for the heat.

She continued to drive, taking the paved road toward the mountains, past McCreedy Ranch and Lucky's burgeoning cowboy camp. Ray must be rolling in his grave knowing how well Lucky Rodriguez had done for himself. Even in Los Angeles, she'd kept up with his progress. *Sports Illustrated* had done a spread when he'd hung up his bull riding spurs. And

God bless Facebook, where you could stalk a person from the comfort of your own living room.

When she got to her destination, she pulled off to the side of the road. Nothing but fields and trees and mountains for as far as the eye could see. At night you could hear faint sounds of the highway. But in the light of day, only the birds and the breeze and the river.

A motocross track, huh? Her gut told her Clay, Lucky, and their neighbors would fight it tooth and nail. Both men held a lot of sway in this town. They'd get the variance undone.

See, not my problem.

But finding the gold was. Ray had left detailed instructions, but Raylene had never been good at reading maps. And the only person she trusted enough with the information was Logan. But the timing was bad. If she signed off on the deal—and she'd be crazy not to—Moto Entertainment would send their environmental engineers to examine the land just as Logan was going on his honeymoon. She wouldn't ruin it for Annie. Her soon-to-be sister-in-law had made enough concessions by accepting the dangers of Logan's profession and the frequency in which he'd have to leave the country. No way would she ask them to put their Hawaii trip on hold.

And, hopefully, they'd return to a big pile of money. Annie could get that new living room set she wanted, and Logan that stupid hot tub he kept talking about. Best of all, the new baby would have a college fund.

She zipped her jacket up to her neck and scanned the land. It was a lot of earth to cover in a short amount of time. And God help her if it snowed. But she'd power through. What choice did she have? The money from the property wouldn't be enough to get her business off the ground and honor her commitments. And she'd be damned if she let a motocross company find the gold after losing everything else to Butch. Just the image of her slimy ex-husband made her whack a tree with her handbag.

"Hey, ma'am, are you okay?"

Raylene spun around, startled, and found a young girl standing there, staring at her as if she were a lunatic. "You scared me."

"Sorry."

"Who are you?" The closest neighbors were the McCreedys, and Raylene had a sneaking suspicion who the girl was.

"Harper Matthews. You probably know me as Hope."

Raylene didn't know her at all, but she was Emily's daughter, the one who had been kidnapped and rescued.

"Who are you?"

"Raylene Rosser. Does your mom and stepdad know you're out here?" When she was the girl's age, she used to run wild through these fields. But it was ten degrees out, and frankly the child looked lost. And dirty, like she'd been dragged through a mud puddle.

"No. I fell off my horse."

Raylene looked past her but didn't see a horse. "Where?"

Harper hunched her shoulders. "Back there somewhere." She waved at a copse of trees near the McCreedy property line. "You're not going to tell anyone, are you?"

"That you fell off your horse?" Raylene's father, who'd been born in the saddle, had been a tyrant when it came to riding and having the perfect seat. But even he accepted that a person could get thrown from time to time.

Harper's gaze fell to her pink cowboy boots, and Raylene instantly knew she was hiding something.

"You're not supposed to be riding alone, are you?"

"My mother doesn't let me do anything, not even walk to the mailbox by myself."

Raylene could understand why.

"I just want to get better at it, and no one has time to help me. Justin's always with Cynthia and Cody would rather play a video game. Clay's got the ranch to run and my mother is afraid of horses."

Raylene laughed. Last time she'd seen the boys was a few years ago. By now, they were young men. "How are your brothers?"

"They're not my real brothers."

"Are they nice?" Raylene asked.

"Very."

"Then claim them, they come in handy." Logan had been her savior.

"I have a half sister, too. Paige. She's a baby."

Raylene nodded. "Should we try to find your horse?" More than likely it had headed home.

"Yes, or I'm gonna be in big trouble."

"How long have you been gone?" Raylene needed to call Clay, but she felt for the kid.

"I don't know. I wasn't keeping track of the time."

"Five minutes and then we call home, okay?" Harper didn't look too happy about that, but she tacitly agreed. "What's your horse's name?"

"Ginger."

Raylene put two fingers in her mouth and let out a loud whistle.

"How'd you learn how to do that?"

"Practice." She called "Ginger" and clicked her tongue. It was a long shot, but worth trying.

Nothing.

"Were you riding bareback?"

"With a saddle. But I didn't do the thing right and it slid off."

"The cinch?" The girl was lucky she didn't get hurt.

Harper nodded.

"You have to learn how to do that properly before you can ride. We should look for your saddle." The McCreedys had always had nice tack. "It'll be faster in the truck." Raylene helped Harper in, and it struck her that the girl hadn't thought twice about talking to or taking a ride with a stranger.

She started the engine, cranked up the heat, and drove in the direction of the trees. "Keep your eyes peeled."

When they got to the grove Raylene stopped, got out of the truck, and looked around. She could see her own breath and rubbed her gloved hands together to keep warm. "Which way from here?"

Harper pointed south, where the land turned to McCreedy property. There was a split-rail fence separating the two parcels. "You sure?"

"No."

Raylene didn't think so. She stared out over the pasture, trying to think how she would've gone. There was a time when she knew every square inch of these fields and had ridden the backcountry for hours at a time.

"Let's get back in the truck before we freeze."

Harper scrambled in and Raylene turned around. On a hunch, she followed the fence line.

"How come you were beating that tree with your purse? Did something bad happen?"

Raylene slid Harper a sideways glance, not wanting to get into the details of her messy divorce with a thirteen-year-old. "My dad died. But it was months ago."

Harper nodded, her lips pursed like a sage old woman, which made Raylene smile. "It's okay to still be sad," she said, acting all grown-up. "My…the woman who stole me…died before Christmas. It's been really hard."

Raylene didn't want to pry or ask anything that was inappropriate, but she was beyond curious. "Did you care for her?"

"Yeah," Harper said. "Her and my dad. But he wasn't really my dad. He died in a car crash a long time ago."

"I'm sorry. You didn't know that they had kid—taken you?"

"They said my parents had died. I guess I was stupid to believe them."

"Nah, you were just a little kid. No way you could've known. Do you see what I see?"

Harper gasped. "Ginger!"

Raylene applied the brakes and slowly got out of the cab. "Come here, girl." She clicked her tongue and held out her hand, and the mare stretched her neck to see what Raylene had. That's when she reached for the reins and tugged her in. "Good girl. You're such a good girl." Raylene pointed a few feet behind Ginger. "There's your saddle. Go get it and throw it in the back."

Harper hefted it off the ground with both hands and Raylene helped her toss it in the bed of her truck.

"You ready to face the music?"

"What does that mean?"

In Raylene's case, it usually meant a beating for hanging around with Lucky, but she didn't think Clay was like that. His father, Tip, had been one of the nicest men she'd known. She'd openly wept at his funeral. "Probably a time-out." Or maybe Harper was too old for that. Raylene didn't interact with too many tweens.

She tied Ginger to her back bumper and drove at a snail's pace to the McCreedy house. Harper kept up a steady chatter, which indicated to Raylene that she wasn't too afraid of the consequences for sneaking out to go riding. The girl seemed healthy—and fearless, not something you displayed if you'd been abused. Then again, victims of abuse had all kinds of ways of manifesting their pain.

Raylene knew that all too well.

"Do you know a lot about horses?" Harper asked.

"Yep." That was pretty much all Raylene knew about. She'd failed at everything else. Friendship, marriage, managing her money. "When I was a little bit older than you, I was a champion barrel racer." Later, she'd married Butch and left the rodeo circuit. And now, living in Santa Monica, there was no place convenient to stable her gelding. She'd had to leave Gunner in Colorado.

"Really?" Harper's face lit up, and it did something gooey to Raylene's insides. It was nice to impress someone again, even if she was only thirteen years old. "Maybe you can show me some things."

"It's up to Clay and your mom." And dad, Raylene supposed. She didn't know anything about him, or even if he was still in the picture.

"They'll say yes." Harper clapped her hands and Raylene felt guilty for getting her hopes up. Clay wouldn't let her anywhere near his stepdaughter, and she didn't have time anyway. She had a fortune to find.

Raylene kept her eyes on the rearview mirror to make sure Ginger was okay, then took the fire trail back to the main road and headed to McCreedy Ranch. Three big dogs came nipping at her tires, barking as she crawled up the driveway. At least the mare wasn't fazed. Clay, Emily, and a man Raylene had never seen before were standing on the front porch, watching her drive up.

She parked in front of the house and hopped out of the cab to untie Ginger. The stranger and Emily trotted up to the passenger side as Harper started to get out.

"We've been worried sick," Emily said. "You can't just go off like that."

Clay came around to Raylene's side and took Ginger's reins. "Where'd you find her?"

"She found me, actually. I was up the road…on my property." Raylene waited for Clay to ask about the land and wondered if he knew about her buyer yet. She was a little surprised that he hadn't tried to buy the parcel himself. It bordered his ranch, and cattlemen were always looking for new grazing land.

He just grabbed the saddle from the bed of her truck. "Thanks for bringing her home."

"No problem. She had trouble with the saddle and fell off."

He gazed over at Harper, who was getting a good talking to, with what looked to Raylene like a great deal of relief. He appeared to have a deep affection for the girl. "I need to spend more time teaching her." He sighed.

"Is that her father?"

"Yeah, Drew Matthews. He has a place in Sierra Heights and splits his time between here and the Bay Area."

"She's a good girl," Raylene said, not that anyone would take her word for it. "I think she was trying to spread her wings, and she desperately wants to learn to ride."

He glowered, clearly not interested in her opinion. "After what happened… we're protective," he said tersely.

Raylene nodded, not knowing how to respond. She could only imagine how difficult it would be to recover a daughter who'd been ripped from you, only to fear losing her again.

Harper ran over to them, and Emily and her ex followed.

"Raylene said she'll teach me to be better on Ginger. Can she?"

Emily looked at Clay and there was a long silence. Raylene wanted desperately to extricate herself from the conversation, but Drew stuck out his hand and introduced himself. Clearly, he hadn't gotten the memo about her.

"Thanks for helping my daughter and bringing her horse home. She's still learning the ropes."

"Not a problem. My brother's rehearsal dinner is in a few hours, and I need to get home to help with the preparations." She ruffled Harper's blond hair. "You take care, now."

"You're still gonna help me ride, right?"

Clay stepped between them and squeezed Harper's shoulder. "I'll work with you some more, kiddo."

"But Raylene said she would, and you don't have time."

"She's busy with her brother's wedding and then she's going back to LA, sweetheart." Clay shot Raylene a warning look.

Message received.

"Clay's right, I'm leaving soon."

"But you said you can teach me."

"Stop." Emily draped her arm around her daughter's back and drew her in. "It was lovely of Raylene to offer, honey. But we don't want to take advantage. She's here for a short amount time, and probably wants to spend it with her family."

Raylene pretended to check her watch. "I've really got to go. It was nice meeting you, Harper."

She swung into the driver's seat and drove down the hill without looking back, a lump in her throat. The sooner she got out of Nugget the better.

Halfway to Logan's, her cell rang. She took one look at the caller ID and let it go to voicemail.

Chapter 5

Gabe kept his eyes peeled. He and Rhys had been riding around the backcountry for more than an hour.

"This is where you saw them?"

"Yep." Rhys parked his SUV next to a tree and pulled a pair of binoculars from the back seat. "It looked as if they'd made camp over there." He pointed at a thicket of pine trees.

"You think they're growing pot out here?"

"I didn't find any evidence of it, but they didn't look like your garden variety campers, either. But, to be fair, they were too far away for me to get a good enough look. Just a gut feeling."

Gabe wagged his hand for Rhys to give him the binocs. "You said there were three of them."

"One was small. Could've been a child; another red flag, if you ask me."

"I can see that. Maybe they're a homeless family." Gabe scanned the area but didn't see anything but trees, leaves, and a few patches of old snow.

"Maybe, but it would be pretty unusual in Nugget. Too cold. If it was one of our own, we would've heard about it."

Rhys was right. If someone had fallen on hard times, the whole town would've banded together to help. That's one of the things Gabe loved about Nugget.

"Looks like they might've just been passing through." Gabe handed him back the binoculars.

"Yup, could be. I'd appreciate you keeping your eyes open, though. Like I said, something about it didn't feel right. Over the years, I've learned to listen to my spidey sense."

Absolutely. It had saved Gabe's life more times than he wanted to think about. That eerie chill running up his back or that gnawing feeling in the pit of his stomach. In the spec ops world, he'd learned very quickly to pay close attention to that sixth sense. "Roger that."

Rhys restarted the engine and took the rutted dirt road back in the direction of the highway. "Thanks for coming along. Usually, I'd take Jake, but he and Cecilia took a few days to visit one of his daughters."

The detective had five of them. All grown, all hot. All wrapped in caution tape as far as Gabe was concerned. Jake was protective, and Gabe wasn't ready to put a ring on it.

"Cecilia upset about Raylene being here?" he asked Rhys.

"She's Lucky's mother, what do you think?"

The way Gabe had heard it was that Cecilia Stryker had practically raised Raylene when she kept house on Rosser Ranch. "She doesn't seem all that bad to me. Spoiled, maybe, but not as terrible as everyone makes her out to be. And she cares about Logan. I know it wasn't that way in the beginning, but she's come around, and I think it's legit."

Rhys drummed his fingers on the steering wheel. "I always suspected that Ray had her wrapped around his little finger. It was a power thing with him, and she was daddy's little girl."

"Logan says he abused her." Gabe was probably talking out of turn, but there were two sides to every story. He'd seen it firsthand, traveling around the world, fighting wars. "I'm not saying that's an excuse for what she did, but I think she was under his thumb. And later, under Butch's. Truthfully, I think she was scared to death of her ex-husband, and I don't think Raylene scares that easy."

Gabe remembered Denver, when she went nose to nose with Butch as she was leaving him. He suspected she wouldn't have been so tough if she hadn't had two former Navy SEALs backing her up. There was a reason she'd called Logan in the first place. At the time, they weren't on the best of terms.

"I definitely think Butch was calling the shots as far as cutting Logan out of his inheritance. But helping her old man set up Lucky on murder charges...that was cold. Lucky loved her."

That was the thing. Nothing about Raylene struck him as cold. Self-centered? Yes. Destructive? Maybe. Mean? Gabe didn't see it. And he'd been up close and personal with some of the meanest hombres on the face of the earth.

"It didn't work," Gabe said. In the end, Ray Rosser went to prison for killing that cattle thief and died in his cell.

"Because Jake and I are damn good cops," Rhys said.

"And modest." Gabe laughed, because listening to Rhys' bravado while riding shotgun, armed to the hilt, reminded him of being back in the teams with his brothers.

"For Cecilia, Tawny, and Lucky's sake, I want her out of here," Rhys said. "And I'm not the only one. But folks care too much about Annie and Logan to make a scene. So, until they leave on their honeymoon, everyone'll be on their best behavior. After that, all gloves come off. I wouldn't put it past Cecilia to run Raylene out of town."

Gabe sighed. "I hear ya, and I don't think you'll have to wait long. As soon as the wedding's over, I suspect she'll hit the road. My sense is she's not feeling the love."

Rhys chuckled. "She'd have to be pretty warped, otherwise. I hear she talked to Dana today about a buyer for her property."

"I hadn't heard, but I'll take your word for it." Gabe knew she wanted to unload the property and use the money toward her horse ranch or whatever scheme she was cooking up. It was a valuable piece of land, and with the market the way it was, he wasn't surprised she had an offer.

"Hopefully it won't hold her up." Rhys pulled into the square and parked his SUV in front of the police station. "See you around, Moretti."

"Later," Gabe said, and ducked inside the barbershop.

Owen, who'd been threatening to retire ever since Gabe rolled into town last summer, was giving some poor kid a jarhead buzzcut and talking the kid's father's ear off about politics. Gabe tuned him out, learning long ago to avoid that subject. Especially with Owen, who got most of what he talked about wrong.

"You got an appointment?"

Gabe scanned the empty waiting room. "No. Since when do I need an appointment?"

"Since I got a date with a new fishing pole."

"You're seriously wanting to fish in this?" Gabe stared out the window where the condensation on the rooftops had turned to icicles.

"Toughen up, boy. You're not in New Jersey anymore."

Gabe had more than a dozen ways he could respond to that but decided to leave it alone. "You gonna give me a trim or not?" *And don't butcher my hair like you did the kid's,* he wanted to say. But again he left it alone. Diplomacy. He was practicing diplomacy.

"You're next, then I'm closing the shop for the day."

"Where's Darla?" Gabe got a kick out of the hairdresser's colorful clothes, and she was a lot less surly than her old man, though he got a kick out of him too. Everyone in town had their own unique thing going. It was part of the reason Gabe fell in love with the place.

"It's her day off. She and Wyatt went to Sacramento to visit her mom." Owen finished up with the boy and motioned for Gabe to hop in the chair. He squared up with the kid's father at the cash register and returned with a clean cape, which he snapped around Gabe's neck. "You want a shave, too?"

Gabe eyed his chin in the mirror, turning his head from side to side. "What the hell? Go for it."

"That way you won't look like a derelict for Annie's wedding."

A derelict? Gabe had to suppress an eye roll. "What's new around here?" The barbershop was gossip central, and Owen was usually king rumor monger. Sometimes he got it right. More often than not, though, he embellished, putting his own bizarre spin on things. Gabe had learned how to muck through the bullshit in order to glean some semblance of the truth.

"That Rosser girl is all anyone is talking about." Owen pulled a pair of shears from his drawer and started snipping away at Gabe's sides.

"Not too much." He covered the side of his head and Owen slapped his hand away. "What's everyone saying?"

"That she's selling that land behind Rosser Ranch. Folks are worried about what'll go in there. No one wants a Hilton."

Gabe stifled a laugh. A Hilton? As if that was even a remote possibility.

"The Millers are worried a big-box store will come in and put Farm Supply out of business."

"Nugget's population won't support a big box store." That was the other thing about the good residents of Nugget: they had delusions of grandeur.

"Tell Sam Walton that."

"Last I looked, he was dead, Owen."

"You know what I mean." Owen pinned him with a look. "I'm personally concerned that one of those cults will come in, like them Branch Davidians."

Where did he cook this shit up? "A Fantastic Sams would be a welcomed addition." Gabe said it just to get a rise out of Owen.

Owen didn't take the bait, rambling on about all the possible businesses that would vie for the land, including a pot farm, which Gabe thought was more likely than a cult or a Costco. Realistically, though, someone would probably want the land to run cattle. Gabe wouldn't be surprised if the offer had come from one of the local ranchers. Clay McCreedy, Flynn Barlow, even Lucky Rodriguez was a good guess.

"That girl planning to stay?" Owen asked.

"Raylene? Nah, she's going back to LA after the wedding."

"She sure pulled the wool over our eyes. Back in the day, she was a sweet little thing. Rodeo queen, champion barrel racer, volunteer at the Elks annual pancake breakfast, real active in the community. Even so, Ray was hard on the girl, publicly laying into her enough times to make me wonder what was going on behind closed doors. But what do you do? You can't go around telling people how to rear their kids."

Nope, Gabe thought. Not unless you witnessed actual abuse. But in a close-knit town like this...someone should've known.

"Back then," Owen continued, "she and Lucky were attached at the hip. Ray didn't like his daughter trucking with a Mexican boy, especially since his mama was the help. He never made a secret about it, and to tell you the truth it made me sick."

Ray Rosser sounded like a grade-A prick. As far as Gabe was concerned, Logan had dodged a bullet when Rosser refused to claim him as his son. Raylene, not so much. She'd had the misfortune of being groomed by Ray to be his protégée.

It told Gabe more than he wanted to know. He'd always had a soft spot for the misunderstood—not that he was ready to give Raylene the benefit of the doubt. But there was definitely more to the spoiled rich girl than everyone saw. Everyone but Logan. And Gabe had always found his partner to be a good judge of character.

"There you go." Owen twirled the chair around and gave Gabe a hand mirror so he could get a view of the back of his head.

"Looks good."

"You'll pass muster." Owen lathered up Gabe's chin and reached for a straight-edge razor.

"Don't get too wild with that thing."

Owen laughed. "I've been shaving men since before you were born."

The barber certainly knew his stuff. Closest shave Gabe ever had.

Outside, the cold stung his face as he walked to his SUV. It was still too early to head over to the farm, and he wasn't in the mood for paperwork. Out of obligation—at least that's what he told himself—he called Raylene.

"You at Logan's?"

"I'm in my truck, in the driveway. Logan's parents just got here."

"Go in and introduce yourself," he told her.

"Scared."

Gabe's lips tipped up. Nick was a badass, and could be daunting as hell, but that's not what Raylene was afraid of, Gabe knew. It was Maisy, though Raylene had nothing to fear. Even if Maisy wasn't the sweetest woman on earth, she was the one who'd been the so-called homewrecker.

Raylene hadn't even been born when Ray started his affair with Logan's mom. "Meet me for lunch, then."

"Why?"

"Gotta eat."

"Okay. Where?"

"You've got two choices."

Raylene groaned. "Fine, the Ponderosa. I'm not eating at the Bun Boy. Ever."

Gabe laughed. It was too cold anyway. The burger drive-through only had outdoor seating. And the Ponderosa had sort of become his home away from home when he wasn't loitering at Logan and Annie's. Although his little apartment had a full kitchen, he never touched it. "I'm right outside the restaurant. I'll grab us a table."

Gabe crossed the square and felt the warm air as soon as he entered the restaurant.

"Hey, Gabe." Today it was Mariah, Sophie's other half, working hostess duties. Gabe didn't say "better" because the dynamic duo were both great. Smart, beautiful, sophisticated, older, and, unfortunately, not into men.

"What's happening?"

"You tell me."

"Oh, you know, wedding twenty-four seven."

She laughed. "I'm looking forward to it."

He ordered a plate of super nachos and a beer and read the *Nugget Tribune* on his phone while he waited for Raylene. He wondered what she'd been up to all day, besides her meeting at the real estate office.

Ten minutes later, she swept into the Ponderosa in her rhinestone jeans and her turquoise cowboy boots. No frog hogs at McPatrick's in Coronado ever dressed like that. Their look ran more toward spray tans, bikini tops, and flip-flops, which Gabe liked just fine. But Raylene...let's just say he was growing partial to cowgirls.

"You want a beer?" He started to call a server over but Raylene stopped him.

"I'll get a cup of coffee when the waiter takes our order." She took off her jacket and hung it on a hook on the wall.

"So you ran out before meeting Maisy, huh?"

"I got a decent look at her coming out of the Winnebago. She's different than I expected." She unwrapped the scarf around her neck and draped it over an extra chair.

Gabe made a Herculean effort not to check out her rack—and failed. "How'd you think she'd be?"

"I don't know, kind of slutty."

Gabe would've laughed, except they were talking about Logan's mom, a woman he happened to adore. "Cut her a break, Ray. She was barely out of her teens when she met your old man. According to Logan, he seduced her, not the other way around."

Raylene shrugged, her mouth forming an affected pout that had probably won over more than a fair share of men. But Gabe saw right through it. Her whole self-entitled schtick was nothing but an act. Armor for the insecure.

"I heard you had a meeting with Dana McBride this morning."

She flipped through Gabe's menu. "Word always did travel fast in Bumfuck."

The nachos came and Gabe handed her one of the small plates the server had left on the table. "What else did you do?"

She took a sip of water and stared at him over the rim of the glass. "Trespassed."

"Yeah?" He arched a brow, trying to act disapproving when for him B&E was just another day at work. "Where?"

"Rosser Ranch." She scooped up one of the cheese-laden chips, dipped it in a mound of guacamole, and popped it in her mouth.

"I hear Flynn Barlow is a good shot." He and his wife, Gia Treadwell, owned Rosser Ranch now. While Flynn wouldn't shoot Raylene on sight, he wouldn't be too happy about her roaming his property. "What were you doing over there?"

"Checking it out."

This was exactly the reason Logan had put Gabe on Raylene duty. Leave the woman alone long enough and she'd cause an international incident.

"Not the best idea, don't you think?"

"It was my ranch first." She pouted again, and Gabe got the sense she was lying. Not about the ranch being hers first—that was uncontested—but about how she'd spent the day. She was trying to throw him off.

"What'd you think of that new addition they put on the house?"

"Tacky."

Yeah, she was lying, all right. There was no new addition. The place was already large enough to fit an entire battalion. Raylene was up to something, and his sixth sense told him that whatever it was, it was no good.

He arched a brow. "Tacky, huh?"

Raylene started to say something, then her attention snapped to the front of the restaurant, where Tawny Rodriguez had just come through the door. A couple sitting by the window, wearing matching bear hoodies, waved to her. She waved back and walked straight to the bar, presumably to pick up a takeout order.

That was the thing about a small town: you couldn't avoid your enemies.

"Shit," Raylene muttered.

"Are you planning to kiss me again?"

She snorted and snatched up the menu to hide her face, trying to make herself as small as possible.

Gabe tilted his head. "With those turquoise boots, she can see you from a mile away." Especially because Tawny was a boot designer and had footwear radar. Her custom shit-kickers donned the feet of celebrities, athletes, and a veritable who's who of the West. And probably the East, North, and South. "I'm guessing those"—he pointed at her feet—"are not hers."

"Good guess, New Jersey," she sneered. "Tell me when she's gone."

"Seriously? You're going to sit in the corner and cower? I thought you were tough, Ray."

She gave him a middle-finger salute, then feigned interest in the condiment caddy. He scarfed down a few more nachos, took a swig of beer, and waited for Tawny to leave before declaring the coast clear.

"What are you planning to do at the wedding? Hole up in the head?" Between Maisy and Tawny, Raylene was already running scared.

She let out a breath. "I haven't figured it out yet." She swiped a chip and pointed it at him. "I'm trying not to make a spectacle out of myself. Believe it or not, what you saw in Denver isn't who I am."

Who was she kidding? From everything Gabe had heard—and seen—it was exactly who she was. "Really? Folks are still talking about your episode at the Gas and Go."

"I was drunk."

"It's okay, Ray, we've all done our fair share of regrettable things." Lord knew he had. One of his had been a redhead with a pissed off boyfriend. He'd like to say another was babysitting the blonde across the table, but he was enjoying himself too much.

"Like what?" She sat up.

"I went off to war and made my mama cry."

She rolled her eyes. "You steal that from a country-western song, New Jersey?"

"I don't listen to that shit. Classic rock, mainly." He leaned across the table and brushed tortilla chip crumbs from her sweater. "I got my high school sweetheart pregnant." He never talked about it, but the words had tumbled out of his mouth, and now he was stuck with them.

"And let me guess, you joined the Navy to do your patriotic duty and stuck her with a kid to raise, alone."

"Cynic doesn't look good on you, Ray. Actually, Bianca lost the baby, then I ran off to join the Navy." That wasn't the whole story, but that was all he was telling her.

They both had their secrets. And tomorrow he was going to find out what hers were.

Chapter 6

Raylene loaded a shovel and a pickax into her truck early the next morning. Between Annie and Logan, there was no shortage of tools in the garage, which saved Raylene a trip to the hardware store. Logan and Annie had taken Maisy and Nick to breakfast in town, so Raylene figured it was okay to help herself.

Maisy had turned out to be a delight, Nick hysterical, telling one joke after another. Neither seemed to hold any ill will against Raylene, despite the fact that originally she'd tried to cut Logan out of his inheritance. God, she'd been too stupid to live back then, and often wondered why God hadn't sent down a lightning bolt to strike her over the head.

With the map tucked securely under her floor mat, she felt like a 49er, setting out to strike it rich. Nugget was a Gold Rush town, after all. She put some Garth Brooks on the stereo, turned it up loud, and headed out, hoping to find Levi's Gold before tonight's rehearsal dinner. Then she could tell Dana to accept Moto Entertainment's offer and be watching a Santa Monica sunset by Monday.

Two hours later, she cursed the cold, hard dirt under her feet and flung the stupid map onto the driver's seat. She felt a blister on the heel of her left foot. Despite the old song lyrics, her boots were not made for walking. They were made for a pair of sterling silver-studded stirrups.

She bent down and held her knees, trying to catch her breath. It was twenty degrees, but her skin was clammy with sweat from digging. Knowing her luck, if she worked without a jacket she'd catch pneumonia.

Raylene straightened up and poked at her hand where the skin had cracked. If she'd been thinking, she would've worn gloves.

Only one hundred and ninety-nine acres to go. I'll be crippled by then.

She got in her truck and examined the map again, then peered out at the land. If she was reading it right, the gold was somewhere in the vicinity of the very trees she was standing under. Raylene was starting to think Levi, her great-great-grandfather's brother, was a real dipshit. Why couldn't he have just put the gold in a suitcase and stowed it in the attic? Or, even better, gotten a freaking safe deposit box?

According to legend, Levi had been bad to the bone. Unsatisfied with the modest—but steady—income from selling beef to the prospectors, he started out stealing horses from miners and selling them across state lines in Nevada. When that wasn't lucrative enough for him, Levi became what the Australians called a "night fossicker." He spent his days sleeping and his nights pilfering gold from the richest claims. It didn't take long for the miners to catch on, and soon they gathered a posse to come after him. Ashamed, his family wouldn't take him in. So Levi buried the gold on Rosser land, planning to excavate it as soon as the heat was off him. That day never came. He was shot and killed after drawing down on a sheriff's deputy who'd been trying to bring him in.

When Raylene had asked her granddaddy why he'd never searched for the gold, he'd rolled his eyes and said the lore was worth more in the ground than in his pocket. But Ray swore by the story, and had even shown Raylene historical accounts of the gold in various newspapers and books. From time to time, Ray had had to shoo enthusiastic treasure hunters off the property. But most people, including Butch, thought the story was a crock, something told around the Thanksgiving table for shits and giggles.

"Sell the fucking land, Raylene, and forget that bullshit," Butch had told her before the divorce. "We need the money to pay off your goddamn Neiman Marcus bill."

Well, he wasn't getting a dime of it now. Not the proceeds from the sale of the property or the gold, when she found it.

She got out and leaned against the hood, surveying the fields. The last rain had left the grass green and the river full. And she could smell pine and eucalyptus and the moss of the river rocks. She walked to the embankment, crouched down, and tried to skip a stone over the rushing water. It was so peaceful she could hear her own heartbeat. In the distance, the mountain peaks were white, covered in snow, and the sky so clear she could see to eternity.

No wonder Ray had never developed the land. Her father had been a ruthless bastard, but he knew a good thing when he saw it. She let out a breath. What if she didn't find the gold? What if it didn't exist? She was down to her last few thousand dollars, not even enough to cover the lease on her beach house or a first and last month's deposit on an apartment.

Unless she could find a job training horses or giving riding lessons, she had no skills. Nothing that would earn her a living wage, anyway. She supposed she could learn to wait tables or clean houses. But there were others to consider, people who needed the money even worse than she did.

Nope, holding on to the property until someone more suitable than Moto Entertainment came along to buy it was out of the question.

Don't stand in the way of progress.

She walked back to where she'd left the shovel on the ground and got back to work. After the wedding, she'd return on Sunday with gloves and a metal detector. Not bringing one today had been shortsighted. But she didn't think Logan and Annie had one, and she didn't know where to rent such things.

"Digging your own grave, or someone else's?"

She jumped, then turned to see Gabe leaning against her truck. He looked as though he'd just walked off the cover of one those soldier of fortune magazines. He wore a green army jacket and camo cargo pants, a boonie hat, and a pair of Gatorz sunglasses. He held a thermos in his hand, and the sweet smell of coffee wafted through the air, making her mouth water.

"Why are you always sneaking up on me?"

"I wasn't sneaking." He pointed at her shovel. "You were distracted."

"Well, now that you're here, make yourself useful." She grabbed the pickax and shoved it at him. "Start here." She tapped the toe of her turquoise boot a few inches from where she'd been digging. From the looks of the map, the gold could be buried anywhere in the general vicinity. Or, she could've been reading it upside down.

"Not until I know what I'm digging for." He took a swig of the coffee.

"Soil samples. I've got a buyer interested but they want soil samples. Be sure to dig deep."

He continued to drink his coffee and survey the hole she'd dug. "Let me see the map, Ray."

She jerked in surprise. "What map? I don't know what you're talking about."

He didn't say anything, just stood there, drinking his coffee, watching her dig.

"Seriously, you're just planning to stand there?"

"Yep, unless you're willing to admit that you're looking for the gold."

The man was insufferable. Logan didn't even know about the legend. "How'd you figure it out?"

He reached in his pocket and held up his phone. "Google. I saw you digging, wondered why, and did a little research. Most of what I read said the story's more than likely bullshit."

Ray didn't think it was. "How'd you know I was here?" She stood up and leaned on the top of her shovel.

"I was in the neighborhood."

"The neighborhood, huh?" She stared out into the distance, where a mama deer and her two babies ran across the pasture. Besides being insufferable, he was a lousy liar. "Have you been following me?"

He laughed. "A little high on yourself, aren't you, Ray?"

She noticed he hadn't exactly answered the question. "Well, now that you know about the gold, are you at least going to help me find it?"

He put his thermos and cup down on the hood of her truck and examined the pickax. "We have a rehearsal dinner to go to."

"Not for hours." She searched for his SUV but didn't see it. "You hike in?"

"Why here?" He toed the hole she'd been digging. "Why this spot?"

"Just a hunch." Raylene shrugged her shoulders. She didn't want to show him the map or let on that she even had one. Just because he was Logan's best friend didn't mean she could fully trust him.

"There's a lot of land here, Ray. You need more than a hunch, unless you're planning to excavate the entire parcel with heavy machinery."

She didn't have the money to do that, and, furthermore, it would look weird to her buyer, like she was trying to destroy something, or cover it up. "Ray said it was here."

He held her gaze, his brown eyes assessing. "Hmm, was he around in eighteen forty-nine?"

Gabe wasn't going to make this easy for her, which was all the more reason to dig in her heels. The prospect of money made people greedy. Look at Butch. He and his lawyer had robbed her blind.

"The story's been passed down from generation to generation. Ray told me about the gold when I was old enough to walk. I would think he'd know, Gabe."

"Then why didn't he dig for the treasure himself?"

"It was his own personal savings account. An account he didn't have to declare to the government."

He folded his arms over his chest. "Not buying it."

"Fine! Then run along." She shooed him away.

He didn't budge. She picked up the shovel and started digging again. At least before her hands were numb—now they were ice cold. That's what she got for stopping to chitchat with G.I. Joe. He thumbed through his phone while she worked, which made her grind her teeth in annoyance.

"There's a hardware store in Graeagle where we can rent a metal detector."

She gazed up at him over the handle of her shovel. "When we find the gold, I'll give you a percentage. But don't get any ideas that we're equal partners in this."

"I'm not worried about it." He tugged off his sunglasses and hooked the earpiece on his breast pocket. "You know why? Because we're not going to find any gold."

"Just as long as you know up front: my property, my claim."

"Aye aye, Captain."

Fine, let him mock her. What did she care, as long as she was getting a strong back and muscles out of the deal? Her own muscles were on fire.

"Why don't you get the metal detector while I continue to dig?" No way was she leaving him alone with her gold.

"Not today." He shook his head. "Today is rehearsal day, tomorrow's the wedding. We'll do it on Sunday."

She didn't want to wait that long. Dana needed an answer on Moto Entertainment. Raylene feared that putting them off too long could risk losing the sale.

She slipped her cell out of her jacket and looked at the time. "By my calculation, we have more than six hours. What's the matter, Moretti, you have an appointment for a perm and highlights?"

He came toward her and yanked the shovel out of her hands. For a second she could feel herself cower, waiting for the blow that never came. Instead, he started digging, making three times the progress she had with his long, hard strokes. She watched for a while, because she needed a breather and because...he was something. Strong and efficient. For a second, she wondered what it would be like to have his big hands work her like he was working the ground. Just as quickly, she shut down the image and grabbed the pickax.

She tried to heft the thing high enough to get a good swing, but it was heavy. And awkward. Eventually, he pulled it out of her hand.

"There's nothing here, Ray. You're either digging in the wrong place or there's no gold. I vote for the latter."

"How can you know that? You've barely started." But her gut told her he was right. She'd been at it for a few hours and wasn't feeling any cosmic connection with the gold. It didn't mean she was willing to quit, though. She wanted to study the map again, but not with Gabe peeking over her shoulder.

"I've got to pee," she said.

He stopped digging and nudged his head several yards away, at a tree on the other side of her truck. "Knock yourself out."

She crawled onto her front seat, found the map, shoved it in her pocket, and pretended to rifle through her purse.

"What are you doing?" he called.

"Looking for a tissue." She climbed out of the cab and held up a mini pack of Kleenex. "Got it," she said, and headed for the tree.

It was a towering oak with thick branches, and she had a sudden flash of a past Valentine's Day. She searched the tree's trunk, and, sure enough, it was still there. With her finger she traced the heart that Lucky had carved into the bark fifteen years ago with his penknife. *Raylene + Lucky.*

She shut her eyes for a second and let the memory wash over her. They'd snuck out here on horseback. Ray had forbidden her from seeing him, threatening to fire Cecelia if Raylene didn't obey.

You stay away from that Mexican trash. He only wants two things from you: a piece of ass and your money. If I ever catch you with him, I'll send his mama packing and make you and Lucky pay. You don't want to test me on this, Raylene. You don't know what I'm capable of. So find yourself an acceptable boy if you know what's good for you.

That acceptable boy had been Butch, who, as it turned out, only wanted Raylene for her money. *Not even a piece of ass,* she thought, wryly. He'd gotten that from her best friend and anyone else willing to spread their legs for him. Remarkably, many women had been.

She sat on the ground with her back to Gabe and retrieved the map from her pocket. Flattening out the page with the palm of her hand, she studied it closely, even tried turning it upside down. As far as she knew, Levi hadn't actually drawn the diagram. It had come from her great-great-grandfather, who knew where Levi buried the gold but was too fearful to dig it up, worried that people were watching the ranch. He died of cholera shortly after Levi was shot to death. The map had remained in the family over generations. Ray had made copies and had stashed them all over the house. Before he went to prison, he made sure Raylene and Butch found every last one of them before the new owner took possession of Rosser Ranch.

"Hey," Gabe called. "You okay over there?"

She folded up the map and shoved it back into her pocket. "Coming."

Gabe had taken off his jacket and stood surveying the hole he'd dug in a waffle-weave Henley that stretched across his chest. He rubbed his forehead against his shoulder to wipe away the sweat.

"This is insane, Ray. Let's come up with a new plan, like grabbing lunch."

She couldn't blame him for wanting to throw in the towel. He was right: it was pretty insane. But she wasn't giving up. Her father had been a lot of things, but naïve dreamer wasn't one of them. He'd been a shrewd business man, making a fortune in the cattle industry while other ranchers scraped by. He'd always had an uncanny knack for reading the beef market, knowing when to cull his herd and when to add to it. Besides livestock, he'd profited mightily from real estate, mineral rights, and California oil. All this was to say: he wasn't the type of guy to believe in a myth.

"But you'll come back on Sunday, right?"

Gabe wiped his face again, pulled off the boonie hat, and scrubbed his hand through his hair. He stared out over the two hundred acres and let out a breath. "If it'll keep you out of trouble…and we can go and have lunch."

Just the mere mention of food made her stomach growl. She'd skipped breakfast to get an early start before Logan and Annie returned home. "Fine. But Sunday we're renting that metal detector. Make sure the store's open."

He flipped out his cell and checked. "Yep. So, can we go now?"

She gathered the pickax off the ground and placed it into the bed of her truck. "As long as it's not the Ponderosa. I'm getting sick of it."

"That leaves the Bun Boy." He grinned.

"There's a good Mexican place in Clio. What do you say we go there?"

Gabe tossed the shovel next to the pickax. "I'm always game for Mexican. How about we drop your truck off at the farm and I drive?"

She had no problem with that, as it didn't make sense for them to go in two vehicles. "You're not afraid to be seen with me?" She smirked. "People around here might start getting the wrong idea. I wouldn't want to hurt your reputation."

"Too late for that." He winked and got into her passenger seat. "Let's bust a move, I'm hungry."

"Where's your SUV again?"

"Down the road about two miles."

She started the engine and slid him a sideways glance. "You were spying on me, weren't you?"

"Damn, Ray, you've got a suspicious nature."

She sure the hell did, and for good reason.

Chapter 7

It had only taken Gabe fifteen minutes to figure out what Raylene was up to. He'd been sitting at the corner of Ralston and Pine, waiting for the light to turn green, when she'd zoomed by in her F-150. On a lark, he'd decided to follow her. When she turned up Rock and River Road, it didn't take much to deduce that she was headed for her property. He almost hadn't come, figuring she was meeting her real estate agent or her buyers.

But after catching her in a lie the day before, curiosity won out. So he trailed her up the road from a distance, parked his SUV on the shoulder, and humped the rest of the way in. There she'd been, digging in those tight Western jeans and turquoise cowboy boots.

Gold. He suppressed an eye roll. Hell, he liked local lore as much as the next person, and these mountains were full of stories. From the Donner Party to the Western Pacific Railroad, there was no shortage. Cannibalism, hangings, people striking it rich. There was a reason the town was named "Nugget."

But after all this time—after earthquakes, floods, and fires—that gold, if it had existed, would've turned up by now. Raylene was wasting her time.

"What are you thinking about?" She reached over Gabe's console and poked him in the leg.

"Whether I want a burrito or a chimichanga. How 'bout you?"

"A torta, probably. They make really good ones, at least they used to."

"How long have you been gone exactly?" He turned down the radio, a station out of Reno. He knew she'd moved back a couple of years ago for just long enough to wreak havoc on the town, then returned to Denver to reconcile with Butch. That sure hadn't lasted long.

"Off and on, seventeen years." She was quiet for a while, then said, "I left right after high school."

"You didn't miss it?"

She sighed. "Not really." But there was something in her voice that said she had, maybe just a little bit. "A lot happened and it didn't feel like my town anymore."

"Like what?" He pulled off the highway and took the road into Clio, heading for the restaurant.

She turned to look at him. "Stuff with my dad, stuff I don't talk about."

"Okay, fair enough." Gabe was surprised she'd even said that much. Ray was usually a forbidden topic, and Raylene usually answered every question with a sarcastic retort. He'd noticed that about her. The truth was he'd noticed too much about her, including the way those Western jeans of hers had molded to her ass when she was shoveling the dirt.

He parked his truck in the dusty parking lot and went around to get her door. She jumped down before he could help her out.

"I'm starved," she said, and rushed off ahead of him.

The restaurant was more like a taco stand with a drive-through, an inside walk-up counter, concrete floors, and a few tables covered in oilcloths. Bright Mexican tiles and Day of the Dead skulls adorned the walls, and a big sombrero hung over the door. In the corner was a drink station, offering *aguas frescas* and *horchata* in big jars. It reminded him of his Navy days in San Diego.

The owner, who'd been in the kitchen, came up to the front and greeted him. "*Hola, amigo.* Where's your friend?"

"He couldn't come today. This is his sister." Gabe slung his arm around Raylene, mostly because he knew it would annoy her.

"What does such a beautiful woman want with you, *amigo?*"

"Ah, Victor, I have many hidden charms."

Victor leaned back and laughed, then pulled two Coronas from the cooler and handed them to Gabe and Raylene. "It's on the house. *Hasta la vista, amigos.*"

He disappeared into the kitchen and the young woman at the counter took their orders. Gabe pulled out a chair for Raylene and they waited for their food.

"The place is empty," Raylene said. "It didn't used to be."

"It's a little late for lunch, and too early for supper." When he and Logan came, the place was usually packed. "We're having steak tonight at the rehearsal dinner. Flynn's beef."

Raylene pulled a face. "It's not as good as Rosser beef used to be, but whatever. So his wife doesn't have the talk show anymore, huh?"

"Gia now runs the Iris Foundation, a charity that helps women who are down on their luck get back on their feet."

"I know," she said. "I read about it." A former celebrity like Gia got her name splashed all over the tabloids.

"Are she and Flynn buying your land?" It made sense that either they or Clay McCreedy would, since it sat between their two respective ranches.

"Nope." Raylene got up and poured herself a glass of hibiscus *agua fresca* and came back to the table.

"If not Flynn, who?" he asked.

"No one from around here."

Their food was up, and Gabe went to the counter to get it. He handed Raylene her torta and took his burrito. He excused himself to go to the head to wash his hands. Raylene had used one of those wet wipes on the ride over. Even in the teams, he'd been a fanatic hand washer. As a result, he rarely got sick, despite the nasty shit they'd breathed and ate during deployments. When he returned to the table, he noticed Raylene had waited for him to eat. Growing up in the Moretti household, you waited to eat, you went hungry. There were too many of them to stand on ceremony. Their table was like a circus, his sibs and steps all talking at the same time, passing food—and gas—fighting over the last dinner roll or strip of bacon, and joshing each other endlessly. It was the best.

He supposed being an only child, Raylene had had a completely different experience. And there was the fact that her father was an asshole. So, yeah, it wasn't the Moretti house.

"Dig in," he told her, and took a big bite of his burrito. "Is it as good as you remember it?"

"Uh-huh," she said around a mouthful. "Maybe better."

"I didn't discover Mexican food until the Navy. At home, it was either Italian, Irish, or some combination of both."

She nodded, pushing a piece of pork back inside her sandwich. "Logan said you guys were like the Brady Bunch…a blended family."

"Yep. My real old man ran out on us when I was two and died a year later from a stroke. My ma met Tino Moretti a few years later and that's all she wrote. Bada bing, soulmates. He adopted me and my baby sister, brought his own brood into the mix, and they had a few of their own. Big Italian family."

"But you're Irish?"

"Half and half. Biological dad was Italian. After him, Ma swore off Italian men. Obviously it didn't stick."

She dredged a tortilla chip through a bowl of salsa. "You're still close with everyone?"

"Like glue. We're spread across the country but that doesn't stop us from Skyping and texting each other every day."

"Wow. Nice. I wish Logan and I could've been like that growing up. Good ol' Ray made sure that didn't happen." She pushed her sandwich at him. "You can have the rest, I'm full."

He held her gaze until she blinked and turned away. "You tried to screw him out of his inheritance, Raylene."

In a voice barely above a whisper she said, "And for that I'm eternally sorry."

He didn't know how sorry she was, but she had dropped her suit contesting Logan's share of Ray's living trust. In the end, Logan had gotten a nice chunk of change. Logan didn't hold a grudge against Raylene, so why should Gabe? But the thing was, he did.

On the way out of the restaurant he asked her, "What are you planning to do with all that gold when we dig it up?" It wasn't as if she needed the money, she'd been left a small fortune. But he wanted to know if her so-called eternal remorse extended to splitting her bogus buried treasure with Logan, who was as much a Rosser as she was.

"Don't worry, I'll make sure you get your share."

He laughed to himself, because his share of nothing was nothing. "Wrong answer."

Raylene turned away, swishing that fantastic ass of hers in the air, and got into his SUV without saying a word. As they drove to the farm, she turned on the radio and, to piss him off, flipped the dial from his classic rock station to country music. When Dolly Pardon's "Jolene" came on, Gabe sang along.

"Raylene, Raylene, Raylene, Raylene, I'm begging of you please don't take my gold."

She slugged him in the shoulder and muttered something about him being an idiot. When they pulled up to the house, there were a couple of cars in the driveway that weren't Logan and Annie's and Gabe could feel Raylene tense. He shut off the engine and grabbed her by the arm before she could flee.

"Tonight's just family, so you can relax."

"Gia and Flynn will be there. Flynn hates me, and I hate him." That was Raylene, always on the offensive. Gabe knew it was her coping mechanism.

Flynn had been old man Rosser's estate attorney. He thought Raylene was a spoiled brat and never hesitated to voice that opinion out loud. The fact that he and Gia now owned Rosser Ranch was probably another thing that stuck in Raylene's craw.

"Gia's in the wedding, Ray. It only stands to reason that she and her husband would be included in the rehearsal dinner."

"I know," she said, trying to sound conciliatory. Yet Gabe saw the same vulnerability that had been there the night of the potluck streak across her face. And damn it, it brought the protector out in him. No matter how much he tried to look at Raylene as an assignment, she got to him. And despite his better judgment, he pulled her over the seat into his lap.

"You'll be fine, Ray."

She straightened her spine. "Damned right I'll be fine."

He smiled because the woman was as stubborn as he was—and as proud. So damn proud he couldn't help but admire her. "That's the old spirit."

They sat there for a few seconds, her legs awkwardly splayed across the console, and it seemed like the best thing to do in that moment was kiss her. He cupped the back of her head, pulled her in, and claimed her mouth. That was the thing about Ray, she couldn't resist a dare. And the kiss was definitely a dare. *I dare you to kiss me back.* And she did, long and slow, exploring his mouth with her lips and her tongue.

He tugged her in closer and took charge, letting his hands wander a little. Even through her jacket, he could feel firm breasts and the curve of her waist. If she wasn't such a pain in the ass, he'd say she was near perfect. And a phenomenal kisser. She tasted good, too, like Mexican food, hibiscus, and her own brand of sass.

He moved over her, taking the kiss deeper, sifting his fingers through her hair. It was soft and fine and smelled like lavender. Her lips were also soft, and he liked the way she gripped his shoulders, clutching him as if she never wanted to let him go. He continued to devour her mouth and heard Raylene whimper. It took all his willpower not to take her right there, in the front of his SUV. But he heard a little voice reminding him that they were in Logan's driveway, and that Raylene was his best friend's sister, and he managed to pull away.

"We should probably go inside," he said, adjusting himself.

She scrambled back to her side and opened the door before nudging her head pointedly toward his crotch, where he was so hard it hurt. "That's for your moronic version of 'Jolene.' Jeez, Moretti, you know how many times I had to put up with that in junior high?" She slid out of the passenger seat, gave his package one more glance, and smirked. "Consider us even."

He wanted to shout that he was the one who'd put the brakes on, that if it wasn't for him she'd be on her back right now with him inside her. Sweet relief. But that would've been even more junior high school than his rendition of the song, so he suffered in silence.

* * * *

Raylene got through the rehearsal dinner without a drink, which was a staggering achievement. She thought Wednesday's potluck had drained every ounce of her willpower. That night in the bathroom, she'd gone as far as to touch her mouth to the edge of the glass until wine lapped at her lips. The taste had been sweet with the promise of escape. Or better yet, oblivion. But a voice inside her head had reminded her how awful she and alcohol mixed, and the last thing she wanted to do was get drunk, make a fool out of herself, and ruin Logan and Annie's big week. So, she'd forced herself to dump the wine down the toilet just in time for Gabe to come banging on the door.

Ninety days sober.

She wiggled her toes, hitting the iron footboard, and let her eyes adjust to the light. According to the clock on the side table, it was a hair past six o'clock. Despite growing up on a ranch, she'd never been an early riser, languishing in bed sometimes well past nine. That's what happened when you didn't have a job or much of a reason to get up in the morning.

She gazed around the room. The walls were a cornflower blue, the curtains a tattered sunny yellow. Rag rugs covered the floor and a chipped white French provincial dresser flanked a black salvaged fireplace mantel. Old, empty picture frames had been glued to the door. Though a hodgepodge, it somehow worked, wrapping Raylene in a great big bear hug every time she entered the room. It was all Annie. Everything her brother's fiancée did was done with love. Raylene had never known anyone like her.

Growing up, Raylene's mother had hired a legion of decorators in their mammoth log home on the ranch. Custom cabinetry, marble countertops, handmade linens, museum-quality Navajo rugs, and Olaf Wieghorst paintings. Everything top-of-the-line, because Ray had to have the best.

If I wanted cheap I would've married a whore, then at least the sex would be good.

Her father had been a real class act. Raylene's mother should've told him to go to hell and back, but she was Ray's personal servant. Raylene couldn't blame her, because she'd also done Ray's bidding no matter how morally bankrupt it was. Whatever Ray wanted, Ray got. She'd once seen a documentary about Jim Jones, and icy fingers had crawled up her spine because she understood with such frightening clarity why all those people had blindly taken their own lives in his name. She understood because for her entire life she'd belonged to the cult of Ray Rosser.

And when it came time for her to build her own house with Butch in Denver, she'd followed the same philosophy. Bigger is better, glitzy is glamorous.

In the end, both houses had been soulless mausoleums, so cold and loveless they made you feel frozen inside. All the money in the world couldn't buy what Annie had accomplished with a full heart and few trips to a thrift store. A real home.

Raylene stretched, threw her legs over the side of the bed, and padded to the window. The sun had barely risen, but it looked like a promising day. Not the summer wedding Annie had wanted, but clear and breathtakingly beautiful. Even as an indulged girl who thought she was too good for a railroad town in the middle of nowhere, Raylene had known these mountains were special. Even magical.

Pressed against the glass, she wished Gunner was here and she could take him for a ride across the fields and up the hills. But Gunner was in Colorado and Raylene had a wedding to attend. A wedding that started in less than eight hours.

She showered, dressed, and made her way downstairs. Logan's truck was gone and Raylene figured he and Annie were already at the Lumber Baron in town, making sure everything was in order for the ceremony. Chad and Annie's parents appeared to still be sleeping and the Winnebago was dark.

Perfect. She could slip out without being noticed. Five minutes later, she was cruising down the highway with Carrie Underwood singing about bashing out her cheating man's headlights with a Louisville slugger and hummed along. It had been a while, but she found Donner Road without any trouble and climbed the steep grade. A recollection of her and Lucky parked up here in the woods, the windshield of his old rusty truck fogged from their make-out sessions, flitted through her head. Their adolescent kisses had been sweet and clumsy—nothing like Gabe's. The man was too practiced for his own good and had gotten her hot and bothered. She wouldn't let that happen again. As far as reminiscing about Lucky, she quickly shut it down. She didn't deserve a walk down memory lane.

She deserved nothing.

The driveway was a craggy mess from last week's snow and she slowly nosed down, careful not to get stuck in a rut. There was a spot next to Gabe's SUV and she slid in, surprised to find him awake, lifting weights on his front porch. She sat awhile, watching his muscles bunch as he hefted what had to be at least three hundred pounds. His skin glistened with sweat and a picture of him kissing her, the way his hands had deftly moved over her breasts, popped into her head. *Stop it!*

She hadn't been with a man since Butch, who never made it past the eight-second bell anyway, and she told herself that was the only reason Gabe had affected her like he did. With abstinence from sex *and* alcohol, she was simply hard up. Then she took another look at Gabe, shirtless, muscles flexing under all that golden skin, and knew she was a big fat liar.

He put the barbell down and came over to her truck and motioned for her to unroll the window, which she did. "Hey, Ray, here for a booty call?"

For a second, she feared that he'd read her mind. "I came for coffee. You better have some, Moretti."

He eyed her for a second, opened the door, and waved his arm for her to get out. "I could probably make that happen."

She skipped down from the running board and felt the morning chill bite through her jeans. "Aren't you freezing?"

"Nope."

The man thought he was a superhero, working out in twenty-degree weather.

"Come in and I'll put a pot on before I shower."

She followed him into his tiny duplex apartment, surprised to find that it was quite tidy. Other than a sixty-inch flat screen that made the small room appear even smaller and a black leather couch, there weren't a whole lot of furnishings. A couple of cheap posters and a hideous Nagel print of a short-haired woman with sunglasses hung on the wall.

"Where'd you get that?" She took a closer look and shuddered. "A nail salon?"

"A mobbed-up Russian gave it to me. It's my most prized possession."

She shook her head, because she didn't know if he was being sarcastic or not, and trailed him into the kitchen "I don't even want to know."

He flicked a switch on a Mr. Coffee and pulled down a couple of mugs from the cupboard, handing her the one that said, "A fun thing to do in the morning is not talk to me."

"I'll be out in twenty," he said, and disappeared behind a door Raylene assumed was his bathroom. Right off the kitchen was a funny place to have it. But the duplex was an old railroad apartment that was designed like a mid-century rail car. There were a number of them in Nugget. The town harkened back to the Gold Rush, but later became a hub for the Western Pacific Railroad. Now, it was a crew-change site for the Union Pacific.

She took the opportunity to snoop, first taking in the kitchen, which was even more sparse than the living room. Other than a few boxes of cereal, a container of protein powder, and a six-pack of beer, Gabe didn't have much food. He had even fewer pots and pans. His dishes were an assortment of mismatched pieces that reminded Raylene of dime-toss prizes from the county fair. Again, everything was spotless.

His bedroom showed more promise. Pine log furniture, reminiscent of the rustic pieces at Rosser Ranch, filled the room. The bed was neatly made with a crisp plaid duvet, which had been turned under the mattress to form perfect hospital corners. A seaman's chest with Gabe's initials carved in the wood sat at the foot of the bed. At least a dozen framed photographs of what Raylene presumed was his family lined his dresser. She examined each picture individually. Pretty people smiled back, and Gabe's parents looked so in love it took her breath away. The photograph was nothing like the Rosser family portraits her mother paid a high-priced San Francisco photographer to take. The sessions had been comical—and not in a good way. The three of them would dress in their Sunday Western attire and stand stiffly while the photographer snapped their pictures. Halfway through the ordeal, Ray would start complaining that he didn't have time for "this bullshit." One of the pictures, which Raylene liked to call *American Gothic II* because she and her parents looked equally as unhappy as the couple in the painting, hung above the fireplace until Ray was forced to sell the house to pay his dream team of lawyers. Raylene had no idea where the photograph was now.

"You don't mess around, do you Ray?" Gabe entered with a towel wrapped around his waist and a second one slung around his neck and blew a catcall. "Straight to the bedroom without even buying me a cup of coffee."

She eyed him, trying to act unaffected by his bulging biceps and his six-pack abs. "It's *coffee*, not *cawfee*."

"That's what I said." He removed the towel from his neck and snapped it at her, then pointed at the picture she was holding in her hand. "That's my stepsister, Marie. She's a bigwig at Morgan Stanley. You go through my underwear drawer, too?"

She would've if he hadn't walked in when he did. Raylene put the picture down, squeezed by him, and went back in the kitchen to fill her mug with coffee. She filled his too and checked the fridge, hoping she'd missed the milk on her first pass. No such luck.

Not long after, he came strolling in, dressed, droplets of water still clinging to his light-brown hair. He leaned against the counter, dripping on the linoleum floor, making the kitchen shrink before Raylene's eyes.

"So you want me to lug this thing all the way to the farm?"

"You said you would."

"And I will." He reached for the cup of coffee she'd poured him and took a sip. "I'll install it too but I'm putting my name on the card."

She rolled her eyes. "Fine, take half the credit, even though I did all the work." It had taken her a month to come up with the right design. Nothing too flashy but with just enough zing. She'd had to consider Logan's more conservative taste with Annie's quirky sensibility and find a happy medium. And then there was the question of a name. After the Rossers sold the property to Lila Stone years ago, the property had become known as the Stone place. Since Logan and Annie bought it, everyone called it The Farm. So that's what Raylene went with. The Farm. She'd worked hand in hand with a metal artist to get the gate and sign just right, incorporating Annie's logo into the motif. The gift had cost an arm and a leg, depleting much of Raylene's reserves, but it had been worth it.

"I'm okay with that." He winked and something in her chest fluttered.

"We better get going then. I want them to have their present before the wedding."

"Let me at least finish my coffee." He continued to lean against the counter, holding and blowing on his cup.

She noted the size of his hands. Large, like the rest of him. Butch and her father, they'd had large hands, too. Raylene remembered feeling the sting of them across her face too many times to count.

"Hurry up." She took her mug to the sink, washed it, and set it on the drainboard. "I still have to get ready."

"You've got hours still."

Annie had hired a local stylist to come to the house at eleven-thirty to do her, her mother's, Maisy's, Gia's, and Raylene's hair. There was a time when Raylene would've spent hours in front of a mirror, primping for an event like this. As the reigning Plumas County rodeo queen three years in a row, she had a reputation to uphold. And Ray liked her to make an impression. It wasn't enough for her to be smart or pretty or an accomplished equestrian; she had to be the girl all the other girls wanted to be and all the boys wanted to bed. Unless that boy was Lucky Rodriguez.

Gabe put down his cup and grabbed his jacket. "Let's do it then."

Together, they went to Gabe's storage shed where they loaded the framework, gate, and sign into both their trucks.

"Thanks for storing it here for me." She'd arranged to have it shipped to his house.

"You're welcome." Gabe tied everything down in the bed of Raylene's Ford while she dragged a bag of quick-set concrete out of the storage shed.

"You sure this will dry in time?"

Gabe grabbed the sack from her, his hands brushing hers, sending a shiver down her spine. She told herself it was the cold.

"Yep," he said. "I'll follow you."

"Hey, King of Covert, how do we do this without getting caught? I want it to be a surprise."

He opened her driver's door and shooed her in. "We've got an hour."

"What do you mean an hour?"

"I've got Chad diverting them at the Lumber Baron while we get this sucker up."

"So all this time we were drinking coffee we could've been installing the gate?" She scooted into the cab and started her engine to move him along.

"I like living on the edge." He hung his hands off the roof of her pickup, leaned in, and pecked her on the lips. "Chillax, Ray."

She slugged him in the arm, reversed out of the driveway, and smiled all the way back to the farm. If she didn't hate all men, she might've actually liked him.

Chapter 8

Drew Matthews stared out his kitchen window. "Did you see that?"

His wife, Kristy, lifted her head from the screen of her laptop. "See what?"

"I could've sworn there was someone out there." He continued to search his wooded backyard.

"Maybe it was maintenance." She returned to her laptop.

It was Saturday. He'd never seen anyone from the development working on a weekend, unless it was on the golf course. Hell, he rarely saw his neighbors. Other than the family of deer that lived on the property, no one came around much. They'd chosen Sierra Heights to be close to Harper. He got her on the weekends, but the four-hour drive each way to the Bay Area was a bear, so he and Kristy opted to get a second place in Nugget.

The developer, who was friends with Emily and knew Harper's story, had given them a great deal. The house was palatial compared to what they had in Palo Alto, and Harper was looking forward to the community pool in summer. Having his daughter back after seven years of not knowing whether she was dead or alive…well, it was a miracle. And everyone agreed that her transition would be easier if both sets of parents lived in the same town, even if Drew and Kristy were only part-time. They were both lawyers in Silicon Valley, 276 miles away. So they tried whenever possible to work four days in the office and telecommute the rest of the week from Nugget.

The situation had worked out well with Harper, but it had put a significant strain on his marriage. Not the part of having two residences. Kristy had instantly fallen in love with Sierra Heights and their home, a rustic chalet with an open floor plan, walls of windows, a chef's kitchen, and an en suite master bedroom as large as half their Palo Alto home. She liked inviting their Bay Area friends up for weekends and using the community's state-of-the-art amenities, including a fully stocked gym. But living only a few miles from Drew's ex had proven awkward for Kristy, and the complexities of reintroducing Harper to life after abduction were beyond difficult. And then there was the constant tension of trying to get pregnant. After three rounds of IVF, nothing.

Kristy felt like a failure, and Drew felt helpless in convincing her otherwise.

"Or a trick of the light," he said, returning to the odd sense that someone was back there. "Nonetheless, I'm going to take a look."

"Okay," she said, distracted by the case she was working on.

He grabbed his jacket off a peg in the mudroom and called to the breakfast nook, "What do you think of having lunch at the Ponderosa later?" Harper was going to a wedding with Emily and her family, so he and Kristy had the day to themselves.

"We'll see."

He sighed and shut the door behind him to explore the backyard. The house sat on an acre of land, which was defined on one side by his garage and the other by a split-rail fence, shared by him and his closest neighbor. The back was wide open, ending at a greenbelt, which fronted another row of houses. There was a good chance that one of his neighbors had innocently wandered onto his property to chase a ball, a dog, or whatever. But having his daughter snatched from his and Emily's backyard seven years ago had made him hypersensitive about security, even in a small, relatively crime-free town like Nugget.

Drew walked the perimeter, the cold lashing through his thick jacket. He dug in his pockets for a pair of gloves and pulled them on. They'd only had the house less than a month and hadn't yet acclimated to the change in weather from the Bay Area. So far, though, he was enjoying building fires and snuggling with Kristy and Harper under a mound of throw blankets.

The sun filtered through the gaps in the trees as he walked to the greenbelt without finding anything amiss. Like he and Kristy, most of the residents were part-timers, who came up on weekends and holidays to golf or take advantage of the ski resorts only thirty minutes away. After Christmas, though, the place had cleared out and felt a little like a ghost town. Drew assumed they'd be back soon for Valentine's Day.

Feeling silly, he started back when something shiny peeking out from under a tree caught his eye. He walked closer to get a better look. Someone had left a ragged army green backpack with tarnished silver buckles lying on the ground. A closer inspection revealed a canteen less than two feet from the pack, which made Drew think that whoever left it planned to come back.

It could've been hikers or campers who'd wandered off the trail. The development was surrounded by state park land. It was nothing, he told himself. But by the time he got inside the house, he still couldn't shake the feeling that something about it was odd.

Perhaps he was making a mountain out of a mole hill, but he dialed the police anyway.

"What's going on?" Kristy found him a few minutes later in the mudroom. "I heard you on the phone."

"It's probably nothing, but I found a backpack and canteen in the yard. I'm pretty sure it belongs to the person I thought I saw."

"But you didn't see anyone when you were out there?" He shook his head. "Did you check the pack? Maybe it has identification in it."

"I'm leaving that to the police."

"That's who you were on the phone with? Seems like overkill, don't you think? It's just a backpack, for God's sake." She laughed. "Unless you think the Taliban planted a bomb in Sierra Heights."

He pinned her with a look and she immediately became contrite. "I'm sorry. That was insensitive of me, but…"

"But what? You think I overreacted because of Hope…Harper? You're damned right." He walked away, because he didn't want to fight with her.

She didn't follow and he heard the bedroom door slam.

Fifteen minutes later, the police chief pulled up. Drew had only met him a few times and knew Emily thought the world of him. Even so, Drew prepared himself for what he knew was coming. It was a small town and the chief had to appease the citizens to keep his job. But he'd passive aggressively let Drew know that he'd wasted his time. Seven years of dealing with law enforcement while searching for Hope had taught him that.

Drew got off the couch and opened the door as Chief Shepard came up the slate walkway. He wasn't in uniform and Drew noted that he had a sports coat on. No jacket. "Thanks for coming."

The chief nodded. "Nice place you've got here."

"Thanks." He ushered Shepard in. "It's around back."

The chief wiped his boots on the mat, took a curious look around, and followed Drew to the kitchen.

"I was getting a glass of water here when I saw…a shadow, I guess. I can't say for sure whether it was a person."

Shepard joined Drew at the sink and peered out the window. "How far away was it?"

"Near that tree." He pointed at the grove. "Not much light comes in there, so it's hard to see."

"But you thought it was a person? Man or woman?" There was nothing flippant in the questions, at least not that Drew could detect.

"Difficult to tell," he said. "The knapsack is over there." He motioned to where he'd found it.

"Let's have a look." Shepard waited for Drew to lead the way.

They walked through the yard together, leaves crunching under their footsteps. The chief was taller than Drew and broader through the shoulders. His gait was brisk and efficient, making Drew wonder if he was in a hurry to get this over with.

"Did you touch it?"

"No. Look, I know this seems crazy. It's a planned community for God's sake. But..."

"You don't have to explain." The chief stopped and turned so he faced Drew. "People should follow their guts." He continued to the spot where Drew had found the pack.

As they came up on it, the chief stuck his arm out to stop Drew from walking, pulled out his phone, and snapped a few pictures, first of the backpack and then of the canteen. He hiked around the area, checking the ground and the trees. Then he slipped on a pair of latex gloves and proceeded to rifle through the bag's contents. Drew wondered if it was an elaborate charade to mock him.

Shepard circled the site and snapped a few more photographs.

"Do you think there is something sinister here?" Drew asked, feeling stupid for having gotten the ball rolling in the first place. He was starting to wonder if the chief was a nut.

"Not necessarily. You were smart to call, though." He picked the pack up by its strap and grabbed the canteen. "I'm going to take these with me. You'll call again if you see anything suspicious." He didn't pose it as a question, but Drew nodded anyway.

Instead of going through the house, the chief walked around the side of the garage to the driveway, where he opened his tailgate and dropped the items in his trunk. "You take care now," he drawled in an accent that seemed to come and go. Maybe the south, Drew couldn't tell. And with that, Shepard drove off.

Chapter 9

Raylene rubbed her hands together. Even with gloves on, her fingers felt like they were about to fall off.

"Bet you wish you were in LA right now." Gabe came down from the ladder and stood back to view the sign. "Looks good."

"It does, doesn't it? You think they'll like it?"

"Are you kidding? They'll love it. Nice gift, Rosser."

"Thanks for putting it up for me." That was twice in the span of only a couple hours that she'd thanked him, and it struck her that she didn't usually show appreciation. Most of her life she'd been waited on. By Cecilia, the stable boys, the ranch hands, even by her mother. She'd been raised to think it was her God-given right to be pampered. Even married to Butch, there'd been housekeepers, gardeners, a pool boy. For a while, she'd even had a personal assistant. Of course, the woman had turned out to be one of Butch's girlfriends who'd needed a job.

"You're welcome. You want to go back to the house or wait until they return from the Lumber Baron and watch their reaction when they see it?"

The gate and sign formed an archway over the driveway right before the house. Every ranch in the Sierra Nevada had one. As far as Raylene was concerned, it was a requirement. Her own heart had always filled with pride when she passed through the curlicue iron gates of Rosser Ranch, her family's brand burned into the big metal sign.

"Let's wait, but in the truck."

He put his hand at the small of her back and directed her to his SUV, where he immediately turned on the heat. "Logan'll think it's an ambush."

"You guys are weird."

He chuckled and checked his watch. "Only a few more hours to showtime." The wedding.

"Yep." She had butterflies in her stomach. The potluck had been bad enough, but now she'd be forced to face the whole town. Worst of all, Lucky, Tawny, and Cecilia.

He slid her a glance. "Just stick with me. It'll be over before you know it."

She hoped so, but time seemed to grind to a standstill when you wanted it to move fast.

"You dance?" He turned sideways in his seat. "They're having some kind of swing band."

"Why, you asking if I'll be your partner?" Lord knew no one else would.

"Don't worry, I'll dance with you, Ray." He winked and she marveled at how he'd turned it around to make it seem like she was asking him.

"I'd rather maintain a low profile."

"Why? You afraid Tawny Rodriguez will beat you up?"

Raylene wouldn't blame her if she did. She'd treated the woman like crap in high school, teasing and taunting her until Thelma—that was Tawney's real name—had cracked like glass. Until recently, she'd never realized why she'd had it out for the girl. It wasn't like they ran in the same circles or that Raylene had to compete with Thelma for Lucky's heart. Back then, he didn't even know Thelma existed. Half the time, Thelma didn't come to school because she had to take care of her sick dad. They lived in a rundown house in a neighborhood Raylene's mother called skid row.

One day, Raylene saw Thelma and her dad at the flea market at the Grange Hall. He fixed and refurbished old clocks for a living, when he wasn't coughing up a lung from all those cigarettes he smoked, and was probably trolling for deals. Unlike Ray's shiny cowboy boots and big silver buckles, Mr. Wade wore faded overalls and scuffed work boots. Ray called him an "Okie from Muskogee" on account of his Oklahoma accent.

At the market, both she and Thelma fixated on the same bracelet-making kit. It came with leather bands and eight stamp design tools, and Raylene thought of all the pretty bracelets she could make for her and friends. When she asked Ray to buy it for her, he laughed. "What do you need that for? I'll buy you a damn bracelet."

"But I want to make them, Daddy."

"Raylene, you never made a goddamn thing in your life, except a mess." He walked away to talk to one of his cattle friends.

Mr. Wade rifled through his wallet and dumped out at least three dollars in change. The man didn't have two sticks to rub together, but he bought Thelma the bracelet kit. Raylene observed the whole transaction, pea green with envy and a dose of awe. All she could think was someone had finally bested Daddy and had made him look like a cheap toad.

But when Mr. Wade handed Thelma the dusty box and said, "Here you go, sugar. Make me something as pretty as you," something in Raylene's chest twisted until she found it hard to breathe. And from that day on, she made it her personal mission to make Thelma Wade pay for every rotten thing Ray Rosser had ever called Raylene.

She poked Gabe in the chest. "I don't have to worry about Tawny beating me up, because I've got a guard dog."

He grinned in that placating way that said she was crazy and tilted his seat back. "Don't press your luck, Ray. I like Tawny Rodriguez and consider her a good friend."

She wondered what he considered her. A chore? A favor to Logan? Someone to play around with in his spare time?

She wanted to ask why he was still single but didn't want him getting the wrong idea. Besides, she already knew why. Gabe Moretti liked to play. He was the quintessential man-child. Raylene ought to know, having been married to one.

Her cell rang and she fished it out of her jacket pocket to look at the display. "Ugg, why can't he leave me alone?"

Gabe sat up to look. "Want your guard dog to handle it?"

"My gawd dawg," she mimicked, and swiped his hand away from the phone and answered. "Stop bothering me, Butch."

"Well, what do you know? The crazy bitch lives. I was starting to wonder if you'd given yourself rabies and died."

She balled her hands into fists and kicked herself a thousand times for answering the phone. "Make this quick, Butch, I've got stuff to do."

"I hope one of those things is picking up your horse, because there's no more room at the inn. If he's not out by tomorrow, I'm selling him to the highest bidder."

She'd been offered fifteen thousand dollars for the gelding and Butch knew it. And he was just mean enough to sell her prized horse right out from under her.

"Tomorrow, give me a break. It's Sunday. The deal was you'd keep him until I found a stable to board him."

"Not indefinitely, and your time is up. Get him or kiss him goodbye. I'm not kidding, Raylene. I've been trying to reach you for days. I've got two new quarter horses that need that space."

The man was a jackass. "If you sell Gunner I'll go back to court, so help me God."

"Good, talk to the judge, Raylene, because I'm not listening." Click.

Gabe watched her tuck the phone back in her pocket. "What was that about?"

"He's giving me until tomorrow to get my horse from his ranch in Colorado or he's threatening to sell him."

"You got a plan?"

She lifted her face to the roof of his SUV and let out a sigh. "No. I don't have a trailer, a driver, or a place to board him." Or any money. "And I've got my brother's wedding in three hours."

* * * *

With three phone calls, Gabe solved the problem. But just for kicks he'd like to fly to Denver himself and beat the shit out of Butch. He got it; Raylene was no cake walk. But only a special kind of douchebag threatens to sell a person's beloved pet.

"Weezer said he'd do it?" Logan flipped the toggles on a pair of cuff links.

"Yep. He's living in Boulder now and can score a trailer. He also said 'fuck you' for not inviting him to your wedding."

"Seriously? The fire marshal cut us off at one hundred and fifty people. Annie has a million friends." Logan nudged his head at the longneck Gabe held between his legs. "You going to drink that?"

Gabe handed it to him. "Nervous?"

"Nope."

"Then how come you're sweating?"

"It's hot in here."

Gabe got up and cracked a window. "We just need a place for Wilbur, and I'm guessing Annie doesn't want him eating her crop of hay, so the farm's out of the question."

"Maybe Flynn or Clay have room at their places until we can build a corral."

"We?" After the wedding Logan and Annie were on their way to a sandy beach in Hawaii. "Don't worry, I'll handle it." The problem was he didn't know if Flynn or Clay would be accommodating once they learned it was for Raylene. Lucky was certainly out of the question. But Logan didn't need to worry about Raylene's horse less than an hour before his wedding.

"How's it going in here?" Nick came through the door, dressed in a tux, looking like a million bucks.

"You two need some alone time?" Gabe asked.

"Yeah, beat it." Nick opened the door and squeezed Gabe's shoulder on the way out.

Gabe figured Nick wanted to do some father-son bonding before Logan took his vows and went in search of something stiffer than a beer. Downstairs, he found Chad stuffing his face with cheese and crackers.

"What? I'm starved."

"I didn't say anything." Gabe opened the pantry, grabbed a bottle of Glenlivet, and poured himself two fingers. "You want one?"

"No thanks."

"Where are your folks?" He hopped up on the counter and sipped his drink.

"They left with Logan's mom for the Lumber Barron. Is that Dink guy really performing the service?"

Gabe laughed. "That Dink guy is the mayor." And a vaunted member of the Nugget Mafia. Why Annie chose the old coot to officiate was beyond Gabe. But she danced to the beat of her own drum. "You see Raylene?"

"She and my sister are already at the inn. What's her deal, anyway? She's hot."

"She's not for you, son." Gabe clapped him on the back and tried to remind himself that she wasn't for him either. But he had to admit that hanging out with her these last few days hadn't been the burden he'd expected. Truth be told, he thought about her a lot. Naked. Not something he wanted to share with his buddy Logan.

"Should we head out?" Chad put the cheese in the fridge. "Logan's riding with Nick."

"Let's do it."

Gabe straightened his tie in the hallway mirror and grabbed his keys off the hall tree. They made it to the square four minutes faster than it usually took to get downtown. Annie and Logan had decided to hold the ceremony at the Lumber Baron because it would be too difficult to turn the farm stand around fast enough for the reception.

Gabe had to admit the place was beautiful. Big stained-glass window in the entry, a staircase that knocked his socks off, and fancy moldings that wouldn't quit. His mother would've gone apeshit for the inn.

He wandered around, looking at the pictures on the wall. A bar had been set up so guests could have drinks and a few nibbles before the ceremony got underway. Annie's idea. Otherwise, a hotel like this...well, it might've felt stuffy.

Dink had set up a podium near the altar. Rows of seats had been swagged with ribbons and bows and flowers. There was even an organist who'd come all the way from Yuba City, where the Sparks family went to church.

He still couldn't believe Logan was getting hitched. A year ago, they'd been in some shit hole in Afghanistan, freezing their balls off, talking about starting their own security firm. And here they were. Logan never could've predicted that they'd set up shop in a small mountain town in the middle of nowhere, though. Strange as it was, it had been a good choice.

"Hey." Rhys sidled up alongside him. "Where's the groom?"

"On his way with his stepdad. The inn looks great." Rhys' wife, Maddy, and her brother, Nate, owned it.

"It's a nice spot for a wedding." He grabbed a stuffed mushroom off a platter and popped it in his mouth. "I got a call this morning. Drew Matthews thought he saw a stranger in his yard and found a knapsack and canteen under a tree."

"In Sierra Heights?" The planned community seemed like an odd spot for a hiker or camper. "You think it's related to the trio you spotted?"

"Don't know. Could be related, could be nothing."

"What was in the pack?" People were starting to arrive, so Gabe pulled Rhys into an alcove.

"A couple of IDs I'm running down, a hunting knife, a necklace, and forty bucks."

Gabe heard murmurs of congratulations and suspected Logan had arrived. "Hey, I've gotta perform best-man duties, but keep me in the loop."

"Jake's back, but I'll let you know what I find from those IDs. In the meantime, keep your eyes open."

"Will do. Hey, before I forget, you think it would be weird to ask Clay if he'd board Raylene's horse for a while?" When Rhys looked at Gabe like he didn't know what he was talking about, he said, "It's a long story."

"You'd have to ask him, but no one's in a hurry to help that woman, not after the mark she left on this town. I thought she was leaving right after the wedding anyway."

"She is," Gabe said. "Only her horse is staying. We just need a place to stash it until we can get something built at the farm."

"Talk to him, but don't be surprised if he says no."

Gabe was surprised. It was no secret that Raylene was persona non grata in Nugget, but her horse? The one thing he'd learned in the short time he'd lived in Nugget was that the residents would give you their left nut if you needed it, and above all else they loved animals. Gabe nodded like he understood, even though he didn't. Clay surely had enough room for one more Wilbur in his barn. It wasn't like the horse had done anyone wrong.

But now wasn't the time, so he went in search of Logan and found him and Nick in a plush room off the lobby.

Gabe noted the big medallion on the ceiling and the marble fireplace. "Nice digs."

"Hell yeah." Logan stared at himself in the full-length mirror behind the door.

Gabe watched him preen like a peacock and affected his best Billy Crystal impression. "You look marvelous. Ready to do this?"

"Never been more ready in my life." Logan got the same look on his face that he did while free falling during a HALO parachute jump. Pure adrenaline rush. "Hey, do me a favor and check on Annie."

"You afraid she's finally come to her senses?" Gabe mussed Logan's hair and took the long staircase up to the bridal suite.

His best friend was getting married. Every time he came to the realization it jolted him like an exposed electrical wire. Not the part about sleeping with the same woman for life—if she was the right woman that could be nice. It was the overwhelming responsibility of keeping someone happy. He'd tried before and hadn't been up to the task. The results had been devastating. Another reason to avoid unhinged women.

"Everyone decent?" Gabe knocked.

"Come in," Annie called and opened the door.

"Look at you." Gabe spun her around. The dress, white lace and poufy, was the most conventional thing Annie had ever worn. "Where's the combat boots?"

"I'm saving them for the honeymoon."

Gabe grinned, knowing that Logan loved those combat boots.

Raylene came out of the bathroom and he sucked in a breath. She looked like sex in Western wear and he felt his blood travel south. Her blond hair had been curled till ringlets bounced down her back. And her dress was an off-the-shoulder lacy number that showed a good amount of thigh. But what really got him were the white cowboy boots. Dallas Cowboy cheerleader meets a Boot Barn ad.

He held her steady blue gaze, but he didn't see confidence there—she looked as if she wished she could fade into the carpet. *You made your own bed, sweet cheeks.* Yet part of him—probably the part between his legs—felt sorry for her. The evening wasn't going to be easy, and if he were Raylene he would've worn a flak jacket under that dress. She'd need it.

Chapter 10

Drew gazed around the Ponderosa while Kristy was in the bathroom. It was only their second time dining in the restaurant. The first had been with Harper. An evening of bowling, then hot fudge sundaes. The place didn't seem as crowded as usual. Then again, it was late for lunch and early for dinner.

Drew liked the quiet, anyway. In the Bay Area you were hard pressed to find a table at a good restaurant without a reservation, let alone one where the acoustics didn't make the place sound like a rave. Even though the Ponderosa was the only sit-down restaurant in town, it was fairly decent. Simple food done well, with friendly service.

Before meeting Emily he'd been content to eat frozen dinners and bad takeout. His ex-wife was a cookbook author and a phenomenal chef. Another thing Kristy felt threatened by. These days, it didn't take much.

When he'd first started seeing her she'd been his rock. The first two years after his daughter's disappearance had been so bleak that there were days when he didn't know how he'd go on. Emily had fallen into such deep despair that they barely said two words to each other that didn't have to do with Hope's disappearance. They hired private investigators, did media interviews, and followed up on every lead, no matter how preposterous. And at the end of the day, they were so exhausted, so distraught, that there wasn't any energy left for their marriage. In the third year they divorced, and in one fell swoop, he lost his daughter and his wife, the love of his life.

Then he met Kristy and she made him live again. The pain of losing a child never subsided, but he no longer felt suffocated by grief. He didn't have to face it every morning by watching Emily, once a vibrant woman, wither away to nothing. With Kristy he laughed, and little by little he healed.

And now their relationship had taken a hit, and he worried that it might not survive.

"Apparently, the place is empty because of the wedding." Kristy returned to the table and took her seat. She motioned to the street. "It's at the big Victorian inn…what's it called again?"

"The Lumber Baron."

"I heard two women in the restroom talking about it. The reception's at a farm stand near McCreedy Ranch. That's different."

"Sounds interesting…nice."

"Want to crash?" She was kidding of course, but for a second Drew caught a glimpse of the old Kristy. Just as quickly, her expression drooped, losing its twinkle of mischief.

"Why not? Who would know we weren't invited?"

"Uh, the bride and groom."

A waiter came and took their orders. Drew chose a bottle of wine for the table. For a country saloon, it had a rather nice list, including some of their favorite cabernets from the Napa Valley.

"What did the police chief say about your sighting?"

They hadn't discussed it on the drive over. Kristy had been consumed with a text her paralegal had sent her. And she'd made it perfectly clear she thought he was acting irrationally to have called the police in the first place. The chief hadn't thought so, though. Either that or he was a good actor.

"He said it was good that I went with my gut." The wine came and the waiter poured them both a glass. When he left, Drew said, "He took the backpack and the canteen."

She didn't say anything, staring off into the distance. "Is Harper staying with us tonight?"

"If they get home from the wedding early enough, Emily said she'd bring her over. Otherwise, tomorrow morning in time for breakfast."

Kristy absently swirled her wine. "I was thinking of going home tomorrow. This case…it would be better if I worked from the office. I'll take the Volvo."

They'd left it in the mountains so they'd have an extra car to drive when they rode up together.

"Seems silly. I'd only be a few hours behind you." If it was really work, he didn't want to push. Lord knew he'd spent enough time away from home, pulling all-nighters on a motion or a brief. But work had become a convenient excuse.

"I don't want you to feel rushed," she said. "As it is, your time was cut short with Harper this weekend."

He and Emily had agreed that they wouldn't be draconian about the schedule. It was more important that Harper settled in here, made friends, and engaged in social activities. The transition had been hard enough. She'd had a whole world in Idaho. Despite what those monsters had done, they'd given Harper a wonderful life. In Morton, she'd been involved in clubs and activities and had dozens of friends. Uprooting a child in normal circumstances was difficult enough, but the transition continued to be a maze of complications.

"Harper and I could go somewhere so you'd have the house to yourself to work. That way we could at least make the four-hour drive together." He tried to take her hand but she quickly reached for her wineglass.

Their food came before she could respond, and Drew saw her working up a good excuse in her head.

"I know this is difficult, Kristy. I want you to know how much I appreciate everything you've done—the house here, the driving back and forth, dealing with a very confused thirteen-year-old—to accommodate me and Harper."

"I'm your wife, Drew. Really…it's insulting."

He wasn't allowed to appreciate her? To tell her he knew this was beyond trying for anyone, even people who loved each other deeply?

"There's no need to be defensive, Kris. Jeez, I can't win for losing with you. Clearly, you're unhappy with the setup, and I can't blame you. But what do want me to do?"

"Shush. You're making a scene."

"There's no one in the damn place." He grabbed his fork and picked at his salad. "We used to talk, Kristy. Now, we're hard pressed to carry on even a mundane conversation about the weather."

"I'm trying to make partner. You should know what that's like." She ignored her food and took another drink of wine.

He huffed out a breath. "You know what the doctor said?"

She turned in her chair and stared daggers at him. "I hadn't realized you were listening, because if you were, you'd know that we missed this month's window of opportunity. I was ovulating last week when you decided to race up here because Harper had a toothache."

He was screwing this up. Badly. "You didn't tell me, Kristy. If you had told me—"

"I shouldn't have to, you should know." She squeezed the bridge of her nose. "Let's not do this now."

She was right. He'd put the entire responsibility of tracking her cycle on her. Between the ovulation kits and fertility monitors, she had it down to a science. All he needed to do was show up. But lately, the whole goddamn thing had become a chore. No longer was their lovemaking spontaneous; everything was done to schedule. Sometimes, she'd call him in the middle of the day to rush home from work and perform like a monkey. On the nights when he felt romantic, she put on the brakes, fearing that it would decrease his sperm count for when "it mattered."

And the worst part of it was: he wasn't entirely sure he wanted a baby. This was a crucial time for Harper. She needed him. The demands of an infant would only take him away from the daughter he was just getting to know.

"We've got to do it sometime, Kristy." If they didn't talk this through, their marriage would only get rockier.

"Not in a restaurant in a town where everyone knows your ex-wife."

"This has nothing to do with her. This is about us. Only us."

She cut a piece of meat and regarded it for a few seconds without taking a bite. "That's not really true, and you know it. She's Harper's mother and, whether I like it or not, a part of our life."

"I suppose that's true to some extent, but there's no reason for you to feel threatened by it."

"I'm not threatened," she said, and pushed her plate away. "I just feel like I've suddenly been thrust into a commune."

He couldn't help himself and laughed, because it wasn't altogether untrue. "What do you want me to do? Abandon my daughter?"

"No, of course not. But maybe I shouldn't come so often...I feel like a third wheel."

He touched her arm. "You're not a third wheel, you're the love of my life."

Her eyes watered. "I know. And finding Harper...my God, Drew, it's miraculous. I'm just having trouble figuring out what my place is."

"Your place is always with me...with us. It'll get easier, you'll see." But the truth was he didn't know that for sure. The day his daughter came home, all his priorities changed. It was a lot to ask her to change hers to meet his.

* * * *

The dress was all wrong. Too short, too revealing. No doubt everyone thought Raylene was trash. Why she'd chosen it, she couldn't remember, only that Annie said she could wear whatever she wanted and this is what Raylene had pulled out of her closet. There was a time when she wore provocative clothing for attention, and Butch had even paid for a breast enhancement. She'd enjoyed men's stares and women's jealous remarks.

Now she preferred jeans and sweatshirts and to go incognito. Better yet, invisible. The truth was she used to live to be in the spotlight, but in recent months she'd learned a lot about herself, including that she was more of an introvert than she ever thought possible. She actually enjoyed staying home and reading a book or going to the movies by herself. It should've been lonely, but it was liberating. No one to impress, no one to perform for, and no one to have power over her.

Gia, Annie's maid of honor, tapped her on the shoulder. "You ready?"

"Uh-huh." They were supposed line up behind the stairwell so they could start the processional. Raylene sucked in a breath. The thought of walking down the aisle while all of Nugget watched—and whispered behind her back—made her feel woozy.

"Hey." Gabe came up alongside her and hooked his arm in hers. "Samantha said to wait until Nick and Gia are in their places before we start walking. She wants to drag it out for drama."

Samantha Breyer, her husband, and the police chief's wife owned the Lumber Baron. A party planner by profession, Sam had helped Annie coordinate the wedding and had overseen the rehearsal. While she hadn't been outright rude to Raylene, she hadn't been friendly.

"Drama's my middle name," Raylene said under her breath.

"Not tonight, okay?" Gabe squeezed her hand, and any resentment she felt at his comment drifted away. "Hear that? They're playing our song."

A string quartet had started the opening chords of "Don't Stop Believin'" and Raylene rolled her eyes.

"I still can't believe Logan picked this." At least Annie had gone with Etta James' "At Last," for her walk down the aisle.

"Didn't you see *The Wedding Singer?*"

"Shush." Sam appeared with a clipboard and whispered, "On the count of three." She held up one, two, then three fingers.

Arm in arm, Raylene and Gabe glided down the aisle. She tried to focus on Logan, who stood at the altar, looking so handsome in his black tuxedo. But seeing Cecilia in the third row, staring daggers, tripped Raylene up and Gabe had to steady her.

They took their places—Gabe alongside Nick and Raylene next to Gia—and she let her gaze drop to her boots before she saw disapproval in anyone else's eyes. Without Gabe as her wingman, she felt exposed. But when the whole room rose to watch Annie's father give away the bride, Raylene lifted her head and audibly sighed. Annie looked like an angel. Radiant, and so in love it made Raylene tear up with emotion.

From the side, she caught Gabe watching her and wondered how anyone could take their eyes off Annie. Raylene, who'd never been the weepy type, wished she'd brought tissues, because she cried throughout the entire ceremony.

After Logan kissed the bride, Raylene and Gabe followed the recessional to the hotel lobby where they were supposed to pose for pictures. But the bride and groom kept getting delayed by well-wishers.

"That was nice," Gabe said in that nonchalant way guys talked when something momentous happened.

"It was better than nice." Raylene jabbed him in the arm.

"I didn't take you for the sentimental type."

"That's because I'm not." She grabbed a glass of champagne from one of the servers, almost forgetting that she no longer drank. It would've been awkward to return it, so she held the flute, praying that the mere smell of the bubbly wouldn't seduce her.

By the time they got to the farm stand, which had been transformed into a gorgeous dance hall complete with twinkle lights, ruffled tablecloths, floral arrangements of dahlias, eucalyptus, peonies, sweet peas, and a Western swing band, Raylene craved something stronger than sparkling wine. She used to be a vodka girl, but tonight called for whiskey. Hell, Everclear might not even do the trick. Twice she'd overheard someone calling her a bitch, which wasn't as bad as being snubbed by Wyatt Lambert, who used to worship her in high school. Gabe had taken off to parts unknown, leaving her alone to face an angry mob. Okay, maybe she was exaggerating, but she could feel the hostility emanating in the air.

Please, God, just let me get through tonight. Then I'll be on my merry way, hopefully with pockets full of gold.

Even though it was twenty degrees outside, she wanted air and made her way through the crowd, looking for the back door. There had to be one. Every farm stand had a back door, right? As she jostled her way through the crowd, she searched for Gabe. Given that he was at least two heads taller than the average human, he shouldn't be hard to find. But there was no sign of him. Maybe he'd run off with one of the caterers. The thought made her stomach pitch, which she immediately blamed on the shrimp.

Today, he'd been her hero, rescuing Gunner from TAB, who would probably sell the gelding to a glue factory just to spite her. Watching Gabe work the phone and call in favors had been impressive. And it had saved her bacon. Her horse was everything to her. She didn't want to think about what would've happened if Butch acted on his threat. Of course, Gabe had done it for Logan, to save her brother from having to bail her out of trouble—yet again. But that didn't make her any less grateful. He'd gone above and beyond. Now all she had to do was figure out how to pay him back. The horse trailer alone would cost a big chunk of change, not to mention gas for the driver. And once he got Gunner to Nugget, she'd have to find a place to keep him. Not a lot of options there, considering her popularity in this town.

She'd worry about it tomorrow. Tonight was about Logan and Annie. Boy, the expression on their faces when they'd seen the ranch gate and sign had been priceless. Pure delight. A rush of joy had filled her as they oohed and aahed over the surprise. "Oh, Raylene, this is perfect, absolutely perfect," Annie had gushed, her eyes watery. In her whole life, Raylene couldn't remember ever giving anyone a gift she'd put this much thought or care into. But the ranch gate represented home to her, and she wanted Logan and Annie to have the happiest of homes.

That was her last thought as she slammed into the broad back of one of the guests. He sloshed red wine all over the woman standing next to him. When they turned around, her heart sank. Lucky and Tawny.

"I'm so sorry." She frantically looked around for a napkin or anything to mop up the mess. "I wasn't looking where I was going."

"You did it on purpose." Cecilia rushed to Tawny's side, and even with the din of the crowded room people heard her and their heads began to turn. A server brought towels, and Cecilia used them to pat Tawny's dress dry.

"No, I didn't, I swear." She'd been so busy scanning the room for Gabe that she hadn't been paying attention. "It was an accident."

"Of course you did." Cecilia's face twisted with anger and she said something in Spanish Raylene couldn't understand. But it wasn't good. "In a room packed with people, you just happen to bump into Tawny? You expect us to believe that wasn't intentional?"

"Mom." Lucky held his hand up. "Not here, not now."

"I'll pay for the dress to be professionally cleaned," Raylene said. Everyone was staring to see what the commotion was, and Raylene wanted to die. She wanted to fade into the woodwork and disappear. But she wouldn't cower—the Rosser in her wouldn't let her. She put steel to her spine and, with as much grace as she could muster under the circumstances, said, "Please, just send me the bill."

"You're damned right you'll pay. And if the stains don't come out, you'll buy her a new dress. You're the same old Raylene. *Desgraciada.*"

"Mom, enough." Lucky got between them.

At only a few inches taller than Raylene, he was still an imposing man. Despite his jaw-dropping good looks, she didn't feel her old attraction for him, only a hint of nostalgia. And a deep remorse for the things she'd done and the pain she'd caused.

Raylene's eyes met Tawny's, and suddenly they were back in high school. Raylene the mean girl and Tawny, awkward, skinny Thelma Wade.

"I am truly sorry," Raylene said, and there was a world of meaning in those words. Because she was sorry for all of it.

Gabe pushed through the crowd, and she didn't know whether to feel relief or doubly embarrassed that he might've witnessed the scene. At the very least, someone had alerted him to it and told him to run interference and clean up Raylene's mess.

Just don't turn Logan and Annie's wedding into your personal drama. His words rang in her ears.

And here she was, on stage, being bitch slapped by Cecilia, the woman who'd practically raised Raylene, for the whole town to see. Raylene's stomach pitched.

"We all good here?" Gabe directed the question at Lucky, the context clear: *Make this go away, now!*

That was the thing about Gabe, he was commanding in the most charming of ways. But Cecilia had never been one to be bulldozed, by a charmer or anyone else. She got up in his face as much as a woman half his size could.

"She owes Tawny a dress."

Gabe draped his arm around Cecilia's shoulders. "I'll make sure that happens. You have my word."

"I trust your word, Gabe, not hers. And she's the one at fault here."

Cecilia's husband joined the fray and Raylene's heart sunk lower. Jake Stryker was the cop she'd mouthed off to a few years ago at the Gas and Go when she'd been back in town—drunk and belligerent.

Do you know who I am? Yep, she'd actually said that. Embarrassment from the memory burned her cheeks.

"Let's take it down a notch." Jake herded them into a corner, where they'd be out of earshot of the rest of the guests, and pierced Raylene with a stern look. "No need to disrupt Logan and Annie's wedding reception."

Gabe stepped in front of her. "The wine was an accident, Jake. The space is tight, and I'm sure Raylene isn't the only person to have bumped into someone. She'll take care of Tawny's dress first thing tomorrow. Now can we all get back to having a good time?"

Cecilia started to say something but Jake stopped her. "That's an excellent idea." He put his hand at the small of his wife's back and directed her toward the buffet table, leaving the four of them alone.

Lucky draped his jacket over Tawny's shoulders, doing his best to cover the red splatters on her emerald green dress. The dress matched her eyes to a tee and not for the first time, Raylene noted how much Tawny had changed. No longer a gangly outcast, she was as gorgeous as the boots she made. Sophisticated and sparkly enough for everyone in the room to take notice, but not so glittery to be garish.

Tawny linked her arm through Lucky's and they started to walk away. Then Lucky turned back to Raylene, and through gritted teeth said, "Don't bother with my wife's dress, just do us all a favor and leave Nugget. The sooner the better, before you poison us all."

It was no less than she deserved, yet the words caught her off guard and she could feel her body tremble. She searched for a door, any door, the impulse to run so urgent she'd go through a window if she had to.

Sensing her desperation, Gabe gently reached for her arm.

"I need some air." Either that or a drink. Or two or three. The temptation was so strong it came over her in waves. Just one sip, she told herself, anticipating the warmth that would spread through her chest and stomach. How just one swallow would melt the tenseness away and then, sweet release.

"I'll go with you."

"No, stay. Logan might need you for something." Nick was the best man, but Gabe was Logan's right hand.

"Nah, I'll come." He started to lead her away.

"You afraid I'll make another scene?" All she wanted to do was flee the party and be by herself. It was one thing to know the people she grew up with despised her. But it was entirely different to feel that hatred emanate from their every pore. Even now, she could see them pointing at her, talking behind their hands, telling their friends she was garbage.

"Yeah, I am." He pulled her away from the crowd and pushed her inside a dark alcove. "Don't expect me to believe that was just a shitty coincidence. Of all the gin joints, in all the towns, in all the world… One night, just one fucking night, and you can't go without being the center of attention. Haven't you done enough to Lucky and his family? At least have the decency to show your brother a little respect… Give us all a break."

"Okay, I will." She turned and nearly tripped over her own two feet in her rush to get away.

Gabe was right behind her. "Don't do this. Pretty soon it'll be time for the toasts and Logan will be looking for you."

She spun around. "You shouldn't have left me alone." It was a ridiculous thing to say, not to mention pathetic. As if it was his responsibility to keep her from walking into people, but she couldn't help herself. Just like everyone else, he thought the worst of her. "If I hadn't been searching the room for you, I would've seen where I was going."

He lifted one sardonic brow. "Missed me that much, huh?"

Her eyes were starting to well and she was a hair away from losing it. "Is everything a joke to you?"

He maneuvered her out of the way so a waiter carrying a tray of hors d'oeuvres could get by. She brushed by him and found refuge in the stock room, which the caterers had been using as a staging area. It was empty, and she took advantage of the quiet to catch her breath. She found a napkin and blew her nose, dabbed at her eyes, and tried to gather her courage to go out again.

Tawny, Cecilia, Lucky, the whole town could hate her all they wanted, but she wouldn't let them run her off. Not on her brother's wedding night. She remembered all the times she'd been kicked at or thrown by a horse. Yet she'd always gotten right back in the saddle. She'd survived Ray and Butch and AA. *Ninety days sober.* She could make it a few more hours.

Raylene searched through her clutch for a mirror and lipstick. There was nothing she could do about the town's hostility toward her. What was done was done. But she could at least put on a good face.

Gabe walked in.

"Will you leave me alone."

"Tomorrow," he said, and shoved her cosmetics back inside her purse. "Tonight, I'm your handler, and it's time for the toasts."

"I don't need you to handle me." She tried to squeeze by him. Ordinarily, she liked brushing against his big, hard body, but he'd hurt her by believing the worst. Maybe they hadn't known each other long, but she'd been fooled into thinking that he got her. "Move."

The big lug finally stepped aside, but just as she started to leave, he grabbed her arm and forced her chin up. "Please play nice."

"Please unhand me." She jerked her arm away and walked out of the stock room on her own.

Chapter 11

Gabe spent the rest of the night watching Raylene from a safe distance. He didn't know what to make of her run-in with the Rodriguezes. Her reaction to seeing Lucky and Tawny on those two occasions at the Ponderosa didn't jibe with someone who would intentionally look for a confrontation, especially at her brother's wedding.

The one sure thing he could say about Raylene was that she cared for Logan and Annie and wouldn't deliberately try to mess up their party. He propped his hip against the wall and observed her talking to Harper Matthews, Emily's little girl. They were over by the dessert table, eating wedding cake. Gabe was too far away to hear what they were saying but it looked animated. Raylene smiled at something the kid said and her whole face lit up. Even from the wall, he could see those baby blues of hers sparkle like the Pacific Ocean. Despite her reputation as a viper, she was a knockout. This morning, as she'd snooped through his bedroom, he'd been sorely tempted to go for another kiss. And when her sweater and jacket kept hiking up as they hung the ranch gate together, he'd had a powerful urge to touch all that creamy skin.

Soon, she'd be leaving. Until then, he better check those urges. Tomorrow, they'd hunt for her stupid gold, and when they came up empty she'd see the search for what it was: an exercise in futility. It's not like she needed the money. Her father had left her a pile of cash, and Gabe assumed Colorado was a community property state and she'd gotten her share in the divorce. In any event, he'd go along with the treasure hunt but wouldn't feel too bad when her gold didn't pan out. Then he'd find a place to tuck her horse and she'd be on her way out of here. The town would likely throw a ticker-tape parade when she was gone.

Jake joined him on the wall with a drink in his hand and flicked his gaze at Raylene. "She's a real piece of work."

Gabe simply shrugged, because his allegiance was to Logan and that was his sister Jake was talking about. "For what it's worth, I don't think she deliberately did it. I'll admit, I did at first, but on closer examination not so much anymore."

Jake leaned his head back and laughed. "She's bewitched you, too, huh?"

If Gabe hadn't respected the hell out of Jake, he would've told him to take a swan dive off the Golden Gate Bridge. But Gabe was man enough to know when he'd heard the truth, and the truth was Raylene had bewitched him. Not to the point where he was blind to her faults, just enough to occasionally close his eyes to them.

"It's happened to the best of us, buddy." Jake slapped him on the back. "I'm a career homicide detective and have heard every lie under the sun. Yet a beautiful woman still has the power to make me question my instincts. Take some advice from a man who's been married four times." He nudged his head at Raylene. "That woman is toxic. She'll burn a hole through your heart faster than a cigarette lighter." With that, he pushed off the wall and headed for the bar for a refill.

Gabe waved across the room to one of Annie's friends and went back to watching Raylene. She was still talking to Harper, which was interesting. Raylene didn't strike him as the maternal type. Then again, the kid was probably the only person in the place who would give Raylene the time of day. Still, she seemed pretty invested in whatever they were talking about, nodding her head and gesturing with her hands and giving Harper, who even from a distance appeared to be talking a mile a minute, her full attention.

Gabe thought about joining them, but they had a good thing going and he didn't want to interrupt. Besides, Raylene had made it crystal clear she was pissed at him. He couldn't exactly blame her. He'd rushed to judgment. But, like his mom liked to say, "If it looks like a duck, swims like a duck, and quacks like a duck, then it probably is a duck." And her collision with Lucky certainly had looked like a duck to him.

He took a visual lap around the room. The party was winding down, and there was no sign of Lucky and Tawny. He suspected they'd left shortly after the incident. Out of his side vision, he saw Clay approach Raylene and Harper. Gabe's ability to read body language was above average, saving his ass in the field more times than he wanted to remember, and Clay's was sending off all kinds of warning signals.

His assessment was proven correct when a few seconds later Clay grabbed Harper's hand and led her away, leaving Raylene standing alone.

Apparently, he didn't want his kid picking up any bad habits from the wicked witch of Nugget, even if their only crime was eating cake and laughing. It wasn't as if Raylene was teaching Harper how to build a nuclear bomb. Cold, man. Gabe thought Clay was cold.

The bride and groom were getting ready to leave, and the wedding party was supposed to hand out sparklers and little bags of rice. The sparklers had been Sam's idea but Annie's family grew rice, so no way were they cutting that particular tradition out of the wedding, even if it was allegedly dated. For the last three months, Gabe had gotten a blow by blow of every detail from Logan, who'd been drowning in wedding planning hell and wanted to share his pain.

Gabe deliberated on whether to act as Raylene's escort for Logan and Annie's grand exit or to leave her alone. He'd all but decided to give her space when his protective side won out and he circled around to get her. She was finishing her cake.

"You ready?"

"Jeez, you're like a bad penny, Moretti."

"I figured after the Lucky incident you might need a bodyguard. The knives are out."

She sighed and put her cake plate down on an empty tray. "You saw Clay, didn't you?"

"Let's walk this way, so we can grab a bunch of sparklers." He steered her toward the door. "Yeah, I saw. Maybe he just didn't want the kid getting hopped on sugar."

"Good try. But I saw Donna Thurston go over to him, whisper something in his ear, and next thing I know he's swooping Harper up like I'm Ted Bundy."

"Now that you mention it, you kind of look like him."

"Thanks," she said. "And thanks for believing the worst of me tonight. I really appreciate that."

She was trying to pass it off as if she didn't care, but he could tell she did.

"Give me a break, Ray. What would you think if in a room filled with more than a hundred people, I happened to plow into my archnemesis and knock his wine out of his hand?"

She put her mouth close to his ear. "Everyone here is my archnemesis."

Raylene had a point. No question that the good folks of Nugget hated her guts.

"Someday, you're gonna tell me the whole story."

"I told my whole story to the police. Now I'm done talking about it. Forever."

They scooped up the rice and send-off sparklers and Gabe made sure everyone in his general vicinity got one. Gia and a few of the kids handled the rest. They went outside and everyone formed two rows for the bride and groom to pass through on their way back to the Lumber Baron, where they planned to stay the night before leaving the next day on their honeymoon.

A cheer went up and the crowd began waving their lit sparklers in the air and chucking rice at Logan and Annie as they walked the path.

When Logan got to Gabe and Nick they shouted, "Hooyah," and pounded on each other's backs. Logan picked up Raylene and swung her around while Annie hugged Gia. There were a lot of kisses and crying and congratulatory embraces and two weepy mothers who fussed.

"It was a beautiful wedding," Emily told Annie.

"Thank you for making the cake. It was the star of the show." Annie gave Emily a squeeze.

"No, you were."

Gabe walked the newlyweds to Logan's truck and tucked Annie's dress in the door. "You kids take care, now. Bring me back something nice."

Logan whispered in his ear, "Take care of my sister."

"You got it. Godspeed, John Glenn."

He watched them drive off with strings of tin cans tied to their bumper and a "Just Married" sign taped to their tailgate, thanks to Chad and a few of Annie's friends. The guests milled around for another half hour or so, but by eleven Annie's farm stand-turned-wedding venue emptied out.

He and Raylene loaded his truck with gifts and Chad caught a ride to Annie and Logan's with his parents.

"I guess I'm taking you," Gabe said, since Raylene had ridden with the Sparkses to the reception.

"Either that or I'll walk." It wasn't too far, only about a mile up the road, but no way in hell was he letting her get home on foot in the dark.

"Hop in, Ray. We've got a long day tomorrow."

"I'll go first thing in the morning to get the metal detector."

Clearly, she wasn't too mad to let him off the hook. More's the pity. Gabe could've done with a day at home, watching football instead of digging in the dirt for rocks with an off-limits temptress. *Take care of my sister.* If Logan only knew.

"I'll get it." That way he could grab some breakfast before she came banging on his door. "And meet you at the property at ten-thirty."

"Ten?" she whined.

"It's Sunday, Ray. The hardware store doesn't open before ten."

That seemed to appease her. The truth was he didn't know what time the hardware store opened, only that he didn't want to wake up at dawn's early light. He'd seen enough sunrises and wanted to sleep in.

Gabe pulled up to the house and before he could put on his emergency brake, Raylene jumped out of the SUV.

He rolled down his window. "What? No kiss goodnight?"

She waved her middle finger in the air and climbed the stairs of the front porch. His mouth quirked as he admired her backside in that tight dress. Gabe waited for the foyer light to come on and started for home when he remembered he'd left his boots in the office. He'd need them tomorrow for their dig, and he rolled his eyes. Flipping a U-turn, he took the driveway past a row of privacy trees Annie had planted and pulled into the carport at L&G. With the engine running, he dashed into the building, punched in the alarm code, found his boots, and was halfway to his truck when a he heard a crackle in the neighboring woods. It sounded like the snap of a twig and then a cough. Probably an animal or a figment of his imagination. But after more than a decade in the spec ops world, "probably" wasn't good enough. They stored hundreds of thousands of dollars' worth of security equipment, a cache of weapons, top-grade gear, and ammo in the small compound. And though they had a state-of-the-art alarm system, nothing was impenetrable. Gabe ought to know. He reached in the SUV, turned off the engine, opened the glove box, and pulled out a Sig Sauer P226.

Other than the security motion light on the side of the building, the woods were pitch black. Not a problem; Gabe knew how to find his way in the dark. He circled around the building, entering the forest from the back side of L&G. Better to exercise his assault from the rear than the front, giving him the element of surprise. He crept through the trees, hoping his dress shoes didn't creak. He felt a little like James Bond, doing reconnaissance in a tuxedo. All he needed was a Walther PPK.

With a sliver of moonlight peeking out from behind the mountains, he could see his breath in the cold. He stopped, flattened his back against a tree, and smelled the air. Pine needles, damp dirt, oak leaves, and something that didn't quite belong. Nothing Gabe could identify, but whatever it was didn't feel right. Fetid, like unwashed bodies. He stood there listening for a while, but all he heard was the sound of the night. Trees rustling in the breeze and an owl. He suspected if anyone had been there, they were gone now.

Still, he snuck closer to his SUV, searching the woods for shadows or clues. The ground looked recently trampled, like someone or something had compressed the sodden dirt near the perimeter of the carport. He got up close and used the flashlight on his phone. Tread marks from a tennis or hiking shoe had left an imprint. It was too small to be Gabe or Logan's, but it could've been Annie's, who had access to the building. It wasn't unusual for her to stop by in the middle of her farming chores to say hi or to use the gym. In the dark, Gabe couldn't tell how fresh the prints were.

By the time he got to his vehicle, he'd half convinced himself that his instincts were wrong.

Let your gut be your guide. It'll keep you alive. The words of his commander rang in his head.

Well, his gut wanted to believe he was overreacting, but in an abundance of caution he slipped inside headquarters and cued up the last hour's security footage. Logan had gone a little crazy with cameras, so they had eyes on practically every corner of the compound—from the carport to the shooting range. He sat in one of the office chairs at a bank of screens and flipped through the frames, alternating between cameras. Nothing looked amiss.

He went back to the footage of the carport and went through it slower this time. *Nada.* More than likely the noise he'd heard was a deer or a raccoon. Could've even been a bear cub, though most of them were supposed to be hibernating. He was about to shut the screens down when he saw something. Just a flash of color, but the hairs on Gabe's arms went up. He rewound and paused the footage at least a dozen times when he spotted it again, zoomed in, and blew up the frame. It was too blurry to make out. He played with it for a while, using various software programs to get a clearer image. Finally, he was able to hone in on the picture and get a decent view of what he was looking at. It was a tennis shoe. A child's red high top, if he wasn't mistaken.

Alarm bells sounded in his head. Gabe sent the frame to his phone and fired it off to Rhys in a text.

"Your elusive trio may have been snooping around L&G. Call me when you get this."

It was after midnight, and he figured Rhys was sound asleep. To be safe, he decided to camp out in his office. If anyone was out there, he'd be prepared.

* * * *

Raylene paced the kitchen. Where the hell was Gabe? He was supposed to be here an hour ago. Chad and his parents had headed back to their Yuba City farm at the crack of dawn. After breakfast, Nick and Maisy had loaded up the Winnebago and took off for Vegas. That left Raylene, who'd cleaned up the dishes and was raring to go.

She shot a text to Gabe.

Did you oversleep?

Chill, I'm on my way, came his response, with an emoji of a steaming cup of coffee.

Did he want one, or was he stopping off at the Bun Boy to bring her one? She took out the filters she'd just put away and made a new pot, in case. The man was beyond high maintenance. He did look good in a tux, though. She'd give him that. Ah, hell, who was she kidding? Gabe would look good in overalls, covered in mud. And despite his cryptic emoji, he was fairly agreeable.

But like everyone else in this town, he thought she was no good. *Someday, you're gonna tell me the whole story.* Maybe she was no good, but the fact that he sided with her critics made her indignant.

She heard a car and looked outside to see Gabe pulling up. A wave of anticipation at seeing him again spread through her and she quickly willed it away. He got out and she could see that his hair was still wet and that he'd dressed for manual labor. Worn Levis, work boots, and a fleece hoodie peeked out of his jacket. There was no sign of the straw cowboy hat he liked to wear. When she found the gold, she'd buy him a felt one.

"Hey." He came through the door. "You make coffee?"

"Yes. Did you get the metal detector?"

"Yes," he mimicked her, and made a beeline for the kitchen. "Is there anything to eat?"

She let out a sigh and pulled eggs, milk, and cheese from the refrigerator. "There goes getting an early start. There's bread in the cupboard."

He retrieved the loaf and put a few slices in the toaster, then stuck his head in the fridge. Juggling the butter dish, an orange juice container, and a plate of leftover banana bread, he made his way to Annie's old farm table.

"Did everyone get off okay?" he asked while setting them places at the table.

"Yep. I already ate. Hours ago."

"Then you can eat again and keep me company." He flashed her a mischevious grin.

She made him an omelet because it was one of the few dishes in her cooking repertoire. Butch used to complain that the only thing she was good for was spending his money. Since a good portion of it had been her money, she'd offered to hire him a cook. She'd gotten the back of his hand for her "smart mouth."

"You don't have to do that; I'll make it." Gabe took over the pan.

"I figured it was the least I could do." She returned her own mischevious smile.

"Nah, when we strike it rich you'll be giving me lots of gold." He laughed and she rolled her eyes.

"You're gonna be sorry for mocking me."

"I doubt it." He sprinkled a good heap of cheese on the eggs she'd already started. "Weezer should be here by Wednesday. We'll have to figure something out in the meantime."

If she could find someone to board Gunner it would take the last of her savings. Between feed, care, and barn fees, stables didn't come cheap. Plus, she owed Gabe, or this Weezer guy, for transportation costs. They'd better find gold.

"How much trouble would it be to build something here?" It still didn't solve who would take care of her horse until she could buy her own place. At the rate she was going, she wondered if that would ever happen.

"It's not a lot of trouble, it's finding the time. I've got other stuff on my plate. Maybe you could hire Colin Burke to do it. Do you know him?"

"No. He's married to Harlee Roberts, right?" She barely knew Harlee but assumed she was in the Raylene Rosser Hater Club. Hell, she'd be in it, too, if she were them.

"Yep. He's a good guy, builds furniture and does a lot of construction around here."

"All I need is pipe corralling and someone to put it together." It would be a lot cheaper than boarding, but she'd still have the issue of Gunner's care. God, she hated Butch. He'd agreed to keep the gelding in exchange for using the horse on his cattle ranch in Crawford. But Butch never met a promise he didn't go back on—their marriage vows of fidelity being the perfect example.

"I'll see what I can do. In the meantime, we have to find temporary housing." He flipped his omelet, and it flopped against the side of the pan and fell apart.

She pointed at some of the melted cheese that had dripped on the floor. "You might want to keep your day job."

"It'll still taste good," he said, in that cocky way she was learning to expect from him.

After plating the omelet, he took it to the table and waited for her to sit before digging in. "Mm, good. You sure you don't want some?" He got up, reached over the counter, and got his toast.

She nodded and poured them both coffees. "What took you so long?"

He looked over the rim of his cup and lifted his brows. "Were you having Gabe withdrawals?"

She snorted. "I can see why you're still single…a little too high on yourself, don't you think?"

Gabe threw his head back and laughed. "Ray, I'm single because I choose to be single."

She didn't doubt it but had no intention of feeding his overinflated ego. The only thing bigger appeared to be his appetite. After devouring the omelet, he ate the toast, slathered with butter, and two slices of banana bread.

She cleared away his dishes, hoping to move them along. Daylight was burning and she needed to find that gold before she called Dana. "You ready?"

"It would help if we had something to go on, like a map." He stared at her pointedly. "All the stories I read said there's supposed to be one. We've only got the metal detector for a day, and two hundred acres is a lot of land to comb."

She thought about it. It would be nice to have someone more experienced in map reading take a look. As a Navy SEAL he probably knew his longitude from latitude, which is more than she could say for herself. And it wasn't as if he didn't know the legend. If he wanted to screw her out of the gold, not having the map wasn't going to stop him. But what finally made her give in was the fact that Gabe was Logan's best friend, and she trusted Logan implicitly.

"Fine," she said, and went to the hallway to find her purse. When she came back Gabe was polishing off the rest of the banana bread. "But it stays in my custody at all times."

"You got it." He winked and she got the distinct impression he was mocking her. The man probably had a photographic memory. He waggled his hand. "Let me see it."

She pulled the map out of her handbag and he spread it out on the table, hunching over it.

He examined it for a while and shook his head. "You're kidding me, right? This looks like something a two-year-old drew. There's no compass rose, no grid, no scale indicator, no nothing. This isn't a map. From what I can tell, it's a sketch made by a drunk. Where'd you get it?"

"My dad. It's been passed down from generation to generation and is based on Levi's instructions."

"According to everything I've read, Levi wasn't the sharpest tool in the shed, so at least the map's consistent with that." He looked at her. "Ray, honey, what's it going to take for me to talk you out of this? Think of all

the ways we can spend the day instead of breaking our backs, digging in
the dirt while freezing our asses off. The forecast said snow. Wouldn't
you rather spend it here, in front of a fire, or in bed?" Gabe tossed her a
cheeky grin.

"I'll do it myself," she said. "Just give me the metal detector."

He huffed out a breath. "Stubborn, just like your flipping half brother.
All right, let's go break rocks in ten degrees." Gabe shrugged into his
jacket and she followed him outside. He opened the passenger door and
ushered her in.

Five minutes later, they were at the site, unloading the equipment. Gabe
was right. It was easily ten degrees outside, and Raylene could feel snow.
Not the best conditions for finding buried gold. But the clock was ticking.
Gabe took another look at the map and cursed under his breath.

"What's this?" He pointed at a row of scrawl, maybe numbers, at the
bottom of the paper.

"I have no idea. It looks like someone was doodling."

He studied the scribbles for a while and shook his head.

She pulled the metal detector from the back and tried to figure out how
the thing worked.

"Hang on, there," Gabe called. "I'm thinking over there." He pointed
to another cluster of trees. "Don't ask me why. It's not like I can make any
sense out of this." He held up the map. "It's just a hunch."

His guess was as good as hers. She carried the detector to the spot and
Gabe brought the shovels and the pickax.

"You do realize that thing will only detect metal a few feet down, right?"
No. "Duh."

"What's the likelihood your gold is buried that shallow? Don't you think
if it was it would've surfaced by now?"

"Jeez, Gabe, you're hellbent on sucking all the joy out of this, aren't you?"

He zoomed in on her pricey sheepskin gloves, a treat to herself from
Rodeo Drive when she'd still had money. "Joy? Easy for you to say, since
I'm the one digging."

"How do you turn this thing on?"

"First, you've got to set up the treasure-vision feature on the touchpad."

She shot him a look. "Ha ha. Very funny."

"It's not a joke," he protested. "See this?" He showed her what appeared
to be a compact computer screen at the top of the detector. "It's an imaging
display and can hone in on a target. Basically, it was invented for treasure
hunting. According to the dude at the hardware store, there are even better

ones on the market, but this is the one they rent out to all the morons who come up to the Mother Lode, looking for buried gold."

He fidgeted with the settings, his expression filled with glee. Even though Gabe didn't believe the gold existed, he sure seemed to love playing with the detector. Raylene suppressed an eye roll. If a gadget with lots of bells and whistles was what it took to get him out here, he could slow dance with the metal detector for all she cared.

She stood on a mound of leaves underneath two massive oak trees and scanned the area. It was at least forty feet from her original spot. A grove of trees had been depicted on the map. They could've been pine, oak, fir, or cedar for all she knew. Gabe was right, the map was so crude it was difficult to distinguish south from north, let alone which species of trees her great-great-uncle had buried the gold under. "Why here?"

"Your original trees had trunks with half the circumference of these. I'm no tree expert, but Levi buried the gold nearly two centuries ago, right? I'm guessing those weren't even around back then."

She hadn't thought about that. "All right, makes sense. Brawn and brains, who would've thought?"

"Hey, ungrateful girl, watch it." He grinned, and it made her belly do flip-flops. Brawn, brains, and charm. A lethal combination.

He fired up the detector and they spent the next hour hovering over the small swath of land inside the grove, going back and forth and back and forth. Nothing. Not so much as a soda can. Gabe even chopped at the dirt to break up rocks in case they were getting in the way.

"This must be the wrong spot," she said. "Maybe we should go back to where we were."

"Or maybe we should go home and snuggle up on the couch with something warm in front of a fire." He let his eyes slowly sweep over her and she remembered the kiss, the hot pull of that glorious mouth of his, and got goosebumps.

Gabe was a tease, and this wasn't her first rodeo. There'd been a lot of pleasurable kisses in her past and they'd all ended in pain. Besides, he was her brother's best friend, and messing around with him would be tempting fate. She didn't want anything to come between her and Logan. They'd just found each other and she wanted to hang on to her half brother with all her might.

"How 'bout we keep working, and at noon I'll buy you lunch?"

He leaned both arms on the handle of the metal detector and considered her offer. "I want steak."

"For steak, you can't break until one o'clock, and if we don't find anything by then, we have to change locations when we come back."

"Come back?" He raised his brows. "Sweetheart, I've got other things to do."

"Seriously, you're willing to quit this early in the game? So much for badass SEALs." She flapped her elbows and made chicken noises.

He threw his head back and laughed. "You really think you can goad me into doing this? Raylene, read my lips: There's no gold, and we're wasting our time. The only reason I've agreed to this fool's errand is because I find you highly entertaining."

"Why?" She sat in the dirt, pulling her knees up under her chin. "Is that your way of saying I'm ridiculous?"

"Not ridiculous, though this is." He gazed around at the ground they'd already covered. "All I'm saying is there's never a dull moment when you're around. And as long as I'm on vacation, I could use a little excitement."

"Glad to be of service." She wasn't sure if he was telling her he enjoyed her company or whether it was his measured way of saying she was a giant pain in the ass. She wished it didn't matter to her one way or another. But it did. "You think we could get back to work now?"

"Yes, ma'am." He saluted her and turned the detector back on.

She got to her feet and followed behind him. If they had two detectors they could cover twice as much ground. She was just about to suggest it when the detector went off.

"Oh my God, we've got something."

"Don't get excited yet." Gabe crouched down on the ground and maneuvered the detector closer. "Right here."

She grabbed the shovel, but the ground was like granite.

"Let me try." Gabe took it from her and dug enough of a hole that they could use their hands.

She got down on her knees and pawed at the soil. Gabe grabbed a miniature detector from his SUV.

"The guy at the hardware store told me this would come in handy." He squatted next to her and waved the handheld one over the site until it made a piercing noise. "Right here."

She took off her gloves and went to work on the spot he'd honed in on. He went back to his truck and returned with a trowel and began digging alongside her.

"Can you believe it, Gabe? This could be it."

"Or not." But he seemed as excited as she was. "What're you planning to do with all your loot?"

"Split it with Logan and Annie, pay off debts, and give a big chunk to this women's shelter where I volunteer."

He stopped and stared at her, his mouth slightly agape. "I don't know which one shocks me more: the fact that you're willing to give half your money to Logan, or that you volunteer."

"If I wasn't about to become filthy rich I might actually be offended." She pried a rock loose and tossed it away. "Run that thing over here again."

He waved the small detector over the hole they'd dug. "Sounds like we're getting closer." Gabe picked up the trowel and chipped away at a few more stones. "This is rocky soil, that's for sure."

"Should I get the pickax?"

"I'll get it." He got to his feet and Raylene thought if Gabe were Butch he'd bludgeon her to death with the pickax and run off with the gold.

"Move away," Gabe said, and lifted the pick above his head.

"Be careful. I don't want you damaging the gold."

He rolled his eyes and hammered into the ground, making real headway. "Get the handheld detector again."

She bent over the hole, turned it on, and moved the wand the same way he had. "Oh, oh, I think it's right here."

"I think you're right." He got down on the ground and used the trowel, shoveling out small batches of dirt at a time. "I feel something." He banged the trowel against a hard object in the dirt.

"Is it a box?"

"Can't tell." But five seconds later he pulled up an old rotted log.

"That can't be it."

"Hand me the detector."

She gave it to him and he tested it on the log. "It's in here."

"How can that be?" According to Rosser legend, Levi had buried the gold in the ground, not a tree.

"I don't know, Ray, but we're about to find out. Stand clear." Gabe put the log on the ground and began splitting it with the pickax.

"There's nothing there."

He crouched down with the small detector again, and it signaled on a piece of the log.

"That can't be right." But maybe Levi had hidden gold nuggets inside the tree itself, and over the years the oak had died and parts of the trunk had been petrified under the ground.

Gabe used his knife to dig around in the bark. "Well, I'll be damned." He plucked something out and Raylene held her breath.

"It's it, isn't it?" She looked down into the hole they'd dug. There must've been dozens of rotted logs, petrified wood, and roots down there. How long would it take them to extract the gold? "Let me see."

She held out her hand and he dropped the small orb in her palm. It wasn't as heavy as she would've thought, and it didn't glitter.

"Pretty cool, huh?"

"It doesn't look like gold." She rubbed her fingers over it, trying to clear away the dirt.

"It's a musket ball, probably leftover from the Gold Rush. I got dibs."

She dropped her shoulders, let out a frustrated breath, and handed it over. "It's all yours."

He examined the ball under the sun with a stupid gooey smile on his face. You'd think Gabe had won the lottery. He hadn't shaved and his face was covered in scruff. With a boonie hat pulled over his ears, a pair of camo cargo pants riding low on his lean hips, and endless amounts of rippling muscle, he was every inch the former Navy SEAL. A former Navy SEAL who'd just reverted to a twelve-year-old on Christmas morning.

He gazed over at her, that same silly grin playing on his lips. "Never a dull moment, Ray."

"Glad I could oblige. You ready to get back to work?"

He checked his watch. "I believe it's steak time."

Chapter 12

The minute they returned from lunch, Gabe knew something was amiss. First off, their pickax was gone. At least he'd had the forethought to stash the metal detector in the back of his SUV before they'd left. Not that the middle of nowhere was a high crime area, but the piece of equipment was a rental, and he was careful with other people's tools.

"It was probably Harper, or one of the McCreedy boys," Raylene said. "They're the only ones around here, since I doubt Flynn Barlow or Gia would've taken it. More than likely the kids were out here playing or riding their horses."

Gabe sincerely doubted it. The McCreedy kids were old enough to know better than to go onto private property and walk off with someone's stuff.

"Stay here."

Of course, Raylene ignored his instructions and tagged along as he walked the perimeter of their dig, looking for anything that would give him a clue as to who'd stolen the pick. But there was nothing.

He'd had a lengthy conversation with Rhys that morning about the tennis shoe that had turned up on his security camera footage. They were both of the opinion that it had a connection to Rhys' trio. Too many coincidences, including the backpack found on Drew Matthews' property. And then there was the fact that no local would've been skulking around L&G Security in the middle of the night.

"It's just a pickax, Gabe, not an international incident. We still have the shovel and the trowel."

He didn't feel the need to share the information about the lurking strangers. Other than the missing pick, Gabe hadn't heard any reports of thefts or vandalism. For all he knew they were a homeless family, looking for shelter anywhere they could find it.

"It just seems like a weird place for someone to walk off with your gardening tools."

"Maybe an animal carried it away," Raylene said, and he looked at her like she was nuts.

"Didn't you grow up here? What kind animal runs off with someone's pick? The only one I know is human."

She laughed. "Once a bear took a six-pack from our ranch foreman's cooler. Shit happens in these mountains."

"Yep, shit happens." He caught her around the waist, because he'd wanted to touch her since the moment he'd seen her standing in Annie's kitchen, fixing his coffee. She had on another pair of her tight western jeans and those turquoise boots that revved his engine, her blond hair pulled through the back of a John Deere baseball cap. "Come on, Ray, let's go home before it snows."

"That's exactly the reason we need to finish what we started. Otherwise, it'll be twice as hard tomorrow when everything is frozen over."

He pulled her in and rested his forehead against hers. "You're assuming a lot, sweetheart." Raylene was a kick in the ass, but he didn't plan to spend Monday digging up holes. He could think of a number of other ways to entertain himself. Unfortunately, the first image that popped into his head was getting Raylene naked. *No can do, asshole.*

He reluctantly let go, and to temporarily appease her he got the metal detector and resumed the search. By twilight, they still hadn't found any gold, not even another musket ball. He persuaded her to call it quits for the night and dropped her off at the farm with a promise to reconnoiter first thing Monday. He considered going in the house with her and having wedding leftovers, but decided the safer course of action was to take his horny self home.

On his way to Donner Road, he took a detour to the police station. Surprisingly, Connie was still at the front desk, talking on her cordless headset. She saluted him like she always did.

"You're here late," he said when she ended her call.

"I've got a shitty boss who's a slave driver."

Rhys came out of his office. "I heard that, Connie."

Her lips curved up. The 9-1-1 operator and office manager was always smarting off to the chief, and the truth was Rhys enjoyed it. Despite his gruff exterior, Shepard was a pushover. Gabe only had to see him with his wife and kid to know that.

"Want to get a beer? As of now I'm officially off duty, and Maddy and Emma are in San Francisco. Big Breyer hotel meeting."

"Yeah? A beer sounds good." Gabe could use one.

Rhys turned to Connie. "You can go home now."

"Gee, thanks. Don't forget to feed Emma's fish." She turned off her computer, shrugged into a coat, and headed out.

"Fish?"

"Maddy got her a little tank. Anything new on our drifters?"

"That's what I came in to talk to you about. It's probably nothing, but Raylene and I were on her property today, looking for gold—long story— and when we came back from lunch a pickax was missing."

Rhys zipped his jacket, grabbed a set of keys from a pegboard behind Connie's desk, and they crossed the square to the Ponderosa. "You sure you didn't just misplace it?"

Gabe shot him a look. "Yeah, I'm sure."

"Don't tell me you actually believe the gold story? Even when I was a kid we all knew it was bullshit. It was something Ray used to brag about when he wasn't bragging about everything else. Let's face it, if he'd believed it himself, he would've dug up the entire ranch looking for it."

Gabe shrugged. "Raylene believes it."

"And she dragooned you into doing the heavy lifting. I didn't realize you were that hard up for female company."

"Hey, I found this." He dug the musket ball out of his pocket and showed it to Rhys.

Rhys rolled it around in his hand. "That's all you're going to find, but at least you're keeping Raylene out of trouble until she leaves."

The derision in Rhys' voice bothered Gabe. He tried to tell himself that it was because Raylene was Logan's flesh and blood, but the damned truth of it was he liked her. Yeah, she was a head trip, but she was also fun. And adventurous. And frankly, despite everyone's opinion to the contrary, she seemed like a decent person. She even volunteered at a woman's shelter, which, admittedly, had come as a shock to Gabe. She'd never struck him as the altruistic type.

Raylene had once told Logan that she was afraid of Butch. But Gabe had always assumed it was a pampered woman's ploy to manipulate her half brother. Get him to help her move her crap out of the Denver house before Butch could claim it in the divorce. Maybe Gabe had misjudged. Maybe Butch used to knock her around. Just the thought of it made him sick to his stomach.

"Yep," Gabe said, and left it at that. "Anyway, as ridiculous as it sounds, someone stole that pickax. It was there when we left and gone when we returned an hour later."

They found two stools at the bar. The restaurant was quiet for a Sunday. There were a couple of TVs playing, but the sound had been turned down. And about half the tables were empty. Rhys flagged down the bartender at the other end of the bar and ordered them a Sierra Nevada.

"You think it's our drifters?"

"Could be. I can't imagine anyone else taking it. Besides the McCreedys and the Rodriguezes on one side and Flynn and Gia on the other, no one is around for miles. Raylene thought one of the kids might've been playing around with the stuff, but I don't see it."

Rhys shook his head. "Me neither. But I'll call Clay just to make sure." He fished his phone out of his pocket. "I'm texting Wyatt to tell him to cruise the back roads while he's on duty tonight."

Gabe nodded. "I'm sure it's harmless, but Logan's gonna be pissed about his pick disappearing."

Rhys laughed. "I'm guessing he'll be more pissed about the fact that someone was sneaking around your offices."

Gabe took a slug of his beer. "It's a good wake-up call. We've probably been more lax about security than we should. Besides the occasional meth house and cattle rustler, Nugget feels like Mayberry."

"We get a fair share of crime, don't kid yourself." Rhys asked for a bowl of pub mix and swallowed a handful. "Dinner."

Gabe picked through the bowl, snagging a couple of nuts. "Yep, dinner."

* * * *

On the other side of town, Drew loaded the car to make the long drive to the Bay Area.

"We almost forgot your suit jacket." Kristy held it folded over her arm as she locked the front door.

He'd persuaded her to stay longer and to ride home with him. While he'd spent the day with Harper, she'd holed up in the office working on her brief, popping out occasionally for a snack or drink. It had almost felt normal. Almost. But there were subtle ways in which he could feel them growing more distant. The way she bristled every time he touched her, the way she sat on the big reclining chair instead of next to him on the couch, and the way she retreated into herself. With the exception of dinner Saturday night, they'd hardly spoken all weekend.

Of course, he'd spent most of the day with Harper, listening to her chatter on endlessly the way thirteen-year-olds did, leaving no space for anyone else to get a word in edgewise. Slowly but surely, she was adapting to her new home, her new life, to him and to Emily. But even still, his daughter was as fragile as glass, trying to make sense of the loss of the people who'd stolen and loved her and a new beginning with her real parents who were no longer together. It was a lot for an adult to handle, let alone an adolescent.

"You ready to go?"

Kristy threw his jacket in the back seat and got up front. "Yep. Hopefully we won't hit all the ski traffic on the way down."

For as cold as it had been, they hadn't gotten that much snow. But on a Sunday evening there was bound to be plenty of cars on the road. Lots of folks returning home from a weekend in the mountains.

"Keep your fingers crossed," he said, and started the engine.

"What's this about Harper wanting to ride?"

Harper had complained that Emily and Clay wouldn't let her have a lesson from the woman who'd brought her home the other day after her spill from Ginger. Raylene was her name. Drew was surprised that Kristy had overheard the conversation, and even more surprised that she'd raised the topic. Of late, she'd become reticent when it came to Harper, afraid of overstepping her bounds. Drew wished she would play more of a role but hadn't brought it up, not wanting to rock an already wobbly boat.

"This Raylene woman, who is apparently quite accomplished with horses, offered to help Harper. I don't know all the details, but Emily and Clay have a problem with her."

"A problem? What kind of problem?"

Drew chuckled. "Something about her screwing over one of their friends. It sounds like a lot of small-town *Peyton Place* crap, nothing I wanted to get involved with. In the five-minute contact I had with her she seemed nice enough."

"So it's not like she's got a criminal record?" Kristy turned up the heat.

The forecast said snow, and Drew wanted to get to the pass before the roads got icy.

"Nothing like that." He reached across the console and threaded his fingers through hers. "She doesn't live in Nugget anymore and was only here for the wedding. She's leaving soon, so it's probably best that Harper doesn't get attached to her anyway."

"And how does Harper know her in the first place?"

Drew told Kristy about Harper's unfortunate fall from Ginger and how Raylene had come to the rescue. He left out the part about Emily freaking out over Harper sneaking off with the horse. Kristy thought they were both too overprotective, but she hadn't gone through the trauma of losing a child. It was a topic they steered clear of. There were so many subjects that they now tiptoed around that Drew had lost count.

"Harper appears to be very taken with the woman," he said.

"Why do you think that is?"

Drew chuckled again. "I'm guessing partly because she looks like a teen idol. Kind of Daisy Duke meets Hayden Panettiere."

Kristy cleared her throat. "Sounds like you were quite taken with her, too."

"Jealous?" He patted her leg teasingly.

"Should I be?" She laughed.

It was the closest they'd come to being playful with each other since the police had found Hope at Christmastime. Drew found it encouraging.

"Nope. I'm a one-woman man." He changed lanes to get out from behind a semitruck. "I also got the impression that Harper liked talking to her. The way she put it was, 'Raylene doesn't treat me like a freak or a victim.'" He supposed most people, nervous about saying the wrong thing, handled Harper with kid gloves.

"They had that much of a chance to talk? I thought you said she brought Harper right home."

"Yeah." Drew nodded. "But then Harper saw her again at the wedding. Clearly, the woman has made a big impression."

"How soon is she leaving? It seems silly not to let Harper take a lesson. What harm could it do?"

"That was my thought, but Emily's pretty adamant about it."

Kristy turned to stare out the window.

"Kris? What's on your mind?" He didn't have to ask, really. Emily had become another one of their off-limits topics.

She sighed. "You're Harper's father. Shouldn't you also have a say in what's right for your daughter?" She leaned her head against the seat and pinched the bridge of her nose. "I don't know why I get involved. It's between you and Emily, and that's the problem, Drew. I'm not part of this. You want me to be, but every time I open my mouth, it's Emily-this and Emily-that. She's Harper's mother, I get that. I get that I'm the interloper here. But it's hard to sit back and watch you smother that beautiful little girl. What happened all those years ago was beyond monstrous. Your child was stolen from you. My God, Drew, it's every parent's nightmare. But the fact is, Harper had a good life. She was loved and cared for and raised like any normal child. I'm not giving her abductors a pass. What they did is unimaginable…and unforgivable. All I'm saying is that Harper is a well-adjusted girl. It's her parents…" She paused, then went back to staring out the window.

"Go on and say it. It's her parents who aren't well-adjusted."

"And how could you be after what the both of you went through? I understand that, Drew. I feel every drop of your pain. All I'm saying is, don't transfer all that anguish to Harper. Don't suffocate her; let her be a thirteen-year-old, and let her pick her own idols."

In his heart, he knew she was right. But loosening up and letting go was easier said than done.

"I want to talk to you about something else," she said, and he stiffened. The tone in her voice signaled the gravity of whatever she was about to say.

"I want to do another round of IVF," she continued. "I know with the expense of the new house we really can't afford it, but I was thinking we could take out a second mortgage on the Palo Alto house. We have plenty of equity, and we can put that bathroom remodel we were planning on hold."

"I thought we already put it on hold to buy the Nugget house." The truth was he didn't want to do another round of IVF. He didn't think he could live with Kristy's disappointment. "Babe, you heard what the doctor said."

"She said she couldn't predict what would happen."

"But as long as there was no remediable explanation for failure after three attempts, she didn't recommend a fourth one." The doctor had indeed made it clear that she no longer thought IVF was a viable option for them, but Drew wondered that it was his convenient excuse to stop trying.

"So we just give up? Is that what you're saying?"

"No, what I'm saying is we go back to the old-fashioned method."

"That hasn't worked either," she said with an edge in her voice. "I don't care what Dr. Melly says. There's new research showing that two-thirds of women who undergo six or more cycles of IVF get pregnant. It just came out, and it's legitimate, not some fly-by-night study."

He let out a breath of frustration. She spent hours trolling the Internet, reading whatever she could get her hands on. Research that said you could increase fertility by standing on your head, painting your headboard yellow, eating royal jelly, and drinking baboon urine. Drew had lost count of all the ways.

They hit a bottleneck in Sacramento, and he considered pulling off at the next exit and waiting out traffic at a restaurant. He hadn't eaten since breakfast, and was hungry.

"You want to get dinner?" he asked.

"Is that your way of changing the subject?"

"No, it's my way of asking if you want to eat."

"I don't want to eat; I want to finish our conversation."

"Okay, you want to finish our conversation, here goes. I don't want to do a fourth cycle of IVF, and I'm definitely not doing six. So if you don't want to eat, we'll drive."

And they did, in silence.

Chapter 13

Raylene thought she heard a car door slam. Deciding it was a dream, she rolled over and went back to sleep. A few minutes later, she heard it again. This time it sounded like the squeak of a tailgate.

She quickly sat up and lifted the lace curtain next to her bed. It was too dark to see the driveway below her bedroom, so she pressed her ear to the glass and listened. Maybe it was the sound of snow hitting the tin roof of the shed, or a raccoon rummaging through the trash. She started to lie back down when she heard it again.

A rustle and a thump and something that sounded like whispering. But maybe that was just the wind wafting through the pines.

She tried to convince herself that it was merely being in a big house alone. There was an alarm—Logan was over the top when it came to security—but she hadn't thought to set it after Gabe had dropped her off. It was Nugget, after all. The only person she'd ever been afraid of here was her father, and he was dead.

She got out of bed and padded to another window, hoping there'd be more moonlight at that end of the room. The view proved to be just as dark, and she wished she would've thought to turn on one of the outside lights before she'd gone to bed.

Too spooked to go downstairs, she went into Logan and Annie's room at the end of the hall and peered out their windows. She still didn't see anything, but she could've sworn she heard a creaking sound coming from her truck.

She thought about calling 9-1-1, but by the time anyone got there she'd be lying in a pool of blood. Plus, she didn't want to have to face Jake Stryker again. Rhys Shepard lived down the road, but he was no fan of hers either.

She'd rather take her chances on her own.

She crept down the stairs. First thing she'd do was activate the alarm, then shine a light on the driveway. It seemed like a sound plan until she heard what was for sure the slamming of a door.

Shit!

She ran back up the stairs, dove into her bed, grabbed her cell phone off the nightstand, and hit automatic dial.

Wake up, wake up.

"Hello."

"Someone's in the driveway. I think they're stealing my truck."

"Where are you?"

"In my room. I started to go down there but got scared."

"Stay where you are. Better yet, go into Logan's room. He keeps a Sig P226 in the closet. You know how to use a handgun?"

"It's been a while, but Daddy taught me."

"Go!" he said, and she could hear him moving. "As soon as you get it, call 9-1-1 and stay in your room. I'll be there fast as I can."

"Hurry."

"Call 9-1-1, you hear me? And Raylene, don't shoot us when we get there."

She found the gun in Logan's closet and sat in there, wondering if she was a complete paranoid wackadoodle. What if no one was down there and all she'd heard was the wind and snow, playing tricks? But she'd heard what she heard. And it wasn't the weather. She'd slept through Sierra blizzards; she knew the difference.

She gritted her teeth and called the police. An operator told her someone was on their way, and she prayed it would be Wyatt or that new woman in the department. Anyone but Jake.

Then she waited.

It seemed like forever until she heard a siren, and then a car. She left the gun where she found it and went downstairs when someone rang the bell.

"It's Chief Shepard."

She answered the door and let Rhys in.

"Gabe's on his way." She didn't know why she'd offered that information and felt the need to add, "I called him first."

He merely nodded. "Did you see anyone?"

"No, but I heard someone in the driveway. You didn't see anyone when you drove up?"

"Nope." Great, he didn't believe her. "Let me have a look. Wait here."

He went outside and she shut the door to keep the cold out. A few minutes later, she heard Gabe's SUV pull up and felt instantly better. Safer. She watched out the window as the two men conferred. They were looking at something near her truck. She ran upstairs, found her ski jacket, slipped into her cowboy boots, and went outside.

The front porch was covered in snow and she was careful not to slip. Gabe lifted his head from his and Rhys' huddle and motioned for her to join them. He met her at the steps and gave her a hand down.

"Come take a look at this."

She followed him to her truck.

Rhys had turned on his headlights and part of the driveway was illuminated. He made room for her so she could peer inside the cab and swept a flashlight over the interior. "Don't touch anything."

Her glovebox was open and its contents were scattered on the passenger seat and floor.

"Did you leave it like that?" Rhys asked.

"No." It had been so long since she'd opened the glovebox that she didn't even know what was in there. She kept her vehicle registration and proof of insurance clipped to her visor and her phone charger in the center console. "So I didn't imagine the noises?"

"Doesn't look like it," Rhys said, and she noted his hair was smooshed and the shirt peeking out of his jacket was inside out. He must've come straight from bed.

"What do you think they were looking for?" Gabe asked.

"Cash, a credit card, I don't know." She checked to make sure her stereo was still there, then scanned the space behind her back seat. Her sweater, a pair of gym shoes, and a nylon shopping bag didn't appear to have been touched. "You probably interrupted them before they could steal anything."

"Take another look and tell me if you see anything missing," Rhys said, and began taking pictures of the glovebox and the stuff spilling out.

"I don't keep valuables in my truck." Not since moving to LA. "You think it was kids, screwing around?" She couldn't imagine anyone breaking into cars in Nugget.

Rhys and Gabe exchanged glances.

"Could be," Rhys said. "Were you able to make anything out in the dark?"

"Not a thing. But they were loud enough to wake me."

Gabe turned to look at the house, which was still dark. In her haste to answer the door, she hadn't even turned on the porch light.

"Whoever it was probably thought no one was home," he said. "Just about everyone in town knew Logan and Annie were going on their honeymoon."

"Nothing appears to be missing." Even so, Raylene was creeped out that a stranger had pawed through her stuff and nervous about being here alone.

Rhys walked around her Ford, sweeping his flashlight over the ground. "Come see this," he told Gabe.

They both crouched down in the snow, and Raylene went over to see what had caught their attention.

"Footprints," Gabe said. "It looks like two different sizes."

"How do you know they're not yours and mine?" She and Gabe had crossed the driveway several times as they'd loaded his SUV for their treasure hunt that morning.

"Because there wasn't snow on the ground when we walked here."

Good point. She hadn't thought of that. Gabe and Rhys exchanged another glance, and she was starting to get the feeling that they knew something she didn't.

"What?" she asked.

"Nothing. I'm just thinking whoever it is also has our pickax."

The possibility hadn't entered her mind, but she supposed two crimes in one day wasn't a coincidence. And suddenly she was struck with the idea that this might not be random. "Do you think I'm being targeted?" Perhaps these were pranks to scare her and get her to leave town sooner.

On second thought, it didn't seem like the Rodriguezes' style, and they were the ones with the biggest ax to grind against her. Tomorrow, she planned to put a check in their mailbox for Tawny's damaged dress. Perhaps she'd go straight to their house and ask them face to face.

Rhys combed his hand through his hair. "Let's just keep our eyes out, okay? Tomorrow morning, someone will come by to take prints. Would you mind staying out of your truck until then?"

"I guess." She didn't like the idea of being without wheels. She'd wanted to start searching for the gold first thing in the morning and had to meet with Dana at some point in the day. "You think it's that big of a deal?" As far as she could tell, the thieves hadn't even gotten anything.

"You never know" was all Rhys said. He turned to Gabe before heading to his police vehicle. "I'll talk to you later."

"Roger that. Thanks for coming out."

Rhys waved his hand in the air, got in his SUV, and drove away.

Gabe walked over and shined a flashlight on her flannel pajama bottoms and lifted his brows. The pants had little horses on them and said, "I'd rather be riding."

"They're warm." She'd stopped wearing sexy lingerie around the time Butch started making her skin crawl.

"They look hot with the boots."

She rolled her eyes.

Gabe's mouth slid up. "Let's go inside, it's freezing out here."

He slung his arm over her shoulder and guided her up the stairs with his light. "You okay?"

"Just a little weirded out." She flipped on the heat as soon as they got inside. Before she'd gone to bed she'd turned it off, and it was nearly as cold in the house as it had been outside. "Can you stay the night?"

"Yeah," he said, his voice gruff. Raylene waited for one of his standard-guy come-on lines, but he just opened the door, turned on the light switch, and headed for the kitchen. "Is there anything to eat?"

"Tons. What are you in the mood for?"

He glanced at her, letting his caramel eyes take a stroll down her body, then quickly turned away. "Some of that smoked ham from the wedding."

Inexplicably disappointed, she pulled the ham out of the refrigerator, along with a container of stuffed mushrooms and some potato salad. He got down two plates and they took turns warming the mushrooms in the microwave.

"You want a glass of wine?" He perused the rack in the sideboard and pulled out a red. "It might help you get back to sleep."

"No thanks." And, for no reason she could understand, she told him what she'd never told Logan. "I'm an alcoholic." *Ninety days sober.*

He took that in, mulled it over for a second or two, and nodded. "How about a soda or a glass of water?"

"Tea," she said, and started a flame under Annie's kettle. "You want some? It's peppermint."

He scrunched his nose. "Nah, I'll stick with water."

They sat in the kitchen, eating in silence until it drove her nuts.

"Go ahead and say something."

"About what?" He snagged a stuffed mushroom off her plate because he'd eaten his. "About you being an alcoholic? Clearly you're doing something about it; I haven't seen you touch a drink since you've been here."

"I'm ninety days sober."

He held her gaze, a world of pride shining in his expression. "That's a big deal, Raylene."

Her chest squeezed. It was the best thing he could've said, because it was a big deal. Not touching a drink in three months had taken every ounce of strength and courage she had. Each day was still a struggle.

"Logan doesn't know…about my drinking. And I would appreciate it if you didn't tell him."

"What happens between us, stays between us." This time there was something else shining in his eyes. Something a little playful and a little suggestive.

She never knew whether his flirting was bona fide interest or him just playing the horndog, a role he'd apparently perfected in the Navy.

"In that case, let's not tell him about his pick either," she said. "I'll get a new one tomorrow at the hardware store before we go back to the site."

He'd started to take their plates to the sink and stopped in the middle of the kitchen. "It's time to give up on that, Ray."

"Uh-uh, I'm not leaving until I find it. I don't care if someone's trying to scare me off, I won't go without the gold."

"Then you'll be here forever, because there is no gold."

"You're wrong." She got up, took the plates from him, and stuck them in the dishwasher. "It's there, and I'm going to find it."

He pinned her in at the sink. "What makes you so certain?"

"My dad wouldn't have told us about it if it didn't exist." Ray was a bastard, but he wasn't prone to believing in fairy tales. If he said the gold was there, it was there.

He exhaled. "Suit yourself, Ray. But I think you're wasting your time."

She shrugged. "I have to find a place for Gunner before I can leave anyway."

"Yeah, about that." He moved in closer, completely boxing her in. "You got any ideas? Because I'm thinking after Tawny's dress situation, Nugget isn't feeling too hospitable toward you and Wilbur."

"I was told by Harper Matthews that there's a stable at Sierra Heights. Do you know the guy in charge there?"

"You mean Griffin Parks?" He lifted her chin with his finger, so she'd have to look up at him. "The same Griffin Parks who owns the Gas and Go where you had your famous incident with Jake Stryker? I believe he was there that night."

"Oh jeez." She'd been in rare form that night. Raylene squeezed her eyes shut, trying to block the memory. But it all came rushing back.

"Have you been drinking, ma'am?"

"No. Have you?" She flashed a little boob, and when he didn't take the bait, screamed, "Don't you touch me!"

Jake ignored the accusation. "Ma'am, I'm gonna need to see your license."

"Uh...I don't think so."

"If you want to drive away, you'll have to take a sobriety test, and I'm afraid that starts by you giving me your license."

"Do you know who I am?" She jabbed her finger at his badge.

"More important, do you know who you are?" Jake said, and Griffin had laughed.

"I'm calling my father," she said, and tottered backward on her high-heeled boots. "In case you didn't know, he's Ray Rosser of the Rock and River Ranch."

"I think that's a good idea, call him," Jake told her. "That way he can drive you home and you can sleep it off."

She dumped her purse on the floor, looking for her cell phone. She found it in a pile of makeup and tampons, made a big show of pounding in a number, then staggered off to a private corner of the store.

Lucky had come in and gotten her that night, and they'd had a big fight on the way home. If she had to guess, he'd already fallen in love with Tawny by then.

"Well, there goes that idea," she told Gabe. Was there anyone in Nugget who hadn't witnessed her acting badly? Raylene didn't think so.

"I'll talk to Grif. He's a good guy. If there's room in the barn, he'll give your horse a temporary home."

She'd still have to come up with the money to pay for it, and find someone to feed and water Gunner until she could afford a permanent situation. Even so, she'd be eternally grateful. "Thank you."

"You're welcome." He leaned down and kissed the tip of her nose, then drew a deep, unsteady breath. "Now, what are we going to do about the fact that we really want to have sex with each other?"

She snorted. "Speak for yourself, bucko." But even to her own ears the retort sounded weak. Especially when she continued to stand there, one inch away from plastering her boobs against his chest.

He thought so too, because he rolled over her denial like an eighteen-wheeler by hooking his arm around her waist. "Logan won't like it. In fact, he'll probably cut my balls off."

"I thought what happens between us, stays between us," she mimicked and then wondered what she was doing, egging him on like that.

"I can't lie to my best friend."

"It's not lying, it's omitting information that's none of his business to begin with." Okay, this was insane. She was practically begging him to have sex with her. She closed her eyes and pretended to be naked with Butch, hoping the visual would make her sufficiently sick. Nope, all she saw was Gabe, which made her entire body tingle, even her hair.

"It really isn't his business, is it? I mean we're both consenting adults—hardly innocents." Gabe looked to her for confirmation.

She nodded, and once again questioned her sanity. But she wanted him, and she hadn't wanted a man in a long time.

He lifted her onto the counter and stared into her eyes, silently telling her it was her move. She wrapped her legs around his hips and pulled him closer. He kissed her. It was more intense than before, like the buildup to this moment had left him so wanting that he was out of control. The idea that she could do that to him was heady.

"Let's get this off." He fumbled with her zipper, and she had a feeling that he was usually defter at it.

She shrugged out of the down jacket and let it drop to the floor, leaving her in a sleep camisole that was thin and lacy—a weird contrast with the horse pajama pants. But she hadn't planned for anyone to see her sleepwear tonight. Gabe didn't seem to mind. He'd stopped kissing her to stare, a sexy smile playing on his lips.

"Damn, you're hot, Ray."

She tugged him in and got his jacket off. He had on a thermal shirt that clung to his torso like a second skin. She could see the ridges of muscle in his abdomen and couldn't help herself. She ran her hand over his stomach. Everything was hard as granite, and she felt him shudder at her touch.

"Jeez, Moretti, you've let yourself go to pot."

He chuckled, knowing exactly how ripped he was. Then he cupped the back of her head and captured her mouth with another kiss. She clung to his shoulders, her body igniting and her breasts tightening.

His hands trailed up her sides and slid back down in slow motion, teasing her senses. Her pajama bottoms became constricting, and she longed to take them off. He shifted to her ribcage and worked his way up to her breasts, stroking her nipples over the flimsy material of her top. She whimpered, and in one quick swoop he lifted her off the counter.

"Where we going?"

"To find a bed." The words came out like a croak.

He carried her upstairs, found her room, and laid her in the middle of her rumpled sheets. She still had her boots on and scrambled to the edge of her bed to pry them off.

"Later, the boots stay on." He slapped her hands away and tugged them off himself, then fell on top of her, the hard bulge in his jeans pressing against her belly.

She inched her hands under his shirt and explored his chest. It was solid like the rest of him and slightly furred. "Take this off."

"You first." He winked.

Raylene had never been known for her modesty, but she suddenly felt shy. When she stalled, he took over, dragging the hem of her camisole over her head.

"Damn," he said, and weighed each breast in his hands, then took one in his mouth.

She let out a moan, the sensation of his warm lips and hot breath so exquisite she thought she'd never felt anything this good. And then it only got better. He squeezed her other breast with his hand, rubbing his thumb in circular motions over her nipple. She arched her back, giving him better access, and nearly came off the bed. The mattress was only full size, and Gabe was a big man.

"Good?" he asked, and her entire body answered with a quiver. "Yeah," he whispered.

His hand slid inside the drawstring waist of her pajama bottoms and his fingers moved over her. One dipped inside. "You're so wet."

"Mmm" was all she could manage, and went for his belt buckle.

He pushed her hand away and tugged the flannel pants over her ass until she lay completely naked. Gabe turned on his side and went up on one elbow to gaze down on her. His eyes slid up and down her body, taking her in from head to toe. "I'm going to say it again: damn!"

"Now your turn." She rucked his shirt up and he finished the job, tossing the thermal somewhere past the foot of the bed. The man was Italian Renaissance-statue perfect. She kissed his chest and worked her way down to the waistband of his jeans, trying once again to unhook his belt.

He unfastened it himself and lifted his hips to pull his jeans down. They got stuck around his boots and he kicked them off, using his foot to get his pants the rest of the way down. All Raylene could do was stare. He was thick and long and hard and so purely male it made her mouth water.

"I was in a rush," he said about the fact that he'd been commando under his jeans.

"I'm not complaining." And then she did the rare thing—at least for her—by taking him in her mouth. He tasted salty and musky and…so good.

"Ah, shit, Raylene. Honey…" He brought her head up. "I want you to do that…but later." Gabe rolled onto her and pressed his erection between her thighs.

She bowed and moaned as he slid up and down against her. The friction was working her up to a fever pitch. "Gabe?"

"Huh?" His hands were underneath her, squeezing her butt, driving her even higher.

"Please."

"Yeah, okay, let me get a condom." He was out of breath.

The entire time he'd dug up her land, looking for the gold, she hadn't seen him so much as break a sweat. But this—she—had undone him. The thought heightened her excitement even more.

He leaned over the bed, got something off the floor, and before she knew it he was suited up and entering her. For a second, she froze.

"You okay?" He started to pull out.

"No, don't stop. It's just been awhile."

He went slow, rocking into her a little at a time. The sensation of him filling her was so erotic that she nearly climaxed right then and there. It had been more than a year since she'd had sex, and even longer since she'd had an orgasm. Even the self-administered kind.

"Mmm."

"Better?" he asked.

"So good."

He quickened the pace and laved her breasts with attention. Her body grew more accustomed to his size, and the extra stimulation loosened her up. Soon she was matching him stroke for stroke, moving to their own special rhythm, so in sync that the pleasure rocketed through her like a current of electricity.

He grunted, calling out her name, whispering endearments and describing the things he wanted to do to her in explicit detail. The words, and his caresses—both dirty and sweet, rough and gentle—took her to a new plateau. She wrapped her legs around his hips, wanting him deeper. Faster. Gabe pumped harder, stroking every erogenous zone on her body with his hands and his lips.

"Ah," he called out. "You close?" He reached between their joined bodies and worked her with his finger while he tongued her nipples.

She felt it low in her belly, and then her whole body began to tremble as she called his name. The orgasm ripped through her in a forceful rush, rocking and rolling like a seven-magnitude earthquake. He continued to pound into her, prolonging the sensation until her body felt limp and sated.

Gabe pistoned his hips a few more times, threw his head back and shuddered, then fell on top of her like a rag doll.

"Wow," he said, coming up on both elbows. "You alive down there, Ray?"

"Just barely." She was exhausted, but all her nerve endings purred.

He rolled to his side and pulled her into his arms. "A little shut-eye, then round two. What do you say?"

She was already asleep.

Chapter 14

The sun was shining in Gabe's eyes, and for a second he couldn't remember where he was. Then he felt something warm and curvy nestled against his front and instantly got harder. If his memory served him right, he and Raylene had done it a total of three times during the wee hours of the morning, not counting some extracurricular activity before they couldn't stay awake any longer.

He glanced at the clock on the nightstand. Ten AM. Shit. He was usually an early riser. Then again, he'd been up since right before dawn. Raylene wiggled her butt in her sleep, and he had to keep himself from entering her from behind. Instead, he draped his arm over her shoulder and fondled one perfect breast. Raylene had an amazing rack. Pert, firm, and the size of ripe peaches. He loved her long legs and her shapely ass, not too skinny. Nope, the woman had a little junk in her trunk, just the way he liked it.

When she didn't stir, he tweaked her nipple, making her stretch against him. He'd woken up many times with naked women in his bed. But this... well, this was something he could get used to. And that wasn't good, because Raylene was Logan's sister and, more important, she was leaving, and he wasn't.

"Hey, sleeping beauty, wake up."

"Uh-uh. Make us coffee...and breakfast."

"Okay. But what about this first?" He rubbed his erection against her backside and she whimpered. "You like that, huh?"

She arched, pushing her ass against his groin, and he almost lost his mind. He spread her legs, reached inside, and stroked her until she was ready for him. He reached over to the nightstand and remembered that they'd already used his last condom.

Gabe pushed away her long blond hair and kissed the back of her downy neck, continuing to stroke her with his fingers. She moaned and made little panting sounds that drove him crazy. He couldn't recall a woman ever getting him this hot. It was as if Raylene's body was made for his. The way he could arouse her with a single touch or kiss, the way she came apart when he was thrusting inside of her...it was a huge turn-on.

"Gabe?" She looked over her shoulder, those baby blues so imploring it made his chest expand.

"We're going to do it this way. It feels good, right?"

"Uh-huh." She sank against him. "But I want you...in me."

He slid a finger inside her and rocked against her. "We're out of condoms."

"Oh, oh, Gabe...so good. I'm dying here. Don't worry about it, I'm on the pill."

He started to push into her and stopped, his balls aching from the sudden denial. He wanted her so badly that every muscle strained with it. Just this once, he wanted to throw caution to the wind, but Raylene was Logan's sister. She was also too impetuous for her own good.

"Shush." He turned her onto her back, spread her legs wide, and crawled between them.

She fisted the blankets with both hands as he covered her with his mouth, licking and sucking until she practically came off the bed.

"Good?"

She tried to say something and squeaked instead. His interpretation was that she was enjoying herself. *Ditto*, he thought as he reached up to fondle her breasts. She shuddered, her whole body quivering like he was rocking her world. And that right there made him come, too.

She tipped her head back on the pillow and he slid up to kiss her on the lips. "Hopefully that worked for you." He couldn't help himself from flashing a cocky grin. "You ready for breakfast?"

"I don't know if I can move yet."

He rolled over to his side and ran his fingers through her hair. It was silky and looked sexy all rumpled and tangled.

"Take a shower and I'll strip the bed," he said.

"And you'll make coffee, too?"

"Sure." She cocked her head to one side and he said, "What?"

"Nothing, you're just awfully accommodating."

What was the big deal? Both chores would take him less than five minutes. "That's the way I roll, baby."

"Are you still planning to help me find the gold?"

He sighed "I thought we talked about that."

"You talked, and I made it clear I wasn't giving up that easily because I'm not a quitter." She emphasized "quitter," clearly hoping to get under his skin and taunt him into assisting her with her ridiculous hunt.

There were a million things he'd rather do than shovel dirt and chase his own tail, but the crazy truth of it was he enjoyed hanging out with Raylene. Besides the fact that she was really great in the sack, she was funny, tough, and stubborn. All qualities that topped the Gabe Moretti list of must-haves. She was also a woman with plenty of issues, and ever since Bianca, he tried to steer clear of those. He hadn't been too surprised that she'd been a heavy drinker. From her prior actions and some things Logan had said, he'd read between the lines. What he was surprised about was the fact that she'd copped to it and was working through her addiction.

She sat up, pulled the blanket over her, and waited for him to respond.

"Fine, I'll help you. But today's the last day, Ray. Tomorrow, I've gotta work." There was always shit to do in the office, and with Logan gone he was pulling the weight of two people.

"Thank you." She leaned over and kissed him softly on the lips.

"Go take a shower." If they kept this up, they'd never get out of bed. "Daylight's wasting."

She dropped the blanket and walked to the bathroom buck naked. He watched, enjoying the view, then got up, put on his jeans, and carried a pile of bedding to the laundry room. The house had to be seventy degrees, and he turned down the heat before starting breakfast.

The refrigerator was full of leftovers, and he considered warming up some of the mini quiches but decided to make pancakes instead. Growing up in the Moretti household, every kid had one meal specialty. His was pancakes. Even in the teams, he was the flapjack king. He started the coffee, then pulled out his ingredients before heating the griddle. Annie kept her kitchen well-stocked, unlike his.

By the time Raylene came down the stairs, the table was set, the batter ready to go, and the coffeepot filled to the brim. Raylene filled them both a mug and took a long sip, warming her hands on the cup.

"I thought of something while I was in the shower," she said. "Logan has a security camera on the front of the house. Maybe it got some pictures of the person who broke into my truck."

"Too grainy to see anything in the dark. I already checked." He swiped his phone off the counter and showed her the footage.

She watched attentively, pressing the rewind button a few times. "It's just shadows."

He took the phone from her and pointed at one of the frames. "See here? There's two of them."

She focused on the picture and shook her head. "I don't see it."

"Take my word for it. There were two." He put the phone down and spooned four dollops of batter onto the now hot griddle.

"Did you tell Rhys?"

"He knows." They were both of the opinion that it was the vagrants Rhys had seen wandering the backcountry. Gabe suspected they were looking for anything of value they could pawn or sell. "Lock your truck from now on, okay?"

"I will, but it'll be a first in Nugget, I can tell you that."

"There's crime everywhere." He didn't bother to point out that her father had received a life sentence for killing a man only a few miles away.

His phone pinged with a text and he picked it up to read the message. "Weezer says he's making good time and should definitely be here by Wednesday, which means we have to find a place for your horse, ASAP. I'll call Griffin as soon as we finish breakfast."

He flipped the pancakes over and grabbed a plate. Five minutes later, they were sitting at the table like an old married couple. He'd had plenty of mornings after with the women he slept with. The difference now was he wasn't in a rush to leave, which wasn't good.

"These are delicious," Raylene said around a mouthful. "I haven't had pancakes in…I don't know how long."

"We used to have 'em for dinner some nights when I was back in the teams. We were stuck using that artificial maple crap, but they were still good, even if it was weird to eat breakfast for dinner."

"Not really," she said on another bite. "It's comfort food, and you guys saw a lot of bad stuff in Afghanistan and Iraq. You needed some chicken soup for the soul."

That was the understatement of the year, but she had an insightful point about the comfort food. He'd never looked at it that way. Back then it was just food, and it was a hell of a lot better than an MRE.

"How about you? You ever have pancakes for dinner?" Somehow, he couldn't visualize her and Butch sitting around a cozy supper table, laughing over a stack of hotcakes. The one time he'd met Butch, the dude had struck him as a colossal dickweed with anger management issues. He'd said a few choice words about Logan's mother, and Gabe had to pull his best friend off the moron. Anyone with half a brain could tell that if Logan hit you, you're weren't getting up. Ever.

"Not that I can remember," she said. "Cecilia used to make *chilaquiles* sometimes for dinner when I was a little girl. They're traditionally for breakfast."

"Yeah?" he said as he watched the memory wash over her. Now Cecilia would probably poison those *chilaquiles* if she got the chance. "So, you and Lucky Rodriguez, huh?"

She looked down at her half-eaten stack of pancakes. "How's his daughter, Katie? Last I heard she was in remission from the leukemia."

"She's good." He'd only lived in Nugget since summer, yet he knew everyone's life story. That's how it was here, and he liked it. In a way, the town was sort of like the Morettis: always bickering but as tight-knit as a sweater. "You're not going to talk about it, are you?"

"What's there to talk about? I screwed up with him, like I have with everything else in my life."

"So there are still feelings there?" Now why the hell was he asking that?

She lifted her gaze from her plate. "Not those kinds of feelings, but he was the only person, except for Logan, who every truly cared about me. And look how I rewarded that."

"By setting him up on the night of the murder?"

She nodded. "My father told me to send a text from Lucky's phone to my dad's to make it sound as if the shooting was Lucky's idea. Ray said Lucky wouldn't get in trouble, that Gus was a cattle rustler and the whole town would back Lucky and my dad. So I did it. But when Ray wanted to show the police the text to help him with his defense, I threatened to tell the truth. Then, later…I let him use it against Lucky."

"Why?" Gabe asked.

"Because Lucky picked Tawny over me." She put her fork down and turned away, gazing out the window into the distance. "Lucky could've been charged with a capital crime because of what I did. I never would've let it get that far, but the damage was already done."

Gabe shouldn't have sympathized with her. What she'd done to Lucky was an incredible betrayal. But Gabe, too, had caused irreparable damage to someone he'd cared for. And what did the good book say?

Do not judge, or you too will be judged. For in the same way you judge others, you will be judged, and with the measure you use, it will be measured to you.

Amen to that.

* * * *

Raylene would never forget the night Lucky confronted her. She'd met him at the rodeo arena at Nugget High School, thinking he'd asked her there to reconcile. But a part of her had always known the truth: she didn't deserve someone as good as Lucky, because at the root of everything, she would always be her father's daughter. Bad to the bone.

She'd slid into his truck in a black leather dress, hoping to seduce him into loving her again. But he was angry. Angrier than she'd ever seen him.

"I know you sent the text, Raylene."

"Is this why you called me out here in the middle of the night?" She started to get out of the truck, but he stopped her.

"Why'd you do it, Raylene? Why'd you set me up?"

"I don't know what you're talking about." She refused to look at him, but she didn't leave, because deep down inside she knew she had to come clean.

"The phone was in the kitchen when the text was sent. It's time stamped, and I have an alibi. One of my ranch hands was out by the corrals when I got there. I didn't have my phone on me, so I asked to borrow his...to check on Katie. He's ready to go to the police. So cut the shit, Raylene, and tell me why you did it."

"You're crazy, you know that?" Raylene spat out the words, but her heart was folding in half. How could she have done this to him?

"Get out of my truck." He reached over and pushed open the door. "You heard me, get out. I'm going to the police. Planting evidence...you'll go to prison, Raylene."

"He made me do it," she blurted, and her eyes filled with tears.

"Who made you do it?"

"My dad. He said you wouldn't get in trouble. That Gus was a cattle rustler and that Clay McCreedy would back you and my dad. He wanted to show the police the text right away, to help him with his defense, but I threatened to tell the truth. Then, later...I told him he could."

"Why?" Lucky asked, his eyes searching her for answers.

"Because you didn't love me anymore." She started weeping uncontrollably, and Lucky found a stack of napkins in the glove box and shoved them at her. "You picked Tawny over me."

"Raylene, do you hear what you're saying? Murder-for-hire is a capital crime. You'd see me executed for something I didn't do because I'm with someone else?"

"No." She blew her nose. "I wouldn't have let it get that far. I just wanted you to feel the pain I was feeling."

"Jesus." Lucky hit his hands on the steering wheel. "When you married Butch, I went on a month-long bender. I was getting up on bulls when I couldn't even see straight. But I never would've hurt you. Ever."

"I know," she said, and choked on a sob. "That's why it hurt so bad. Because no one ever loved me like you did. Not my mother. Not my father. Not Butch. No one." She swiped at her eyes, smearing her mascara. Lucky pushed more napkins into her hand. "I'll go to the police, Lucky. I'll tell them the truth."

"You shouldn't have let it get this far. What? Did Ray panic after he shot Gus and ask you to steal my phone and send the text?"

She started crying all over again. "He sent me over to your house to do it. He was angry at you for calling him an abusive father and husband. And livid about Gus taking his cattle. All day he paced and shouted how no one messed with Ray Rosser, yelling, 'Not Gus. And not that bastard Lucky Rodriguez.' Then you made it easy by leaving me and your phone alone in the kitchen."

Lucky took a while to process that, then very softly said, "You were a vision, sitting there on the hood of your truck that night. Looking as beautiful as I'd ever seen you. I knew we were over—we had nothing to say to each other anymore—but even then I loved you." Lucky tilted his head against the backrest and shut his eyes. "Get out of my truck."

"Lucky, please—"

"If you're not out of my truck in two seconds, I'll physically remove you."

She opened the door and put one foot on the running board. "I'll go to the police right now and tell them the truth. I swear."

And she did. But it was too late. She'd already lost two of the most important people in her life: Lucky and Cecilia. They had never talked to her again, a punishment that had crushed her black heart. She'd betrayed them and her entire hometown, losing everything that mattered. At least she'd been able to redeem herself in Logan's eyes, and for that she thanked her lucky stars. Her half brother was the best thing that had ever happened to her, and she planned to hold on to him with both hands.

Gabe cleared away the breakfast plates. "Let me jump in the shower and we'll get going. I'll call the hardware store and tell them that we're keeping the metal detector an extra day, and check with Griffin about stable space."

She rose to help him clean the kitchen, walked over to the sink, and covered his hand with hers. "Thank you, Gabe."

"*De nada.*" He stared into her eyes, and then he kissed her, his lips softly brushing hers while he held her close. It wasn't the most passionate kiss she'd ever experienced, but there was something about it that was deeply intimate, and a dozen unwelcome emotions swamped her.

Her cell buzzed with an incoming call, interrupting the moment. *Thank God.* It was the area code for Nugget. Not Butch. Hallelujah.

Raylene took a deep breath and answered, "Hello."

"Raylene, it's Dana. The buyers want to know where we're at on their offer. Technically, our deadline to respond was an hour ago." Raylene didn't say anything. "Are you there?"

"Uh, yeah, sorry. So if we accept, when would they start their inspections?" She needed time.

"They'd start right away. Typically, they have seventeen days to get it done and drop their inspection contingency. Because they want the property for commercial purposes, they may ask for extra time, but you don't have to be here for that."

She may as well have said, *And don't let the door hit you on the way out.* The whole town couldn't wait for Raylene to leave, and she didn't blame them. She'd be out of here as soon as she found the gold.

"It's not that; I was just wondering about the timing."

Dana audibly sighed. "If you'd rather not see the land turned into a motocross park, we could hold out for other buyers." Her voice sounded hopeful.

A dirt bike track wouldn't go over well, though it would bring revenue to the town. And lord knew Raylene couldn't afford to be choosy. She had a hefty rent payment due first of the month, a horse to board, and Lucy's House was counting on her. If they didn't get her donation, they'd have to close their doors, and then how many women would suffer?

"No, let's accept," Raylene said. She'd just have to work faster to find the treasure.

"Okay. I'll let them know." For a woman who stood to make a fat commission, Dana didn't sound the least bit happy. "Can you come in today to sign paperwork?"

"Uh, how about this evening, about five or six?" Later was better, so she could take advantage of the daylight to continue the hunt.

"That'll work," Dana said, and signed off.

"What was that about?" Gabe hung up the dish towel and leaned against the counter.

"My property. I accepted an offer, which means we have to find the gold before the buyer starts his inspections."

"Afraid he'll get to it first?" He could laugh all he wanted now. When they were sitting on a big pot of money, she'd have the last laugh. "Who is it, anyway? Someone I know?"

"Nope. They're from out of town."

He pulled off a glove with his teeth and cracked his knuckles. "Ranchers?"

"Uh-uh. They're in the entertainment industry."

His expression turned into a giant question mark. "What do you mean by 'entertainment'?"

"Racing." She grabbed the sponge and began scrubbing pancake batter off the stovetop.

He let out a whistle. "Thoroughbreds, huh? I would've thought cattle, but yeah, racehorses make sense. Plenty of room for them to run."

She couldn't stand it. Being vague was one thing, misleading him was…well, it was lying. She used to be quite accomplished at stretching the truth, even mangling it for her own purposes. Not anymore. Not since Lucky almost took the fall for what her father had done.

"Not horses," she said. "For a motocross track."

He gave it a second to sink in. "Wow. You like twisting the knife, now don't you?"

"It's not my place to decide what someone does with the land once it's theirs." Even to her own ears she sounded too defensive. Moto Entertainment was offering her full price; she'd be a sentimental idiot not to take it.

"Nope, but you could sell to someone else. The constant noise, the smells, the traffic…it'll be untenable for the neighbors. But I suppose this is your ultimate fuck you…to Lucky…Tawny."

"I doubt they'll even be able to hear it."

"Really, Ray? They're not even a mile away." He put away the griddle, slammed the cabinet door shut, and strode away.

Chapter 15

Gabe felt sucker punched. Just when he was starting to think Raylene wasn't the evil witch everyone thought she was…a motocross track. A goddamn motocross track. Sure, it was her property to sell to whomever she wanted to, but really? It was certainly an effective way to get back at everyone who'd been hateful to her. But he'd sort of gotten the impression that her trip here was as much about redemption as it was about Logan's wedding.

Well, you were wrong, sucker.

He turned the water as hot as he could take it and stepped into the shower. Logan and Annie had redone the plumbing and gotten one of those tankless water heaters, so maybe he'd stay in here for the rest of the day.

He heard the door creak open and pulled the shower curtain open enough to see Raylene standing there.

"It's not what you think," she said. "I don't want to sell to Moto Entertainment, but I need the money."

He pulled the curtain closed, wanting his shower in peace. "You've got loads of it, Raylene. More than most people will ever have in a lifetime."

"That's the thing: I don't."

He didn't want to hear her bullshit now. He just wanted a little time to himself to wash her away and get his head on straight. "I'll help you look for the gold today if you promise to be out of here after we find a place for your horse." When the neighbors caught wind of who she was selling to there'd be hell to pay, and he was duty bound to Logan to defend her.

"Can't we talk about this?"

He could hear a tremble in her voice and thought she might be crying, but he wasn't going to let her tears sway him. "There's nothing to talk about. Let me finish my shower and we'll go."

She drew the curtain open. "Please."

"Out!" he shouted, and she jumped. Gabe didn't like yelling, he didn't like scaring her, but he had nothing to say. "Please go away."

By the time he got dressed she was gone, and so was the metal detector he'd stowed in the garage.

He found his phone on the floor of Raylene's bedroom and called Griffin.

"Yo," he answered on the second ring.

"I've got a favor to ask." Gabe sat on the edge of the bed, which Raylene had remade, and explained the situation with her horse.

"There's room," Griff said, "but the stable is for residents only. I'm a resident and could presumably sponsor her but…"

"I know, I know." Gabe pinched the bridge of his nose. "Look, the sooner I can square away her horse, the sooner she leaves, which would be best for everyone. It'll just be until Logan and Annie get back from their honeymoon and we figure out a more permanent situation."

"All right. But who's going to take care of the horse in the meantime? I'm looking to hire someone, but until then everyone takes care of his or her own animals."

That was step two in Gabe's nonexistent plan. "Still working on that. But having a place for the horse in the interim is half the battle. Thanks, Griff. I owe you big time."

"You don't owe me a thing—Raylene does. And she can pay me back by leaving Lucky and Tawny alone."

Wait until he heard what good ol' Raylene had in store for her former neighbors. Not that it was the horse's fault, so why should he suffer?

After he hung up with Griffin, he called the hardware store. His last call was to Rhys, to see if there was anything new on their overnight break-in. Earlier, before Raylene had woken up, Gabe had spied one of Rhys' officers outside, processing her truck. No matter how much he wanted to convince himself that it was the work of the homeless trio Rhys had spotted, something about it—them—felt weird, like there was a missing piece to the puzzle.

Rhys wasn't in, so Gabe left a message, then headed out.

Raylene was digging a few feet away from where they'd found the musket ball when he got to the property. She was covered in mud, and her pants were wet from kneeling in the melted snow. It was a hell of a day to be searching for buried treasure. Even though the sun was out and the temperature was a balmy fifty degrees, the ground was still slushy and, in the shady spots, blanketed in a layer of ice.

She gazed up at him. "I don't need your help."

From where he was standing, what she needed was to have her head examined. Wasn't it enough that she'd make a small fortune from the entertainment company who wanted to buy her land?

"I told you I'd help you, and I keep my word."

"Maybe I don't want you around." She sounded like a petulant child.

He grabbed the shovel out of her hand. "Let's get this over with. Where's the map?"

She stomped off and came back with the map a few minutes later. So much for her not wanting him around.

"FYI: I found a temporary home for your horse. Griffin said he'd sponsor you at Sierra Heights. You're welcome."

Her eyes filled and he turned away so he wouldn't see her cry. He was feeling pretty low on sympathy for her but Raylene had a way of sucking him in. Not today, he told himself. He was standing firm, despite their night together.

"I don't know how to thank you."

"Hire someone to care for him and go back to LA." Out of the side of his eye, he saw her flinch.

He took the map and spread it out on the hood of his SUV, looking for something he might've missed the first time. Of course, there wasn't anything he'd missed, because there was no gold. But at least if they covered enough ground, he could persuade her to call off this fool's errand.

She sat on a log and kicked at a berm of snow. "I'm broke. Last I looked, I had two thousand four hundred and fifty-two dollars and fifteen cents in the bank. That's it."

He knew how much Logan got from Ray's will, and it was a hell of a lot more than a few thousand dollars. They'd built L&G Security with Logan's inheritance.

"I think we should start looking over there." He pointed to a new spot on the other side of the grove of trees. There was nothing on the map that indicated the gold might be there, but it was as good a guess as any.

"You don't believe me?"

He didn't know what he believed, but it was best not to get too involved in her crazy life. "So being broke is a good excuse to get even with your old boyfriend?" Lucky's dude ranch wasn't likely to survive with a motocross track next door. His guests didn't pay hundreds of dollars for the privilege of noise pollution. They could get that at home in the big city.

"I'm not trying to get even with anyone, I'm just trying to come through for a worthy cause."

"The women's shelter?" It sounded a little too convenient to him.

"Lucy's House. It's had some financial problems and will shut down without enough funds to keep it running. It's a good place, and without it there will be one less shelter for women in need."

Gabe had heard enough. He swiped the metal detector from the tree where Raylene had left it resting and turned it on, hoping she'd take the hint. End of conversation. He didn't know what to believe where she was concerned. What he did know was that she shouldn't be using the shelter as an excuse to hijack her neighbors, even if said neighbors hated her guts. She'd brought that on herself.

He moved the detector halfheartedly across a new swath of land, forcing himself not to look at her. Occasionally, he'd get a hit. So far, he'd dug up a few quarters and an old tackle box. Raylene had planted herself at their original search spot, trawling through the snow and mud.

Gabe heard a motor over the low hum of the detector and shielded his eyes from the sun. In the distance, a pickup truck was coming toward them. Raylene stopped what she was doing and looked up.

"You expecting company?"

She shook her head. He tried to make out who it was, but with the sun reflecting off his shades he couldn't identify the truck. He hid the detector and shovel behind a tree, not wanting anyone to think he was gullible enough to have fallen for the foolish legend. Raylene quickly shoved the map in her jacket.

As the truck got closer Gabe saw who it was. A few minutes later, the Dodge Ram screeched to a halt, and the first thing to exit the cab was a pair of custom boots. Then two hundred pounds of angry cowboy. Gabe moved swiftly in front of Raylene.

"We don't want your money." Lucky flung a white envelope at her. "I just saw Dana in town. Is it true?"

Well, that hadn't taken long. Then again, Gabe knew that news traveled faster in Nugget than the speed of lightning.

Raylene shuffled out from behind Gabe's protective cover and stood nose to nose with Lucky. "The money is for Tawny's dress."

Gabe had to give her credit. She was taking the bull rider by the horns, so to speak.

"I don't give a shit about the dress. I'll buy Tawny a new one." Lucky stared her down. "Are you selling your land to a company who wants to build a motocross track?"

Gabe wondered if she'd tell the truth. She had with him, but he hadn't had as much to lose as Lucky.

"I'm considering it, yes. It's the only offer I've got and, frankly, I'm in need of the money."

Okay, Gabe had to give her points for being straight up, even if he didn't necessarily believe that she was as broke as she said.

"I'd hoped that either you, Clay McCreedy, or Flynn Barlow would've made an offer," Raylene continued, holding her ground, while Lucky looked ready to mow her down. "I'd prefer for one of you to have the land."

"Would you now? Cut the crap, Raylene. If you think I don't see what you're doing, you're out of your mind."

"What am I doing, Lucky?" She asked it with such composure that anyone would've thought she was as self-possessed as the queen of England. Anyone but Gabe.

He saw the slight tremble in her left hand and imagined that right about now she was wishing she had a drink. Lucky fisted his hands at his side and his jaw clenched. Gabe wedged himself between the two of them.

"Let's take it down a notch, okay?"

Lucky threw his head back and let out a bitter laugh. "Take it down a notch? She doesn't know when to quit. First, she wanted to send me to prison for crimes I didn't do. And when that didn't work, she decided to financially ruin me and my family. So *you* take it down a notch." He got up in Gabe's face, close enough for Gabe to feel Lucky's spittle.

Ordinarily, that would've been a colossally bad idea, but Gabe liked Lucky.

"Everything isn't about you, Lucky." Raylene stepped up and nudged Gabe aside. He didn't know whether she was trying to protect him or Lucky. "If you'd like to make an offer, I'll give you first priority."

"So you can use my bid to jack up the other one you've got, or vice versa? You're a nasty piece of work, Raylene."

"I said I'll give you first priority."

"I don't have that kind of money, and even if I did, I wouldn't give it to you." He spat the words with such venom that for a second Gabe thought Lucky might hit Raylene. "Know this," he continued, "Clay, Flynn, Gia, and I will fight a motocross track with everything we've got. Be sure to disclose that to your buyers."

"Clay, Flynn, and Gia are free to buy the land themselves. And just like you, I'll give them first priority."

"You're not going to extort us into buying your land," Lucky fired back. "When we're through with you, no one will buy it." He turned around, got back in his truck, and peeled off.

Gabe watched the Ram disappear in the distance. "What do you mean by giving them first priority?" He wondered if it meant the same thing Lucky had accused her of—creating a bidding war. That's what a good business person would do. It's what Ray Rosser would've done. But it wasn't necessarily how a good neighbor would play it. Then again, Lucky hadn't been very neighborly.

"Moto Entertainment made me a full offer. I'll take that from Lucky, the McCreedys, the Barlows, or anyone else from Nugget who wants to run cattle."

Gabe didn't know how much she was asking for the land, but two hundred acres of prime California riverfront property couldn't be cheap. Lucky, the McCreedys, and the Barlows were far from paupers, but he didn't know if they had that kind of cash to throw around. Lucky had said he didn't have the money.

And even if I did, I wouldn't give it to you.

Nope, Gabe thought. *This looks like flat-out war.*

* * * *

Feeling dejected after meeting with Dana, Raylene took a drive. She'd put off signing the real estate papers by giving Dana a bullshit excuse about Butch and how she needed her divorce attorney to look everything over first. The truth was she wanted to give Lucky, or any of the other locals, time to step up. Plus, she still hadn't found the gold. Lord knew if she ever would. Gabe certainly didn't think so.

Gabe.

The man was an enigma. Shutting her out one minute, having her back the next. Lucky had been spitting mad during their confrontation, but he'd never hurt her. Not physically anyway. Yet Gabe had rushed in to keep her safe. No one but Logan had ever done that for her. Once upon a time, Lucky had. But they'd just been kids. Now when she looked into his big dark eyes all she saw was hatred. And at the rate she was going, Gabe would detest her, too.

She certainly had the golden touch where men were involved. Come to think of it, women, too.

Raylene drove aimlessly through the backcountry. Even after all the time she'd been gone, she knew these roads like the back of her hand. Up ahead was the swim hole where she and Hannah used to ride their horses and swim naked out to the big rock in the middle of the river. There, they'd lie in the sun until their skin turned golden brown. She passed Buckie Graham's house and remembered that time in high school when his parents had gone out of town and they'd thrown a giant kegger. Raylene had gotten so drunk she'd thrown up on the Grahams' bearskin rug. Wyatt's family lived out here somewhere, too. As a teenager he'd been madly in love with her, but she'd been dating Zachary Baze, captain of the football team. A more suitable boyfriend than Lucky, in her father's eyes.

As she continued to drive, she eventually found herself in the most familiar place of all. Most of the thousand-acre spread was fenced for cattle, but there were places a person who knew her way around could get in. She took the fire road to the back lot, parked near a small graveyard, and got out of the truck.

Though she hadn't meant to visit, something pulled at her. Ghosts? Things that still needed to be said? The cemetery had been here since the Rossers settled this land during the Gold Rush. They'd come to sell beef to the miners. Even though the Rock and River belonged to Gia and Flynn when Ray died, they'd allowed him to be buried with his ancestors—and his prized horse, who had died a few years earlier.

She swung open the gate and wandered the grounds, reading the tombstones. As kids, she and her friends used to come on Halloween and try to psych themselves out. Back then, Ray hired a crew to weed and place flowers on the graves. Now brambles and scrub grew rough, making the little cemetery look like something out of the Wild West.

She kicked at the dirt with the point of her boot. "Hey, Ray." She sat on the cold, hard dirt and pulled her knees up to get warm. "You down there, or did the devil turn you away for being more evil than him?

"Lucky's married now. Despite all you tried to do to him, he's happy. And alive, unlike you. He's got a nice daughter and a big old ranch and he's the longest reigning world champion in the history of the PBR. Remember when you said he'd never make anything of himself? Guess you were wrong.

"I loved him, Daddy. And you made me do terrible things to him. Hateful things. I don't even know how I live with myself after what I did."

A tear leaked down her cheek and she swiped it away. "Butch and I are divorced now. The man was a cheating, vicious piece of shit. I should've known what he'd be like when you picked him for me. He was just like you, Daddy."

She wiped away another tear, then just let them come until they poured down her face. "Logan's ten times the man you ever were. Funny how you wished I was a son when you already had one. But you wouldn't even claim him. You let him grow up without a father. For what? To protect your stupid name? A name that's dirt now. That's right, Daddy, you ruined the Rosser name. You dragged it through the mud until it meant nothing. Everything Papa and Grandpa worked for, you ruined. And Mom, you beat her down to nothing. She's a shell of the woman she used to be."

She tried to collect herself, but she wasn't done yet, not by a long shot. "Everything you built is gone now. And me? You had me under your thumb for so long, I didn't know up from down. Good from bad. But I'm trying to change that. I'm even selling the last of your land and moving on. You know what helps me sleep at night? Knowing that you'll never be able to hurt anyone again."

Raylene took a long, deep breath, got to her feet, and leaned over Ray's grave. "See you in hell, Daddy."

Chapter 16

By Wednesday, Drew was seriously considering marriage counseling. Since their drive home Sunday night, Kristy hadn't said more than ten words to him. Most of the time, they were like two strangers passing in the night.

She left for the office before he got out of the shower in the morning and spent her evenings working overtime or at the gym. Tonight, she'd locked herself in their home office.

He'd grilled a couple of steaks in hopes that at least the smell would lure her out and they could talk. But she'd emerged only long enough to make a plate and go back to her computer. Sullen, he'd moved to the den and turned up ESPN as loud as his ears could take it. Not a proud moment, but he couldn't think of any other way to grab her attention.

Before Hope had gone missing, he and Emily had rarely fought. And when they did it was always about something minor. He hadn't taken out the trash. She didn't stand up enough to her mother. The usual things that husbands and wives squabbled about.

After the abduction, everything changed. He and Emily had become so despondent they were barely recognizable to each other. Emily, who'd been with Hope the day the Lanes stole her, had blamed herself, and Drew hadn't been able to handle her self-incrimination.

After the divorce, Emily agreed to sell their home, the home where Hope had been snatched from the yard. Emily had been steeped in so much grief there that she was slowly dying. On a whim, she'd moved to Nugget, a place neither of them had ever heard of, met Clay, and fell in love. From what Drew could tell, they had a strong marriage, though he suspected that Clay was suffering from some of the same insecurities Kristy was. In a way, they were outsiders, looking in on a family that had been ripped apart by tragedy. And when Hope—the Lanes had renamed her Harper—had come back into their lives, their new spouses had to learn to assimilate as much as their little girl did.

At this point, he gave Emily and Clay's marriage a better chance of surviving than his own. He turned down the TV and flipped through the channels. It was only eight, too early for the glut of *CSI* shows. The phone rang, and when Kristy didn't pick up in the other room, he checked the caller ID and smiled.

"Hey, how's my cowgirl?"

"You'll never guess what!" Harper said, and didn't wait for him to try. "Raylene is keeping her horse, Gunner, at Sierra Heights. Technically, she's not allowed to because she doesn't live there, but Griffin Parks said she could, as his guest. And guess what else?"

"I give up."

"She wants to hire me to take care of him."

"Oh yeah?" It seemed like a big job for a thirteen-year-old, but Drew didn't know much about horses. "What does your mom think about that?"

There was a long stretch of silence, which told Drew everything he needed to know. "Harp?"

"She and Clay don't want me to. But Justin said he'd give me rides back and forth and, Dad, she's going to pay me fifty bucks a week just for feeding and watering him. Once a week I have to muck out his stall. Can you believe it?"

Drew chuckled. It was nice to hear his daughter so enthusiastic for a change. Her moods were as mercurial as Northern California's weather. The counselors said some of it was puberty, but a lot of it they attributed to her adjusting to a new life.

"Sounds like a good gig." He felt a little disloyal to Emily saying that, but what would be the harm? "How come your mom and Clay don't want you to do it?"

"You know how they are." He could practically see her rolling her eyes. "They think it'll interfere with my schoolwork and my chores on the ranch. Silly, right?"

"I don't know, Harp. Your mom's pretty smart about these things." He didn't want to go against Emily's rules, but at the same time, he thought the responsibility would be good for their daughter.

"Will you talk to her? Please."

He didn't want Harper to get into the habit of running to him every time Emily said no. Yet Kristy's words rang in his head.

Don't suffocate her; let her be a thirteen-year-old, and let her pick her own idols.

"I'll talk to her and Clay," he finally said. "But, Harper, don't get your hopes up. When you're with Mom and Clay, it's their rules."

"That's not fair. What about when I'm with you? Can I do it on the weekends?"

He needed to know more about this Raylene woman before he signed on to anything. Emily didn't like her, and he trusted his ex's instincts. "We'll see. How was school today?"

"Good. It was pizza day. Cody ate four slices and threw up on Katie Rodriguez's backpack. It was seriously gross."

"Sounds like it. Is he okay?"

"He's fine. Mom gave him ginger ale when he got home and Clay still made him do his chores. Are you coming up Friday?"

He wanted to. It was hard going five days without seeing his daughter. But a lot would depend on Kristy and what she wanted to do, since it meant telecommuting for work. It was hard to know when they weren't communicating with each other.

"I'm planning to," he said. "Just have to check with the boss."

"Will you talk to Mom and Clay in the meantime? I've got to give Raylene an answer soon or she'll have to find someone else."

"You bet. But, Harper, remember what I said. You're not going to play us against each other, got it?"

"Yeah." She dragged the word out like it was tremendously taxing to agree, which made him chuckle to himself.

"You do your homework?"

"Yes. Justin helped me with my math, and we're dissecting a frog in science. I'm lab partners with Sam Shepard. He's totally annoying."

"Totally annoying, huh? I'm sorry to hear that."

"It's okay. He's a good lab partner, at least."

"That's important. I'm looking forward to seeing you this weekend. What do you think of checking out Glory Junction? It's a cute town, and Kristy's never been."

"Whatever," she said. "Call me when you get here. I want to visit Gunner at the stable."

"Will do. Night, sweetheart, sleep tight."

After signing off, he texted Emily to call him when she got a chance and went to check on Kristy. It was high time they had it out.

* * * *

Gabe leaned against the stall door and watched Raylene fawn over her horse like the two were long-lost lovers. If he wasn't so conflicted about her, he'd be jealous. After the scene with Lucky on Monday, she'd made herself scarce. He didn't like her staying alone in the farmhouse at night, so he'd been sleeping on Logan's couch. There'd been no invitation otherwise, and it was best to keep it that way, though he'd be lying if he said she didn't tempt him beyond belief. The last three evenings, they'd eaten wedding leftovers together, watched a little TV, and then she'd go up to bed, leaving him to toss and turn on the sofa.

She was still looking for that goddamned gold, and it really did seem that she wasn't leaving without it. He hadn't asked her whether her property was in escrow yet, but the scuttlebutt around town was Moto Entertainment was moving in. According to Owen, citizens were planning to pack the next city council meeting to fight the motocross track.

"It'll be a damned public nuisance," Owen had said. "That land should be zoned for agricultural use only. But that Ray Rosser was a slick one. He always knew how to get around the rules."

Gabe was trying to remain neutral. Raylene had given Lucky and the rest of them an opportunity to buy the land at fair market value, and it did seem unrealistic of them to expect her to hold out for a buyer they deemed acceptable. At the same time...a freaking racetrack?

He gazed around the barn, a new addition to Sierra Heights to appeal to potential buyers who wanted the security and convenience of a gated community and the cache of horse property. In the last year, the real estate market had boomed, and folks priced out of Glory Junction and the other Sierra ski resort towns had found Nugget. Though they were thirty minutes from the slopes, the area had rivers and lakes and enough nature to make weekend warriors happy. Griffin was finally selling houses in the white elephant subdivision he'd bought from bankrupt developers as an investment.

The barn, a traditional gambrel style with a symmetrical two-sided roof and an open center loft, had more than a dozen stalls that opened to a large corral. Everything was freshly painted gray, and there was even a bathroom for humans. Gabe didn't know much about stables, but he thought this was a pretty nice one. Raylene seemed pleased with it. Then again, beggars couldn't be choosers.

Unfortunately, Weezer hadn't been able to stay for a visit. He'd dropped off the horse the day before, returned the trailer in Reno, and caught a flight out. Gabe would've liked time to have caught up with his old SEAL buddy.

"This gonna work?" Gabe asked.

"Are you kidding?" Raylene glanced around the barn. "It's fantastic. I'm hoping Harper comes through."

Raylene had seen the kid in town with her stepbrothers and had offered her the job on the spot.

"I guess once you get old Gunner here settled in you'll be taking off." Gabe scratched the horse's nose.

"That's the plan. Just have to find my gold." She flashed him a tight smile as if to say: *You might not think it exists, but I know it does.*

"Happy hunting." He wasn't going to get into it with her. If she wanted to waste her days digging in the dirt, far be it from him to stop her.

Outside, he heard a truck pull up and a door slam, then boots crunching gravel. A few seconds later, Clay came through the barn doors.

"I want to talk to you." He jabbed his finger in the air.

"I'm here." Raylene opened Gunner's stall, walked to the center of the barn, and put her hands on her hips. "Talk."

"If your old man knew what you were doing he'd roll over in his grave. Even he wouldn't have sold that land for a motorcycle park, and Ray always put business first. Everyone knows you're a spoiled brat, leaving a trail of destruction wherever you go. But this, even for you, is beyond the pale." Clay reached under his cowboy hat and scrubbed his hand through his hair. "The one thing I thought we had in common was love for this land...for our ancestors and for the legacy they left us. Guess I was wrong."

He started to walk away when Raylene said, "Make me an offer. Like I told Lucky, I'll sell it to you for the same price. It's good, fertile land. Good grazing for cattle."

Clay turned and glared at her. "If I could afford it I would, for no other reason than to get you out of here."

"You won't have to wait long for that," she spat. "But I think you have a hell of a nerve. You don't know my situation, you don't know anything about me, yet you think you have the right to decide who can purchase my property and who can't. Just like you can't afford to buy it, I can't afford not to sell it. Yet according to you, I'm the one in the wrong. Three words, Clay: Get. A. Loan."

Gabe continued to lean against the stall, watching the match. So far, he'd say Raylene was winning, though Clay had lobbed some doozies. But Gabe pushed off the wall when Clay started coming toward Raylene.

"Let's keep this civil, folks," he said, and moved to Raylene's side. Gabe didn't think Clay would pick his hands up to a woman, but he could see steam coming out of Clay's ears.

Clay shot him a look, then did an about-face and walked out.

"Making friends and influencing people, aren't you, Ray?" He watched all her earlier confidence dissipate like a puff of smoke.

"I wouldn't do it...I wouldn't sell unless I had to."

"How broke are you, really?" He was starting to think she hadn't been exaggerating her money situation.

"Exactly what I told you before."

"How can that be, Raylene? I know what Logan got when your dad died."

She nodded. "First thing Butch did when I got my money was buy hundreds of thousands of dollars' worth of equipment for his ranch. Guess who isn't listed as one of the owners of said ranch?"

"Where was your lawyer in all this?"

"He fought for me. He fought hard, and when everything was hashed out in court I owed him more money than Butch had stolen from me." She let out a breath. "And the sad truth is I've always been bad with finances, because when I ran out of cash there was always more...from Daddy... even begrudgingly from Butch. I used to call it hush money, to overlook his infidelities...his abuse. After moving out of our Denver house and racking up an enormous bill at the Four Seasons, I rented a beach home in Santa Monica for twenty-thousand dollars a month." When Gabe did a double take because he wasn't sure he heard her right, she rationalized, "It was built for a silent film star."

"Oh, well in that case..."

"I thought nothing of spending three hundred dollars on a pair of jeans or eating at Urasawa," she continued. "In one month, I bought a new truck and a Mercedes Roadster. The next, I booked a week at a spa in San Diego. Then one morning I woke up and there was no more money and no one to tap for a loan."

"Did you tell Logan?"

"No, and if you do I will kill you in your sleep."

He sat on a bench near the tack room, trying to comprehend how someone could be that irresponsible...that extravagant. "You're telling me you pissed through your entire inheritance?"

"Yes, though there wasn't much left of it after Butch got through with me. The only thing he wasn't able to get his grubby dukes on was the land. In exchange, he got a lot of other stuff."

Gabe was guessing that the other stuff was even more valuable than the land and that, unlike Raylene, Butch knew the legend of the gold was bullshit.

"What about the Mercedes? Can you sell it?"

"Repossessed."

"But you're out of the beach house, right?"

"It's a lease." She sat next to him and huffed out a breath. "I've got two more months on it."

It just kept getting better. "Will selling your land cover you until you can make some money?"

She didn't answer, letting the silence stretch until he couldn't take it anymore. "Raylene?"

"Sort of, except I kind of promised some of the proceeds to Lucy's House."

"How much?" She really was batshit crazy.

"Half. But it won't matter, because when I find the gold—"

"There's no fucking gold, Raylene. Did you cut a deal with these Moto Entertainment people?" He didn't think so, because if she had she wouldn't have offered the land to Clay.

"Not yet."

"What are you waiting for?"

More silence. Then finally, "I don't want them to have it."

He didn't see that she had a choice, unless she moved in with Logan and Annie and lived off them until she got a job and patched her finances together. Raylene was the definition of a hot mess. And yet he couldn't stop himself from trying to help her.

Chapter 17

By Friday morning, Raylene had a new game plan. Instead of searching the land around the copse of trees on the lower end of the property, she decided to take a stab at the top end. The entire two-hundred-acre parcel was dotted with small, wooded groves. Anyone of them could've been Levi's hiding place, and the ones she'd already searched had all been duds. At thirty bucks a day for the metal detector, she needed to find something soon or give up.

She drove the length of the property, bumping along the rutted fire trail, taking Gabe's advice to look for the older trees. The day was gloomy and cold and, in her rush to get out of the house, she'd forgotten her hat. Gabe had left a stack of folded bedding on the couch and had been in the kitchen, eating, when she'd ducked out. At least twenty times during the night she'd considered going downstairs and crawling under the covers with him, but he'd made it abundantly clear that their Sunday hookup had been enough for him.

When she crested the top of the hill, her mouth fell open. Someone had trenched a five-foot-deep hole around a cluster of oak trees. *What the hell?*

She punched Gabe's number into her phone. "Did you come looking for my gold on your own?"

"What are you talking about, Raylene?"

"Someone was here…on the property, digging."

He was quiet for a few seconds. "It wasn't me." He had an iron-clad alibi. Her. "What do you mean, digging?"

"Hang on, I'll send you a picture." She parked, got out of her truck, snapped a few images of the trench, and hit the send button.

"I don't think gophers did that," she said.

"Nope. Do me a favor, wait in your truck until I get there. And, Raylene, lock the door."

For once, she didn't think he was overreacting. From the looks of it, someone, or several people, had been here all night to have dug a channel that deep and that long. It had to be at least forty feet wide. But who? Everyone in town knew the lore of Levi's Gold and had had ample opportunity to sneak through the fence and search the property. But like Gabe, most everyone thought the gold didn't exist. Occasionally, a treasure hunter would trespass, but without the map there wasn't much point in it. As it turned out, even with the map, the gold had remained as elusive as Bigfoot.

She hopped up on the hood of her truck and waited, not wanting to disturb any potential evidence. The thought did cross her mind that maybe Clay or Lucky were trying to mess with her, but she quickly dismissed the idea. What would they gain from digging a huge hole on her property? Furthermore, vandalism wasn't their style.

Gabe came over the hill in his SUV, pulled in alongside her, and got out. A pair of wraparound sunglasses covered his eyes, but his body language told her all she needed to know. He was pissed.

"I told you to wait in your truck."

"No one's here, Gabe, relax."

He searched the horizon, then crouched down to have a better look at the hole. "Has anyone seen you out here?"

"Only Lucky. No one comes up here. McCreedy Ranch has its own road, and guests of Lucky's cowboy camp enter off Highway Seventy. But it's no secret I've been up here looking for the gold. By now, you have to know that nothing in Nugget is a secret."

He acknowledged that with a half grin, then whipped out his phone and sent a text. "I'd say this was the work of a pickax. Our pickax."

"You think it's the same person who broke into my truck?"

His head came up. "Where do you keep the map when you're not using it?"

She patted the breast pocket of her jacket and he let his eyes linger on her chest, then snapped them away.

"You think that's what he was looking for?"

"I don't believe in coincidences," he said and took the map from her for safekeeping.

"How would anyone know I have the map?" Only people in Ray's inner circle knew of its existence, one of them being Flynn Barlow, who knew everything, because he'd been Ray's estate lawyer.

Gabe shrugged, but she saw the wheels in his head turning and suspected he had a theory. She turned at the sound of a car and subconsciously moved closer to Gabe. He hooked his arm around her in a protective manner and the contact sent shivers down her spine. It was the first time he'd touched her since their night together, and her body instantly responded.

He absently stroked her arm until a Nugget PD SUV sent a cloud of smoke into the air.

"Did you call the police?"

"Rhys," he said.

Rhys was Clay's best friend, so she wasn't counting on him caring much about someone trying to stake a claim on her gold. And yay! Jake was riding shotgun. The two of them stepped out at the same time. Unlike Rhys, Jake was in uniform, and Raylene didn't miss him shooting her a dirty look.

Rhys followed the trench to where it ended at a gnarled old oak tree and stared down into the hole. "Raylene, what time did you get here?"

"About nine, give or take a few minutes." She hadn't been watching the clock.

"Gabe says you were with him yesterday morning at Sierra Heights and then you came over here. What time did you leave?"

"Just before it got dark."

"About six, six-thirty?" Jake said.

"That sounds right." Gabe had been making dinner when she got to the farm.

"You didn't come back any time between then and now?" Rhys asked, and she wondered if he was trying to accuse her of digging on her own land. How ridiculous would that be?

"No."

Rhys exchanged a glance with Gabe. Was he actually looking for verification?

"You see anyone or anything suspicious while you were here?"

"Just me and my metal detector." She motioned at the back of her truck and saw Jake glance at the bed.

"Anyone besides Gabe know what you've been doing here?"

She rolled her eyes. "I'd wager a guess that all of Nugget knows what I'm doing here. But the only person besides Gabe who's seen me here is Lucky."

That perked Jake up. Apparently, he hadn't known that his stepson had confronted her.

"Why was Lucky here?" Rhys asked.

"To talk to me about the sale of my land; it had nothing to do with the gold." She could feel Jake watching her, drilling holes through her with his laser eyes.

"When was that?" Rhys pulled out a notebook.

She looked to Gabe. "Monday?"

"Yeah, I think so."

"You were here when that happened?" Rhys asked Gabe.

"Yep."

"Lucky didn't have any part of this." Raylene nudged her head at the trench. She didn't know that for sure, but it seemed awfully unlikely. Besides, she didn't want to make trouble for him—not that Rhys and Jake would take her side over Lucky's.

Rhys glanced over at Gabe and he nodded, confirming what she'd just said. Clearly, her word wasn't good enough.

"You have any idea who might've done this?" Jake asked her.

"Zero. The story of the gold has been out there a long time. I don't know why the sudden interest."

Jake cocked his brows. "Why are you suddenly interested?"

Because I'm broke and desperate. "Call it a last-ditch effort before the new owners take over." She looked at him, and then at Rhys. "Why are you even taking this seriously?" Unless there was an actual theft, or worse, she would think digging holes in someone's vacant field wasn't the top priority of a small police department that was already strapped.

Rhys contemplated the question. "We think this"—he eyed the trench—"and your break-in may be connected to something else."

"Like what?" From all the weird body language she was witnessing, there was a whole conversation going on here that she wasn't part of.

"A home invasion in Green River, Utah."

A home invasion. How in the world had they come to that conclusion, and why would someone committing a home invasion in Utah know about her gold in Nugget, California? "Why do you think that?"

"It's purely supposition at this point," Rhys said, sidestepping the question. "But until we eliminate that possibility, you shouldn't come out here alone."

She darted a look at Gabe, wondering if he was following this. He gave nothing away. His face was completely deadpan.

"I'll come with her," he said. Four days ago, he'd tossed the metal detector in the trunk of his SUV and told her he was "done with this bag of dicks." Apparently, that was Navy slang for an extremely odious task.

"What kind of home invasion are we talking about?" she asked.

Rhys hesitated for a moment, then said, "Robbery and murder."

* * * *

Drew started his Friday morning with a heated discussion with his ex-wife.

"Raylene is selling the neighboring property to a company that wants to turn the land into a motocross track. Isn't that reason enough?" Emily asked, her voice raised.

He gazed around the Ponderosa, hoping no one had heard her. Ten minutes ago, he'd thought it was a good idea to meet at the restaurant—neutral ground—for a rational discussion over why she was so adamantly against their daughter taking on the small task of feeding a horse.

"Let me get this straight. The woman's not allowed to sell her land to someone you disapprove of, and therefore our thirteen-year-old daughter can't spend time with her horse?"

"Disapprove of? Drew, the racetrack would be next door to us. Every day, we'd be forced to hear dozens of motorcycles driving in circles for hours. What part of that nightmare don't you understand?"

"I sympathize with you, I really do. Hire a good lawyer and fight it. But it has nothing to do with Harper, so why punish her for your land dispute?"

"Oh for God's sake, are you that dense? We are feuding with this woman. Clay is beside himself. Our livelihood depends on the ranch; this will make living here untenable. We have a stable full of horses Harper can feed."

"That's called a chore, Emily. This is a job, with a paycheck. Do you remember what that meant when you were Harper's age?"

"I can't even believe I'm having this conversation with you. Raylene Rosser is not the kind of person I want Harper hanging around."

"Why? Is she a felon? A druggie? All I've been able to glean from your story is that she had a lover's spat with a friend of yours and as a result everyone hates her. Jeez, Em, when did you join the real-life cast of *Peyton Place?*"

"A lover's spat? She nearly sent him to prison for a murder he didn't commit. When did you become Raylene Rosser's defender?"

"I don't even know her." Now he was raising his voice, but this argument was ridiculous. "All I know is that she's been good to our daughter, and she's offered her a job that will help Harper adapt to life here…to the enormous changes she's been put through. Harper's practically bouncing off the wall with excitement over it. And the *evil* Raylene won't even be here. That's the ludicrous part of this. You don't want Harper around a woman who lives in Los Angles. Isn't that the whole reason she needs Harper to feed her goddamn horse in the first place?"

Emily started to laugh.

"What the hell is so funny?"

"Just that we never argued like this when we were married."

He grinned, then studied the woman across the table from him, the woman who used to be his wife. "You look good, Em. Happy, healthy, loved."

She reached across the table and took his hand. "I wish I could say the same for you. What's going on, Drew?"

He sighed. "Kristy wants to do another round of in vitro fertilization."

"You don't?"

Talking to his ex about his marital problems was probably all kinds of wrong, but he needed someone to confide in, and no one would understand better than Emily. They'd walked through hell together and had come out the other side. "No. The God's honest truth: I don't think I can handle having another child right now, not when Harper needs me. Not after all we went through to get her back."

"I had similar fears when I first got pregnant with Paige," Emily said. "All I could think was how do I bring another child into the world when I couldn't keep my first one safe? And there was guilt that Paige would somehow replace the memory of Hope." She rummaged through her purse for a tissue and wiped her eyes. "Clay was so upset that I didn't want another child, for a while I didn't think we'd make it.

"Then I had a scare," she continued. "I was cramping and spotting and my OB thought I was on the verge of a miscarriage. In that instant, everything changed. I felt such unconditional love for that baby growing inside me, and every maternal instinct kicked in. Paige was my baby every bit as much as Hope was, but they were two separate individuals. And loving one didn't mean I couldn't still love the other."

"I didn't know it was a difficult pregnancy. I'm sorry you went through that. And now?" He wondered if she and Clay were back on firm ground. They seemed solid, but sometimes people only saw what they wanted to see. And Drew wanted Emily to be happy. Lord knew she deserved a lifetime full of joy after the horror they'd lived through.

"Things couldn't be more wonderful." Her face positively glowed, and Drew knew her well enough to know she couldn't fake it if she tried. "And it will be for you, too. This is just a hump, Drew. What do they say about marriage? Peaks and valleys."

He stirred his coffee. "I don't know. This is more like Mount Everest. She didn't even come with me to Nugget this time."

Emily leaned across the table. "Do you want to work things out?"

"Of course I do. I love her, Em."

"Then you'll make it work. Hear her out on the IVF, Drew. There's room in your heart—in your life—for two children, take it from me. The day I met Justin and Cody was the day I started healing."

"I'm glad. You've made a good family, and Clay's a good man."

"And Kristy's a good woman. You'll work through this, I know you will."

He grinned. "The question is can you and I work through this issue with Raylene's horse? Come on, Em. It would mean a lot to Harper."

"I don't know." She played with the spoon on the table. "I think the responsibility would be good for her, but why does it have to be Raylene's horse?"

"Because she's the one offering Harper the job. Really, what would be the harm? I'll take her to the barn on weekends, and Justin's volunteered to do it on the weekdays. She'll never be without adult supervision, and… it seems petty to say no because of your personal differences with this woman."

"You don't know the history, Drew, but since Raylene won't be here I'm inclined to say yes and see how it goes. If it interferes with Harper's schoolwork or her after-school activities, then Raylene will have to find someone else."

"Sounds fair enough. What do you say I pick her up from school and give her the good news?"

"All right." She looked at her watch. "I promised to relieve Clay of Paige by eleven, which means I've got to get going. Do you want Harper to stay with you tonight?"

"If you wouldn't mind. Since Kristy didn't come, I'd like to get an early start on Sunday, maybe get home to the Bay Area in time to take her to dinner."

"I don't mind. I'll check in around bedtime."

Drew nodded. So far, they'd done a good job of co-parenting, though Emily spent the most time with Harper. Secretly, he'd hoped that eventually he could make Nugget a more permanent base, which would be another bone of contention with Kristy. She liked it here, adored the house in Sierra Heights, but she was a city girl at heart. If it wasn't for Harper, he wouldn't consider relocating to such a rural place either. But surprisingly, Nugget had begun to grow on him. He liked knowing his neighbors, being part of a close-knit community, and walking out his door to find deer on his lawn.

"Okay. I've got what she needs at the house. I was thinking about taking her to Glory Junction tomorrow. You think Cody would like to join us?" He was a fine kid, and he looked out for Harper.

"That's so sweet of you. I'll ask him, but that boy's social calendar could rival the royals'."

Drew laughed. "This is a good place for kids, isn't it?"

"It is." She gave him a pointed look. "Something to keep in mind. We all look out for one another."

They just don't look out for Raylene Rosser, he thought to himself. "I'll take care of this." He covered the check with his hand. "You get going."

He paid the bill, then strolled around the square for a little while, killing time before Harper's school let out. The sporting goods store was having a sale on bikes, and he popped in to have a look. He'd been meaning to get Harper a bicycle for the Sierra Heights house so she could ride to the community pool in summer. Little by little, he was growing more comfortable with letting her do things on her own. Kristy was right: they had to stop smothering Harper.

He took out his phone to see if Kristy had called or texted, but there was nothing. He tried her cell and got voicemail. "Hey, it's me. Just wanted to say hi and that I love you. I'll try to get home early Sunday. Maybe we can go to that seafood restaurant you like."

Drew hung up and continued to walk down the bike aisle. There wasn't much of a selection for kids. They mostly carried adult mountain and road bikes. He helped himself to a complementary cup of cider by the camping gear and headed back outside. It was a good twenty degrees colder than Palo Alto, and he stuffed his hands in his jacket pockets, trying to keep them warm.

He started toward the Lumber Barron Inn when he bumped into the police chief. Rhys bobbed his head in greeting.

"Hey, did you ever find out any more about that backpack?" Drew asked him.

"I did, and I was going to call you about it, but since you're here why don't we go over to the station?"

Drew thought it sounded serious—then again, this was a small town, and the police were probably more conscientious about public relations.

"Sure." Drew had nothing better to do, and he was curious about what the chief had found.

The station wasn't much, just a non-descript building on the other side of the greenspace from the inn. Inside was equally bland, with a reception desk, a row of work stations, and a glass office in the back that belonged to Rhys.

"Have a seat," the chief said, and Drew took one of the wing chairs in front of the desk. Rhys took the other. "There were a number of IDs in the pack, and it turns out that one of them holds a connection to a home invasion homicide in Utah."

"A connection?" Drew was an attorney; he knew when law enforcement was being intentionally nebulous.

"That's all I can say right now, but keep your eyes out. And if you see anything suspicious, call me or 9-1-1."

"I have my daughter staying with me this weekend. You can't give me more than that?"

"The identification belonged to the victim. There could be an innocent reason why the owner of the backpack had it, but until we can find the person and question him or her, we don't know."

"What about the other IDs? Do they belong to victims of other homicides?"

"We're in the process of hunting that down."

"Do you have reason to believe the person I saw is still in Nugget?" Drew's hope was that he'd moved on, because the idea that a killer might have been in his backyard was very disturbing.

Rhys took a while to answer, then finally said, "Yes. At least, as of last night."

"What happened last night?"

"Someone dug up Raylene Rosser's property."

Either Drew wasn't following, or he was missing a big piece of the story. "As in vandalized it?"

Rhys exhaled. "It's a long story, so I'll give you the *Reader's Digest* version. There's an old legend that Raylene's ancestor stole a gold claim from one of the miners in 1849, buried it on Rosser land, and was shot and killed by a sheriff's deputy before he could dig it up. Raylene's getting ready to sell the parcel, and we think whoever you saw in your yard is here to find the gold before she or the new owner does."

"You're kidding me, right? This sounds like a bad TV show."

Rhys brushed a fly away. "Welcome to Nugget."

"Then you don't believe this gold exists?"

Rhys' mouth quirked. "About as much as I believe in the tooth fairy. But from time to time we get a few yahoos up here who have read the story of Levi's Gold and hope to strike it rich."

"What's the link between the gold and the home invasion, other than the ID you found in the backpack?"

"Don't know. We can't even say for sure that the treasure hunter is even the same person you think you saw. But it's a lot of coincidences."

"Like what?" Drew wanted to know.

"You're not the only one who's had a sighting."

"But other than trespassing, there've been no crimes committed?"

"Someone broke into Raylene's truck the other night. They didn't take anything, but we think they were looking for the map."

"A map to the gold?" Drew laughed. "This just keeps getting better, doesn't it?" But if this so-called treasure hunter was involved in a homicide, it wasn't the least bit humorous.

"Just keep a lookout," Rhys said. "But rest assured we're on top of it."

Drew didn't know how reassuring that was, but he planned to watch Harper like a hawk and turn the security alarm on tonight. "Thank you, Chief. I appreciate you giving me the lowdown."

As he drove to Harper's school, he thought how there was always something. He supposed Nugget had less crime than the big city, but even the bucolic hamlet wasn't an island. People had to remain vigilant wherever they were.

He pulled into the pickup lane in front of the school, where cars had already begun queueing up. There were a couple of women standing outside their SUVs and Outbacks, chatting while students burst through the school's front door, searching for their rides. He saw Harper walking and talking with a couple of girls and tapped on his horn. Maybe he'd imagined it, but her face seemed to light up at the sight of him. *Progress*, he told himself. In the beginning, she'd been reticent to let him or Emily in, and for weeks would only call them by their first names.

He unrolled the window. "Hey, kiddo. I'm your ride today."

"You're here!"

"I'm here." He leaned over and opened the door.

"What about Cody?"

Shoot, it hadn't occurred to him to offer to take Cody home, too. "Let me call your mom and see what she wants me to do. Justin's not driving him?"

"He's got practice."

"Okay." He dialed Em just as Cody came up to the door.

"Hi, Mr. Matthews."

"Hey, Cody. I'm checking with Emily to see about giving you a ride home." He held up his hand. "Em, I'm at the school, and Cody's here. You want me to run him home for you?"

"It's out of your way."

"So? I've got nothing else to do."

"Then yes. It would really help me out, because I'm running late."

"No problem." He hung up and motioned for both kids to get in the car.

"Where's Kristy?" Harper asked.

"She had to work, honey." It wasn't a complete lie. The last thing he wanted was for Harper to think they were fighting because of her. "You buckled in, Cody?"

"Yes, sir."

He pulled out and took the back road to McCreedy Ranch. It was a pretty drive, and he enjoyed listening to Harper and Cody talk about school and their friends. He'd missed out on a significant part of her life, and to have her back, to hear her chatter about her day…well, he didn't want to miss a minute more.

"Hey, Cody, you interested in joining us tomorrow? We're planning to check out Glory Junction, maybe grab sandwiches at that bakery everyone talks about and spend an hour or two skating." A couple of the resorts had outdoor rinks.

Drew watched in his rearview mirror as Cody checked something on his phone.

"I think I can rearrange my schedule," he said, and Drew had to stifle a laugh. The boy had charm. Both of Clay's sons were good kids; they adored Harper and looked out for her. "Thanks for inviting me, Mr. Matthews."

"Hey, Cody, you can just call me Drew."

"Okay."

When they got to the top of Emily's driveway, two big dogs came out to greet them. Cody opened the door and shooed them away. In the beginning, when they'd first brought Harper to the ranch, she'd been cautious of the animals. Now, she got out of the car, scratched one of the dog's heads, and ran up the front porch stairs.

"I'll be right back," she called.

"Thanks for the ride." Cody took off after her, his backpack flapping up and down.

A few seconds later Clay came out and waved. "You want to come in, have a cup of coffee or a soda? Emily ran to the store."

Drew got out of the car. He didn't want to be antisocial, but he was anxious to spend what was left of the day with Harper. "Thanks for the invite, but I'm fine." He gazed up at the clear blue sky. "Beautiful day."

"Yep, we've been enjoying mild weather for a change." Clay came down from the porch and joined Drew on the driveway. "Thanks for bringing Cody home."

"My pleasure." Other than the kids, they didn't have a lot to talk about. Drew didn't know anything about ranching or livestock, and he assumed Clay wasn't all that interested in Internet law. "Emily told me about the possibility of a motorcycle park going in near the ranch. If you're looking for an attorney, I might be able to recommend someone."

Clay nodded. "I appreciate it. Flynn Barlow, another neighbor who will be affected, is a lawyer, and I think he's talking to someone about representing us. In the meantime, we're appealing to the city, hoping they'll block it."

From everything Drew had heard from Emily, Clay McCreedy held a lot of influence in Nugget. His family was one of the original founders, and his cattle ranch was one of the largest in Northern California. Drew's money was on Clay and his neighbors coming out on top.

Harper came out. She'd changed out of her school clothes into exercise pants, a sweater, and sneakers and was toting a small suitcase.

"Honey, you already have stuff at my house." Harper was a bit of clotheshorse, changing outfits a few times a day. Her closet at the Sierra Heights house was just about full.

"I know, but I don't have anything at your house to wear skating."

Clay smothered a smile and ruffled Harper's hair. "You have a good time."

"Tell Cody we'll pick him up at ten," Drew said, and loaded Harper's case in the trunk.

When they hit the main road he said, "I talked to your mom today, and we both agreed you could take care of Raylene's horse."

"Seriously?"

"Seriously. But only if you keep up your schoolwork and don't let it interfere with your after-school programs."

"I will and it won't, I promise. Can we go to the barn and see Gunner? Please?"

"Sure. But let's stop home first, drop off your stuff and get a snack. What do you think of having dinner out?"

"Can we go to the Bun Boy?"

"Great minds think alike." He draped his arm around Harper's shoulder. "Kristy'll be jealous."

But when they got home her BMW was parked in the driveway. Something told him her surprise visit wasn't going to be good.

Chapter 18

"Do you know how crazy this is?" Gabe wanted to throttle Raylene until she came to her senses. "Let the police handle this."

"It's my land, and I'm not letting anyone get my gold." She filled her thermos with coffee.

"Is there another one?" He started searching through Annie's cupboards for a second thermos. It looked like he was doing surveillance tonight. "And we're taking my SUV; it's more comfortable."

"Who said anything about you going?"

He stopped rummaging through the cabinets and threw her some shade. "Don't be one of those people."

"What people are you referring to?"

"The kind who try to act all badass when they're clearly out of their league." No thermos, but he found a travel mug. He took the coffeepot from her and filled the tumbler. "Give me ten minutes to get supplies." Including his Sig and NVGs. He planned to see the bad guys before the bad guys saw them.

He spun her around. "Stay put, you hear?"

She rolled her eyes. "You're bossier than anyone I know."

And she was the biggest pain in the ass. This was supposed to be his friggin' vacation. He drove to L&G instead of walking, to save time. He collected his trusty Stingray to track cell phones in the area and a Range-R radar device in case he wound up chasing the dirtbags. Using radio waves, the detector could pinpoint even the slightest motion inside a building from fifty feet away. Gabe gathered up a few other necessities and hightailed it back to the house, fearful that Raylene would leave without him and blow any chance of going in quietly and staying out of sight. No, she'd be more like a bull in a china shop, as his mother liked to say. And these people had the potential to be dangerous, especially if they were connected to that homicide in Utah. The whole thing was a mystery, and he wasn't about to let Raylene go charging in like Wonder Woman.

He found her waiting on the porch with enough gear to go camping for a week. "What the hell is that?" He pointed at two quilts she'd obviously heisted from the house as she tossed them in his back seat.

"In case we get cold."

He laughed. "Did you bring your horsey jammies, too?"

She got in the front seat and socked him in the arm. "Just for that, I'm not sharing." Raylene held up a small ice chest.

"What's in there?" He tried to lift the lid, but she slapped his hand away.

"Food, and it's all for me."

"We'll see about that. Buckle up, buttercup." He stepped on the gas and took a shortcut to Raylene's property.

"What are you doing? This isn't the way we go."

"It's the way I go, because we're parking over at Rosser Ranch. Up on that knoll right behind your land. There's a water tower there, and I figure we can take cover behind it and still have a clear vantage point if anyone comes back to Rancho Raylene tonight."

"Flynn will run us off his property with a shotgun if he finds out."

"He'll run *you* off, not me. He likes me. I'm not trying to depreciate his property values with a motocross track." He flashed her a tight grin.

"I'm not building a motocross track. I'm selling my land to folks who made me an honest offer. He's a big-deal lawyer. He can fight it, or he can buy the property himself. Here's an idea: if it's such a problem for Lucky, Clay, and Flynn, why don't they go in together and buy it from me?"

"Maybe they don't want to be jacked up like that."

"Look, my father got a variance for the land a long time ago that would let it be used for something other than agriculture. They should've raised a fuss then, or raised the funds to buy the land. What am I supposed to do, let them determine who can and who can't buy my property?"

He shrugged, because she made a valid point, yet he sympathized with the neighbors. Having a motorcycle track in your backyard would suck.

He pulled off the road and cut across a field, bouncing every time his tires hit a rut. Good thing for all-wheel drive. Raylene didn't seemed phased by it, and he figured she'd probably taken similar routes to look after her father's cattle.

"Kind of reminds me of the terrain in the Hindu Kush," he said, remembering the years he spent near the Afghanistan-Pakistan border.

"Was it hellish?"

"Not a lot of creature comforts." He didn't really know how to answer that question. It was war. He lost friends, saw people get blown up, and watched a lot of brothers go home forever changed. But he was proud of what they'd accomplished and how he'd served his country.

"Do you miss it?"

The truth was he was still doing a lot of the same kinds of missions as a contractor. They were just more under the radar. But he missed the camaraderie of the teams. He still had Logan, though. His brother from another mother. "Nah, all the red tape was a drag. And the money is better in contract work."

"Do you ever think of doing something less dangerous?"

"What's up, Ray, you worried about me?" He slid her a sideways glance.

"Definitely about Logan. You?" She shrugged. "So what happened with the pregnant girlfriend after she lost the baby?"

"Nothing I want to talk about. Let's talk about you instead. You find someone to take care of your horse?"

"I sure did. Harper's on."

"Nice. I guess you'll be leaving soon." Finally, his babysitting duties would come to an end. Somehow, he couldn't work up the relief he knew he should be feeling. Raylene was a royal pain in the butt, but she kept things interesting. Sleeping with her had been wrong on a dozen levels, but he'd be lying if he said he didn't want to do it again.

"As soon as I find the gold."

"Then you must be staying for good."

She jabbed him with her finger. "Why do you think our trespasser dug at the top of the property?"

"Beats the hell out of me. You think he's onto something?" he asked, half mocking. The other half of him had wondered the same thing. From his reading of the map, such as it was, the gold had been buried at the other end.

"It's funny, because my plan this morning was to try my luck exactly where the trench was dug."

"Are you sure the map never got out?"

"How do you mean? Like publicized in an article or something?"

"Or Ray maybe gave it to other people. Any chance your ex is somehow involved in that trench?"

"I doubt it," she said. "He knew about Levi's Gold but, like you, he thought the story was bogus. Otherwise he wouldn't have given up his rights to the property."

Gabe wasn't a hundred percent convinced. From everything he'd heard about Butch, the man was the picture of self-entitlement. If he thought there were any riches to be found, he'd want to get there first—before Raylene sold the land.

Gabe pulled up behind the water tower, found a few trees for camouflage, and parked his vehicle there. If he climbed up on the tower he could see clear to Nevada. Below sat Raylene's two hundred-acre parcel with a bird's-eye view of the trench. Gabe suspected the digger would be back to finish the job.

"I'd forgotten about this spot." Raylene handed him the travel mug and poured herself a cup of coffee from her thermos. "I used to play here sometimes and pretend the tower was a fort. Ray caught me climbing up the tank once, and said if he ever saw me doing it again he'd tan my hide."

There was a ladder, but the top of the tank was a good distance from the ground. A little kid could do some serious damage, or even die, falling from that kind of height.

"I'm going to climb up and have a look," he said, and jumped down from the driver's seat to scope out the area.

"I don't think that's such a good idea in the dark." Raylene got out, too, hugging her arms around herself to ward off the cold.

He winked. "I operate best in the dark." Just to prove it, he climbed the ladder like a monkey. With the night-vision goggles, he could see as far as the McCreedy ranch, including a few cattle grazing in the distance. But no suspicious gold diggers lurking around. He stayed up long enough to get a lay of the land, then took the ladder down.

"Well?" Raylene asked.

"Nothing yet. Get back in the truck before you turn into an icicle." She'd at least dressed warmly, with a bulky sweater under her ski jacket. Those signature tight jeans, hugging that outstanding ass of hers. And the boots, which practically glowed in the dark. "Turquoise isn't a color I would've picked for a stakeout."

Her eyes fell to her feet. "I guess I should've gone with the black ones, but these go better with the jacket."

"Yeah, I hate when my camo clashes with my footwear."

She laughed. "Are you ever serious?"

Only when he had to be. He opened the passenger side door and motioned for her to get in, then went to the base of the tower, crouched down, and scanned Raylene's land from that angle.

"It's still early," he said as he climbed into the SUV and removed his NVGs. "I suspect if anyone returns it'll be past midnight. I also wouldn't be surprised if Rhys or Jake was here doing exactly the same thing as us."

"Wouldn't they have told us?"

"Nope."

She grabbed one of the blankets and wrapped it around her.

"Cold? I'd turn on the heat, but I don't want the sound of the engine to scare anyone away."

"It's okay." She reached behind her. "You want the other one?"

"I'm good." Being in such close proximity to Raylene was as good as a bonfire. She warmed his blood. He tried to remind himself that touching her flame meant third-degree burns. "You might want to catch some sleep; we've got a long night ahead of us."

"It's only nine."

"In surveillance situations, you sleep whenever you can. Go ahead, I'll take the first watch."

"I'm not tired."

He didn't argue with her. Realistically, he was going to be the one to do this. No way was he letting her climb up on the water tank in the pitch black.

He leaned his chair back. "Then tell me a story."

"I've told you enough stories. You tell me one."

"PG or X?" The fact was he had sex on the mind, which was a first on a stakeout.

"About your life," she said.

"Then definitely X."

Even in the dark, he could see her roll her eyes. "Besides your Jersey girl, you ever have a serious girlfriend?"

"Nope. Was sort of busy fighting a couple of wars. Why you so interested in my love life?"

"I don't know, it's something to talk about." She was quiet for a while, then said, "I think you'd make a good boyfriend."

"You asking me to go steady, Ray?"

"Hell no. See this?" With her finger she drew an imaginary circle around her face. "Man-free zone."

He laughed. "Didn't seem like that a few nights ago."

"That was just meaningless sex."

"Ah, you trying to hurt my feelings?" He said it sarcastically, but her words had hurt his male pride. Meaningless was even worse than ho-hum, which he definitely wasn't. A slew of frog hogs could vouch for that.

"Oh, come on. It didn't mean anything to you either. But when it does…I mean with someone else…you'll be the loyal, doting type."

He wasn't going to correct her about their night together, but it had meant more than she thought. Quite frankly, he hadn't been able to stop thinking about it. About her. "What makes you so sure that I'm such a prize?"

"This, for one thing." She wagged her hand at him and the outside. "Sitting up all night, waiting to nab a trespasser…this is above and beyond. I know it's for Logan, but it shows the extent of your dependability."

"Or maybe it just shows that I love doing shit like this, otherwise I wouldn't have made it my profession. But keep going…tell me how great I am." His lips ticked up.

"You try to act like everything's a big joke, but at the heart of it you're a really good person. I'm sorry Jersey Girl lost your baby. You would've made a good dad, even if you were too young to start a family."

He didn't say anything and let the statement sink in. "She lost the baby because she took sleeping pills—an entire vial. Her sister found her unconscious and called 9-1-1, but by the time the ambulance got her to the hospital, she was dead." He didn't talk about it. Not then, not later, not ever until now, because he wasn't a good boyfriend. Not even close. "She didn't want to have the baby, but I pressured her to go through with it. I didn't even love her…jeez, we were barely eighteen. Who knows what love is at that age? We grew up together, came from the same neighborhood, same Italian families. Back then, I thought it was enough to get married and raise our baby together. But she knew better. She knew I was dooming her to a life of unhappiness."

Raylene adjusted her seat upright. "It sounds like you're blaming yourself for her suicide. With all due respect, she didn't have to marry you if she didn't want to. She didn't have to have the baby, or she could've put the baby up for adoption, or let you raise it. She had choices. Would it have been better if you'd walked away from her?"

"I don't know," he said. "I've spent the last fifteen years wondering."

"Well, stop wondering. You stepped up because you're a good man. My guess is she was fighting a lot of demons to have swallowed all those pills. You can't shoulder that kind of responsibility."

He thought about what she said. It wasn't anything he hadn't told himself a dozen times, but the guilt never subsided. Still, it was good to hear the words, to be absolved. Lord knew he hadn't been able to forgive himself.

"It taught me a valuable lesson," he said. "I don't ever want to be responsible for someone's happiness. Ever."

"You shouldn't have to be. Everyone should be responsible for their own. I had to learn that the hard way."

"Butch was that bad, huh?"

"Butch, my father, you name it. I won't do it again."

"What? Get married?"

She let out a mirthless laugh. "Never. But I was talking about getting attached. It's not worth the pain or the trouble."

"Hear, hear." He checked his watch and opened his door. "I'm going to do another sneak and peek."

He climbed the tower again and peered out over the pastures and trees with his night-vision goggles. Everything remained quiet, though he thought he spotted some movement on the border of the McCreedy spread and Raylene's land. Gabe took a closer look and suspected it was Nugget PD surveilling the situation from that vantage point. It wasn't as good as the water tank tower—not as high or as remote—but Gabe was an expert at scouting out prime locations for reconnaissance missions. He'd certainly done it enough times.

He sat on top of the tank for a while, keeping his eyes peeled. The cold was biting, but he needed the air. The inside of the vehicle had gotten a little confining. He wasn't used to spilling his guts, though Raylene had been a good ear. Not too touchy-feely or pitying, yet comforting in her own way. At least they were simpatico on the commitment thing. Who needed all those emotional complications?

He did another scan of the area, hauled himself up, and scrambled down the ladder.

"It's freaking cold out there." He got in the truck and quietly closed the door. Sound traveled at night. "Give me some of that blanket." Gabe pulled the quilt across his lap. Raylene moved closer so they could both huddle underneath it.

"You didn't see anything?"

"All quiet on the Western front, as Rhys likes to say. You should hop in back and get some shut-eye." He turned around and folded down the seat. She could use the other quilt for padding. It wasn't the ideal bed, but he'd slept in a lot worse.

"I'm okay. Why don't you go and I'll keep watch? If I see anything I'll wake you up."

"Nah. I don't want you climbing up on the tank in the dark, and you can't see much from here."

He expected her to argue, but she didn't.

"Why don't we both stretch out in the back? It'll be warmer, and we won't get cramps in our legs for sitting too long."

It seemed like a good idea to Gabe, since visibility wasn't any better from the front seat. Not as long as they were behind a water tower. The thing about surveillance in the boondocks is a vehicle parked on a country road stuck out like a sore thumb. Not a lot of places to hide in plain view.

"Crawl back there," he said. "I'm gonna go through the tailgate."

While he was out he took another look around, gazing across the field to where he thought he'd seen another vehicle. Nothing. But the night was young, he told himself, and joined Raylene under the covers.

"Did you ever used to go to drive-ins? This reminds me of that." She snuggled closer to him and he slipped his arm under her head to use as a pillow.

"Nah, I don't think we had any. We were all about the IMAX."

"There was one in Reno, and we all used to pile into someone's truck and go. We'd stretch out with blankets and watch the movie from the bed of a pickup."

He bet she was something then. Still growing into her looks but turning the boys' heads. She would've turned his, that's for sure.

"Sounds fun."

"Sometimes the Lamberts used to hang a sheet in their yard and show movies. We'd build a big fire and roast marshmallows and make s'mores."

"Country living." He laughed. They didn't do shit like that where he was from.

"Did you have a lot of friends back then?"

She shot him a look and he realized how it sounded. "I wasn't trying to be sarcastic, but…"

"I wasn't the town pariah, if that's what you meant. I was the most popular senior girl at Nugget High, I'll have you know. Homecoming queen, Sweetheart of the Mountains, and Plumas County rodeo queen."

"Impressive."

She socked him in the arm. "What were you? JROTC geek of the year?"

"Nope, I was in a band. It was a cross between Bon Jovi and Springsteen."

"How very New Jersey. Were you any good?"

"God awful. Couldn't carry a tune to save my life, and played the same two chords over and over again." He laughed at the memory. "We actually got gigs, though. And groupies."

"Then you went into the Navy?"

"Yep. Met Logan my first day of BUD/S. We've been inseparable ever since."

"I never did thank you for coming to Denver with him and helping me move out."

"That was some house." He whistled, because it was the ugliest house he'd ever seen. "It reminded me of Tara."

She shuddered. "What can I say? I had really bad taste back then. And I think part of it was sadistic…I went forty-thousand dollars over budget building that house. It almost gave Butch a coronary."

Gabe chuckled, though it sounded like Raylene had a significant spending problem, which made him think of her finances. "What happens if you don't find the gold? Will you be okay financially?"

She blew out a breath. "I don't think I'll be able to buy a ranch for my horse farm with only the proceeds from the property, but I'll survive."

From the hesitance in her voice, it sounded like she'd still be on shaky ground. "You still planning to give a chunk of change to that women's shelter?"

"Yep. They're counting on it."

She was a contradiction, to be sure. The world thought Raylene was a vain, self-indulgent, spoiled brat. Yet it seemed there was a side of her no one knew—no one but him.

"How long have you been involved with this operation?"

"It's a battered women's shelter, not an operation. Since I moved to Santa Monica. I was walking around the neighborhood—yes, people actually walk in LA—and saw it. At first, the big 1920s Mediterranean looked like any of the other stately single-family homes in the area. But on my daily walks I started to notice different women coming in and out. Some of them had toddlers on their hips or a small child's hand in theirs. And all of them looked hauntingly familiar." She paused. "Because they looked like me."

"Butch abused you?"

"My dad, Butch…it's a pattern, you know?" She turned on her side so he could no longer see her face in the dim moonlight.

"You seem strong to me, Ray, not like someone who would put up with that shit." It was the wrong thing to say, because she sprang up.

"I am strong, and I didn't, as you say, put up with that shit. But you try stopping someone twice your size, someone who has the power to cut you like a knife with a single sentence, someone who holds your financial well-being in his hands, to be nice. He was my father, Gabe. It took a long time to realize that the way he treated me wasn't normal. My entire childhood I thought the things Ray did and said were simply tough love. Later, I thought if I was a good wife to Butch, who my father handpicked, I'd make Daddy proud and he'd love me more."

"I shouldn't have said that." He gently nudged her back down. "I have no idea what it was like for you…what I said was stupid." His parents had been the gentlest people on earth. They were big on praise and short on disapproval, unless he or his siblings deserved to be put in their place. He had no concept of what it was like to be in an abusive relationship.

"A lot of people think it's easy to walk away. I can attest that it's the most difficult thing I've ever done. But I did it, and now I'm helping other women do the same."

"That's huge, Ray. You should be really proud of what you've accomplished. The booze, too. I was right about you being strong, that part I didn't get wrong."

"I am," she said. "And every day I'm getting stronger."

He flipped over on his side and brushed away a strand of hair from her face. "I'll miss you when you leave. Between you and me, you might even be more fun than Logan."

That made her smile. "You can visit me in LA. I'm sure we can find someone to surveil or shadow."

He couldn't help himself. He leaned over and kissed her. All night he'd wanted to, but not more than now. She wrapped her arms around his neck and pulled him closer, returning the kiss with equal fervor. Next thing he knew, he was on top of her, pressed between her thighs. She unzipped his jacket, reached under his thermal shirt, and rested her palms against his chest. Gabe wondered if she could feel the rapid beat of his heart. He ground against her, wishing they didn't have so many clothes between them.

He sucked in a breath as her hands trailed down his abs to the waistband of his jeans. "We gonna do this in the back of the car?"

"Mm." She rubbed against the hard bulge in his pants. "May as well."

He had to laugh at her feigned indifference, because her body told a different story. Even through her jacket he could tell her nipples were hard, and he'd bet his last nickel she was wet. To test the theory, he unbuttoned her jeans and slid his hands inside her panties. Wet didn't begin to describe it—soaked was more like it. He played for a while, watching her tremble as he dipped a finger inside her. When he used two fingers she whimpered, the sound so arousing it went straight to his groin.

He struggled with her clothes, trying to remove them, but in the cramped quarters nothing seemed to cooperate. She somehow managed to shrug out of her jacket while still kissing him. He got his off and tossed it up front, then went to work on her sweater, dragging it over her head. Her bra was black and lacy and he took a few seconds to admire it—and her breasts. She tore at his shirt and he slapped her hands away, laughing.

"I'll get it." He pulled the thermal over his head and began trying to pry her boots off. "You have to be a damned contortionist back here."

"Don't worry about those." She peeled her pants and underwear down and managed to jerk them past her boots. "Yours now."

Gabe grinned. "I'm not done looking yet."

He lay beside her, pulled down the straps of her bra, and traced his finger across the tops of her breasts. She shivered as he kissed her, first her mouth, then her cleavage. Her bra had one of those front clasps, and it took him a few seconds for him to figure it out. There were goosebumps on her skin, and he pulled the blanket over both of them.

She reached for his fly and he helped her get his jeans off.

"Hang on a sec." He grabbed his pants before she tossed them and searched the pockets for his wallet and a condom.

"Hurry."

"I'm moving as fast as I can." He hit his head on the roof and muttered a curse. "I'm too old and too big for this."

Her lips curved up in a teasing smile. "Want to stop?"

"Hell no." He rolled on top of her and she encircled his hips with her legs. He rolled the condom down his length and entered her in one powerful thrust, grunting as her heat enveloped him. "You feel good."

She moved under him, her hips rocking back and forth. Gabe repositioned himself, pulled out, and plunged back in, going deeper than before. Then, with long, even strokes, he brought her to climax, feeling her come apart in his arms.

Raylene arched up and kissed him. "Your turn," she said, and nudged him onto his back, straddled his lap, and rode him.

Watching her like that, her breasts bouncing, her body swaying, those turquoise boots...it was the ultimate turn-on. And something more. Something that made his breath hitch and his emotions do somersaults, like he was under a spell. He held her hips and directed her to move harder and faster while he surged into her, letting her feel every inch of him.

"This is so good." She tipped her head back and he kissed her throat while fondling her breasts.

He was so close, but he wanted it to last. For her and for him. "Slow down just a little."

She decreased the pace, draping herself over his chest. He rubbed his hands up and down her back and combed his fingers through her hair. The windows had fogged, and he mentally kicked himself for dropping the ball. He should be paying attention, watching for the trespassers to reappear. But this would probably be their last time together, and he wanted to savor every minute of it.

Her too. Because she sat up, her eyes filled with a tenderness and longing he'd never seen before, and in a barely audible whisper said, "Oh, Gabe."

His breath caught, and she started undulating, finding a rhythm that suited them both. He slipped his hand between her legs and rubbed her center with his finger, touching her slick folds. She cried out and he pumped harder until he felt his body quake, filling a need in him so powerful he hadn't been aware he had it. He captured her mouth with his and held her against him, afraid to let her go, afraid to end this perfect moment. For a while she just lay on top of him while he stroked her hair.

"You cold?" He readjusted the blanket to make sure it covered her back.

"No, are you?"

He couldn't feel his arms or legs, let alone the temperature. "I'm good." But he wasn't. He was conflicted, and he didn't understand why. Good sex had never done that to him before.

"I should go outside and check on things. You okay for a little while?"

"Of course." She felt around the bed of the SUV for her clothes.

He pulled on his shirt and jeans and tugged on his jacket as he opened the tailgate to climb out. It was at least ten degrees colder and felt like snow. He climbed the water tower, got into position with his night-vision goggles, and scanned the countryside. Other than the wind howling through the trees and the call of a lonesome owl, the land was still. Not even a car on the highway. He gazed out over McCreedy Ranch and spotted a flicker of light so faint anyone else would've missed it. A cellphone, perhaps.

He fished the Stingray out of his pocket and turned it on. The device worked as a high-powered cellular tower. Because cell phones were programmed to connect to a tower with the best signal, he could use it to intercept calls, locate devices in the vicinity, and collect personal data. The military and cops used them all the time, but they were highly controversial. Big Brother and all that. It took him only a few minutes to determine that the only cell phones in the immediate area were his, Raylene's, and Rhys'.

Bingo.

He raised his Stingray in a salute to Rhys, who was likely the source of the movement he'd spied earlier. Rhys probably couldn't see Gabe sitting up on the water tank, but the police chief undoubtedly knew he was out here somewhere.

Gabe checked his watch. It was approaching one in the morning, but he was getting the feeling their gold diggers would be no-shows. Too damned cold. *And too damned dark*, he thought as he looked up at the sky. Not even a sliver of moon tonight.

He should go back to his SUV and get warm. But he continued to sit there, letting the cold lash his face and bite through his jeans while he tried to clear his head. This thing between him and Raylene had taken on a life of its own. He hadn't prepared for that, but when she left, she would surely take a piece of him with her.

Chapter 19

Raylene woke up cold, with a crick in her neck and her hair tangled on a piece of loose carpeting next to Gabe's wheel well. She'd fallen asleep sometime during the night and couldn't recall Gabe ever coming back after he'd gone outside for watch duty. The space next to her was empty.

She extended her arm and felt around, thinking he might've rolled closer to the other side. Of course, that was ridiculous, because the back of his SUV was about the width of a twin-size bed.

It took her a while to unhook her hair. When she finished, she sat up and tried to get her bearings. Everything was a little hazy—except the amazing sex. Sex that changed something between them. It had suddenly gone from recreational to deeply meaningful. Perhaps it had been happening all along, but last night she'd felt a definite shift in the universe. She'd like to say she'd been down this road before, but she hadn't. As much as she'd cared for Lucky, their relationship had been puppy love, fraught with complications and her ultimate betrayal. Butch had always been her father's pick, not hers. And all the lousy choices in between had been her desperate attempt to fill the gaping hole in her heart.

Gabe was different. She, on her own, had begun to heal that hollow place in her soul a little at a time, and she'd planned to keep at it until she was completely whole. She had herself for that. But Gabe had a way of filling everything else. He made her laugh, he made her feel beautiful, he made her feel clever. But most of all, he made her yearn for tomorrow and all the adventures it could bring.

And they had absolutely no future together. He'd built a life in Nugget, and she'd destroyed the one she'd had here.

"Morning." Gabe twisted around in the driver's seat.

"Have you been there all night?" She rubbed her eyes.

"Here and the water tower. I didn't want to wake you."

"I guess I'm pretty shitty on stakeouts."

He flashed a sexy grin. "I wouldn't say that."

"No sign of him, huh?" She figured if the thief had shown up, Gabe would have had him tied up and begging for mercy by now.

"Nope." He shook his head.

"What if he's already gotten the gold?" The thought had weighed on her. There was nothing to say that someone else hadn't succeeded where they'd failed.

Being the naysayer that he was, Gabe huffed out a breath and made that face he always made when she spoke of Levi's Gold. But their phantom digger confirmed for her that it really did exist. Someone knew she was selling the property and wanted to get the treasure before it was too late.

"He...they...got exactly what you got. Nothing."

"How do you know that, other than the fact that you don't believe in the legend?"

"I don't for sure, but it seems to me that the trench is too shallow and too even. Like whoever dug it knew where he was going and was just getting started."

"Like he was digging a tunnel?"

"Yeah. I also think we would've seen more of a disturbance in the ground, where someone hefted out a box or whatever storage unit was used for the gold."

For all she knew, Levi had simply buried the nuggets in the raw dirt. Still, for the kind of weight they were talking about, the thief would've needed something to transfer it from the ground. A wheelbarrow, wagon, even a backpack. There would've been some sort of markings in the dirt. But why hadn't the thief come back to finish the job?

"Why do you think he didn't return last night?"

Gabe shrugged. "Too cold, too dark, he had a date. Who knows?"

"He's got to realize we're onto him."

"Another reason he may not have returned." He brushed a strand of hair away from her eye, the gesture so tender it made her chest squeeze.

"You think he's gone and not coming back?" she asked, trying not to let him distract her from the conversation.

"I don't know, Ray. But we can't surveil the place twenty-four seven."

"That's why I've got to find the gold today."

He scrubbed his hand through whiskers that hadn't been there the day before. "You mind if we shower and eat breakfast first?"

"No, and I have an errand to run." Not exactly an errand, but she was leaving on Monday and needed to get it done. Sunday she planned to spend teaching Harper how to care for Gunner. Raylene also wanted to take the gelding out for one last ride before she left.

He didn't ask about her so-called errand, which she was thankful for. Otherwise, he would've tried to talk her out of it.

When they got to the farmhouse Gabe dropped her and went home to get a change of clothes. He hadn't been to his duplex apartment in a few days, and Raylene supposed he had things to catch up on. Still, his absence left her feeling melancholy. *Get used to it*, she told herself, and made a call to Lucy's House.

Wanda answered the phone. Like Raylene, she was a volunteer and had graciously taken Raylene's Saturday shift. Unlike Raylene, Wanda had been married to a wonderful man who'd been killed two years earlier in the line of duty while responding to a domestic violence call. Helping at Lucy's House had been Wanda's salvation, something the two women had in common.

"How's everything going?"

"You tell me, girl. How was the wedding? Any fireworks?" Raylene had given Wanda the entire 4-1-1 on her history in Nugget.

"I got through it unscathed and have lots of pictures of Logan and Annie to show you. That asshole Butch threw me a curve ball with my horse, but I'll tell you about that when I get home."

"Ooh, you better. I love me some TAB stories. That man deserves a hot poker up his ass."

Raylene laughed. Wanda always had the power to make a terrible situation not feel so bad. That's why the women at Lucy's House loved her.

"Any changes there?"

Wanda sighed. "Jenny's waiting to hear on whether any of the grants she applied for will come through, but she isn't optimistic. A lot of organizations need money, and there's not a lot of it to go around. What we need is a wealthy benefactor."

"I'm working on it." Raylene was no longer wealthy, but two hundred thousand dollars would be enough to hold the non-profit over until they could raise more.

"I know you are, girl. I'd give 'em DeRon's pension if I didn't need it to live on." In Los Angeles, a cop's pension didn't go far.

"I got a good offer, Wanda. I just need to close escrow." She still had to sign the papers. *Today*, she told herself.

They talked a few minutes longer. Afterward, Raylene climbed in the shower, dressed, and grabbed a quick breakfast. On her way out, she texted Gabe to meet her at the property at noon.

The last time she'd been to Lucky's ranch, he'd been living in a single-wide trailer, waiting for workers to metamorphose the place into a full-service dude ranch—a cowboy camp, as he called it. She hadn't believed it possible. Once a church camp, the place had fallen into disrepair. The outbuildings were mostly rotted, the big lodge infested with rodents, and the land strewn with old tractor parts.

Today, it looked completely different. A big ranch gate and sign had been erected at the entrance with Lucky's brand and "Cowboy Camp" in big letters. Spiffy split-rail fencing stretched around the perimeter of the property and pavers took the place of dirt on the long road to the office and parking lot. All the buildings had new roofs, new siding, and new front porches. Raylene didn't remember any front porches from before. In the distance, she could see river rock had replaced the crumbling chimney on the big lodge. And rows of corrals, barns, and an arena with metal bleachers now sat where there once was a weathered horse ring and amphitheater.

The trailer was gone, and in its place was a big cabin with a front porch, complete with a row of rocking chairs and an outdoor fireplace made from the same river rock as the lodge's chimney. A wooden sign on the door said, "Welcome and Check in Here."

She found a parking space next to a Toyota Prius, took a deep breath, and tried to steady her shaking hands.

God grant me the serenity to accept the things I cannot change, courage to change the things I can, and wisdom to know the difference.

This was it. This was the very spot she'd stabbed Lucky in the back.

She slowly got out of her truck and forced herself to take eight long strides to the cabin. There was a young man behind the counter who Raylene didn't know.

"Howdy, you checking in?" The man craned his neck to look behind her, presumably wondering where her luggage was.

Someone ought to tell him that no one said "howdy" in California.

"No, I'm looking for the Rodriguezes."

"Sure." He picked up a cell phone. "You have an appointment?"

"No."

"Okay. What's your name and what company are you with?"

Raylene hesitated for a minute. She didn't want to lie, but she knew if she told the truth Lucky might refuse to see her. "Lucy's House."

The guy didn't seem to notice that she hadn't given a name—perhaps he thought she was Lucy—and punched in a number. "Hi, someone's at the front desk from Lucy's House. Okay, I'll let her know." He put down the phone and turned to Raylene. "Someone will be here in a few minutes. Would you like something to drink while you wait?"

A vodka tonic would be good. "No, thank you."

He motioned for her to take a seat on one of the big kilim sofas. Whoever decorated the place had serious talent. It was rustic and Western without being Country Bear Jamboree, and despite the soaring ceilings and massive space, the room felt cozy. There was a credenza in the corner with two large coffee urns, a set of ironstone mugs, and a tiered plate of cookies. Raylene smelled hot apple cider coming from a separate dispenser. Navajo rugs covered the wide-plank floors and two Stickley chairs hugged the fireplace, a larger replica of the one outside. She gazed around the room at the pictures of Lucky riding bulls. A couple of his championship buckles had been framed in shadow boxes and hung on the wall, along with a *Cowboys and Indians* magazine cover that featured Tawny's custom boots.

A Randy Travis song played in the background, and outside she could see it had started snowing again. During the night they'd gotten an inch or so. Hopefully, they wouldn't get much more. Otherwise, it would be a bitch for digging.

A couple wandered in out of the cold and fixed themselves each a cup of coffee. They were dressed in Western attire that looked straight off the rack and boots too nice to ride in. They examined the buckles for a few seconds, then seemed to notice her for the first time and smiled.

"Are you going on the ten o'clock trail ride?" the woman asked.

"Uh, no," Raylene said. "I'm not a guest."

The woman took a seat on the sofa across from Raylene. "Then you must be a local. We love it here, don't we, Rob?"

"Yep." Rob was immersed in reading one of the pamphlets at the desk about things to do in the Sierra.

"We already made a reservation for summer," she continued. "This time, we're planning to spend a couple of days at that Victorian hotel in town."

Raylene nodded, too rattled by nerves to give the woman her full attention. The lady kept up a steady stream of conversation, unaware that Raylene wasn't really listening.

The door opened and Lucky wiped his boots on the scraper before coming in. He'd caught her off guard the other day when he'd come to yell at her about the motocross park. Now, she took the time to really look at him. He was as gorgeous as ever, maybe even more so. His face had always been arresting, but the years had whittled away his full cheeks, leaving a profile that was raw and rugged and breathtaking. There were a few streaks of silver in his dark hair that hadn't been there a few years ago. And his body had lost some of its ranginess from his rodeo and PBR days. But what she noticed most was that he looked happy, like a man at the top of his game, blessed with people who loved him.

He scanned the lobby, and his expression went from bright to dark the second he spotted her. To her advantage, he couldn't banish her from the property in front of his two guests. She rose, calculating how to play this.

"I was hoping you, Tawny, and I could talk."

He nodded a greeting at the couple, put his hand under Raylene's elbow, and walked her out of the cabin into the parking lot.

"Before you kick me out, let me say what I've come to say." Step nine out of twelve. She'd already made amends to Logan and to all the others she'd hurt, leaving the Rodriguezes for last. With them, she had the most justice to restore.

"Unless you're here to tell me you're not selling to a motocross company, we've got nothing to say."

"Please, Lucky, it won't take long."

He dropped his hand and squeezed the bridge of his nose. "I'd hoped you'd left by now."

"I'm leaving Monday. And you'll never have to see me again, I swear. Just give me a few minutes."

He looked at his watch. "You've got eight seconds." The length of time a bull rider is required to stay on a bull's back to receive a score. Basically, a death-defying eternity for a cowboy. She hadn't missed the reference, or the jibe.

"I had hoped we could do this inside...with Tawny, too."

"Nope. You've just used two of your seconds."

"I came to make amends," she said.

He made a bitter sound in his throat that she presumed was supposed to be laughter. "We both know there's no way you can do that."

"I can't undo what I did, but I can own up to every horrible piece of it." She shuffled her feet. The snow was coming down harder now, and she was so cold her lips were numb.

"How about you make good on your promise to leave Monday, never come back, and we call it amends." He took her by the arm again and started walking her to her truck.

"I'm sorry, Lucky. What I did to you, Tawny, your mom...I can't even live with myself it was so awful."

"Yet here you are…living."

She flinched. She deserved every drop of his vitriol, and then some. "I'm not asking you to forgive me, and I know I can't make it right, but I'd like to make restitution."

She and her sponsor had spent a considerable amount of time deciding what would be appropriate compensation. Money had seemed crass, and anything of her father's Lucky would spit on. In the end, they'd settled on a generous donation from her property sale proceeds to Lucile Packard Children's Hospital Stanford in the Rodriguez name. It was the hospital where their daughter, Katie, had been treated for leukemia.

"There's no restitution in the world that will cover what you did to me… to my whole family."

She dropped her gaze to the ground. "I understand that, and I'm not trying to buy your forgiveness. I know I can't have that. This is for me, proof that I've changed and the key to my recovery." And that's when she knew what she had to do. "You can have my land for two hundred thousand dollars."

He reeled back as if he wasn't certain he'd heard her right. "Your land, two hundred thousand dollars?" It was worth over a half a million.

"I'd give it to you for nothing, but the two hundred thousand dollars is already spoken for. You won't have to worry about Moto Entertainment, and can expand your cowboy camp or raise more stock. Whatever you want to do with it."

He studied her for a while, and Raylene thought he was trying to decide what her objective was.

"And then you'd feel absolved?" he asked.

She nodded.

He curled his lip, looking as angry as she'd ever seen him. "Then no. I don't want any part of your *recovery* gift. Now get the hell off my property and don't bother any of my family members."

Raylene left before she was physically escorted away.

* * * *

"You spent all night crammed in your wife's car and you're here on a Saturday morning?" Gabe took the liberty of walking into Rhys' office uninvited, sinking into one of the wing chairs, and stretching out.

"You made me?"

"Hell yeah, I made you. Were you lighting a joint at one in the morning or was that your cell phone?"

"I didn't see you."

"Of course you didn't." Though Gabe had been sloppy as hell, starting with the fact that he'd spent much of the night rocking his SUV naked with Raylene. "You think they're gone?"

Rhys made a rim shot off the garbage pail with a Nerf ball. "Don't know, but there haven't been any sightings of late. Though it seems highly unlikely they'd leave before tearing that property apart if the gold is what they came for."

"What other reason would they have?" It wasn't as if Nugget was a major attraction off the interstate.

"Don't know that either. Best working theory is that they caught wind that Raylene was selling the place and wanted to get in before the new owners break ground. It's not like Levi's Gold is a big secret, even if the story is a ridiculous fable."

Gabe tilted his head from side to side.

"Oh, for Christ's sake, don't tell me she's got you believing it."

"No, but she sure believes it. She swears by it, and she won't quit until she finds it. I'm supposed to meet her over there at noon so we can start digging again." Gabe rolled his eyes. "I'm hoping the snow will dissuade her." And the fact that neither of them got much sleep last night.

"Watch yourself." Rhys got up to dig his ball out of the trash. "If any of them had anything to do with that home invasion killing in Utah, they're dangerous."

"I will, but I think they're gone. My guess is they realized how difficult it is digging that rocky soil, didn't like camping in the cold, and decided to call it quits. Otherwise someone would've seen them by now."

"Could be, but don't lower your guard."

"Never do."

"So where were you, anyway?"

"Last night?" Gabe stifled a grin. "I'm like a ghost, dude. And if I told you, I'd have to kill you."

Rhys shook his head. "Save it for Owen. Were you up on the water tower?"

"Did you see me up on the water tower?"

Rhys threw the Nerf ball at Gabe. "Go dig up Levi's nonexistent gold. The sooner Raylene leaves, the sooner I can cross off quelling a riot from my to-do list."

"If they don't want her to sell to those motocross people, they should buy it themselves." Enough was enough. She wasn't selling to spite anyone; the money from the property was her only livelihood.

"As the police chief, I'm staying out of it, though having motorcycles speed around a track all day is going to wreak havoc on my family's quality of life, not to mention our property values. I'm just on the other side of McCreedy Ranch, if you remember?"

Gabe knew, and sympathized with all of them. "Hopefully the city will stop it from happening."

"I wouldn't bet your money on it. Revenue for the city is a hard thing to turn down just because a few nimbies are complaining."

"You mean some of the most influential residents in the community." Gabe hitched his brows in challenge.

"I don't know about that. What I do know is, as much as I don't want a motocross track next to my home, or the crime and nuisance it might bring, the money it'll generate will buy the department a few more officers, after-school programs for the kids, and a host of other things this town needs. It'll also lose the city a bunch of money if Moto Entertainment decides to sue because the town blocks it from coming in. Damned if you do, damned if you don't. For me, personally, things would be best if they stayed the same, if the land was kept for agricultural purposes."

Raylene didn't have that choice, unless one of the local ranchers stepped up.

Gabe got to his feet. "I'm off to search for gold."

"Good luck with that." Rhys beaned him in the back of the head with the ball.

Chapter 20

On Sunday morning, Harper showed up at the barn in her pink cowboy boots with a baggie full of apples and her dad in tow.

It was so cute that Raylene's mood instantly lifted.

Drew Matthews followed his daughter around the stable, listening to her chatter on endlessly.

"This horse's name is Sugar," she told him. "She used to have thrush in her hoof. That's like this really gross infection. But the farrier—that's kind of like a foot doctor for horses—came and trimmed her hooves and now she's better."

Drew turned to Raylene. "Harper's been hanging out here a lot."

"I can tell. Between this and McCreedy Ranch, you're an expert, huh, Harper?"

"Not as much as Justin and Cody. They know everything about horses and cattle, and even chickens."

"You'll get there." Raylene gave Harper's ponytail a little tug. "How's Ginger?"

"She's good. Clay gave me a lesson yesterday."

"That's great." Raylene suspected he wasn't thrilled about his stepdaughter working for her. At least Drew didn't seem to have a problem with it.

"You want to watch me next time?" she asked her dad.

"I can't think of anything I'd love more." He kissed the top of Harper's head, making Raylene wonder what the world would be like if everyone had a father like Drew Matthews.

Gabe would be that kind of dad. Attentive, nurturing, proud. She mentally kicked herself for going there and tried to focus on the task at hand.

"You ready to learn the routine?" she asked Harper, who bobbed her head enthusiastically.

"First, you break off a flake of hay." Raylene walked Harper to the hay loft and showed her how to snap open a bound bale of alfalfa by twisting a hook in the wire that held it together.

Drew watched closely, and Raylene got the impression he'd be taking over this part of the chore. It didn't take that much strength if you did it right, but the hook was sharp and could cause a serious injury if you weren't careful. She'd grown up using them and had never had an accident.

"It'll break off like this." She demonstrated.

"I know. I do it at home all the time."

"Excellent," Raylene said, and showed Harper which trough was Gunner's. "Always make sure his water is filled."

"I know how to do that, too." Harper climbed up on the fence. "Can I give him some apple slices?"

"Sure. Then I'll show you how to feed him his oats. Only once a week, though."

"Okay." Harper stuck her hand inside the stall and held her palm perfectly flat so Gunner could take the apple without nipping her fingers.

While she fed him a few more slices, Drew joined Raylene at the fence.

"I hear you're heading home tomorrow."

She'd never really thought of Los Angeles as home, but she supposed it was the closest thing she had to one anymore. "Uh-huh." She just had to officially accept Moto Entertainment's offer. "Thanks for letting Harper do this. It'll help me sleep better knowing Gunner is in good hands."

"Are you kidding? Look at her, she's thrilled."

It was funny, because Harper lived on a working ranch with plenty of horses to care for. Raylene supposed this was the girl's first job and a way of showing some independence. She gathered that after what had happened, Emily was extremely protective of Harper. And who could blame her?

"You taking off tomorrow too?" Raylene asked, knowing that Drew and his wife lived somewhere in the Bay Area.

"My wife and I are leaving this afternoon," he said. She got the impression he wished he could stay longer. It must be difficult leaving his daughter after only recently being reunited with her.

"Safe travels."

"Thanks." He watched Harper fawn over Gunner for a few seconds. "Would you mind if I bowed out of the rest of the lesson? I think I got enough of the basics to jump in if she needs help. I should really help Kristy pack up. I know Harper wanted to watch you ride Gunner in the ring, and I don't want to deprive her of that before dropping her off at Emily's."

"Of course. I'll take her to your house when we're done here."

"Great. We're just on the other side of the development. Harper can show you, but it's not even a half mile away."

"Not a problem at all. And again, I can't tell you how much I appreciate her doing this." She handed him Harper's first payment. "I wasn't sure if I should give it to her or to you."

Drew smiled. "You should give it to her. It'll be nice for her to see what it's like to earn her first paycheck."

"All right." Raylene slipped it inside her jeans. She'd give it to Harper when she dropped her home. Between the weekly checks and Gunner's feed, she'd be eating into what was left of her money faster than she wanted to think about.

Drew went over to Harper to tell her he was leaving, then he drove off. Raylene showed Harper how to dole out Gunner's weekly grain ration and saddled the gelding for one last ride before she left. Later today she was going to take another stab at finding the gold. They'd gotten more snow on Saturday, but with the sun out today it had already started melting and she fervently hoped the digging would be easier. Yesterday had been rough, and once again they'd come up empty.

Gabe had bitched and moaned the entire time, but he had stuck with her until it was too dark to dig anymore. She hadn't told him about her awful meeting with Lucky. There was no sense reliving her humiliation—her shame. Lucky hated her so much he wouldn't even accept her land, which in her mind was asinine. He could've hated her while sitting on two hundred prime acres of real estate.

Her sponsor had warned her that some of the people she'd hurt wouldn't readily accept amends, but Raylene thought it was important to at least try to make restitution any way she could. Nothing could undo the trouble she'd caused, but she'd spend the rest of her life willingly paying penance. And that meant leaving tomorrow, with or without the gold. Her visit here had clearly upset the balance of Lucky's life, which was the last thing she wanted to do.

She checked her phone to see if Gabe had texted. Nothing yet. She'd spent the night in his arms, this time in a real bed. Leaving him tomorrow…well, she wasn't going to let herself face all the things she felt for him because there was no happily-ever-after in their future. Examining it too closely not only wasted energy, it was unhealthy. She couldn't change her past and all the reasons she had to leave Nugget, so pretending there was even an iota of a chance with them would only set her up for disappointment. Besides, as attracted as Gabe seemed to be to her, he'd never indicated that the past two weeks had been anything more than a fling.

"You ready to take him out?" Raylene stuffed her phone in her pocket and handed Harper Gunner's reins to lead him out to the arena. She'd give Gabe her ETA later.

"Can I ride him?"

"Sure. He hasn't been out in a while, so let me first."

It was a great ring, and they had the entire barn to themselves. Tucked away on the other side of the main road from Sierra Heights, the stable was convenient to the community center where the pool, tennis courts, and rec room were, but not too close to subject everyone to the smell. To Raylene it was a good smell—the gamey odor of a working ranch would forever be ingrained on her soul, even if she did live in a big city now—but not everyone felt that way. Especially city folks up to enjoy a summer weekend lounging by the pool or a snowy day in the spa. Or so she presumed. The barn and arena backed up to Redwood State Park, where there were more than a dozen riding trails, which made it even more enticing to residents of the planned community. She'd heard Griffin was searching for someone to manage the stable full-time. That way boarders didn't have to do it themselves or hire caretakers.

Raylene took a few turns in the arena. If she had more time, she'd double up with Harper and ride through the park. Harper sat on the top row of the fence and watched Raylene kick Gunner into a lope. Her boy had a lot of pent-up energy and she wanted to tire him out before Harper climbed into the saddle. She rode him until he worked up a nice lather, then got down to give Harper a turn. They'd take it nice and slow at first, to make sure Harper could handle him. He wasn't a horse for beginners, but Raylene would be right here in case he started acting up.

Once Harper got up, Raylene adjusted the stirrups. "Walk him around first, nothing fancy."

Raylene watched as Harper rode in a wide circle. She had a nice seat. Raylene figured Clay had worked with Harper on that. "You're doing great. How does he feel compared to Ginger?"

"Bigger." Harper looked down and Raylene laughed.

"A little bit. But you're a natural."

"You think? I'm always kind of scared. Clay said a horse can sense that."

"It's true. But it's good to be on guard, yet confident. You have to be the boss, or else he'll take advantage." Just to prove it, Gunner stopped to nibble on a few weeds under the fence. "Give the reins a little jerk, but not too hard. Just enough to tell him to stop it."

Harper successfully tugged his head up, and with a nudge to his flanks, he was walking again.

"Good job!"

"Thanks for letting me ride him."

"You're welcome." Raylene thought she was getting even more enjoyment out of it than Harper. Maybe someday, when she finally got her horse farm up and running, she'd give a few riding lessons to kids. Though the ranch would be a pipedream without Levi's Gold. After she donated part of her property sale proceeds to Lucy's House, she wouldn't have enough for the land, let alone the capital to get the business off the ground. Not unless she left California. And even then it would be a stretch. "He likes you."

"You think?"

"No doubt about it. You ready to call it a day?"

"I guess so. My dad and Kristy probably want to get going. It's a four-hour drive."

Raylene helped Harper get down and led Gunner toward the barn to unsaddle and groom him.

"Don't worry about feeding him tomorrow morning." Raylene wanted to see him one more time before she left. "And this is for you." She slipped the check in Harper's jacket pocket.

Harper's face lit up. "Thank you."

"Don't spend it all in one place." Raylene squeezed Harper's shoulder. The girl was just so darn cute. "Let's get done here and get you home."

She carried the saddle to a small tack room at the rear of the barn while Harper brushed Gunner with a curry comb. Taking a second to look around, she marveled at how neat everything was. Gabe had saved her bacon by sweet-talking Griffin into letting her keep Gunner here. For all her sins, the universe had sent her an angel in Gabe. She wondered if he would keep in touch with her after she left, or if she would simply go back to being Logan's high-maintenance sister.

She left the tack room, making sure to lock it behind her, and it struck her that she should make Harper a copy of the key. "Hey, Harp—"

Raylene stopped dead in her tracks. There were three people with Harper, one of them a small woman who at first glance looked like a young girl. On closer inspection, all three looked homeless and rough. The hairs on Raylene's neck went up. Something didn't feel right. She stuffed her hand in her pocket and fumbled around for her phone.

"Hi there," one of them, a man with stringy hair, a beard, and clothes that looked as if they hadn't been washed in a month, greeted her, then wrapped his arm around Harper's shoulder. Though he smiled, nothing about his demeanor was friendly. "Your friend said it was okay for us to pet your horse."

Raylene palmed her phone, keeping her hand casually inside her pocket. First, she wanted to put herself between Stringy and Harper. She didn't like his familiarity with Harper, and from the looks of it the frightened thirteen-year-old didn't either.

"Sure," Raylene said. "Harper, can you get me the hoof pick in the tack room?"

"Uh, okay." But Harper hesitated. Sweet little Harper didn't want to leave Raylene alone with their threesome.

"Go on." Raylene nudged her head toward the back of the barn, hoping Harper would take the hint and run to get Drew or the first person she could find. Her creep meter was way off the charts.

Harper started to move, but Stringy pulled her back. "Don't go yet. What's your name?"

"Her name is none of your goddamn business. Let go of her. Now!"

Stringy put his hands up in the air. "Why do you have to be so hostile?"

The other two laughed, drawing Raylene's attention to the small woman who she'd initially mistaken for a child and a man who was slightly taller than Stringy. He had beady eyes and reminded Raylene of a ferret. She couldn't decide who of the three was the biggest threat, but her money was on Stringy.

"We come in peace," he said, and again the other two laughed.

"Well, we're packing up here. My boyfriend's on his way to pick us up." And he's a former Navy SEAL. "You have to be with a resident to stay in the barn, so you've got to leave." Raylene tried to usher them out the entrance, but they didn't move.

Stringy went back to draping his arm around Harper's shoulders, as if he hadn't heard a word Raylene said. That's when she knew this really, really wasn't good. She eyed the hay hook and calculated how long it would take for her to get to it, wondering if she'd be better off trying to surreptitiously unlock her phone and dial 9-1-1. Hard to do without looking.

The tiny woman caught the direction of Raylene's gaze and shook her head. "Don't even think about it."

Raylene could take her with one arm tied behind her back. It was the two men she wasn't so sure about. They weren't large, both well under six feet and on the waifish side. One on one, she might've had a chance, but not all three of them at once. And she had Harper to worry about. If anything happened to her, Raylene couldn't live with herself.

"What do you people want? We don't have any money."

Ferret gave her a once-over that made her skin crawl. She had to get Harper out of here. Pressing the home key on her phone, she felt the surface of the screen, trying to spatially figure out where the numbers were to punch in her passkey. She was so nervous her hand shook.

"What are you doing?" Tiny grabbed her arm.

"Get your hands off me." Raylene pushed her, a tactical error because Stringy tightened his arm around Harper.

"Don't push me again, bitch." Tiny reached in Raylene's pocket, found the phone, and threw it against the barn wall.

Time for another plan. The problem was Raylene didn't have one. And Harper...not again... Raylene wouldn't let them put her or her parents through any more trauma. They'd already been through so much.

"What. Do. You. Want?" she asked through gritted teeth.

"We want the map." Tiny backhanded Raylene across the face. She might have been small, but the slap stung so hard Raylene's eyes watered.

The map? It took a few moments for her to process what they were asking for, then it all became clear. They were the ones who'd stolen the pickax, broken into her car...and possibly killed someone in Utah during a home invasion robbery. That third piece of the puzzle chilled her to the bone.

"I don't have it with me." Raylene held her throbbing face, trying not to look at Harper, afraid her fear was so palpable she'd scare the girl even worse.

"Well, that's a problem, isn't it?" the woman said, and Raylene knew she'd miscalculated. She, not Stringy, was running the show. Tiny exchanged a glance with Stringy and he stroked Harper's arm.

"You're not going to get it unless you let her go," Raylene said, knowing it was an empty threat. The more she protested on Harper's behalf, the more they'd use Harper to their advantage.

Tiny laughed before turning to Ferret. "Search her."

He took his time, emptying Raylene's pockets and running his hands under her clothes. Her purse was in her truck. The map was in Gabe's. *Gabe.* She silently prayed that he'd show up here, instead of her property.

"Nothing," he said.

"Check the truck," Tiny demanded.

"My boyfriend has it." Raylene tried to block Ferret. "Let me call Gabe. He'll bring it, and you can leave us alone."

"You mean the boyfriend who's on his way?" Tiny snorted and signaled to Ferret that he should search Raylene's Ford.

With him gone, Raylene considered her odds against Tiny and Stringy. She wished she had something she could use as a weapon, and scanned her immediate area as discreetly as possible. During the commotion, Gunner had wandered closer to his stall. The curry comb sat on the mounting block, but Raylene didn't think it was capable of doing any real damage. Her fear was she'd only antagonize the trio and they'd take out their anger on Harper. Whatever she did had to be enough of a distraction to give Harper time to make a run for it. Before she had any more time to contemplate it, Ferret came back, holding her purse.

"It's not in here, or anywhere in her truck," he said.

"Give me that." Tiny swiped Raylene's handbag and started sifting through it herself.

In her frightened state, Raylene couldn't estimate how much time had passed since Drew had left. An hour? Ninety minutes? Something like that. She held out hope that when Harper didn't show up home he'd come looking for her. Sneaking a glance, Raylene was surprised to find that Harper was holding it together. Stringy no longer had his arm around her, and she'd managed to put a half-foot distance between them. Raylene tried to communicate with her using her eyes.

When I say go, you run! Don't look back, just get help.

Harper gave Raylene an imperceptible nod. Good girl. Now Raylene had to come up with something. What would Gabe or Logan do? Who was she kidding? They'd beat the living daylights out of all three of them. None of them appeared to have a weapon, and if it wasn't for Harper, Raylene would've taken her chances by hightailing it out of there.

Tiny threw the purse at Raylene. "Where is it, bitch?"

"I told you, my boyfriend has it. Just let me call him and you can have it."

Ferret looked at Tiny, and Tiny's lips curved up in a sick smile that made Raylene's blood curdle. "Fine. I'll wait here with you, and these two will take your little friend to a secure location. She doesn't go free until I safely have the map."

No way in hell was Raylene letting the two men take Harper anywhere. Furthermore, she didn't believe Tiny. Neither of them was going free, otherwise she and Harper would blow the whistle and the authorities would nab Tiny and her two friends while they dug for the gold.

"That won't work," Raylene said. "She and I stay together, that's nonnegotiable." Probably not the best idea to challenge three psychopaths, but what choice did she have? She wasn't leaving Harper alone with any of them.

That's when she saw it. A pitchfork leaning against the wall next to the mounting block. How she'd missed it before, Raylene didn't know. It was less than three feet away. All she had to do was stretch out her arm and grab it. But could she wield it against the others and hold them off long enough for Harper to get away? And did she have the stomach to actually stab someone with it? To assure Harper's safety she thought she could...no, she knew she could. No one was going to hurt that sweet little girl. No one.

Stringy turned slightly to say something to Tiny and that's when Raylene made her move. She lunged forward, clutched the handle of the pitchfork, and brandished it like a sword, jabbing it first at Stringy. Then she swept it through the air, thrust-and-parry style, at the other two.

"Run!" she shouted to Harper, who faltered at first, then took off out of the barn as fast as her small legs would carry her.

Ferret started to go after her, but Raylene stuck him with one of the prongs of the pitchfork, buying Harper more time. He yelped, which brought the other two to action.

All Harper had to do was make it across the road and to the first house she saw. *Go, Harper, go!*

With the three of them coming at her at the same time, it was difficult to keep them herded together inside pitchfork range. But in her desperation, she was able to swiftly sweep the pitchfork in wide arcs, jabbing at each one of them as they individually dove for her. *Just a few more seconds*, she told herself as her arms began to tire from the weight of the pitchfork and the constant motion. Just a few more seconds to help Harper get to safety, then she'd deal with the fallout.

She pierced Stringy hard enough to draw blood and tried to stick him again, hoping that if she could incapacitate at least two of them she could get away, too. It was a tactical error, because while she focused on Stringy, Tiny managed to move out of range, circling around like a pouncing tiger. Raylene pivoted to fend off Tiny, tripped over the mounting block, and went down with a hard thud, nearly knocking the wind out of her. The pitchfork went flying and suddenly there was a pistol pointed at her head. Where had that come from?

"Get up," Ferret said as Stringy ran outside.

Raylene slowly rose, trying to catch her breath.

"She's gone." Stringy came in and threw Raylene against the barn stall. "You stupid bitch."

"What do you mean she's gone?" Tiny said. "She's probably hiding in the trees. Go out there and look again."

Stringy went to do Tiny's bidding, leaving absolutely no doubt in Raylene's mind that she was the boss of this rag-tag operation.

"By now she's called the police," Raylene said, hoping upon hope it was true. "You better leave before they get here."

Tiny backhanded her again, and this time Raylene's lip started to bleed.

"We've got to go." Tiny took the gun from Ferret and poked the muzzle in Raylene's gut. "You're coming with us."

Apparently, Stringy also realized that with Harper gone they were in deep shit, because he rushed into the barn, frantic. "She's nowhere, man. We've got to move out."

"We'll take her truck." Tiny waved the gun at Raylene, motioning for her to lead the way.

They got outside and Tiny held out her hand for the keys.

"I don't have them," Raylene said. They were in the purse Tiny threw at her but she was trying to stall, knowing that getting in the truck with them would be the kiss of death.

Tiny nudged her head at Stringy. "Find them in the barn."

"Are you like her man slave?" Raylene asked, trying to create a division.

She got a sharp elbow in her side from Tiny. "Shut your stupid blond mouth." Tiny turned to Stringy. "Go!"

Stringy trotted off and returned a few seconds later with Raylene's fob.

"Get in the passenger seat." Tiny aimed the gun at Raylene's head. "You two ride in the bed and keep down."

It was illegal to ride in the open bed of a pickup, and Raylene's only hope was that Rhys or one of Nugget PD's other cops would pull them over and she could scream the truck down. But the likelihood of that happening was next to nil. She presumed Tiny wouldn't be driving Raylene's truck down Main Street or taking any of the other major roads.

Tiny got in the driver's seat, headed south past the turnoff to Raylene's property, and hung a left on a winding county access road. Raylene didn't think it had an official name, but everyone up here called it Dover Trail. It was a rarely used byway to Lake Davis; it usually washed out in the winter from rain, snow, and mudslides. There was nothing up here, as far as she knew. Maybe a few deserted trailers and a couple of fishing cabins.

Gabe would never think to look for her here, and the sad truth was the people who might wouldn't care that she was missing. As soon as Tiny and company figured out that the map to Levi's Gold was a useless piece of crap, they'd kill her and bury her body in the woods.

"How'd you know about the map?" she asked Tiny, who had one eye on the rearview.

"Did I ask you to talk? No. So shut the hell up."

Raylene noted the outline of the gun in Tiny's ratty pocket—the pocket next to the driver's door. Her only hope was to make Tiny crash and, in the confusion, grab it. But before she could devise a workable plan, Tiny pulled off onto a dirt road that wound through the forest. Raylene had never seen it before. The road—you couldn't even call it that—was in worse shape than Dover Trail, rutted so badly even her all-wheel drive bounced and hurled until Raylene thought her truck axles would break.

"Where are we going?"

Tiny's fist connected with Raylene's cheek so fast Raylene didn't see it coming. "What did I tell you about talking?"

The woman was really starting to piss Raylene off. But her face throbbed so hard she kept her mouth shut. Tiny drove about a mile more, then skidded to a halt in front of a dense thicket of overgrown brambles. Other than that, there was nothing there but trees. The two men jumped down from the truck and the gun appeared in Tiny's hand again.

"Get out."

Raylene did what she was told and tried to focus on her surroundings instead of the burning pain in her cheek. She thought she could smell the lake, but the trees made it difficult to see. There was more snow on the ground here than there'd been at Sierra Heights, but Raylene chalked that up to the area not getting much sunlight. It didn't seem as if they'd climbed any higher into the mountains. By Raylene's estimation, they'd driven less than fifteen minutes, and, given the rugged terrain, they couldn't be far from where they'd started.

Tiny jabbed her in the back, indicating that she should follow Stringy and Ferret, who had disappeared through a break in the brambles. There was an old blue Chevy Impala parked in front of a shack so rundown Raylene was surprised it was still standing. Stringy opened the front door, and it was just as bad on the inside. Exposed siding where electrical wires poked through, floors that had been eaten down to the foundation by critters or termites, and a ceiling where you could see daylight.

Despite the cabin's condition, the trio had made themselves right at home. An open can of Vienna sausages sat on a three-legged table and a couple of bedrolls lay on the floor. There was a pile of equipment in the corner, which included her pickax.

"Sit." Tiny pushed her into a folding chair.

Ferret swiped the can of sausages off the table as if Raylene, in the midst of fearing being murdered—or worse—would find them so overwhelmingly irresistible she'd gobble them up. The idiot should be more concerned about the pickax. It wasn't a match for the gun, but she could do some real damage with it—if she could only reach the handle.

"We need those numbers," Tiny said, and Raylene squinted with confusion. "Did you hear me, Blondie? We need the numbers."

"I don't know what you're talking about. I already told you, my boyfriend has the map. He can drop it off, or meet you somewhere with it."

This time, Tiny pressed the muzzle of the handgun into Raylene's forehead. "You're not listening, Blondie. We're not calling your boyfriend. Give us the numbers."

"I honestly don't know what numbers you're talking about."

"The numbers on the fucking map." Stringy pulled Raylene out of the chair and slammed her against the door. "We know you got to it before we did. We spent all night digging, wasting our goddamn time, and I'm sick of freezing my ass off in this piece-of-shit shed. So stop dicking us around and give us the damn numbers. By now you've memorized them, so stop with the 'I don't know what you're talking about,' because we both know that you do."

Suddenly, she remembered the chicken scratch at the bottom of the map, the scrawl she and Gabe had thought were meaningless doodles. But what did that have to do with anything? Longitude and latitude? Some sort of a location key?

"All I have is the map my father left me. If you say there are numbers on it, I believe you. But I never paid any attention to them. Even if I had them, the authorities are looking for me. They'll stake out the property where the gold is; you can't go back there without getting caught. Your only hope is to let me go."

Tiny laughed. "Either you're a good actress or you're the dumbest blonde I ever met." She pushed Raylene back into the chair and stuck her face so close their noses were almost touching. "We already have the gold, we just need the numbers. We couldn't find them in the ground where they were supposed to be buried with the map. So give them up. Now!"

"What do you mean you have the gold?" Raylene didn't care. At this point they could have everything she owned as long as she walked away from this alive. But she was so confused she didn't know how to help herself.

"Enough of this bullshit," Stringy said, and belted Raylene in the side of the head. "I'm going to keep hitting you until you give us the numbers. When I get tired of that, I'm going to start shooting. First your toes, then your fingers."

He slugged her again, this time so hard it knocked her out of the chair. She was starting to feel dizzy and nauseous, like maybe she had a concussion.

"All right, all right." She held her head. "I'll give you the numbers, but you have to give me some kind of guarantee that you'll let me go."

Stringy pulled his foot back. It was the last thing she saw before everything went black.

Chapter 21

It amazed Gabe how fast everyone had come together to organize, but he was afraid it wasn't fast enough. According to what he'd learned from Harper, Raylene's captors hadn't done anything to hide their identities. As soon as they learned Raylene didn't have the map, they'd have no further use for her. Gabe knew what that meant, and it made him shudder. He'd never felt more powerless than he did now.

The worst part was they could be anywhere. He figured they had at least a forty-minute lead time, and no one knew what direction they'd gone. Their only hope was that they'd stayed in the area.

"We're trying to locate her position through the GPS in her truck," Rhys said. "Unfortunately, it'll take a little time."

"We don't have time." Gabe felt his shirt sticking to his back. It was thirty degrees out and he was sweating. Extractions were his specialty, but for the first time in his life the stakes were so high he was filled with a paralyzing fear. "Let me talk to Harper."

"Gabe, she told us everything she knows." Rhys paced the floor. Every one of his officers had been called in, including Jake. Despite Jake's issues with Raylene, he hadn't balked at working the case.

It was a small-town department, but Rhys and his people were pros.

"Chief." Connie popped her head into Rhys' office. "Clay and Lucky are in the lobby. They want to head up a search and rescue. What do you want me to tell them?"

"Send them back."

Rhys waited for them to file in and closed the door. "I appreciate your offer, fellas, but this is a police operation."

"I thought I'd take the plane up and see if I can spot her truck."

Gabe knew Clay was a former Navy fighter pilot and owned a couple of planes. He was all for the idea. It was better than nothing, and he didn't give a rat's ass about protocol—not when Raylene's life was in danger. "I think he should do it."

"What happens if they hear Clay buzzing around, spook, and do something rash?" Rhys didn't have to say what he meant by "rash." Gabe knew.

"Look, because of Raylene, my stepdaughter's safe and sound. I can't sit around doing nothing."

Lucky nodded. "I was thinking a couple of us could go out on horseback, search the hard-to-get-to places in the backcountry. Flynn's already getting the trailer ready."

"This isn't a lost hiker," Rhys said. "These are dangerous people."

"We can handle ourselves." Lucky pushed off the door. "Knowing Raylene, she's mouthed off enough that they can't wait to get rid of her."

Gabe got in Lucky's face. He needed to punch something, and Lucky had just made himself the perfect target. "You think that's helpful, asshole?"

Lucky held up his hands. "I didn't mean anything by it. It's my way of dealing with a stressful situation. I wouldn't be here if I didn't care what happened to her. She tried to make amends by selling me her property for a song and I told her to go to hell. This anger I have…I'm letting it go." He let out a breath. "Let's find her."

Gabe didn't know what Lucky was talking about, and frankly he didn't care. They were wasting time in Rhys' office. "I'm out of here."

"Where you going, Gabe?" Rhys tried to block him. "You're just planning to aimlessly search for her?"

"Better than sitting around here with my thumb up my ass. What about the backcountry where you first spotted them—we're all on the same page that it's the same people, right?"

Rhys and Jake nodded. "I've got Wyatt out there and Sloane on the other side of Sierra Heights," Rhys said.

"Sounds like a good enough spot to start." He headed out and Clay caught up with him.

"We can cover more ground in my plane."

"Works for me. Is it at your ranch?"

"Nervino. Want to follow me?"

"Let me swing by L&G first and grab some equipment." A chute, because he wasn't waiting for Clay to land if and when they spotted Raylene's truck.

Twenty minutes later he was at the airport, boarding Clay's Piper Cub. Clay used the antique plane to scan the mountains for his cattle. It was a sweet aircraft, and under normal circumstances Gabe would've liked to spend more time checking it out.

Unlike most planes, the Cub's seats were tandem instead of next to each other. The captain piloted the aircraft from the back seat, another idiosyncrasy.

Clay started the engine outside from the prop, pulled blocks away from the front tires, and wedged himself inside the cockpit before taking off. Gabe presumed Clay had worked out a flight plan before Gabe got there with his gear.

From the front, he had a bird's-eye view of the mountains and valleys. But, like the cliché went, spotting Raylene's truck would be like finding a needle in a haystack. There were a lot of pickups in these parts.

"Any ideas where we should start?" Gabe asked. Clay was the local; presumably, he'd know the best hiding places.

"I say we work from Sierra Heights, south. It's a lot of territory to cover, but that's where I'd go if I needed to lay low."

"Roger that."

They flew low, about two thousand feet above ground. That was the beauty of a Cub, and probably why Clay had chosen it for ranch work.

"Thanks for doing this," Gabe said. Clay wasn't a member of Raylene's fan club either, but he was a standup guy.

"We take care of our own here. And according to Harper, Raylene took on all three of those bozos so my stepdaughter could get away. Emily and Drew…well, you can imagine."

"I'm glad she got away. How's she doing otherwise?" Gabe would imagine Harper was pretty traumatized.

"Better than you would expect. She's mostly worried about Raylene. To hear it from Harper, Raylene was like a mama grizzly, putting herself between Harper and those men. To tell you the truth, it surprised me. The Raylene I used to know looked out for herself. Period."

All the bad-mouthing had started to irritate Gabe. As far as he was concerned, if anyone really knew Raylene they would've seen an abused young woman.

You can't go around telling people how to rear their kids. Owen's words rang in his ears. Maybe not, but Raylene had become a product of her surroundings. And had turned herself around without anyone's help. She was something. People around here didn't know it, but Gabe did.

"What was Lucky talking about when he said she offered to sell her land to him for a song?"

"First I heard of it." Clay handed him a pair of binoculars. "Keep your eyes peeled."

They flew over the tops of trees, giving Gabe a filtered view below. "What are those houses down there?" He thought he recognized the geography. It was somewhere between Grizzly Peak and Sierra Heights.

"We're coming up on the stables. I wanted to start there and work our way out."

"Good plan." Gabe trained the binoculars on the ground. As they got farther away from Sierra Heights there were fewer homes to see and the land became more rugged. Nugget was surrounded by remote pockets of fields, forests, streams, and lakes. And nothingness for miles and miles. So many places to hide that it boggled the mind. And for all he knew they were holed up in town at the Lumber Baron.

"Rhys spotted them the first time not far from your area, up in the hills."

Gabe drew a map in his head. If they were talking about the same people, which seemed all but certain, they'd lost their backpack on Drew Matthews' property, had broken into Raylene's truck at the farmhouse, and had been to her land at least twice. All three locations were just a few miles apart.

Gabe theorized that Raylene's abductors must've been watching her to know she was at the Sierra Heights stables alone with Harper. There'd never been any evidence that they'd traveled in a vehicle—no tire tracks, no engine noise the night Raylene caught them at the farm, no sign of a deserted car at the barn—which meant they were on foot and had been camping out somewhere within a few miles' radius of all three locations. With wheels they could've gone anywhere, but Gabe didn't think they would. Roaches typically crawled back to their hidey-holes.

"You got a map?" Gabe asked Clay.

"In there." Clay nudged his head at a flight bag. "There's land and aerial, take your pick."

Gabe found a pen, grabbed a land map, and spread it out on his lap. He immediately found Sierra Heights and used it as a reference to pinpoint Logan and Annie's farm and Raylene's two hundred acres, then drew a circle, representing three miles around all three locations.

"I think they're somewhere in this vicinity." He handed Clay the map with his scribbles. "Can you find it from the air?"

"Not a problem. But a good portion of what you've got there is Lake Davis." Clay pointed to the blue on the map.

Good, less land to cover. "What's out there besides the lake?" Gabe had gone fishing there a few times with Logan and a local arson investigator named Aidan McBride, but, being relatively new to Nugget, he didn't know the area as well as Clay.

"Not much. There's a trailer park where a few railroad workers used to live, but it's vacant now, and in bad disrepair. Rhys has been all over the city to clean it up. Other than a couple of hunting and fishing cabins, I can't think of anything else. You think they could be holding her in one of the trailers?"

"Yep. I'll let Rhys know what I'm thinking; you circle." Gabe shot off a text.

"What about spooking them if they hear the Cub? You heard what Rhys said."

Gabe weighed the risk. To his mind, the bad guys had been spooked the minute Harper got away—she could identify them. Every second that ticked by was borrowed time for Raylene. They couldn't afford to tiptoe.

"As soon as we think we're close, I'm going in." He tightened the straps on his parachute harness.

Clay shook his head. "This ain't a free fall from a Blackhawk, buddy. You ever jump from a Cub before?"

Gabe grinned. "There's a first time for everything."

Clay didn't try to dissuade him, though he shook his head again. Gabe went back to peering through the binocs.

"What's that?" Gabe pointed at what appeared to be a wooden structure built into the side of a mountain.

"An old mineral mine."

"A good place to hide?"

"I don't think so. The front's completely open, and it's not far off the main drag to the lake." Clay made a slow turn. "See that? That's the trailer park."

"Can you get a little lower without drawing too much attention?" Gabe wanted to see if he could find Raylene's truck.

Clay slid him a get-real glance. They were already low enough to be loud. Besides, the tall pines made it dangerous.

"From up here the place looks like a ghost town," Gabe said. "What's that over there?" In the distance, the sun glinted off blacktop.

"The highway, and past that, the railroad. I'd say they're less than a mile as the crow flies from the trailer park. The workers used to walk."

"So maybe not the best place to hide."

Clay shrugged. "Around here, you can still be close to civilization and feel remote as hell." He circled around the park again. "Take another look."

They were too far away for him to use his Range-R radar device to detect motion in any of the trailers, but he didn't see anything to indicate signs of life.

"What's closer to the lake?"

"A campground, and those fishing and hunting shacks I told you about."

"Let's take a look over there."

Clay turned the nose of the Cub toward the lake and pointed at a densely wooded area. "I'd be looking down in there. Fishing shacks tend to be empty this time of year. A while back, a wanderer OD'd in one of the cabins around here. His skeletal remains floated down the Feather River and wound up not far from Nugget High School."

Gabe kept his eyes rooted on the area, but it was difficult to see with all the trees. "Where's the best place to let me out?" At this point, he'd be better off on the ground.

"Not a lot of good places in the forest. Our best bet is the lake."

Gabe had spent enough time in the ocean to be unfazed by a relatively small fishing lake, even if it was the dead of winter. "Let's do it." They were running out of time.

"You sure about this?"

He'd never been surer about anything in his entire military career. Failure wasn't an option. He was bringing Raylene home…her life depended on it. "Yep. Do me a favor, as soon as I'm on the ground, have someone get ahold of Logan. He's staying at the Honua Kai in Maui."

He had no idea what kind of shape Raylene would be in when he found her, but she'd need her family. And him. He'd be there every step of the way.

"Will do." Clay flew over the lake, and to anyone watching they looked like sightseers. At least for now.

"If you know of a hidden area where I can jump, that would be good."

"Already on it." Clay directed Gabe's attention to a sandy bar that reached out like a finger from a corner of the lake to a strip of land less than a football field from the Feather River. It would be an excellent place for him to land. "That look okay to you?"

"Perfect." Gabe unhooked his seat belt, double checked his gear, and prepared to jump from the open cockpit. He collected the map and stuffed a few other necessities, including his Sig, into his tactical vest. "Just give me the signal."

A short time later, he hit the ground. He reached for his compass and took a few seconds to get his bearings. He wanted to go back to where those fishing shacks were. His phone vibrated with a text, and he held his breath. Maybe they'd found her.

The message was from Rhys. **Where are you? We may have gotten a hit from her GPS.**

Gabe punched in his coordinates and the question: **Where?**

In the general vicinity of where you are, at least according to the last time the satellite got a ping off her GPS. That was about thirty minutes ago.

Shit. Anything could've happened between then and now. Hell, with the right kind of transportation they could be all the way to the Mexican border. Gabe plugged in Raylene's coordinates. According to his GPS, it was about a klick away.

Roger that, he wrote back, and cut a path through the woods.

Rhys signed off with, **Sending backup.**

If Raylene was there, Gabe wouldn't need backup.

* * * *

Raylene's head pounded as she watched her three captors fight. She'd done her best to sow discord in the group, and now they were turning on each other like a pack of angry wolves. Perhaps it hadn't been the best strategy, because Ferret was on a homicidal rampage and Stringy wanted to keep Raylene alive so he could continue to pummel her until she "broke."

She didn't know how much more she could take. She was pretty sure she had a few broken ribs, a concussion, and her face was so bruised and beaten it felt numb. She wanted Gabe. That was her only thought as Stringy delivered one punishing blow after another.

Even though giving them the numbers they so desperately wanted would be akin to a death sentence—they would no longer need her around—she would've done it if she knew what they were. She had never realized that the digits at the bottom of the map were anything other than illegible handwriting.

Tiny and friends obviously knew something she didn't. She'd tried to ascertain where they'd gotten their information—or the gold—but hadn't been given a clue. And really, what did it matter? Every second that passed, she was living on borrowed time. Even Ferret, who appeared to have the IQ of a hazelnut, realized they couldn't remain here much longer. None of them had gotten the memo that Raylene was public enemy number one in Nugget, and they believed there was a huge manhunt on the rise.

The only person she knew for sure was searching for her was Gabe. He was the light at the end of the darkest tunnel she'd ever been forced to walk through. It was odd how the universe worked. She'd come here never expecting more than to celebrate her brother's wedding, to make amends to the people she'd hurt, and to shut the book on her past. And in walked Gabe Moretti. Even now, she could hear his New Jersey accent. *Cawfee*. That deep laugh that seemed to reverberate from the bottom of his stomach. And the way he looked at her, really looked. Like she was special, instead of head case Raylene Rosser: self-indulged, backstabbing bitch.

"I say we take one more crack at her," Stringy said. "If she doesn't give it up, we move to plan B."

No one had to tell Raylene what plan B was.

"We don't have time," Tiny said. "I say we cut our losses and get the hell out of here."

In their debate over what to do next, they'd forgotten Raylene, who sat propped up in the folding chair like a punching bag. She moved her legs, an experiment to see if they still worked. Then she tried her arms. The movement made her chest ache something fierce, but she still had a little life left in her and she didn't want to die. She wanted to welcome Logan and Annie's baby into the world. She wanted to raise the best cutting horses in California. But most of all, she wanted to tell Gabe that she'd fallen for him. Even if he hadn't fallen for her, she wanted him to know how she felt. How amazing he was.

While Tiny and the boys continued to fight, Raylene made her move. The gun, which sat on the windowsill across the room, was too far away. But the pickax was within reach, just a few stretches in front of her. All she had to do was lean forward and grab it with both hands. *Stretch*, she told herself. *Stretch*.

With her eyes swollen and her head muzzy, it took all her focus and strength to wrap her hands around the wooden shaft, stand up, and swing the pick with all her might. She heard herself let out a primal scream and, like a deranged animal, began launching her attack. Hacking and hammering in wild strokes, blindly bludgeoning anyone in her way. The only goal was to get out. She ran to the door, made it outside and into the sunshine.

Lake. Houses. People. Gabe.

Those were her only thoughts as she stumbled past the brambles that hid the cabin from view. She followed the crude road they'd driven from Dover Trail and ran toward the water.

Lake. Houses. People. Gabe.

It became a silent mantra as she tore through the woods, her body protesting at every step. Her lungs devoid of air, gulping oxygen like it was water to a person dying of thirst. But she could hear them, yelling, chasing after her. They were so close she considered falling on the ground and begging for mercy. No, she wouldn't let them kill her while she pleaded for her life. Gabe would tell her to keep running...to keep fighting.

She pushed forward, envisioning Harper. Sweet little Harper. Raylene wanted to teach her how to ride. And Lucky and Tawny's girl, Katie. She wanted to make that donation to Children's Hospital in their name. And Donna Thurston...she'd miss the witch. What about Cecilia? Raylene would never get to tell her she was sorry face-to-face. Or Jake, for getting up in his grill while she was drunk. And what about one hundred and twenty days sober? She'd never make that milestone.

She heard a twig snap, heavy breathing, and sneakers beating the ground behind her. They were closing in and she had nowhere to go, nowhere to hide. Her lungs felt ready to collapse and her legs were caving beneath her. Dizzy, she was so dizzy. But Gabe was in her head, telling her to keep going.

Go, go, go!

Where was the lake? She couldn't find the lake. Just lots and lots of trees. And snow and dirt. And then the earth was pulling her down, her body so light it was like floating.

Boom. Boom. Boom, boom, boom.

The blood, there was so much blood. And sleep, blessed sleep.

Chapter 22

Gabe hated hospitals. The smells, the waiting, the sadness. He shifted in his seat, anxious for an update. Four people had had to pull him off that son of a bitch who'd fired at Raylene. The others…all three of them were lucky to be alive. If Rhys hadn't gotten there when he had, they wouldn't be.

He wanted them to pay for what they'd done to Raylene. The fact that she'd been able to get away under that kind of duress was nothing short of a miracle.

"She's going to be fine," said Clay, who'd been good enough to sit vigil with him while the doctors gave Raylene an MRI and a battery of other tests. "Logan and Annie are on their way home. They're at the airport, waiting to catch a plane to Reno."

"Does Rhys know anything about these jokers yet?"

Clay hitched his shoulders. "He'll get whatever he can."

A couple came into the waiting room, and Clay got to his feet and introduced Drew and Kristy Matthews. Gabe had maybe met them in passing once or twice, but he didn't recognize them. Truthfully, all his energy was focused on Raylene.

Drew pumped Gabe's hand. "How is she?"

"Beat up, but okay. How's Harper?"

"Better now that she knows Raylene's safe. We're deeply indebted to her. What she did for Harper…" He paused, too emotional to continue.

"Ray's tough." And she was good as gold. Better than anyone gave her credit for.

"Is there anything we can do?" Kristy took Gabe's hand in hers. "You name it and we'll do it. Contact relatives…friends. Anything at all."

"Her brother and his wife are on their way. I think we've got everything covered for now, but thank you."

"Harper would like to see her," Drew said. "Emily's with her now, but as soon as Raylene can have visitors, would it be okay?"

"Sure." Gabe had appointed himself Raylene's point person, going as far as to tell the medical staff he was her fiancé. Otherwise, they wouldn't give him any information. "As long as the MRI is okay, they're planning to release her today." Which was insane, in his opinion.

"That's great."

"You could bring her by the farmhouse." But Gabe wondered if that was such a good idea for a kid. Raylene was in pretty rough shape.

"Thank you," Drew said. "I think she needs to see for herself that Raylene's okay."

"You may want to give it a few days, for her face to heal," he said, and saw Drew flinch. Apparently, word that Raylene had taken a bad beating hadn't spread through the mighty Nugget grapevine yet.

Shortly after Gabe had come to the rescue, Rhys, Jake, and two other Nugget PD officers had responded. They'd arrested Raylene's attackers and called for two ambulances. The gunman hadn't gone totally unscathed—Gabe shot him in the arm just before he tried to pull the trigger on Raylene. He'd cried like a little bitch, and was somewhere in the hospital under guard, getting treated.

Everything after that was a blur. At the time, Gabe's only focus had been on getting Raylene the hell out of there. She'd been barely conscious on the ride over, incoherently muttering about love and kindness and how Gabe was the best man she knew. He'd been too shaken to pay attention, and he was pretty sure the paramedics had put a painkiller in her IV, making her goofy.

"We're staying a few more nights, just to be here if Harper needs us," Drew said. "I know Emily is making Raylene a big pot of soup, but if you need anything else, like Kristy said, don't hesitate to call us." He pulled a business card out of his wallet and scribbled a phone number on the back.

Clay walked them to the bank of elevators and an older guy in a white coat came out of a pair of double doors.

"Are you Gabe Moretti?"

Gabe got to his feet. "I am. Is Raylene out?"

"She is, and she's asking for you. Come on back."

"Did the tests come out okay?"

"They did, and we're cutting Miss Rosser loose. I wrote her a prescription for a painkiller, and she should see her primary physician in a week if the swelling doesn't start going down. She should avoid taking ibuprofen for forty-eight hours, ice the ribs, and get plenty of rest."

Gabe wanted to say, "That's it?" In the teams, Raylene's injuries would've been nothing. A few broken ribs and a busted-up face came with the territory, and was nothing compared to getting a limb blown off by an IED, or worse. But Raylene had never been in the military, had never been trained in SERE or how to withstand torture. And make no mistake about it: what those people had done to her was torture.

"Counseling?" Gabe asked.

"I would say as soon as possible. In the meantime, respect her boundaries. If she doesn't want to talk about it, don't push it."

Gabe nodded, feeling sick to his stomach. And pissed. All for some goddamn gold that didn't exist. Rhys had warned him to stay away, but right now Gabe wanted to find out what floor the piece-of-shit gunman was on and wring his damned neck.

He followed the doctor to Raylene's room. She was sitting on the hospital table in green scrubs. Her own clothes were covered in blood. Other than the chips of blue that shone through her swollen eyelids, her face was so bruised it was hardly recognizable. All Gabe wanted to do was hold her, but he forced himself to give her space. After the ordeal she'd been through, she might not want to be touched.

"You ready to go home, Ray?"

She slowly nodded, and, despite his best efforts to give her breathing room, he gathered her up in his arms. "I've never been so scared in my life, Ray."

"I knew you would come. I knew you'd save me," she whispered.

"No, baby, you saved yourself. I'm so freaking proud of you."

She rested her face against his chest. "I thought I was going to die, that I'd never see you again."

"I'm right here, sweetheart." He grazed the top of her head with his lips, never wanting to let her go. "You're safe now. Harper's safe. All because of you. You done good, Ray. You gave me a heart attack, but you done good."

"They had our pickax, Gabe. I stabbed them with it. I think I went a little crazy."

He laughed, even though none of it was funny. The idea of her having to defend herself against three hardened criminals made him want to slam his fist through the walls. But she needed levity and comfort now, not his fury. "Let's go home, Ray."

When a nurse came with a wheelchair, he had a difficult time releasing Raylene, but he held her hand the whole way down the elevator. According to the ward clerk, Clay had gone home. As soon as they got to the lobby, he dashed across the parking lot to pull his SUV up to the circular driveway and helped Raylene get into the front seat.

She fell asleep on the drive home. Gabe carried her inside when they got to Logan and Annie's farmhouse and fixed her a bed on the sofa, afraid she'd wake up if he climbed the stairs. He sat in an overstuffed chair by the fireplace so he could watch over her and send a few texts while she rested, including one to Logan to let him know they were home. Next, he built a fire, wanting her to feel warm and safe.

Not ten minutes after getting a good blaze going, there was a knock on the front door. Donna and Emily clutched boxes, bags, and baskets full of food.

"You planning to feed everyone aboard the USS *Dewey?*" He let them in and helped them with their packages.

"How is she?" Emily peeked around the corner at Raylene lying on the couch.

"She's asleep." He put his finger over his lips, signaling that they should whisper. "Shoot, I forgot to ice her ribs and face."

"Don't wake her," Donna said. "You can do that later."

It was best to do it as soon as possible, but, yeah, he'd let her sleep. They moved into the kitchen and Donna muscled him out of the way like she owned the place, putting a big pot on the stove and making room in the refrigerator. Emily began unloading the dishwasher.

"I can do that," he said.

"That's okay, you focus on Raylene. We made chicken soup. Both of you need to eat."

Donna finished unpacking the food they'd brought. "I'll set the table."

"Clay said she's pretty beaten up." Emily put a stack of plates in the cupboard and turned to face Gabe, her eyes tearing up. "What she did for Harper...there are no words."

"Drew said Harper's doing okay."

Emily sighed. "She seems to be handling it better than Drew and me, if you want to know the truth. Now that she knows Raylene's safe, she's treating the whole ordeal as if it were a big adventure, like one of her Gallagher Girls novels. When I think about all the ways it could've—"

Donna stopped her. "That's why you shouldn't think about it." She came over and rubbed Emily's back. "Harper's safe, Raylene's safe, and Gabe and Rhys caught the bad guys."

There was another knock at the door and Gabe went to see who it was. Lucky, Tawny, and Cecilia. Gabe ushered them into the kitchen.

"Where's Jake?" Gabe asked.

"He's at the station," Cecilia said. "That's all I know."

He and Rhys were probably still interrogating Raylene's abductors. Gabe suspected Cecilia knew more than she let on but had been sworn to keep her mouth shut. In the teams, everything they did was top secret, which could be awfully tough on a marriage. Gabe didn't think cops had to be as close-lipped about their cases, but they also couldn't have their spouses spreading information all over town.

"How is she?" Cecilia asked.

"She's hanging in there." Gabe grabbed a few chairs from the dining room. A day ago, these same people would've crossed the road to avoid Raylene. Now, she was the town hero.

Cecilia turned to Emily. "Jake said Harper's been amazing."

"She's a brave girl, our Harper is." Donna pulled a jug of apple cider from the fridge, got a pot off the rack, and began heating the juice on the stovetop. "And Raylene, she always was—"

"I always was what?" Raylene stood in the doorway, a blanket wrapped around her like a poncho. Her face was blown up like a balloon and had turned a multitude of colors, but she stuck her chin out and held it firm in challenge. "I always was what?"

"Tough as nails." Donna looked her in the eye and something passed between them. Maybe, like Owen, Donna had known more about Raylene's childhood than she wanted to admit, or maybe—just maybe—there was an apology in that gaze.

"Sit down, *mija*." Cecilia made room at the table for another chair.

"Let me get you something to eat." Emily ladled the chicken soup into a bowl.

Soon, the kitchen was a hive of activity, everyone rushing around to make Raylene comfortable.

"Did you really whack one of them with a pickax?" Lucky asked.

"Two of them," Raylene said, and Gabe tried to hide a smile.

She didn't appear to realize that her status had suddenly changed from town exile to town savior. He wondered if by tomorrow her place on the pecking order would revert back to leper.

* * * *

Monday, Drew called work and told them he wasn't coming in for the rest of the week. While Harper was treating the ordeal as a big adventure, and had even gone to school, he couldn't bear to leave her yet. He was having a difficult time letting her out of his sight for even a few minutes.

"Did you see this?" Kristy came into the kitchen with her tablet and showed Drew the headline in the *Nugget Tribune*: "Prodigal Daughter Saves Child, then Herself."

Drew scanned the story and chuckled.

"You're laughing; that's a good thing." Kristy gave him a hug.

"Have I told you how happy I am that you came this weekend...that you were here when this all went down?" She'd been a rock. Frankly, he didn't know what he would've done without her.

She'd shuttled back and forth between Sierra Heights and McCreedy Ranch at least a dozen times, making sure Harper was never alone and watching Paige while Emily and Clay dealt with Raylene's rescue and the aftermath. She'd gone with Drew and Harper to Quincy to identify two of the attackers while the third recovered in the hospital. And she'd called Harper's counselor, just in case their daughter needed to talk to someone outside the family.

"I'm glad I was here, Drew." She poured herself a glass of juice and joined him at the breakfast table. "To be candid, it was the first time I felt like part of this family." By "family," Drew knew she meant him and Harper.

"You were always part of it," he protested.

"I'm not blaming anyone." She held up her hands. "Honest. Under the best of circumstances, blending a family is difficult. And this...well, it was a unique situation." She forced a grim smile, because "unique" was a euphemism for what he and Emily had gone through during the years their daughter was missing. The odds of getting Harper back after all that time was truly nothing short of a miracle. "And as much as I want to be involved in Harper's transition, I understand that you and she need time to catch up and make up for years of missed bonding. It doesn't mean it hasn't been hard on me. At the risk of sounding like a child, I felt left out. Until this weekend." She sipped her juice and let out a breath. "It sounds awful, but it took what happened in the barn for me and Harper to really connect.

"She clung to me, Drew. After she ran home and you went to call the police, she clung to me. And it wasn't because I was the only person around. She knew she mattered to me and I mattered to her. In those few desperate moments, it clicked: I'm her family, I'm someone she can rely on, someone who will always love and protect her. It clicked, and the seismic shift in our relationship stuck, because things have been different between us ever since. I'm no longer an afterthought or a nuisance who takes you away from Harper. I'm someone who is important to her."

Drew swiped at a tear. Between the arrests and ensuring Harper's well-being, there'd been so much going on that Drew hadn't noticed. The truth was ever since reuniting with Harper, he'd been on his own shaky ground as far as reconnecting with his daughter. But while he struggled, Kristy had been relegated to outsider. He'd probably been as guilty of making her feel that way as Harper.

"We're all important to each other," he said, and reached across the table for her hand. "And you...you're my life, Kris. You're my everything."

Her eyes grew wet. "And you're mine. I know it's been rocky between us. The reason I came on Friday was to give you news, talk it out, and hopefully get back to where we were before Christmas." Before he'd been complicit in making her a third wheel. "Friday, Saturday, there was never a good time to talk, and then...Sunday."

When their world had been rocked. But thank God everyone had come out fine in the end.

"News?" he asked.

"News." Her face lit up like sunshine. "I'm glad you're sitting down, because you're not going to believe it. I'm pregnant! Or at least I think I am. I missed my period last week, chalked it up to stress from all the tension, then, on a lark, took a pregnancy test Friday morning. Positive."

Something in his chest moved, and for the first time since Harper came home, the prospect of having a baby wasn't fraught with complexities. It was just...joyful. So freaking joyful that his heart felt ready to burst. "But when? I thought we missed this month's window of opportunity."

She lifted her shoulders. "I'm thinking it was the night we skipped Wendy's dinner because we were fighting."

They'd had incredible make-up sex—the first time they'd been spontaneous in months. His lips tipped up and he couldn't stop smiling. "Well, I'll be damned. No IVF, no fertility monitor, just good old-fashioned sex."

"Just good old-fashioned sex." She laughed. "Are you happy? Be honest."

He pulled her up and danced her around the kitchen. "Happy doesn't even begin to describe it." Funny how life worked. He'd convinced himself that having another child would interfere with getting closer to the one he'd lost. But now, now that it was staring him in the face, it suddenly felt like this had always been the master plan.

There's room in your heart—in your life—for two children, take it from me. The day I met Justin and Cody was the day I started healing. Emily's words reverberated through his head. When had his ex-wife become so sage?

"Really? Because I'd gotten the impression that with Harper...that you weren't so gung ho about having a baby right now."

"I wasn't," he admitted. "At least, that's what my head was telling me. But a second ago, when you said the words *I'm pregnant*...my heart reacted in a way that was entirely different. I want this, Kris. I really, really want this."

She wrapped her arms around him and squeezed. "Good, because I have an idea."

"Yeah." He nuzzled her neck. "What's that?"

"I think we should move here full-time."

He pulled back and did a double take. Kristy had agreed to their current living situation for him, because of Harper, but it never would've been her first choice. She was an urban dweller by nature and loved their life in Silicon Valley.

"Hear me out." She laughed at his dubious expression. "It's cheaper to live here, and if we sell our house in Palo Alto, we'll have a nice cushion if I want to take a year or two off from work for the baby. With a newborn, I don't know how easy going back and forth will be. This way we'll eliminate that headache. We'll be here for Harper, and she'll be able to grow up with her new sister or brother. And despite what happened Sunday, obviously a fluke, this is a good place to raise children. Watching the way the community rallied around Harper and Raylene was nothing short of amazing."

There was no denying that Nugget was a tight-knit town. When Harper had gone missing, Drew's Bay Area neighbors had either looked at him and Emily with recrimination or had been too busy with their own go-go lives to offer succor. Here, the townsfolk stood together in times of need, even with someone as disliked as Raylene. Yep, they certainly took care of their own.

"And given your status as the best Internet lawyer in the land, I don't think you'll have a problem working remotely." She kissed him. "On the days you have to be in the Bay Area, I'll hold down the fort here. We could even buy a small apartment there. And who knows, maybe I'll hang out a shingle and take on a few clients here."

"You've got this all worked out, huh?" He kissed her back. Damn. They were having a baby.

"I want you to be happy, Drew. I want you to feel like you don't have to compromise when it comes to Harper, and I'm hoping you and Emily can find your way to giving her more freedom, even after what happened Sunday."

He exhaled, because the memory of his daughter running toward them, an expression of abject fear on her face, wasn't something he'd likely forget in the near future. But, yeah, she was right. They had to lighten up on the reins, or else Harper would grow up to be a complete neurotic.

"What do you say?" she asked.

"You'll be okay living here full-time?"

"The tradeoff will be worth it, and I'm planning to work hard to make friends here, join some groups, maybe do some pro bono work for that foundation Gia Treadwell founded, the one that helps struggling women get a leg up."

He started to say that Emily could introduce her around, help her find her footing, but stopped himself. Kristy needed to be independent from his ex-wife and carve out her own niche here in Nugget. He got that.

"We could always move back to the city if you hate it," he said. "But everything you've said makes sense. And, Kris, the idea of being here full-time for Harper, for our new baby..." He choked up a little and had to collect himself. "Thank you. Thank you for making the sacrifice."

She looped her arms around his neck and pulled him in until their foreheads were touching. "I'll let you in on a little secret: it's not much of sacrifice. I'll get to experience full-time motherhood, something we never could've afforded in the Bay Area. Besides that"—she paused for emphasis—"I've got everything I want right here."

And so did he.

Chapter 23

Raylene sat so close to Gabe she was practically in his lap. The fact that she'd had to identify Ferret and Tiny in a lineup was beyond ridiculous. Stringy at least had been caught in the act of trying to kill her, so no lineup for him. By the time the police got to the scene, Gabe had had Stringy down on the ground and trussed with his own belt like a runaway hog on fair day. The other two had tried to flee in their Impala, but had only gotten as far as Highway 70 before the police nabbed them.

"Just routine," Rhys said. "Rufus Hawkins is wanted in the home invasion homicide and is being extradited to Utah. The two yahoos you identified today will remain in county until their bail hearing and arraignment. My guess is they'll plead out and you'll never have to testify."

Raylene hoped so. Seeing them today had given her the willies. Gabe reached for her hand, lacing his fingers with hers. He'd stood by her side throughout both lineups. And though Tiny and Ferret were behind glass and under guard, just having Gabe there made her feel safe and confident. Sunday, he'd held her through the night, watching over her like her own personal guardian angel. Because of him she'd actually slept, burrowing into his side, feeling cocooned in his warmth and strength. At one point, she awoke, her head fuzzy from the painkillers, and thought to herself that this was love. Someone who was there for you through thick and thin.

He'd stood by her while she'd stared down a hostile town, had held her hand through awkward social events when the desire for a drink was sometimes stronger than her need to breathe, and had faced down a deranged gunman to save her life. He'd found a home for her horse and had spent hours digging for her gold when he hadn't even believed it existed.

"Did they tell you how they knew about the gold?" Raylene asked. Bits and pieces of her captivity had floated back to her throughout the night.

"Ray apparently bragged about it in prison," Rhys said. "Rufus' brother, Shane Hawkins, shared a cell with your dad the first year of his incarceration. He told Shane that he'd dug up the gold not long after he killed Gus Clamper, knowing that mounting a defense would be costly, and stashed the gold in his safe. Apparently he didn't take it out before selling the ranch to Gia Treadwell."

Raylene was still trying to wrap her head around the fact that Ray had dug up the gold and not told anyone but his cellmate. "They kept asking me for numbers. I had no idea what they were talking about."

Rhys nodded. "Rufus and company planned to break in to Gia and Flynn's house, but they needed the combination to the safe."

"The only safe I know about was Daddy's gun safe." By now, Gia and Flynn had to have cleaned out the safe and stored their own valuables. Raylene turned to Gabe. "I think that scrawl at the bottom of the map was the combination. But it doesn't make sense, because we all knew Daddy's gun safe combo, even Mom."

"I talked to Flynn this morning, and it wasn't the gun safe," Rhys said. "Gia was given the combination during the sale of the ranch. The safe was empty. Your dad had already cleaned it out."

"If he cleaned out his gun safe, then he certainly removed the gold before the house got sold," Gabe said, and Raylene had to agree.

The whole story was bizarre. After all these years, Ray digs up the gold, hides it in a safe, and forgets to cash in before he goes to prison. Raylene wasn't buying it.

"You have the map with you?" Rhys asked.

"It's in my SUV," Gabe said. "Why, you want to see it?"

"No, but Flynn does." Rhys turned to Raylene. "As your late father's estate attorney, he says it's his fiduciary duty to make sure you, Logan, and your mother get the gold…if it exists."

"You don't believe it does?" And if it was in Gia and Flynn's house, weren't they entitled to it? Finders keepers…

Rhys shrugged. "Inmates are known to tell tall tales in prison. Maybe Ray thought the story would buy him friends. In prison, safety comes in the company you keep."

"That would mean it's still in the ground," she said, and Gabe rolled his eyes.

"Before you start digging, I think you should pay a visit to Flynn over at the ranch. He wants to go through the house with you…look for any kind of hidden safe. You grew up there; if anyone would know where to search, it would be you."

"And Cecilia," Raylene said. Cecilia knew every nook and cranny from cleaning the ranch house all those years.

Rhys leaned back in his chair. "Good idea. I'll ask Jake to call her and see if she'd be willing to meet you over there. I'd like to put an end to this ridiculous Levi's Gold legend for once and for all."

Not as much as Raylene would. She'd almost died for that gold; the universe could at least allow her to reap its riches.

* * * *

A few hours later, a small crowd assembled at Flynn and Gia's house. It was weird for Raylene to think of the big, rustic ranch house as belonging to anyone else. For so long it had been her home, and before that the home of her ancestors. Everywhere she looked there were small changes. Her father's hunting trophies had been removed from the wall, as well as his prized Winchester rifle. Some of the heavy wooden furniture had been replaced with sleeker, more modern pieces. And a lot of abstract artwork filled the walls next to Ray's Western landscapes and cowboy paintings. It was Manhattan meets the Sierra Nevada, and while it wasn't Raylene's taste, she could understand how the juxtaposition of the old West with canvases covered in bold shapes and colors might appeal to someone with a more sophisticated sensibility.

In any event, it was gracious of Flynn and Gia to open their doors, allowing her to comb the house, hunting for Levi's Gold.

Someone had tipped off Harlee Roberts, who showed up with her camera and a laptop, presumably pumped to post a story on the *Nugget Tribune's* website as soon as they found the gold. Raylene suspected Rhys was her source, hoping an article would end the intrigue and keep any treasure hunters away from Nugget.

Cecilia had also come. If anyone knew where Ray hid his valuables, it would be Cecilia. Raylene had always suspected that big bad Ray had been afraid of Cecilia. As their housekeeper, she knew where all the skeletons were buried. But because of her financial restraints—a single mother, raising a son—she'd been forced to keep her mouth shut to keep her job.

"You have any ideas?" Raylene asked her. "It's not the gun safe."

"There are only two other safes that I'm aware of. One was in Ray's closet."

That seemed too obvious to Raylene. Wasn't the closet the first place robbers looked? But it was certainly worth a try.

"Is this the combination?" Gabe stepped forward with the map and showed Cecilia the tiny numbers scrawled at the bottom.

"I never knew the combination, *mijo*. But let's try."

"I hope it is," Flynn said. "Gia and I have been wanting to get into that safe since I moved in." He led Raylene and the rest of the crew into the master suite.

Her parents' former bedroom was different now. The heavy draperies had been replaced with blinds, the cowhides with modern area rugs, and the big rough-hewn log four-poster with a metal and wood platform bed. Any trace of Raylene's father had been stripped from the room. She could breathe in here for the first time in her life.

Flynn opened the closet, cleared a row of suits, and tossed them on the bed. "You want to do the honors?" he asked Raylene.

"Let Gabe do it." Her hands were shaking.

Gabe stepped forward and turned the dial on the safe the same way he did everything else—deftly, and with utter confidence and calm. When he got to the third number he winked at Raylene, and it felt like a hundred butterflies fluttered their wings in the pit of her stomach. She was supposed to be focusing on Levi's Gold, not on Gabe Moretti.

"Ready?"

"Do it," she said.

The safe door opened with ease and she held her breath. "Is it there? I can't look."

It felt like a thousand eyes were peering over her shoulder. Harlee began snapping pictures and Rhys pulled her back. "Anything, Gabe?"

"Let me see what we've got." He pulled a stack of paperwork from the safe.

"What is it?" Raylene moved closer.

"Deed to the house, insurance documents." Gabe continued to sort through the pile. "Some pictures." He stopped to focus on a photo of Logan graduating from BUD/S. "Well, I'll be damned."

"Let me see." Raylene took the picture to examine it. A tear leaked from her eye; a jumble of confused emotions swirled in her gut. "You think my dad was there?"

"Don't know. Someone had to have taken the picture. I doubt Maisy would've sent it to Ray. Maybe Nick, just to shove it in your old man's face. But it obviously meant something to Ray, because he kept it."

"I want to give it to Logan," Raylene said. "You think that's okay?"

"I don't see why not." Gabe gazed at the photo. "He was a handsome devil back then. Lord knows what Annie sees in him now."

Gabe went back to the paperwork. "No gold, Ray. Just stuff you don't want to lose in a fire."

"But the combination on the map matched. This has to be it." Raylene moved deeper into the closet to check the safe for any hidden compartments.

"I think your dad snowed everyone on this," Rhys said, ready to be done with the search.

"Where's the other safe?" Raylene asked Cecilia. It was probably futile—the combination matched this safe—but she wanted to explore every option before throwing in the towel.

"It's downstairs. Follow me, *mija*."

The entire entourage trailed Cecilia to the bottom floor. Like the rest of the house, there'd been a great deal of changes. Ray's man cave had been stripped of his hunting trophies, and the dark paneled wood had been painted a dove gray. The bar had been cleared of Ray's clutter, but remained mostly the same.

Cecilia lifted the bar gate, ducked under, and headed straight to the back bar. She ran her hand over the mirrored wall, found the spot she was looking for, and gave it a strong tap with her fist. And just like that, a hidden door popped open and a safe, similar to the one upstairs, appeared.

"I had no idea that was there." Flynn moved in to get a closer look. "Should we try the same combination?"

Raylene thought it was unlikely that her father would use the same number code twice. He'd been more careful about security matters than that. The fact that he had three freaking safes in his house, one so deeply concealed that even Flynn, a former FBI agent, hadn't found it, showed just how anal Ray had been.

"I say we give it a try," Gabe said. "If it doesn't work we'll figure out something else."

Raylene nodded and Gabe turned the dial. This time, she didn't hear the click at the end of the sequence and her heart dropped in disappointment.

Gabe studied the numbers on the map. "Raylene, what's your birthdate?"

She rattled off the month, day, and year and heard Gabe chuckle. "What?"

"This is your birthday backwards." He turned the map so she could see it. "He started with the year you were born, the day, then the month. Not particularly clever."

Yet she wouldn't have thought of it on her own. "Should we try it?" At this point, she was starting to think the whole thing was Ray's idea of a joke. Wasn't it just like him to yank everyone's chain? He was probably laughing in his grave.

"Do you want to do it, or do you want me to try?"

"You," Raylene said.

He turned the dial first to the right, then to the left, then back to the right. *Snick.* The small crowd burst into applause, seemingly more excited that Gabe had untangled Ray's lame number code than the prospect of finding gold. Apparently, Raylene was the only dreamer in the bunch. Or maybe just the most desperate for cash.

Gabe opened the door and reached his hand in. "There's something here."

Raylene craned her neck to see over Gabe's shoulder. He pulled out a black velvet pouch and there was a collective gasp.

"What is it?" she asked, afraid to look.

"You want to open the bag?" Gabe started to hand it to her, but she pushed it away.

"You do it."

Harlee pointed her camera lens past Raylene's face and Rhys reeled her in. "Hang on there, Lois Lane. Let's see what we've got first."

Gabe fumbled with the drawstring on the bag, which had been tied in so many knots Raylene wondered why he didn't just cut it with his pocketknife instead of making a big production out of untangling the strings. This was it. If it wasn't Levi's Gold, the gold didn't exist. She and Gabe had dug up every inch of soil depicted on the useless map. And Tiny and company had come right behind them, searching for the map. If the total of them hadn't found anything, there was nothing to be found.

"Hurry," she urged Gabe. Just rip the damn Band-Aid off.

Gabe finally got the bag untied. "Ready for the moment of truth?" The crowd moved closer.

"Open it, *mijo.*"

Gabe reached his hand into the pouch and Raylene closed her eyes.

"Feels like gold!"

There was another collective gasp and Raylene opened her eyes.

Gabe emptied the purse onto the bar top and Harlee started snapping pictures in rapid succession. Raylene reached out to touch one of the nuggets to determine if it was real.

"I can't believe it," someone—maybe Gia—murmured. "It really exists."

"There's more, right?" Raylene stared down at the small mound of nuggets.

Gabe turned the pouch inside out, producing nothing more than dust. He reached into the safe to check for more, but his hand came back empty. "That's it."

What was on the counter didn't look like much, maybe enough to make a few wedding bands and a small medallion, but it had to be worth a fortune. Right? Raylene wasn't too sure. She turned to Gia, the money expert. "How much do you think it's worth?"

"It depends on the day." Gia grabbed her phone, and Raylene could see her googling something. "Right now, a little more than forty-two dollars a gram."

Raylene's stomach tanked. There couldn't be more than twelve grams in the pile.

"But natural nuggets like these are worth more," Gia said, and Raylene's hopes lifted. "Maybe as much as twenty or thirty dollars more a gram, depending on purity and color."

Raylene did a few quick calculations in her head. Best case scenario, they were sitting on roughly eight hundred and sixty-four dollars' worth of gold. Not exactly a windfall. Hell, it wasn't even enough to cover her Nordstrom bill, let alone her new niece or nephew's college tuition.

Gabe took her hand and pulled her into his side. She suspected he intuitively knew she needed someone to lean on. Didn't he always?

"You solved the legend, Ray. You were right all along."

Yeah, yay her. "I don't know about my mom or Logan, but I'll donate my share to the Railroad Museum." She was trying not to act petulant, but it was hard not to be disappointed, especially while her face still throbbed from Stringy's beating. At least kids might get a kick out of the legend, and getting to see real nuggets from the Gold Rush.

"Let's not be rash," Gabe whispered in her ear. "You need the cash."

Flynn gathered up the gold and stuffed it back in the pouch. "This time it's going to the bank, where I'll make sure it's divided three ways."

"Come on." Gabe slung his arm around her shoulder. "Let's get you home."

On the drive to the farmhouse Gabe squeezed her knee. "I apologize for doubting you, dissing Levi, and mocking the legend. You were right all along."

She snorted. "Give me a break. There wasn't even enough gold to pay for the metal detector."

"Nah, I'd say we're at least fifty bucks ahead of the game." He laughed. "Ah, Ray, where's that 49er spirit that's in your blood? It was fun."

"This," she motioned to her face, "was not fun."

He went from playful to dark in under a second. "I should've beat that son of a bitch within an inch of his life while I had the chance. I'm sorry, baby. I wish there would've been more gold, a million dollars' worth. But you've still got the money from your property."

Except she had yet to sign the papers. Dana had done a good job of keeping Moto Entertainment at bay while Raylene had been stymied by indecision. Why couldn't Lucky drop his foolish pride and buy the damned property from her? Two hundred thousand dollars wouldn't leave her any money to live on, but she'd manage. She didn't know how, but she would, even if she had to move into Lucy's House herself. Her horse farm would have to wait. And Gunner...it was too much to contemplate with a migraine that felt like a stampede through her head.

Gabe parked in front of the garage and pulled Raylene in for a hug. "What are you thinking?"

"That I need to make a phone call."

Gabe gazed out the window at Logan's truck. They were home. "Better do it quick, or else you'll miss my funeral."

Chapter 24

Gabe had had one damned job—take care of Raylene—and he'd failed the mission. Miserably. And if that didn't piss off Logan, the fact that Gabe was pretty sure he was in love with his best friend's sister was going to set Jenk off real good.

"Hey." Logan met them on the front porch. "Where've you been? We got in an hour ago. I'm never flying commercial again."

They'd been waylaid by weather, and then overbookings, finally managing to get a flight out that morning.

"Whoa, shit." Logan bit down on his knuckles. The swelling on Raylene's face had gone down since Sunday, but it was currently every color of the rainbow. "Aw, come here." He gathered his sister in a hug.

"Gabe saved my life," she blurted. Bless her lying heart.

"Nope," Gabe said. "She saved herself, whacked 'em with a pickax. By the way, we owe you a new one."

"Let's go inside." Logan still had on some jacked-up Hawaiian shirt and it was forty degrees outside. "Tell Annie and me everything that happened."

An hour later, Raylene and Gabe told them about Ray bragging about Levi's Gold in prison and Rufus Hawkins and his two psycho friends.

"The dude's actually wanted in a Utah homicide?" Logan asked, and Gabe saw him walk through the what-ifs in his head. Gabe had done it a thousand times and could safely say it wasn't productive. The truth was it made his blood run cold.

"On a good note, you're roughly three hundred dollars richer," Gabe said.

"According to Donna Thurston, Raylene donated her share of the gold to the railroad museum," Annie said, and once again, Gabe was reminded how fast news traveled in Nugget. Like a Lockheed SR-71 Blackbird. "We want to do the same." Annie looked at Logan, and they shared a sloppy love-struck smile that made Gabe throw up a little in his mouth. "Right, hon?"

"Whatever you want to do, babe."

"Ah, Jesus, the honeymoon's over, folks." The whole love thing was making Gabe feel on edge.

I don't ever want to be responsible for someone's happiness. Ever.

"I'm going to take off and let you all have some family time." Gabe rose, even though Raylene's blue eyes implored him to stay.

What did she care? She was leaving anyway.

"I'll walk you out," Raylene said, but Logan blocked her way.

"I'll do it, you stay warm." Logan gave Raylene a gentle squeeze.

Logan grabbed a coat off the hall tree and followed Gabe outside. "Anything else I ought to know?"

"Like what?" *I've got feelings for your sister.*

There was a long pause while Logan shuffled his feet in a patch of semi-melted snow. "Uh…anything else happen to her in that fishing shack?"

It took a few seconds for Gabe to absorb what Logan was getting at. "Ah, jeez, Jenk. No. Hell no!"

Logan sagged against Gabe's truck and let out a breath. "Thank God. Ray and his goddamn big mouth. Why do you think he just left the gold in the safe like that? Why didn't he tell Flynn about it…make it part of his estate? Hell, he could've cashed it in and put the money on his prison books."

Gabe hitched his shoulders. "To a guy like Ray Rosser, it was chump change. He probably forgot about it. Or he liked the idea of the legend so much he wanted to preserve it for the next generation. Who knows? There was a picture of you in one of the safes…BUD/S graduation. I don't know if he shot it himself, but it clearly meant something to him. Raylene took it to give to you."

"I made my peace with the late SOB a while ago," Logan said. He toed the dirt. "Still, there's no love lost. But if it hadn't been for Ray I never would've met Annie…or my half sister. Thanks for taking care of her, man."

"Yeah, I didn't do so good with that."

"She's here in one piece." Logan turned away so Gabe wouldn't see him choke up.

"She's tough. Reminds me of an ex-SEAL I know. She saved Emily's kid, Harper, who was able to flee the barn unscathed." Gabe opened his truck door. "People sure are less pissy about her now. Donna and Emily made her soup, and Cecilia has been clucking around her like a mother hen. Who knows if it'll last." Gabe suspected that once the sale to Moto

Entertainment was final, Raylene would go back to being public enemy number one. "She's leaving town soon anyway."

Logan nodded. Gabe considered telling him that Raylene was broke and had promised a good portion of her earnings from the sale of her property to a woman's shelter. But he'd sworn to keep her secret. Besides, she was perfectly capable of taking care of herself. He supposed he was looking for an excuse to get her to stay, then tried to convince himself that he was merely sleep deprived.

"I'll talk to you later." He climbed into the driver's seat and watched through his rearview as Logan went back inside the house.

Instead of going home, he headed to the Ponderosa for a beer, a decision he reevaluated after four people in succession plied him with questions about Raylene's abduction and Levi's Gold.

"Heard that gold didn't turn out to be much." Owen took the empty stool next to Gabe's.

"Nope."

"Ray always did like his tall tales. How's Raylene?"

"She's okay."

Owen let out a whistle. "Who knew the girl was hero material?"

"I did," Gabe said. He was pissed at how everyone sounded so surprised. The Raylene he knew was giving half her inheritance to a woman's shelter. Should it really come as any big shock that she'd protect a thirteen-year-old? He called to the other end of the bar. "Hey, Mariah, forget that beer."

He got up and left, bumping into Clay McCreedy on the way out.

"Hey, where's the fire?" Clay called as Gabe made a beeline for his SUV.

He needed peace and quiet and time to reconnoiter. Alone time. Yep, that's exactly what he needed.

* * * *

The next morning, Raylene had breakfast with Logan and Annie and went to town to see Dana.

"I got your text, and was frankly surprised you were ready to do this." Dana took one look at Raylene's face and grimaced. "Shouldn't you be resting?"

"I'm okay." Raylene had put this off long enough.

"Let me print it, then." Dana brought up Moto Entertainment's offer on her computer and walked to the back of the office, waiting for the printer to cough up the contract. "Everyone is talking about what you did for Harper."

Apparently, people thought she was such a bottom feeder that protecting a thirteen-year-old had instantly elevated her to Martin Luther King Jr. status.

"Let me ask you something. What's the likelihood of getting another offer...like, soon?"

Dana grabbed the paperwork and came back to her desk. "Well, there haven't been any showings since Christmas, as far as I know. Are you having second thoughts?"

"Yes...no...I have to do this." Raylene took a pen from a mug on Dana's desk that read: "Everything I touch turns to sold." At least it wasn't gold. "Where do I sign?"

"Let's go over it first." Dana started to explain the terms of the offer, stuff she'd already told Raylene having to do with environmental studies, etc., etc., etc. "We can certainly ask for different terms but—"

"The thing is, I promised two hundred thousand dollars to a women's shelter where I volunteer," Raylene interrupted. "It's a non-profit that runs on grants, and this year a lot of those grants didn't come through. In other words, they're pretty desperate for money."

"Uh...okay." Dana seemed at a loss. Either she was shocked that Raylene wasn't one hundred percent Satan, or she'd been thrown by the non sequitur. "This is none of my business, but don't you, uh, like, have a lot of money?"

"Butch got a lot of it in the divorce, and to tell you the truth I'm not the best with money." Raylene let out a long breath. That she was confiding in her real estate agent, a woman she hardly knew, showed how desperate she'd become. "Anyway, I'm not as rich as everyone thinks. Otherwise, I wouldn't be selling to a motocross company. That land has been in my family for generations. To see it desecrated like that...I don't know why I'm telling you this. It's not your problem."

"Maybe you don't have to sell it to them to still get the money," Dana said.

"But you just said there are no other buyers."

"What about taking out a second mortgage on the land? It's valuable real estate."

"I'm afraid it would put me further into debt, and I wouldn't be able to manage the payments."

"Then you want to accept the offer." Dana pushed the stack of papers closer to Raylene.

She toyed with the pen for a few seconds, started to scribble her name on the dotted line, but froze. "I can't." She dropped the pen onto the desk. "I just can't. Tell them no."

The one thing she'd learned in that horrid little fishing shack, as her life flashed before her eyes, was that regardless of whether she lived here or not, Nugget would always be her home, and these would always be her people. She couldn't put a motocross track in their backyard.

Raylene got up and walked out. A short time later, she found herself sitting in Gabe's driveway, deliberating knocking on his door. He must've heard her engine, because he came to her instead. Just opened her truck door, picked her up, and carried her like a bride into his duplex apartment, straight to his bed.

"Clearly, you've got stuff on your mind. What do you say we talk about it later?" He unzipped her jacket.

"Works for me." She helped him take off her clothes and then his, and for a long time they lay there naked together in each other's arms.

Then he moved over her, tasting her lips and caressing her breasts. She held on to him, wanting to take their time so she could imprint this moment on her heart forever. Gabe, like her, didn't seem in any rush. He went slowly, touching, tasting, feeling.

She would miss this, the special kind of intimacy she had with Gabe and no one else. The way he put his whole body into making her feel good. He was the only man for whom she'd never had to wear a coat of armor. With Gabe, she was safe to be herself.

By the time he entered her, she was a jumble of raw emotions. "I love you," she whispered, so softly that he couldn't hear the words. It was better that way, she told herself. Leaving him would be hard enough.

His strokes became needier, more powerful, and she urgently rose up to meet each thrust. Gabe rolled her on top, cushioning her ribs, which were still sore from Sunday. She moved steadily with his hands on her hips, guiding and controlling the pace. Slow and easy. Both of them swaying to the rhythm of a primal dance as old as time. Both of them so lost in each other that nothing outside of them existed.

Their breathing had become heavy, and Gabe's face strained in the sunlight that had seeped through the blinds and left striped shadows on the wall.

"Ah, Ray, I'm not going to make it much longer."

"Try." She leaned over him and dragged her long blond hair down his chest.

"That tickles." His hands clasped her arms and he propped her up. "Are you trying to kill me?"

She laughed, and their eyes met and locked. Raylene traced his lips with her finger and something moved in her chest.

"What are you doing?" he asked.

"Looking at you. Memorizing your face."

He reached up and ever so gently rubbed his thumb along her bruised cheek. She shrugged up her shoulder, holding his hand in place so she could revel in his soft touch.

"Does it still hurt?" he whispered.

"Nothing hurts…all I feel is you."

His eyes heated and he flipped her onto her back, careful not to put pressure on her ribcage. Then he re-entered her in one fluid thrust. Increasing the tempo, he plunged deeper with long, powerful strokes, making her call out, "Gabe, oh, Gabe."

He reached one hand under her butt and used the other between her legs. And all at once she felt herself break into a million pieces as she clenched around him, waves of pleasure washing over her. Gabe let go of the tight grip he'd had over himself and matched her as his own climax stole his breath away.

"Ray…ah, baby." He caught her mouth and kissed her hard.

Afterward, they lay there, tangled up together, gulping for air. Eventually, he found one of the pillows that had been knocked to the ground, fluffed it, and placed it under her head.

"I backed out of the deal with Moto Entertainment," she said, breaking the silence. "I couldn't go through with it."

Gabe rolled to his side and faced her. "What are you going to do now?"

"Get a job, I guess."

He let out a soft chuckle. "What about your women's shelter?"

She exhaled. Another one of her failures, and another name to add to her long list of people she'd let down. "I don't know. But I couldn't sacrifice my hometown. I'll think of something."

"I believe you," he said. "You're just stubborn enough to get the money."

"I'm hoping in spring, Dana will find another buyer. A rancher or a farmer."

"Lucky said you offered to sell it to him for less than half the price."

She didn't say anything for a while, ashamed that the man hated her so much he'd pass up the deal of a lifetime so he wouldn't have to lower himself to take something from her. "I was trying to make amends."

He tipped up her chin with his finger. "That's a hell of an amends. You're a good person, Raylene, who made some mistakes. I think people around here are starting to see that."

"People around here are riding high on what happened a few days ago. As soon as the adrenaline rush subsides, they'll go back to hating me. That's the way it is in Nugget."

"Maybe." He rested his forehead against hers. "Or maybe they're over it. Who can say? But you can leave with a clear conscience."

She wondered if she'd ever be free of the constant guilt that gnawed at her, or if she even wanted to be. Carrying it around was a good way of keeping her honest and off the booze.

Somewhere in the mess of clothes on the floor, a phone rang.

"Is that yours or mine?" she asked Gabe.

"Not my ringtone."

"It's probably Butch calling to tell me he wants half the gold." She rolled her eyes and hung over the edge of the bed to find her cell. "It was Dana. What do you suppose she wants?"

Gabe sat up and scrubbed his hand through his hair. "You think she found a new buyer already?"

Raylene sincerely doubted it. It had been less than two hours since she'd left Dana's office. She hit the return call feature on her phone and held her finger against her lips to let Gabe know to be quiet. "Dana, it's Raylene. I couldn't get to my phone fast enough. What's up?"

"I hope you don't mind, but I told Gia about the situation with your land… how you turned down Moto Entertainment's offer…about your financial situation, and about how you're a benefactor for a women's shelter. She'd like to meet with you." Annie had once mentioned that Dana and Gia were BFFs, and in Nugget nothing was ever a secret anyway.

"All right," she said. Why not? Other than Gabe, Wanda, and Dana, Raylene hadn't told a soul about her money woes. She figured the folks in Nugget would only be too happy to see how far the mighty had fallen. But why not take advantage of her sure to be short-lived good standing while she could? Though Raylene had never watched Gia's show—financial self-help programs weren't her thing—she could use some good advice. And Gia was a millionaire ten times over.

"How about in my office in twenty minutes?"

"Sure," Raylene said, and got there five minutes early.

A short time later, Gia swept into the room, a laptop case slung over her shoulder. For a former talk-show host, there was nothing fluffy about her. Her blond hair was tied back in a smooth ponytail, her face flawless without makeup, and her clothes tailored but not stuffy.

"What's the name of the women's shelter you told Dana about?" she asked by way of a greeting, then set up her laptop on Dana's desk.

"Lucy's House."

Instead of responding, Gia tapped away at her keyboard. "This it?" She turned the laptop toward Raylene. When Raylene nodded her head, Gia continued typing. "It's a 501(c)(3)."

Raylene had no idea what she was talking about.

"It's legit," Gia announced.

Duh. Of course it was legit. Did Gia think Raylene wanted to give two hundred thousand dollars to the Real Housewives of Santa Monica?

"I can help you with this," Gia said. "I can help you with your own finances, too."

"Why? Why would you do that for me?"

"Because you're Annie and Logan's family and I love Annie and Logan."

Okay, that sort of made sense. And perhaps Gia thought if she didn't help, Raylene would stay and mooch off her brother indefinitely. She had zero plans to do that. But if it meant Gia would help her with Lucy's House, Raylene wouldn't disabuse of her of that notion.

For the next two hours they stuck their heads together, and for the first time in Raylene's life she had a strict budget to follow. It included getting rid of her beach house and moving into a cheap apartment with a roommate. Getting a full-time job, which wouldn't be easy given Raylene's lack of skillsets. And selling her truck and buying a used, more fuel-efficient car.

Gia emphasized that none of these cost-saving measures were going to save Raylene. The only thing that would do that was a career with good earning potential. *My horse farm*, she thought to herself. But without the land or the money, it was a fantasy.

By the end of their brainstorming session, Gia had given her an Iris Foundation grant application and a wink and nod that the fix was in for Lucy's House. Apparently, the foundation was so flush, the board had begun awarding money to other women's organizations around the state in addition to the good it already did in Nugget.

When she got back to the farmhouse, she found Lucky in the driveway, leaning against his truck.

What now? she wondered, exhausted from trying to paste together her freak-show of a life. She slid out of the driver's seat. "You looking for me, or Logan and Annie?"

"You."

"It's cold out here. You want to come inside?"

"Nope. This won't take long."

Here we go. She was sure there must be some infraction she'd committed. Maybe he still wanted the money for Tawny's dress. "What can I do for you?"

"Word's all over town that you sent that Motocross operation packing. I just wanted to thank you, and let you know that I'm working on getting a consortium together to buy your land...for full price."

She swallowed hard. This wasn't what she'd been expecting. "Talk to Dana when you're ready."

"You leaving town?" Perhaps it was her imagination, but he sounded a wee bit wistful.

"Yep. Just have to close out a few things." Rhys wanted her to check in before she left and Annie wanted to do a dinner.

She started to head to the house.

"Hey," he called. "We're even now."

"Okay," she said, not knowing exactly what that meant.

"Take care, Raylene." He tipped his hat, got in his truck, and drove away, leaving her feeling lighter than she had in a long time.

Chapter 25

"What the hell's the matter with you?" Logan slapped Gabe upside the head. "For the last ten minutes, you've done nothing but stare into space. If I wanted to have a beer by myself I would've come to the Ponderosa alone."

"I've got stuff I'm thinking about."

"Like what?"

Like your sister, asshole. "Just stuff."

"Oh, stuff. Glad we got that cleared up." Logan glanced up at the TV. "We've got another hour to kill, so do something entertaining."

Annie had kicked them out of the house while she put the finishing touches on Raylene's dinner.

"So she's really leaving tomorrow, huh?" Gabe had struggled with it the entire week, telling himself it was for the best. There wasn't anything here to hold her. No job, no home, only years of bad history.

"Yep. We tried to get her to stay longer, but she and Nugget don't mix."

"Seems like she's mixing better now, wouldn't you say?"

"Yeah. Better than before, that's for sure. It sounds like Lucky, Clay, and Flynn are getting ready to make her an offer on her land. That'll go a long way to putting her back in the black." He shook his head. "I always knew she'd blow through that money, the way she was living."

"She'll be able to buy her horse property." Suddenly, the idea of selling property to buy different property sounded absurd. "Hey, I've got to go."

"What are you talking about? We just got here."

"I forgot something." Gabe slipped off his stool and made it to the door before Logan got any more in his face. "I'll see you tonight," he called across the bar.

As soon as he got out into the square he called Raylene. "Meet me at your property."

"I can't right now. I'm helping Annie peel potatoes for my dinner."

"What if I told you we missed the real gold?"

"I'd ask you how many beers you had with Logan."

"Come on, Ray, meet me at your land. I'll be there in ten minutes." He hung up before she could argue with him, then drove way faster than the speed limit permitted.

The trench Rufus and his two thugs had dug was still there. Gabe slammed the door of his SUV and walked closer, kicking in some dirt. As soon as he could carve out the time, he planned to fill in the hole. Gabe wandered around the lower part of the property, scoping it out. The sun was setting over the mountains and the sky was a vivid red and blue and pink and yellow. It was cold enough to see his breath, but not cold enough to snow. Soon it would be spring and the days would get longer.

He took the trail down to the river and skipped a few rocks, working it all out in his head. The hills wouldn't be good for much, but they did afford the parcel a good degree of privacy. And they were beautiful. Come summer, they'd be awash in flowers. Heather and primrose and a thousand other plants Gabe didn't know the names of. But most of the land was semi-flat—and usable.

He swung around when he heard Raylene's truck pull up, but waited for her to find him. This is what he wanted her to see. The breathtaking views of the Feather River and the mighty Sierra mountains looming in the background.

He heard footsteps clattering through the trees, then Raylene utter a swear word and he smiled to himself. She came around the corner and pushed through the brush in her tight Western jeans and those turquoise boots that never failed to rev his engine.

"What? What was so important that I had to leave Annie with all the work?"

"This," he said, and lifted his arms. "Why can't this be your horse farm?"

She huffed out a breath. "Because it's in Nugget."

He wanted to ask what was wrong with Nugget. It was where he lived, after all, but obviously he didn't factor into her decision. "I get that. And in the beginning, I would've agreed that you couldn't live here. But things have changed; people's opinions about you have changed."

"I don't know about that. But, more importantly, my opinion of this place hasn't changed. I hate it." She sounded too defensive, like someone trying to protect herself, if you asked Gabe.

"It doesn't seem like you hate it. You'd be close to Logan and Annie when they have the baby." And then, because he couldn't help himself, he blurted, "And close to me."

She didn't say anything for a while, just stared down at the toes of her boots. "It would never work. None of my relationships ever have."

"You don't know until you try."

"I've tried, and they still failed."

He didn't know what to say to that, only that he wanted her to stay more than he'd ever wanted anything in his life. But he couldn't force her. "I just thought this would be perfect for you." He stared up at the painted sky. "And the best part is that you already own it."

"Even if it was perfect, I'd still need capital to build a barn, corrals, fences, a place to live. I'd need stock. Where would I get that kind of money?"

"Where would you get it in LA?"

She hitched her shoulders. "I guess I'll invest the money I get from this place, and maybe in a few years I'll have enough."

At least she had a semblance of a plan, though it seemed counterproductive to sell perfectly good land to buy new property. "It's your choice; I had just hoped you'd stay." He wanted to tell her that he'd fallen for her and get down on his knees and beg her not to leave.

But it would mean taking on the responsibility of making her happy, and he just couldn't put himself in that untenable place again.

"You want to follow me back?" she asked. "Dinner is in less than thirty minutes."

"Yeah, sure."

She started to walk away.

"Raylene?"

"Yes." She turned to see what he wanted.

He might as well tell her. "I love you. I didn't want to." He scrubbed his hand through his hair. "But it happened and now I don't know what the hell to do about it."

She stared at him for a while and then shook her head. "Bad timing, I guess." She continued to head for her truck.

"That's it? Bad timing. That's all you're gonna say?" He'd just for the first time in his life told a woman he loved her and she'd walked away. "Hold up." Gabe went after her.

"If we don't get moving, we'll be late," she said when he took her arm. "Annie put a lot of work into this dinner."

"Did you not hear what I said?" He paused. "I love you."

"Then we're in the same boat, because I love you, too, and I didn't want to either. I'm not good at it. Worse, I'm destructive." When he didn't say anything, she reiterated, "I'm like a human wrecking ball, crushing everything in my wake. I don't want to do that to you, Gabe. You're the only man I ever wanted to save from myself. That's how much I love you."

"You've never known a man like me. I can save myself, Raylene. But I don't need saving from you. You know why? Because you're good." He put his hand over her heart. "Right here, you're good. I know you don't think so, but I'm telling you, you're good. Right down to your marrow. You're good."

Tears streamed down her face. "No, I'm not. You only see what you want to see."

"Nope." He shook his head adamantly. "I see what Logan sees, what Annie sees, what Harper sees, what those women at Lucy's House see. I see good. I see so much damn good that I don't even know if I'm worthy."

"You're the worthiest man I've ever known." She choked on a sob. "But you're a little blind where I'm concerned."

"Nope," he said again, and cupped her face with both hands. "My eyes are wide open. And you know what I see? I see the most beautiful woman in the world standing before me. Inside and out. Here." He clasped her face. "And here." He touched her heart. "I want you to stay, Raylene. I want to see where we go. But I understand that you're trying to wrest back control of your life, and I won't get in the way of that. You have to do what's right for you, even if it means going back to LA."

She swiped at her cheeks, wiping away tears. "That's why I love you."

He wanted to say *then just stay*, but it had to be her decision. She'd already had too many men in her life telling her what to do. He wouldn't be one of them. He couldn't be responsible for her happiness, but he wanted her to have absolute fulfillment with every fiber of his body. And that meant letting her go if he had to.

"Let's go eat," he said, and took her hand.

* * * *

There were at least six cars in the driveway when Raylene pulled up to the farmhouse. The dinner was supposed to be a small family affair.

"What's all this?" she asked Gabe, who'd parked alongside her and had come to her truck door.

He shrugged and leaned in to kiss her. "Dunno. Looks like Annie invited a few more people. You okay with that?"

"Do I have a choice?" Since the arrests, and her rejecting the offer from Moto Entertainment, she'd been treated well by her old nemeses. But Raylene knew better than to think that would last. "It's one dinner." By tomorrow morning she'd be on the road to Los Angeles. She felt a pang in her heart and tried to ignore it. "Sit by me, okay?"

"You got it."

Gabe took her hand and together they walked into the house. When they entered the dining room a loud cheer went up. Raylene gazed around the table to see Harper, both sets of her parents, and all her siblings; Lucky, Tawny, and their daughter, Katie; Cecilia and Jake; Gia and Flynn; and Dana and her husband sitting there. She swallowed hard, uncomfortable with the attention. But when Harper begged Raylene to sit by her, a smile blossomed in her chest. Gabe shuffled around some chairs and both of them took places next to Harper.

Logan came over, squeezed her shoulder, and whispered, "What were the two of you up to?"

Raylene started to say something, but Gabe interrupted her. "Private stuff." He locked eyes with Logan in a silent warning.

"Private, huh?" Logan grinned and started to say more, but Annie shot him a death glare.

"Everything is ready." Donna came out of the kitchen. "So sit your butts down."

"I'd like to make a toast before we get started." Drew stood up. Someone filled Raylene's goblet with wine and when no one was looking, Gabe replaced it with a glass of water. "To Raylene, who stood up to the bad guys and who we're blessed to call a friend. To your bravery and quick thinking, and for protecting Harper." With wet eyes he held Raylene's gaze, clearly not wanting to say more in front of his daughter.

"Hear, hear!" everyone shouted.

Logan made the next toast. "To my sister. There's never a dull moment when she's around, and I'm so lucky to have her." He pointed his finger at her and winked. "Don't go changing."

She laughed, then tried to yank Gabe down when he stood up.

"My turn." He raised his glass. "To the best person I know. I love you, Ray. No matter what you decide to do, my heart will be with you." He sat back down and the room went instantly quiet, not entirely sure what that had been about.

Annie, sensing there was something highly personal going on in a room full of people, decided to change the subject, thank goodness. "We're doing this buffet style. Everyone grab a plate and come on into the kitchen."

The guests began moving toward the food. When the coast was clear, Raylene mouthed to Gabe, "I can't. I just can't." But the thought of leaving him tomorrow made her heart fold in half.

"Do what you gotta do," he whispered, and for the first time in her life she didn't feel pressure to bend to someone else's will. This was her choice. She had all the power.

"Let's eat, baby." He guided her into the kitchen where casseroles lined the counters.

Someone had smoked a brisket and there was fried chicken, pork ribs, and grilled vegetable skewers. Annie's refrigerator was already jammed with soups and dishes people had brought while Raylene was convalescing from her attack. Gabe filled her plate, then his, and they went back to the dining room to take their seats.

"You look a lot better," Harper said. She'd been over a few times to visit Raylene.

"Thanks." Raylene had covered some of the bruising with makeup, but for the most part the swelling was gone.

Everyone began talking at once, and the room hummed with chatter as everyone ate. Under the table, Gabe rested his hand on her knee. She laced her fingers through his and they sat that way throughout dinner.

Clay made his way over. "You got a second to talk?"

Gabe started to get up to give them privacy, but she pulled him back down. Anything Clay had to say, he could tell her in front of Gabe. Clay motioned for Lucky and Flynn to join them.

"We'd like to buy your property, if it's still for sale," he said, adding, "at full price."

She thought about all the things she could do with that money, including the debts she could pay, and the fact that she wouldn't have to get a roommate. Maybe she could even keep her truck. Then she thought about leaving Gabe. About how he'd left their future in her hands. How he would always be her hero.

She tried to picture raising her cutting horses in another place and couldn't.

"Did you talk to Dana about it?" Raylene turned her gaze down toward the other end of the table, where Dana was in an animated conversation with Gia and Annie.

"We thought we'd talk to you first," Lucky said, and Flynn nodded in agreement. "Has anything changed?"

Yeah, something had. "I'm not sure I still want to sell it." She looked at Gabe, whose expression was filled with such hope that her love for him soared even higher than she thought possible.

"No?" Clay sounded annoyed, like she was up to her old tricks.

"I'm seeing someone here," she said. "And he's asked me to stay. And, as he pointed out, it would be awfully silly to sell perfectly good horse property just to buy different horse property."

Gabe broke into a grin while Clay exchanged glances with Lucky and Flynn.

"Horse property?" Clay turned back to her. "I'm not following."

"I want to raise cutting horses. Until recently, I'd planned to do it in Southern California. I'm assuming you wouldn't mind a cutting horse farm next door to your respective properties?"

"Nope," Lucky said, and smiled, first at her, then at Gabe. "Cutting horses are good."

"I'm absolutely good with a horse farm," Flynn said.

"Yep, me too." Clay slapped Gabe on the back.

"It won't be for a while. I have to get a job and raise some cash first." She had to find a place to live, a way to make a living…the whole thing was crazy. But when she saw utter adoration shining in Gabe's eyes, she knew she'd made the best choice in the world.

Gabe clinked his fork against his glass. "I'm making another toast." He rose and cleared his throat. "To Raylene, who's decided to stay in Nugget and make me the happiest man alive. We love each other." He met Logan's eyes across the room. "Anyone have a problem with that?"

There was a long stretch of silence, then thunderous applause.

"Then if it's all the same to you, we're going to skip dessert." He grabbed her hand, and together they made their way outside, under a perfect Nugget star-filled sky, to plan their future.

Epilogue

"Eyes up, spine straight, legs relaxed," Raylene called out to her class. "You've got it, Harper. Wrap your legs around your horse's barrel, Josie. There you go."

She stood in the middle of the ring, watching. "Looking good, cowboys and cowgirls."

Three days a week she taught riding classes at the Sierra Heights stable, where she worked full-time running the barn. As part of the deal, Griffin said she could use the stable to house two new broodmares she'd purchased, who'd once been champion cutters. She planned to build her operation little by little by breeding good stock.

"Harper's getting good." Gabe stood at the fence, watching.

"She is, isn't she?" The girl was a natural, but Raylene liked to take part of the credit.

"You decide to take that coaching spot at the high school?"

Nugget High had a phenomenal rodeo team. The head coach had asked Raylene to work with the barrel racers. The extra money would go to her horse farm kitty. "Yep. I'll have to juggle, but I can make it work."

"You have time to juggle lunch?"

"For you, I can cram it in." She beamed at him. Even after five months of living together, he still made her stomach do the jitterbug every time he was near.

"You want to look at that house I told you about?"

"Nope. The rent's too expensive." His small, duplex apartment was no Rosser Rock and River Ranch, or a Santa Monica beach house, but it served them just fine. "I want to save so we can build our own dream house."

"You sure? There's almost enough closet space in this place for all your jeans." He grinned.

"Positive." She walked over to the fence and pecked him on the lips. "But thank you anyway." Gabe wasn't particular about where he lived; he'd found the rental to please her. "I'm doing really great with Gia's budget. If I stick to it, I can start building a stable on my property next year. After that, a house."

"We may be able to speed that up if L&G continues to bring in the kind of contracts we've been getting."

Together, they were making a decent living, especially with their costs being so low. A lot of their food came from Annie's farm. It wasn't the life of riches she'd had growing up or being married to Butch, but it was a life so good she had to pinch herself every day to make sure it was real and not a fantasy. Who needed money when they had Gabe Moretti?

Raylene checked her watch.

"Okay, kids, time to bring it in. You know the drill."

She waited for them to dismount in the barn, then made sure they groomed their horses before turning them out to pasture. Gabe made a few phone calls while he waited for her to finish with the group.

Parents had started to pull up, and within twenty minutes the stable cleared out.

"I finally get you to myself." Gabe helped put away the rest of the tack. In the last few months, he'd learned a lot about horses. Raylene was in the process of hunting for a good gelding for him, one he could grow into as his riding improved. Then again, Gabe was a quick study—and fearless. She'd have to find him a fairly spirited horse.

"Tonight I have to participate in a conference call for Lucy's House." Gia had taken the women's shelter under the wing of the Iris Foundation and Raylene had been appointed to the board. "After that, I'm all yours, though." She waggled her brows.

"Good." He winked. "Because I've got plans for us. You mind if we take a detour before lunch?"

"Okay, I don't have to be back until the evening feeding, so we're good. No work today?"

"Nothing that can't wait." He steered her to his SUV and she scooted in the passenger seat.

"Where we going?"

"You'll see."

But it only took her a few minutes to realize they were heading to Rancho Raylene—that's what they'd taken to calling her property. Over winter they'd filled in the big trench that Rufus and his pals had dug, and today the property was blanketed with wild poppies for as far as the eye could see.

The sight made her suck in a breath. "It just gets prettier and prettier, doesn't it?"

"Yep, and so do you." He hauled her out of his truck and they walked to the edge of the river.

"This is the detour?" It was a good one. She never tired of looking at this land and planning how she would spend the rest of her days here.

"Sort of. Follow me." He wrapped his arm around her waist and led her to the grove of trees where they'd first started digging for Levi's Gold. A picnic table had been set up with a spread of fine china.

"Whoa, fancy lunch." She hadn't been expecting this, but Gabe was always full of good surprises, one of the many things she loved about him.

He waved his hand over the bench for her to take a seat, then dropped to one knee.

She gasped. "You're not…oh my gosh, you are."

His lips quirked. "Damned right I am." He took her hand. "Will you marry me, Raylene Rosser, and grow old with me right here on this land?"

"Yes, yes, absolutely yes! I love you so much, Gabe." And even though he'd said he never wanted to be responsible for another person's happiness, he'd done that for her. These days, she was bursting with joy because of him.

"I love you right back, Ray." He leaned in and kissed her long and hard.

When they finally came up for air, he tugged a velvet box from his pocket, flipped open the lid, and a diamond winked up at her. "The band's made from one of Levi's nuggets. Read the inscription."

She studied the inside of the band where it said, "U were right."

"Of course I was right." She laughed and launched herself at him. "Sometimes it's good to tempt fate. Look what I got."

"An awesome ring?" A smile stretched across his face.

"Nope, I got you!"

About the Author

Photo Credit: Photo by Laura Finz

New York Times bestselling author **Stacy Finz** is an award-winning former reporter for the *San Francisco Chronicle*. After twenty years-plus covering notorious serial killers, naked-tractor-driving farmers, fanatical foodies, aging rock stars, and weird Western towns, she figured she had enough material to write fiction. She is the 2013 winner of the Daphne du Maurier Award. Readers can visit her website at www.stacyfinz.com.

Printed in the United States
by Baker & Taylor Publisher Services